FATHER MICHAEL'S LOTTERY

A Novel of Africa

schaffner
press

Tucson, Arizona

Editor: Andrea Nattrass
Cover designer: Kay Sather
Book designer: Darci Slaten
Cover Photo: Stuart Fox (Gallo Images and Getty Images, Inc.)

Library of Congress Cataloging-in-Publication Data

Steyn, Johan.

Father Michael's lottery : a novel of Africa / Johan Steyn. -- 1st US ed.
p. cm.
"Originally Published in 2005 by University of KwaZulu-Natal Press...
South Africa"--T.p. verso.

ISBN-13: 978-0-9710598-7-0
ISBN-10: 0-9710598-7-X

1. Clergy--Fiction. 2. Poverty--Africa--Fiction. 3.
Hospitals--Africa--Fiction. 4. AIDS (Disease)--Fiction. I. Title.

PR9369.4.S75F38 2007
823'.92--dc22

2007016829

*This novel is a work of fiction, set in a nameless African country. Names, characters, places
and incidents are either a product of the author's imagination or are used fictitiously. Any
resemblance to actual people, living or dead, events or locales is entirely coincidental.*

I STARTED WRITING this novel when antiretroviral drugs were available only to the privileged few. Since then there has been some progress, but in many parts of Africa the conditions described in this novel still prevail and the majority of people living with HIV/AIDS don't have free access to antiretroviral drugs.

Poverty, apathy, a lack of education, the disadvantaged position of women in the Third World, inadequate medical facilities and bureaucratic bungling all play a role in the propagation of the disease. These problems were compounded by the fact that antiretroviral drugs were prohibitively expensive when they first became available.

Botswana is the one country in southern Africa that has approached this pandemic effectively. Here AIDS was declared a national emergency and a dynamic antiretroviral program was instituted, with the aim of making antiretroviral drugs available to every citizen.

Several private individuals have made it their mission to fund treatment for people living with HIV/AIDS. Notable among them are Bill Gates, Bill Clinton and Nelson Mandela.

Unfortunately, in many parts of the world, the pandemic also highlights the divide between the 'haves' and the 'have nots'. The reality of this is that those who can't afford medical care are being left out in the cold.

It is inevitable that my own views on the inequalities in medicine will emerge between the lines. I do not apologize for this.

I WOULD LIKE to thank several people: my long-suffering sister Inez, on whose desk I dropped the various stages of this novel; David Zetler whom I found, red-nosed with 'flu, reading the first draft; Gail Zetler who read the first completed manuscript; Elise Calitz, for her valuable comments; as well as Danie Fourie, David Mead, Lourenza Foghill, Pierre Lucouw, Tienie Myburgh and Pohl de Villiers.

Very special thanks to Andrea Nattrass for the final editing and to Glenn Cowley and his team at the University of KwaZulu-Natal Press.

*For Hannes Meyer — surgeon, mentor and friend
— who always spoke his mind…and cared about
the things that really mattered.*

Father Michael's Lottery
A Novel of Africa

PART 1

1

On the whereabouts
of a dead cat

TO: The Veterinary Department
FROM: Dr John Morgan

I am enquiring about the whereabouts of a dead cat that I dispatched to your office on Monday a week ago. The cat had bitten a man and his two dogs and there is a suspicion that it might have been rabid. Unfortunately the owner of the dogs killed the cat. I sealed the body of the cat in a cool-box, in formalin, and sent it to the veterinary surgeon after discussing the matter with him.

I have not heard anything from your office and I have been unable to trace the veterinary surgeon.

I am sending this message to you with the owner of the two dogs.

Please send me the laboratory report as soon as possible.

TO: Dr John Morgan
FROM: The Veterinary Department

We acknowledge the receipt of your note regarding the dead cat. Unfortunately we have been unable to trace it.

We advise you, for safety's sake, to vaccinate the owner.

The veterinary surgeon is away in the district and will only be back in six weeks' time.

TO: The Veterinary Department
FROM: Dr John Morgan

I have already started vaccinating the owner. Didn't he tell you?

It is difficult to understand how the specimen could have been lost, since it was accompanied by a covering letter and was delivered to the veterinary surgeon's house by the Constable himself.

Please try to locate it, since it could pose a serious health risk if it landed in the wrong hands.

TO: Dr John Morgan
FROM: The Veterinary Department

We have discovered a blue cool-box containing two six-packs of beer.

What color was yours?

TO: The Veterinary Department
FROM: Dr John Morgan

My cool-box was blue.
So where is the cat?

2

Another arrival

MORGAN CLEARLY REMEMBERED the day Mary was brought in. As always, the pick-up truck was spotted even before it started to reverse towards the entrance. The doors with the frosted glass panes were opened, orders were shouted and Rebecca went outside to inspect the cargo before the makeshift ambulance came to a halt. 'Casualty'was chaotic as usual, but Morgan paused and watched.

On the back, wedged between two spare wheels, a drum of fuel, and a toolbox was a bright, multicolored blanket. The head of a girl rested on two white, dust-covered pillows. The truck reversed carefully until it was in the shade just outside the entrance. Rebecca waited, together with two nurses and a trolley. When the pick-up came to a halt, she commandeered two fit-looking bystanders to lift the girl off the back. She had obviously underestimated their enthusiasm and before she could stop them, both men had jumped over the tailgate. One of them scooped the girl into his arms and stood up, holding her like a baby, with her head resting against his chest.

Rebecca straightened her back. She put her hands on her hips.

Due to the noise in the room Morgan couldn't hear what she was saying. Both men froze. The man holding the girl stood like a statue and his comrade carefully climbed down again. Then, with an air of exaggerated gentleness, they passed the girl from one to the other. The blanket slipped away. As it fell to the ground, Morgan saw the thin figure of the girl.

Rebecca moved forward and supported her head. They lowered the girl onto the trolley and Morgan saw a thin arm reaching out as if she were trying to assist in the proceedings. One of the men picked up the blanket and vigorously shook off the dust. It was a patched quilt of red, green, orange and blue. The girl lay flat on the trolley and underneath her flimsy dress her pelvic bones stuck out like wings.

The driver of the truck walked up to Rebecca. He was carrying a brown envelope that he handed to her with both hands. She took it, pointed at the truck and shouted a command. One of the pillows was removed, dusted and placed under the girl's head.

Finally, she was covered with the blanket and the procession moved into Casualty.

'Everyone is coming here today,' Rebecca said as they filed past.

She handed Morgan the discharge summary from yet another overcrowded hospital and took the girl to the resuscitation room.

He removed the file from the envelope, paged through the notes and read about yet another tragedy. The language was cold and impersonal, as always: a young teacher who had had an exploration for an abdominal mass. *Diagnosis: Lymphoma. HIV- positive*, written in red ink. *Patient refused chemotherapy. Discharged on relatives' request.*

The girl had traveled two hundred kilometers.

Why the hell bring her here? No one was going to save this girl, thought Morgan.

'Just help her.' He heard a man's voice above the noise in the room. Morgan looked up and recognized the driver of the truck; a big man with thick forearms, square, calloused hands, and a broad, weather-beaten face.

You fool, thought Morgan. You bring the girl here, on the back of a truck, in this heat, and for what? Do you expect a miracle?

The man seemed oblivious to the noise around him. His calm demeanor reminded Morgan of a rock standing firm amongst swirling waves.

The eyes were innocent, like those of a child.

Morgan stifled his anger.

'Are you the father?' he asked, trying to keep his voice neutral.

'No,' said the man. 'I am her uncle.'

Morgan sighed and shook his head. 'There's not a lot we can do for her,' he said. 'You must realize that.'

'Just do your best.' The man moved forward and grabbed his hand. 'I trust you.'

'You know what's wrong with her?' Morgan asked, holding up the file like irrefutable evidence.

The man nodded. 'I have been told,' he replied.

Morgan shrugged his shoulders. 'We will keep her here,' he said and thought: like all the others, and she will die, like all the others.

The man grabbed Morgan's right hand in both of his and said, 'I know you will try.'

IN THE RESUSCITATION room Rebecca was putting up a drip by the light of an angle-poise lamp.

Morgan moved to the bedside. The girl shifted her gaze towards him and he noticed her calm, undefeated eyes.

She was dehydrated, underfed and exhausted after the journey.

'There you are, my girl,' Rebecca secured the drip and gently patted the thin arm. She was speaking in a soft voice, not her usual harsh-edged Casualty Matron's tone. Morgan looked at the girl's beautiful face and understood Rebecca's sudden tenderness. He smiled and took a history in spite of knowing the story already.

All her words were carefully chosen and spoken in a melodious voice. Without a hint of self-pity, Mary related a tale of woe that had left her body in ruins but had not dented her spirit. 'And that is all,' she concluded simply.

Morgan admitted her into his ward and from that day onwards Violet and her girls nursed her with endless patience.

'Mary must have some pain,' Violet told him more than once, 'but she never complains.'

One day he found her sitting in a wheelchair on the veranda, looking out over the garden that was filled with the cries of weavers darting to and fro amongst the trees.

Mary was adamantly against chemotherapy. 'It just makes me sick,' she told Morgan, 'and I have to enjoy as much as I can.' She smiled faintly, taking stock of her body with the impartial air of a judge and said, 'What use can it be anyway?'

Morgan understood perfectly. Life is there to be lived, not to be prolonged at all costs.

'I know I am going to die,' Mary said, 'but I want to enjoy the good days I still have left.' This was the end of the road for her. Her mother was too ill to look after her, her daughter too young and, apart from her uncle, she had no other relatives to turn to.

She observed the world with the fresh vision of a child, accepting life as a gift in spite of her bedridden state. Morgan tried to forget that their liaison was very temporary.

3

A forty-four gallon drum

MORGAN HAD EXACTLY one hour of sleep on the worn couch in his living room. He had arrived home at ten minutes to five, set the alarm for six o'clock, stripped off his clothes and almost instantly fell into a deep, dreamless sleep from which he woke at two minutes to six. He pressed the button on the alarm clock and sat up feeling surprisingly refreshed. For a moment he stared at the slowly rotating fan below the ceiling and wondered for how much longer the rains were going to stay away. On the wooden table amongst books, a portable radio and a chessboard, lay a ginger cat. Sphinx-like, it stared at him with unflinching green eyes. Morgan stared back and then smiled.

Morgan was tall and lean with an angular face, perfectly level blue eyes above a thin nose and premature lines around his mouth that made him look stern and remote. He did not smile often, but when he did, it came as a complete surprise and transformed his face into that of a mischievous schoolboy.

'So,' Morgan said to the cat, 'I hope you had a more enjoyable night than me.' He bent his legs and rolled off the couch. 'I'm afraid I can't show anything for my efforts.' The cat jumped onto the floor and followed him into the kitchen.

He took a piece of meat out of the fridge and cut it into squares.

'In my next life, Oscar,' he announced, 'I'm going to be a cat like you. I am going to enjoy myself and not give a damn.'

He fed the meat to the cat and made himself an omelet, which he ate at the table while contemplating the moves of a half-finished chess game.

In spite of having fought a futile battle for most of the night, he didn't feel tired. But there was a picture he couldn't get out of his mind; a husband gripping the hand of his dying wife as if he wanted to hold her back from the beyond. Morgan felt the anger stirring inside him. He shook his head to rid himself of the memory.

No use getting angry so early in the morning, he told himself; besides, who is going to listen to you?

He washed down his breakfast with a cup of strong black coffee and lit a cigarette. His hand reached out for the radio but he checked himself and prolonged the early morning quiet with exactly the time it took to smoke the cigarette.

At half past six he ran a bath and slid into the lukewarm water.

A shadow fell across the frosted glass window above his head at the very moment his chin touched the water. There was the sound of hurried footsteps and then loud knocking at the door. Morgan swore vehemently. He ripped a towel from the rail against the wall, tied it around his waist without bothering to dry himself, and strode down the passage, leaving a trail of wet footprints. Through the mosquito mesh he saw the bearded figure of Maxwell, the hospital driver. Morgan pushed open the door with his shoulder and stepped outside.

From within Maxwell's beard appeared a row of uneven teeth with wide gaps between them. He came respectfully to attention and the thin leather belt that suspended his protruding belly seemed ready to snap. A deep, sonorous voice rose out of the depths of his barrel chest and expressed its deep regret at having to disturb a gentleman during his early morning bath.

'Your telephone line is still buggered sir,' he added solemnly.

Morgan gave him a faint smile and said, 'Morning Maxwell. Don't call me sir.'

Maxwell returned his greeting, brought his feet together, fumbled in the pocket of his baggy trousers and produced a handwritten message. Morgan opened the note with one hand, holding onto the towel with the other.

'Come and see a patient,' he recognized Rebecca's handwriting. 'He fell off a trailer and was followed by a forty-four gallon drum.'

Morgan calculated the weight of a full forty-four gallon drum and the result alarmed him, even without taking into account the effect of gravity and the distance traveled. 'One day,' he said to Maxwell, 'you must try to give me good news.'

The screen door slammed behind him. 'Tell her I am coming!' he shouted over his shoulder.

He drew a comb through his hair and ignored his unshaven face. In the living room he pulled on his trousers, searched under the table for his shoes, and ran out the front door, still buttoning his shirt.

He drove down a dusty backstreet, dodging chickens and calves, and swore as he slammed on the brakes, edging past a donkey that wasn't intimidated by the horn. Next to the river, the tin shacks peered through a veil of smoke, dogs ran next to the truck and barked, skinny children played on the bank, women carried loads of washing on their heads, and men in blue overalls recognized his battered truck and waved. Suddenly he felt as if he had lived in the town forever.

At the bottom of the hill he changed into second gear and ignored the whine of the engine as he negotiated the ever-increasing incline, until suddenly the road branched and an exasperated colonial building leaning on tired veranda pillars came into view. The road leveled out and the truck gratefully gathered momentum.

Morgan aimed its nose at an entrance guarded by a dusty bougainvillea and two sad, off-white pillars crying out for a coat of paint. He swerved to avoid the pothole beyond them, cranked the steering wheel sharply to the left, slammed on the brakes and stopped under a tree.

Only when he ran through the entrance to Casualty did he remember that he hadn't drained his bath.

Behind the frosted glass windows of the emergency room darted white-clad figures like fish in an aquarium. In the passage next to the door stood Maxwell, who had already reported back to Rebecca.

He waited until Morgan was within reach, then opened the door, letting the sound flood out into the hallway. In the center of the room, with her regal back towards him, stood Rebecca like the conductor of a chaotic orchestra. Next to her lay a man who was alive only because she had been able to insert a large bore cannula into a constricted vein. His clothes had been slit open like a cocoon—cut away from him with a huge pair of scissors. Around the frayed edges lay a fringe of dust.

Above the noise, Morgan realized with surprise that he could hear the whirring of the ineffectual electric fans that struggled bravely against the heat.

The impact of the drum exceeded Morgan's worst expectations. He noted the fractured femur and the wide bruise running from the man's shoulder, across his chest, and down to his pelvis. He was aware of Rebecca's voice, telling him that the man had spent most of the night traveling on a trailer drawn by a tractor. The tractor was a different version of the same theme. Usually they came on the back of a truck. And they took the river road.

'Just imagine,' she said, 'on that terrible road, and not even a blanket to cover him!' There were two choices: a longer, smooth road or a shorter, bumpy road. It was a matter of priorities, a tradeoff. More time and less pain, or more pain for a shorter time.

There was no time for reflection. The man was bleeding into his belly. His friends had made the right decision.

For more than an hour Morgan had the distinct impression that he was in the middle of a thunderstorm as he and Rebecca revived the patient. Around them nurses ran like frightened rabbits as orders sliced through the stifling morning heat like bolts of lightning.

'The laboratory wants to know if they must crossmatch more blood?' Rebecca shouted at the very moment he shoved a drain into the man's chest and was rewarded by a large amount of dark blood that escaped down the tube like an evil spirit.

'Six units at least!' Morgan answered, and was both impressed and dismayed by the amount of blood.

Then, unexpectedly, there was a lull in the storm.

The man responded to their energetic transfusions.

Voices returned to their normal pitch and harsh words were forgiven. Rebecca regained her sense of humor and a sleepy radiographer with pillow marks still on her cheek handed Morgan an envelope containing X-rays.

Stuck onto the viewing box, they revealed a path of destruction.

A fractured clavicle, fractured ribs, a shattered pelvis and a fractured femur.

That should be enough to keep me busy for most of the morning, he thought. This is a tough guy, he decided; a lesser man would have died hours ago, river road or not.

MORGAN TURNED AWAY from the screen and explained to the man that he would have to operate on him. The man's mouth remained firmly sealed as if he wanted to contain any expression of pain. He consented with a mere nod of his head.

Above him hung drips with clear fluid and blood. Drops fell into drip chambers at a rate determined by Rebecca's watch, which she lifted up from where it was suspended over her left breast.

She glanced down at it through glasses that had shifted down to the tip of her nose.

'Another bad day,' she said. 'Listen to that lot outside.'

Under the shelters outside was the usual early morning bustle.

For the first time Morgan became aware of the outside world. A child was singing 'Beautiful Sunday . . . Beeeaaauuutiiifuuull Suuundaaaaayyyyy!'

It was Tuesday.

'They will have to wait,' Morgan said. 'I can't be in two places at once.' He glanced at his watch. 'Where is Thomson?' he asked. 'He will have to give the anesthetic.' The question was superfluous he realized as soon as he spoke.

'Still in the meeting,' Rebecca said. 'It is that time of the day. He will be only too happy to oblige.'

'Well then, break up the goddamned meeting,' said Morgan.

He observed the man through a surgeon's eye. Short, stocky and muscular. Deep chest. Square pectoral muscles and an abdomen as taut as a trampoline. The breathing only slightly compromised in spite of the fractured ribs. Safer to ventilate him afterwards though, he thought, depending on the surprise package inside the belly.

Rebecca was talking to Thomson on the phone. She interrupted the conversation to convey Thomson's sincere gratitude. 'Tell him to hurry up,' said Morgan.

By noon he had finished operating, and the man was lying in High Care amidst a tangle of drip lines, catheters, drainage tubes and monitor leads that were sorted out by efficient High Care nurses.

The leg was in traction with a pin driven through the tibia and the technician stood at the door with his toolbox, waiting to attach a frame to the bed.

Thomson, oblivious to the mayhem around him, adjusted the ventilator. He watched as the monitor leads were connected. The EKG trace and the figures displayed on the screen conveyed good news, like stock prices recovering after a crash. Morgan sat down at the table and wrote his notes.

The open window did nothing to alleviate the heat inside the room. Outside, the gardener was chasing a cow off the lawn by throwing stones at her. She casually walked through a scruffy flowerbed and pulled out a tuft of grass, indifferent to the gardener's profane words.

Morgan stared out of the window for a moment longer and saw men putting new roof-plates onto a house next to the river. The faint sound of the hammer-blows was delayed, reaching his ears only when the men lifted their arms. He found himself comparing the sound of the energetic hammer-blows to the sound of the monitor. The man's pulse was now slow and regular.

From amongst the bleeping of monitors, the puffing of the ventilator, and the rattling of the air conditioner came Thomson's cheerful voice.

'Well my friend, we've done our bit. Up to him now, and he's looking well, considering.'

Thomson was standing at the end of the table, facing Morgan, who was still dressed in his theater clothes, the imprint of the surgical mask etched on his cheekbones. Morgan's sleepless night had caught up with him and a feeling of weariness settled on him like a cloud. Around them the bedlam continued. The place was packed.

One patient had been moved out to make room for Morgan's newcomer. Nurses were brushing past each other in the cramped space, nimbly avoiding the protruding wheels of drip stands.

Morgan gave Thomson a faint smile. 'At least we've done something useful today,' he said.

'Our leader is not going to be pleased,' Thomson reminded him. 'You should have referred him. New gospel, from the prophet himself.' He sat down and leaned his hairy arms on the table. A smile lingered in his disheveled beard; a surgical mask still hung around his neck and his eyes were a dark shade of mirth.

'Our leader can get stuffed,' Morgan said graciously.

Thomson's smile disappeared and he got up from the table. 'Another day in paradise,' he said. 'Call me if you need me.'

THE DECAY HAD started from the top where the rotten ceiling curved downwards to join the wall. Water seeped in from the leaking roof tiles and lifted the plaster to make bubbles and craters like a moon landscape. The ever-increasing blotches with overlapping borders on the ceiling looked like uncharted continents. Hundred-watt light bulbs hung precariously from rusty sockets. Linear streaks that ran down the wall had the character of a surrealist painting with colors varying from grey to green to cream and returning to dirty white.

In the rainy season, the dampness seeped up from the floor and lifted the paint above the skirting boards. The taps at the washbasin hissed and the water pipes rattled. The rotten wooden frames of the sash windows were held together by a cracked coat of enamel paint. The shelves on the wall sagged under the weight of books and stationery.

There were two desks in the room: a cluttered one, for general use, and a scrupulously tidy one belonging to Violet. The windowpanes of the sash windows were bright and shiny, the plain white curtains hanging next to the decomposing window frames were almost transparent from oft-repeated washing.

The floors were swept, washed and polished almost every day, the linen in the ramshackle linen cupboards was clean, and so were the worn, blue hospital regulation frocks of the women and the ridiculous wide pants and oversized shirts of the men. The cleanliness amongst the decay caught one by surprise, like finding a rotten shipwreck with tidy bunks, polished mess tables and clean cutlery.

It was an exercise in the art of the possible. A mixture of what could be addressed and what was seemingly beyond repair. It translated into a peculiar smell of polish, soap, deodorant and disinfectant mixed with sweat, stale urine from the defunct urinals and the stench from the sporadically blocked drainpipes.

Even the lockers next to the patients' beds were tidy, kept so under the watchful eye of Violet, the ward nurse, who supervised the ward with the same attention to detail as a sergeant major on a parade ground. But she didn't look like a sergeant major; she was beautiful—completely out of place amongst the carnage, a delicate lily growing in a pigsty.

Her face could have come from the cover of a fashion magazine: perfect shape, dark unblemished skin, perfectly curved eyebrows, absolutely regular features and eyes like deep, dark pools in a river. The austere nurse's uniform, instead of detracting from her good looks, managed to enhance them. She bore the burden of beauty with grace and a touch of indifference.

As she made her way to Female Ward, she paused for a

moment at the door and gauged the mood. All the women, it seemed, were taking stock of their own mortality. For a week they had witnessed Morgan's desperate battle, which had finally come to an end just before daybreak. Their only reward was a newcomer who had taken their dead comrade's bed and had arrived a mere two hours after her demise. No one had slept properly during the night and no one felt like sleeping now.

The newcomer was still settling in, like an exhausted bird that had found a safe haven after being battered by a storm.

Most of the women were sitting on their beds, counting their blessings. No one was on the brink of death, not as yet; and that was something to be thankful for. From the bathroom came a woman with a towel tied around her waist, her withered breasts flapping to and fro as she walked. This morning they all talked in subdued voices, in deference to their newly dead friend.

VIOLET STOPPED AT the newcomer's bed and paged through her notes. On the locker against the wall was a dented enamel bowl. She lifted the ill-fitting lid. Inside was a small helping of the porridge served for breakfast and a slice of bread.

'And this?' she asked.

'My food for the day.'

For a moment Violet was puzzled, then she realized what was happening and laughed. 'You don't have to hoard food; we feed you three times a day!'

The woman's precaution was not completely out of place. The matter of the high-protein diets was not as simple as Violet made it sound. Keeping up the supply of eggs, ice cream, milkshakes and protein powder had become a battle of wits between Morgan and Holmes, the superintendent.

So far, Morgan had thwarted every new rule concerning food rationing for the inpatients. A smuggler's chain of deception ran from him to Charles the Senegalese cook, to the stout kitchen assistants, to Violet, and ended with the pharmacist who supplied the tins of protein powder.

'Come on,' she chided the woman. 'Eat that food now, and you didn't have to bring your own bowl!' She looked closely at the woman's bony frame again and then, in her file, she read the name of the poorest village in a one hundred kilometer radius. So that explained it, she thought.

Drought. Dying cattle. Vultures sitting in the trees. Failed crops, children dying of malnutrition and their parents dying of AIDS. This was the report she had received from the clinic nurse some time ago. No wonder this woman was saving her food.

So what was the difference between her and the other women?

Not much.

They all came from villages scattered around the bush, ravaged by disease, ill-fed and carrying their meager possessions in plastic bags. Some of them were barely more than living skeletons. By the time they arrived in the ward, they were jobless, destitute and discarded by their boyfriends. Almost all of them had children.

When they got better, Violet scolded them about their uneducated state.

She urged them to get some form of education at least. But where do you start when you have no money and are suffering from the 'big disease'? Some took her advice to heart and struggled bravely to improve their lot, but in the end their illness caught up with them.

Most of them died.

Violet had lost count of the number of shattered dreams, small victories and crushing defeats she had shared.

She had heard heart-rending tales of loss, related without the slightest hint of bitterness. She had scrutinized faces for traces of anger but found none, listened for words of resentment but heard nothing. There was only sadness about loved ones lost and fears about children to be left behind.

MORGAN'S RESPONSE TO this silent massacre was predictable. Being helpless was foreign to his nature and sometimes, in Violet's office after ward rounds, he swore like a trooper and cursed the complacency of humankind. She tried to pacify him, but understood his anger. And as for her own anger, she had it neatly stored away in a far corner of her ordered mind. Now and again it dislodged itself during Holmes' meddlesome ward rounds. Then her back stiffened, her eyes blazed like those of a tigress guarding her cubs, and with a well-aimed one-liner she put Holmes in his place, her body language sending a clear signal: keep your hands off or else.

As she walked from bed to bed, she hardly needed to consult the notes. She knew more than just the patients' medical histories. In that ward, where everyone had become used to the precariousness of life, there were no secrets. Violet greeted everyone and enquired about their well-being.

The answers were not as spontaneous as usual. Everyone seemed pensive, and she realized they were pondering their own fate. What had happened during the night was a glimpse into their joint future, another episode of a private horror movie.

Janet was sitting cross-legged, repairing a rent in a pair of schoolboy's trousers. The chain of the crucifix around her neck followed an angular path: around the remains of her neck muscles, across the prominent clavicles, and over the protruding ribs just where they joined the breastbone. With nimble fingers she threaded the needle through the fabric and left a neat, evenly spaced suture line, the needle flashing with every flick of her wrist. When Violet approached, she deftly anchored the needle in the garment and carefully put it aside.

Janet's eyes bore a mixture of inner strength and utter vulnerability. She had a mouth that was designed to smile easily with rounded creases that effortlessly encircled her lips. But this morning, a slight angularity had crept into them, just where they negotiated the closure line of her lips.

For a moment Violet pondered the illusion of normality: a mother repairing a naughty boy's torn pants. Janet's slightly slurred speech shattered the illusion. Violet resisted the temptation to ask Janet to open her mouth, so she could examine the tumor of her palate. Not today, she decided. Not after the early morning tragedy.

Morgan would have to do it anyway. Today was reserved for mending a boy's trousers and pretending all was well.

In the last bed next to the window was Mary.

Violet knew that Mary was Morgan's favorite patient, if there was such a thing. In his brusque way, he doted on all of them, but Mary was special. The harsh-voiced Rebecca who hid her big, soft heart under her gruff demeanor brought her a bowl of soup every so often and treated her like a daughter. Morgan visited Mary each afternoon when she sat on the veranda in her wheelchair.

Mary never complained, no matter what. For the past few weeks she had been free of pain and had even gained a little bit of weight. She was sitting on her bed with her back supported by pillows, reading the field guide on birds that Morgan had given her. On the locker next to the bed were two other books: a manual on the principles of flight, and De Saint-Exupéry's *The Little Prince*. According to Morgan, those were the three books a person should never be without.

How can someone so riddled with disease still be so beautiful?

It comes from the soul, Rebecca had said, when Violet posed the question to her one afternoon soon after Mary had arrived.

'The soul is the source,' Rebecca had said. 'Beauty starts there and spreads all over, like an aura.' If you have a beautiful body and a twisted soul, you can wear as much make-up as you please, and it won't be of any use. Even if you have a perfect body. You could even be a film star, but you won't be truly beautiful. You might be pretty, but it's not the same as being beautiful. She had pronounced it 'be-auutifuull'.

Violet smiled and she could almost hear Rebecca say: 'It is something totally different.'

Mary's spirit permeated the room like perfume, but she seemed totally unaware of it. The first time Morgan had found her on the veranda, she was looking at the weavers. She asked him to name the other birds in the garden. Soon she became obsessed with the birds and their habits.

'That girl,' Morgan told Violet, 'is trying to cram a whole lifetime into a few weeks.' In a way he was right. Mary's world was confined to the inside of the ward and the view from the veranda, but she expanded it by reading and listening. That was the key to Mary. She listened more than she talked. And she had a fertile imagination. In a very short while she had become an expert on birds. Not only the ones that frequented the garden, but every other feathered creature in the field guide. She could list eight kinds of albatross, even though she had no hope of ever seeing them in real life.

Morgan explained the principles of flight to her and left her with an aviation textbook. Soon she became acquainted with aerodynamic foils and Bernoulli's law, lift, drag, camber and the different wing designs. Different wing shapes for different purposes. Slow-moving freight aircraft and fast-moving fighter aircraft. The birds in the garden went about their business as usual, unaware that they were being categorized, the camber of their wings noted, their flight patterns memorized, their endurance calculated and filed into an ardent admirer's memory. Her obsession with creatures of flight was probably driven by an intuitive desire to free herself from the cares of an earthbound existence.

She seldom spoke about her illness. A cumbersome, failing body was something that had to be endured, even ignored if possible.

Mary put the book aside and greeted Violet with a smile. All she wanted was to go outside, and she was well as always, thank you.

Violet collected the wheelchair from the far corner of the room and helped Mary into it. As they came to a halt near the edge of the veranda, Mary looked up and almost instantly spotted two Yellowbilled Kites soaring on motionless wings high above the rooftops. 'They are my favorites,' she exclaimed as she watched; her face was turned skyward and her hands clutched the field guide in her lap.

Violet laughed. 'You almost sound as if you own them.'

The kites continued to soar, unaware of Mary's admiration. For a brief while, Violet forgot all about the tribulations of the ward and shared Mary's separate world. Shifting her gaze from the kites she looked at Mary's face. She seemed oblivious to everything around her, completely absorbed in the graceful flight of the birds. What a waste, Violet thought. She is such a beautiful girl. She tried to ignore Mary's frailty and forbade herself to even speculate how much time was left.

The ringing of the telephone at the nurses' desk brought her back to reality.

She gently tapped Mary on the shoulder. 'I have to go now,' she said, and hurried back through the ward. As Violet walked towards the door, she saw the newcomer eating her porridge, cherishing every mouthful.

4

An empty bed

THE KENYAN SAT with his arms resting on the tabletop in Violet's office. On the other side of the glass partition, the final act of a tragedy was unfolding. In the passage were Violet, Oumar the Nigerian, and the parents of the young student who had died after lunch.

Stacked on the nurses' counter were two yellow-covered books: *Electronics, Part One* and *Electronics, Part Two*, which had accompanied the young man on his final journey.

The mother was crying softly, turning her head away and wiping the tears off her face with a tiny handkerchief. The father stood absolutely still, his arms folded in front of his chest. His face was impassive save for the occasional tightening of his jaw muscles.

Oumar's face was solemn as he talked. His white coat looked somewhat disheveled. Through the open door, the Kenyan could hear what Oumar was saying. He was talking in English, and Violet was repeating every word in the local language.

The parents nodded their heads solemnly. The mother struggled bravely to control her tears; her facial muscles twitched, her jaw was clenched and, as he watched, her eyes again filled with tears and she started crying openly and unashamedly. Her husband kept his eyes focused on Oumar, but put his right hand around his wife's shoulder and drew her closer to him. Oumar waited for the woman to regain control of herself and then resumed talking.

Behind them, through the open door of the ward, the

Kenyan saw the bed with the drawn curtains. At the end of the bed, below the curtains, he caught a glimpse of the feet of the nurses shrouding the body. From around the corner came the trolley with its familiar canvas cover, much too fast. The porter leaned his weight on it, planted his feet firmly on the floor and brought it to a halt. Not a moment too soon. The end of the trolley had come to rest only six inches from the mother's rump. Violet raised her hand, palm upward, indicating: 'Stop, not now!' Her eyes flashed like a brief burst of machine-gun fire.

The porter parked the trolley against the wall and waited patiently.

Finally Oumar stopped talking. The man stepped forward, grabbed his hand and thanked him. The Kenyan saw Oumar straighten his back, and noticed his stony features. He could almost read Oumar's thoughts. I know what you feel like right now, he thought. You feel like a traitor.

The parents departed; Oumar returned to the office, and the porter continued his interrupted journey. Oumar sat down opposite the Kenyan and let out a sigh. His shoulders slumped, and the lapels of his white coat sagged.

'How many times am I going to have to do this?' he asked. His usually metallic voice sounded hoarse. The Kenyan shifted in his chair. He was a huge man with powerful shoulders and the long limbs of a Masai warrior. His unexpectedly benign, almost fatherly countenance seemed slightly at odds with his physique. When he smiled, his whole face smiled. 'I know exactly how you feel my friend,' he said, and put his massive hands on the table. 'We like to think we can cure everyone.'

Oumar shook his head rapidly to and fro, as if trying to rid himself of the memory. 'The worst part is when the relatives thank you, and you know you really have done nothing.'

'But you have tried very hard,' said the Kenyan.

'We try, yes,' Oumar said, 'with our hands tied behind our backs.'

The Kenyan didn't answer. He sighed and looked past Oumar's shoulder.

The curtains around the bed parted, and the orderly was helping the nurses to lift the shrouded body onto the trolley. From where he sat, he could see the scrawny men in the beds nearest to the door. They were looking straight ahead, studiously ignoring the grim scene in the third bed. The Kenyan wondered: what was it like to lie in that ward, watching other people die, and waiting your turn?

The porter covered the body with the canvas cover, made sure it fitted properly, then started his return journey. He negotiated the cluttered aisle, steering the trolley like a boat, and narrowly avoided a collision with a nurse who had to turn sideways to allow the trolley to pass.

'You know what I feel like?' said Oumar. 'I feel like an undertaker, not a doctor.'

The Kenyan again said nothing. He knew exactly what Oumar was talking about.

He saw nurses wearing masks and gloves cleaning the plastic mattress with disinfectant. From the locker they took the young man's personal belongings. Violet brought clean bedclothes from the linen cupboard and they made the bed with swift, efficient movements. The speed of the transformation was alarming. In the space of a few minutes, every trace of the young man's presence had been removed.

'An empty bed,' said the Kenyan, and thought, 'an end or a beginning, depending on which way you look at it. Or the beginning of an end.'

Violet came through the door. No cheerful greeting this afternoon, he noted. Her shoulder muscles were taut and her eyes showed no expression. She went out for a moment, brought back the two books and locked away the young man's possessions.

Then from a file she extracted a death certificate and

placed it in front of Oumar.

'Might as well fill it in now,' she said.

Oumar sighed. He took a pen out of the top pocket of his white coat and started filling in the form.

Then he hesitated. The Kenyan knew exactly why. The immediate cause of death was easy. It was either pneumonia, or meningitis, or a tumor of sorts, or TB or any other of the numerous complications of the big disease. 'As a result of' was the problem. Do you write *Acquired Immune Deficiency Syndrome*, or do you replace it with a euphemism that would soften the blow for the relatives but would not fool the statisticians?

Oumar wrote *Immuno-compromised*, signed the form and handed it back to Violet.

Tomorrow or the day after, the relatives would come and collect the certificate together with the body and the belongings. In a week's time, another or maybe two futile battles would have taken place in the empty bed and the young man would have become a mere statistic.

'He was such a nice boy,' Violet said as she pinned the certificate to his file.

A tall man with well-worn, dusty clothes appeared in the passage. He bore the tired look of a traveler at the end of a long journey. His big frame was intended to carry a lot more muscle, but all that remained of his former glory were his bone structure and his clothes, which hadn't kept pace with his fading figure. In his left hand, he carried a fertilizer bag containing his belongings, together with his file from Casualty.

At first he stood against the wall, then saw the wooden bench on the other side of the door. He sat down on it, like someone waiting for a bus, and leaned his head against the wall. Somewhere down the passage a water pipe belched noisily, the tap at the washbasin hissed, a nurse pushed a spindly drip stand into the ward, and the creaky door of the toilet opened and slammed shut.

The man was staring at a fixed point on the floor, indifferent to his surroundings.

Oumar and Thomson were on call, the Kenyan remembered. At least they wouldn't have a problem admitting this man; not with an empty, newly made bed.

'You have a new patient, sister,' he informed Violet.

With surprising agility for his large frame, he stood up and grabbed Oumar by the shoulder 'Come,' he said. 'Life goes on, my friend.'

They parted in the passage. Oumar went back to Casualty to resume an interrupted consultation. At the end of the passage, where the tiled floor with its faded yellow, blue and red lines joined the wooden floor, the sound of his footsteps was replaced by a multitude of voices. It was later than he thought; the afternoon light was already shining through the high windows of the waiting hall.

The overhead fans, which hung from the ceiling like inverted ship's propellers, vibrated precariously on their stems. Underneath them sat the motley afternoon crowd, an assortment of headscarves, multicolored blankets, walking sticks, plastic bags, and anxious faces.

He saw the ripples on the glass pane of Rebecca's office before he heard the sound of her knuckles tapping on it. She was standing behind her desk, calling his name. Behind her, etched against the white bulletin board, he saw the outline of the Constable's cap. Oumar entered the office with a sense of trepidation.

In the far corner of the room, slumped against the wall, wearing only a torn pair of underpants, was the madman. His legs were splayed and his right arm was folded awkwardly behind his head. The Constable stood next to him like a hunter next to a trophy. As Oumar walked in, the madman briefly woke from his slumber and stared at him with dazed eyes. The skin over his left brow was broken and already the eyelid was starting to swell. That will be a nice shiner by tomorrow, Oumar thought.

THE FAN ON Rebecca's desk stirred up a breeze carrying the smell of cheap wine and marijuana.

'Our friend,' said Rebecca, 'is back.'

It must have something to do with the weather, Oumar thought. In less than ten days, most of the regular drunks and other assorted odd customers had passed through Casualty: the epileptic woman who found her medication to be incompatible with the wine she drank at the shebeens; Smirnoff, the intermittent binger; the other marijuana smokers at the mall; and the sly, scruffy beggars who conned the youngsters into admitting them for a day or two so they could get a bath, a shave and a couple of decent meals.

The only ones who hadn't appeared were the husband and wife team who had seemed to be on a crusade to deplete the liquor stocks of all the shebeens in town. They had a legitimate reason though; the wife was dead after her husband had underestimated both the length and sharpness of a bread-knife during one of their drunken brawls. He was serving seven years for murder with extenuating circumstances. It was not clear what the extenuating circumstances were. Was it the liquor, the aggravating, sharp tongue of the wife, or the unexpected sharpness of the bread-knife?

The Constable removed his cap and mopped the sweat from his forehead. He hesitated for a moment and then, probably because of the heat, decided to hold the cap in his hand. He faced Oumar and explained the madman's presence.

At noon, there had been a slight altercation in Mr.

Chiremba's bar. The madman was involved in a fight that resulted in damage to property. Taking the law into his own hands, Mr. Chiremba attempted a citizen's arrest. The madman escaped and was later apprehended by the bar customers whilst running across the street on the verge of total nakedness. No one knew what had happened to his clothes. Mr. Chiremba had had enough of the antics of the madman and laid a charge of drunk-and-disorderly conduct, common assault, damage to property, resisting arrest, indecent exposure, and not stopping for a stop sign.

The Constable was reluctant to press charges. Oumar's gaze moved gloomily from the Constable, to Rebecca, to the madman. He wondered how he had managed to walk straight from a tragedy into a farce.

Everyone was well acquainted with the enigmatic madman. He lived his life in a never-ending circuit. From Casualty he went to the ward. From there he went to the mental hospital where he exasperated the psychiatrists until they discharged him in despair.

Then he returned to the town, loitered at the mall and did odd jobs until he saved enough money for marijuana and liquor. The forces of destiny unerringly led him all the way back to Mr. Chiremba's bar.

'He is mad,' the Constable stated the obvious. 'I don't want mad people in the cells; they cause problems.'

In his corner the madman had sunk into a drunken stupor and was snoring serenely. Without interrupting his sleep, he removed his right hand from behind his head and placed it in his crotch.

The left arm, which ended abruptly at the wrist, was pointing at Oumar like the end of a double-barreled shotgun. The hand had been amputated long ago and even the madman, in his more lucid moments, couldn't remember why.

'What makes you think we want him?' Oumar asked.

The Constable was adamant. 'At least you can treat him,' he told Oumar and pointed out that the madman was injured.

Oumar couldn't dispute the Constable's logic. Besides, the madman had become a tradition in the wards, and provided a certain degree of light entertainment. Everyone inherited him from time to time. So today it is my turn, Oumar thought philosophically.

The madman opened his eyes, pointed his right hand at Oumar and tried to sit up. He spoke to Oumar with a sense of urgency, his eyes imploring him to do something. But Oumar couldn't understand the language. Rebecca and the Constable were laughing.

'He thinks you are the magistrate,' Rebecca said. 'You must please release him because he is not guilty.' Oumar started to say something but the madman had fallen asleep again.

'All right then,' he said to the Constable. 'We'll keep him.'

'I think it is better that way,' said the Constable, visibly relieved. He hurriedly put on his cap and prepared to leave. 'Oh no, ' said Rebecca. 'You wait until I get someone to take him away.'

Oumar entered a cubicle and resumed his long-interrupted consultation. The woman had been waiting patiently. He sighed when he saw the thin clavicles above her dress. He didn't have to enquire about her condition; it was written all over her—in the lean face, the angelic eyes and the wasted temporal muscles. She undressed and he felt her heart beating against her thin ribcage when he examined her. When he wrote up his notes, it occurred to him that the symptoms that he was listing read like a code language that translated into only one disease.

The memory of the young man's last moments still haunted him. Thinking about it, he relived his helplessness. From across the table, the woman was watching him, unaware of what he was thinking. She sat with her hands folded in her lap, awaiting his verdict. Oumar again noticed her slightly accelerated breath rate. Did she know he had just written her death sentence into her file?

'I want to do a few tests,' he broke the silence. Resignedly he wrote out an X-ray form and gave it to the nurse.

'Follow the red line on the floor.' He heard the instruction as the woman left the cubicle.

Suddenly the nurse burst out laughing.

He went out and looked.

The woman was balancing on the line like a tightrope artist, following the nurse's instructions to the letter. The people in the waiting room were enjoying the unexpected entertainment. She froze like a rabbit in the beam of a headlamp, looking back at them with an embarrassed smile on her face.

'Don't laugh!' snapped Oumar.

He took the woman by the arm and led her to X-rays.

'The red line is to show you where to go,' he said and slowed down so she could keep up with him. There was hardly any muscle on the arm that he was holding; she was short of breath just from walking.

'Take your time, my child,' he said, and wondered how she had ever got to the hospital. He made her sit down in a chair in front of X-rays.

'Thank you,' said the woman, holding her file with both hands as if it was going to fly away.

He saw the traces of beauty that remained in her face and eyes, like embers in a burnt-out fire. For a moment he held her gaze and noted her innocent eyes.

'I will have to keep you here,' he said. It was spoken as a request, not an order.

She nodded in quiet agreement and humbled him with her unconditional trust.

5

Cost-effective management

FROM OUTSIDE THE window came the scraping sound of shovels interspersed with the dull, rhythmic blows of picks. The men handling the picks let out their breath with an audible 'unh' each time the picks were embedded in the hard soil. Holmes sat behind his desk and uttered a grunt of satisfaction. The blows were slightly out of phase and he could hear the picks strike the ground a split second apart. The men carrying the spades were having a break, conducting a cheerful conversation.

Suddenly there were cries of consternation and the sound of rain falling on the roof. Holmes walked over to the window and saw a geyser fifteen meters high rising from the far end of the furrow. One of the pick handlers had discovered the main water supply.

Men were running about trying to find the tap that was buried somewhere under the lawn.

Holmes uttered a curse. Even as he watched, a cow came running in from the street to quench her thirst at the rapidly expanding fountain.

Stacked on the lawn were the branches of the huge bougainvillea that was the source of all the trouble. A week before, the gardener had discovered a snake hiding amongst its leaves and unceremoniously killed it with a spade, thereby incurring the wrath of Thomson who loved snakes. Holmes held an entirely different opinion of them.

He ordered the gardener to remove the offending bougainvillea. Where there is one snake, he argued, there might be more. And besides, the shrub was right next to his office. At first, the gardener pruned the bougainvillea, then it was cut off at its base. Holmes was still not satisfied and ordered the roots to be removed.

He observed the chaos outside. The dust-covered trees and hazy, cloudless sky depressed him. He turned away, looked out of the opposite window and was rewarded with the sight of scrawny AIDS patients languishing underneath the trees.

The noise of the air conditioner irritated him. Does it work when there is no water? he wondered. He turned it off and switched on the overhead fan, walked into the adjoining office and asked Rose, the secretary, to report the damaged water pipe to the town council. 'Please ask them to hurry,' he added, and managed to keep his voice even.

The heat was overwhelming as usual and he could feel the sweat trickle from his armpits down the side of his chest.

Holmes had the figure of a benevolent beer drinker: a shiny bald head, gold-rimmed spectacles, a protruding belly, and an affected joviality that didn't fool anyone. Neither his ready smile, nor his smooth voice, nor his expensive clothes could conceal his reptilian eyes, which pierced his benign veneer like gun barrels peeking through a camouflage net.

After a year in the bush, he hadn't changed his dressing habits. His shirts were immaculately pressed and the sleeves held together with cufflinks at the wrist. The shirt and trousers joined exactly at the level of his navel and both were unable to hide his potbelly. He always wore a tie in spite of the suffocating heat, and avoided walking in the streets for fear of ruining his patent leather shoes.

Holmes disliked the town. He hated the dusty streets, the donkeys, the potholes in the road, the noisy marketplace, the mosquitoes that rose up from the river like a cloud, the fine dust that settled on his desk during the dry season, and the oppressive humidity of the rainy season.

His wife complained about the absence of a decent hairdresser, the unavailability of bean sprouts, the condition of the tennis courts at the expatriate club, the flies in the butcher shop, the shocking lack of culture, and the prices at the Indian shop.

'Only another year or so,' he reassured her, 'then we return to the Capital.'

The job was a promotion after all, he reminded her. And he had been hired for his managerial skills. There seemed to be a total lack of proper managers, he echoed the words of the Regional Superintendent. His wife was not impressed. She missed her friends, the boutiques, shopping centers and the other luxuries of civilization. At least once a month and sometimes more often he was forced to take a long weekend to drive her to the Capital. On the way there she regained some of her former warmth and on the way back she was as frigid as the frozen food in the boot of his BMW.

FOR ANOTHER MOMENT Holmes stood in front of the window and watched as the men finally found the tap and turned it off. The geyser imploded. He turned away and sat down at his desk. A fly settled on his head. He waved it away but it returned and landed on his nose. He waved it away again, then looked for something to use as a flyswatter. He picked up a newspaper, folded it length-wise and stalked the fly. It flew up toward the ceiling and settled on a light bulb.

Holmes gave up and tried to concentrate on the auditor's report that heralded the start of a bad week. It was delivered to his office on Monday, telling him that the hospital was ten percent over budget for the second quarter. The same morning the Regional Superintendent had announced a visit scheduled for the following Monday. Holmes had to cancel his planned long weekend and his wife threw a tantrum.

Also, on Monday he received a repair bill for the hospital ambulance that had hit a cow while traveling at night. On Tuesday Lawrence, the hospital administrator, reminded Holmes about the faulty emergency generator that needed urgent repairs. Lawrence was back on Wednesday, asking him to authorize an order for more oxygen cylinders.

'But I authorized one last week!' Holmes cried.

'But this week we have a patient on a ventilator,' Lawrence told him. 'Whose patient is this?' Holmes asked, knowing it could only be Morgan's. He signed the authorization and tried to get hold of Morgan. He was told that Morgan was in theater and refrained from leaving a message for Morgan to come and see him, since the last thing he needed was a personal confrontation.

It was Thursday morning, and he had just returned from the doctors' meeting. His concern about the budget seemed to have fallen on deaf ears. Holmes scrutinized the auditor's report again. The main culprits were the pharmacy and the kitchen—expensive antibiotics and high-protein diets. Why on earth were they spending so much money on antibiotics? He took his pen from the top pocket of his shirt and wrote a memo to the pharmacist, asking him to list the stock level of each drug in the pharmacy. He read the memo and felt satisfied that he had at least made a start in addressing the problem.

The desk was crowded. Holmes lifted his head and glanced around the room. On the opposite wall were the new shelves with box files carrying labels of audit trails, minutes of meetings, budget forecasts, policies and protocols.

Underneath the shelves was an examination couch with a sphygmomanometer for measuring blood pressure mounted against the wall. The lower shelf was mounted above the couch, so close that even the scrawniest patient would not be able to fit onto it.

Directly opposite the desk was a bookcase with glass doors. In it, neatly stacked and catalogued, were old Jenkins' journals. They had been untouched for almost a year, relics from the past.

Holmes surveyed the bookcase as if he was seeing it for the first time. The journals will have to go, he decided, as well as the examination couch. It was a matter of priorities, he told himself. This is an office, not a consulting room. This is what old Jenkins didn't understand. Jenkins had spent far too much time in the wards and in the operating theater.

And what was his reward? 'Early retirement', as it was euphemistically called by the bureaucrats from Head Office, who realized their own jobs might be on the line if they didn't do something about the maverick who had overspent his budget two years in succession and refused to carry out instructions about home-based care for AIDS patients.

Holmes had decided long ago that Jenkins had had no idea of finance. After all, if a cake has to be shared by more takers, the slices become smaller. Jenkins did not seem to appreciate that. His defiance did not further his cause, nor did his violent disagreements with the rule-makers.

His doctors didn't seem to care about finances either. They were acting as if there was an unlimited supply of money, without ever considering the cost of their interventions. That, Holmes told himself, was going to have to change drastically. There are limits to how much can be spent and how many patients can be treated. They would just have to understand.

'Jenkins wanted to cure everyone, just imagine,' the Regional Superintendent had told Holmes on the day he was appointed.

'There simply isn't enough money. He didn't seem to realize that. What did he expect us to do?'

Holmes finished writing the memo, walked through the

door and put it on Rose's desk.

'Could you make me a cup of coffee?' he asked.

'The water has been cut off,' Rose reminded him with deliberate indifference.

He wanted to challenge her and tell her to fetch some from the ward, or the doctors' tearoom, but she had turned all her attention to the letter she was typing, ignoring him completely. Holmes shrugged and returned to his office.

He had inherited Rose. She had become Jenkins' secretary during his last year in office. She made no attempt to hide her dislike for her new boss, and it was an uneasy relationship. Holmes couldn't find an excuse to fire her, since she was very competent.

As for Rose, she needed the job and had to put up with someone she loathed.

He suddenly cursed Jenkins' legacy. This morning everything seemed to remind him of the old man. The way Rose treated him was a case in point that he had been weighed, measured and found wanting—a poor substitute for a living legend.

Holmes knew all about old Jenkins' fights with the authorities. Battles won and battles lost. His biggest coup was a High Care unit that he managed to extract from his reluctant masters after numerous acrimonious conversations and dogfights with the Regional Superintendent.

Holmes remembered the old man from meetings at Head Office. Tall, with an unruly shock of grey hair, black eyebrows and black eyes that exuded boundless energy. A deep, passionate voice, and an incisive intelligence that cut through bureaucratic arguments like the proverbial hot knife through butter. Holmes and Jenkins were on different sides of the fence, so to speak. Holmes abided by the rules laid down by the authorities and Jenkins questioned them incessantly. The old man had a tendency to ask questions that embarrassed everyone sitting around the long mahogany table in the boardroom.

Integrity depends on mundane things, such as household expenses and the importance a man attaches to his bank balance or his continued employment. Or on school fees for his children and his wife's extravagances. Like in the song, most men do owe their souls to the company store. Old Jenkins was a man of independent means, and did not really need his job. A man who can't be bought or a man with nothing to lose can be extremely dangerous.

Jenkins fearlessly questioned the morals of his colleagues. 'Would you,' he once enquired from the Regional Superintendent, 'send your own brother home to die in a hut if you had drugs available to save him?'

He challenged the men around the mahogany table to go out there and see for themselves what they were asking him and his doctors to do: 'Meet the people living with AIDS, look them in the eye and tell them you are sending them to their deaths,' he suggested. The men around the table squirmed; some were angry, others gave lame excuses that the old man refuted without even bothering to hide his contempt.

He became an embarrassment to Head Office, not because he was a bad doctor, but because he was the best one on their payroll. He was both hated and feared by the bureaucrats. His battle around the AIDS patients proved to be his undoing. He started a one-man crusade against what he called the complacency of the authorities.

No one calls his superiors a bunch of smooth-talking, soft-bellied murderers and gets away with it, not in the long run. He had overstepped the mark. And he had blatantly ignored instructions.

Even worse, he seemed to have the unconditional support of his doctors. And that, Holmes had soon realized, was the biggest problem.

It was apparent from the first day he had set foot in the hospital.

The old man was gone by then, but his spirit seemed to pervade the place. Notices written in his tidy handwriting were preserved by the nursing staff, and ward rounds were conducted with the same care as always. At night, doctors facing difficult problems asked themselves: 'Now how would the old man have handled this?'

They regarded Holmes as a mere figurehead. He was unlucky to have to step into the shoes of a man like Jenkins. Besides, his reputation as a Head Office lackey had preceded him.

When he first met the doctors, and announced that he had come to restore the health of the hospital, they measured him with disinterested eyes and reserved their judgment. Soon they realized he had no clinical prowess whatsoever. Since then, they had treated him with the disdain that professionals reserve for amateurs. They were dismayed when he insisted on doing a call every so often to justify his overtime allowance. Each time this happened, it took them up to a week to sort out the complications of his ill-considered interventions.

The staff despised him, but mostly hid their feelings behind a veneer of civility, except for Morgan who had openly defied him from the first day they met. Morgan instinctively did not trust people who wore neatly pressed suits, ties and shiny shoes.

He had a theory about shiny shoes: 'Just look at their shoes,' he told his colleagues, whenever the suit-clad bureaucrats from Head Office came calling for their mindless inspection tours. 'They are shiny and squeaky clean. It means they don't know what is really happening. If they took the time to walk the streets, there would be dust or mud or cow dung on them.'

FROM OUTSIDE HOLMES' window came the sound of a hacksaw. The heat inside the room was overwhelming.

As he got out of his chair, Holmes glanced out of the window and saw a man rummaging through a toolbox. He turned away from the window, unbuttoned his collar and picked up the previous year's budget from the shelf. Back at his desk, he paged through it, and was pleased with himself.

He had managed, in spite of opposition, to stay exactly within its limits. The Regional Superintendent had congratulated him on his efforts. True, he had had to make concessions here and there. There were voices of dissent, as expected.

The nurses had threatened to riot when he tried to cut their overtime allowance, but that problem had been solved. He had instructed the Matron to limit overtime. Morgan complained incessantly about understaffing, since several nurses had resigned.

But it takes time to recruit new staff, he had pointed out. We can't appoint just anyone. So far, the nurses had not been replaced and the hospital carried on as before.

Holmes was interrupted by Rose, who handed him a dictated letter to sign. He took his pen, signed it without reading it and handed it back to her. Stiff-legged, she walked out of the office and shut the door behind her. The heat instantly became worse. 'Please open the door!' he shouted, but his words fell on deaf ears.

He decided to endure the heat for a little longer and returned to the file in front of him. This year was a different matter altogether. The drug bill had soared to new heights in spite of his efforts.

'The doctors are a spoiled bunch,' the Regional Superintendent had warned him. 'The old man's influence will take a little while to wear off.' But he was wrong. The doctors were becoming more and more rebellious—even the benign, soft-spoken Kenyan.

Holmes could trace the insubordination all the way back to Morgan, right up to the time of their first meeting. Not that he hadn't expected trouble. Morgan had been the old man's blue-eyed boy after all. The day they were introduced, Morgan had ignored Holmes' proffered hand and barely acknowledged his presence.

They had violent disagreements right from the start and rarely spoke to each other since the day Morgan, in a fit of rage, called the medical profession a bunch of whores and added that Holmes would be a whore anyway, regardless.

In a rare display of emotion, Holmes had insisted that Morgan apologize.

Morgan reflected for a moment and smiled. 'Of course I take it back,' he said with mock sincerity. 'How could I insult the oldest profession in the world? Whores are honest people; they don't pretend. If you go to a whore, you know exactly what you are going to get.'

Holmes was enraged, 'You will be disciplined! This behavior cannot be tolerated!'

Morgan sneered. 'Do your damnedest; I don't need your job anyway; I will only apologize to the whores. You and your kind defy description!'

Holmes spent two full working days preparing his disciplinary hearing. The night before the event, he went to bed early and fell asleep, only to be woken by a nightmare about a huge snake that was nestling on his chest. He jumped out of bed with a scream that woke up his whole household, and smashed a bed lamp as he tried to kill the snake, which turned out to be his wife's favorite cat that had cuddled up to him in a moment of ill-considered camaraderie.

His destructive behavior didn't endear him to his wife who screamed at the top of her voice: 'I can't understand why I didn't divorce you long ago!'

At that very moment, which was close to midnight, Morgan

and Thomson were making their way back to Morgan's truck. They were on one of their nocturnal excursions into the bush and Thomson was carrying a puff adder to be photographed, weighed, and measured.

'We should release it into Holmes' bed,' Morgan suggested.

'Are you mad?' asked Thomson. 'I could never do that to a poor snake!'

Holmes dropped all charges against Morgan the next day, since his wife had stepped on a shard of glass when she got out of bed. It took the rest of the morning to dress her wound, pacify her, and save his marriage. After that, he had no energy left to take on such a formidable opponent as Morgan. Besides, he was superstitious and regarded the dream as a bad omen.

Holmes realized he needed help to 'turn the hospital around'.

'You do need an ally,' the Regional Superintendent had agreed with him. 'Let's find someone to take the flak so you can concentrate on more important things.'

After much motivation, headhunting and agonizing, a marginally unsuccessful general practitioner was found who had a degree in business administration and had administered his own practice into the ground. Even to Holmes it was not clear why the man was hired. Was it because of his degree, or his successful destruction of an existing practice, or his total lack of personality?

There was no way the man would upstage him, he realized with a feeling of gratitude. It was bad enough to have people such as the Kenyan, Thomson and Morgan to contend with, especially the unruly Morgan.

The most noticeable feature of the assistant superintendent was his extraordinarily slow gait, like a mountaineer at high altitude. At first his colleagues thought he had Parkinson's disease or even a perianal abscess, but then realized that was simply the way he walked.

Rebecca, who hated him instantly, timed him over fifty paces and named him Thunderbird. The name stuck so well that nobody seemed to remember his real name.

'High Care is a thorn in my side,' Holmes had told him soon after his arrival. 'I want you to sort it out.'

Whether Thunderbird wanted to impress Holmes or whether he displayed a profound lack of insight was unclear, but one morning he walked into High Care as Morgan was making his rounds. He reminded Morgan about cost-per-patient-per-day and urged him to discharge his patients earlier.

Morgan took him gently by the arm and led him into the passage out of earshot of the patients. Then he spun him around violently and in a soft, almost amicable voice promised to kill him if he ever set foot in High Care again.

Thunderbird looked into Morgan's eyes and saw the slightly lighter tint of blue around the inner fringe of the irises that made the eyes look as if they were aflame. He suddenly realized that Morgan could probably do exactly what he promised.

Since that day he had avoided Morgan and communicated with him only by memos that were promptly folded into paper airplanes.

Now and again, if he received a particularly irritating memo, Morgan would write him an acrimonious reply that reassured Thunderbird that the internal mail system was working after all.

6

A question for Father Michael

FATHER MICHAEL CROSSED the road to the mall and wondered what had possessed him to wear a cassock on such a hot day, but he could not turn back since he was already late for his appointment.

He avoided the dust blown up by a bus loaded to capacity, starting its journey to the north. On its roof were suitcases, cardboard boxes, brand new toilet bowls, a bed complete with mattress, and a tethered goat.

Vendors selling their wares on the verandas of the shops greeted him as he walked past and weaved his way among canvas shelters, where women sold fruit that ripened rapidly in the stifling heat.

Outside Mr. Chiremba's beerhall, patrons sat under the lover's tree, where an unsuccessful lover had tried to hang himself one night with a frayed rope, and ended up with only a fractured ankle.

A man called to Father Michael and offered him a drink, but he dismissed him with a wave of his hand and a forced smile.

He walked onwards up the hill as fast as the heat would allow and stopped halfway to catch his breath and wipe the sweat off his glasses. He looked down on the river that had receded to a silver line in the middle of its bed.

Women washed clothes and spread them on the gravelly sand, making a multicolored mosaic amongst which ran children, dogs and goats. Skinny, naked boys played in the shallows away from the deep pools.

Father Michael continued his journey. Near the top of the hill he stopped to catch his breath once again, before he entered a lush garden where tomatoes, cabbages, potatoes and mealies grew in neat rows. He knocked on the open door of a house that was tucked away between huge banana trees.

'Come in, Father!' Dorcas, the shebeen queen, called out from the living room. Father Michael's eyes took a moment to become accustomed to the darkened interior of the house. He noticed her white headscarf first, then the blue dress and then her dark face. She was smiling at him. 'Sit down, Father.' She grabbed his arm and led him to a chair. She opened a window but no breeze came through it.

'A beer, Father?'

Father Michael wiped the sweat from his brow as if to justify his indulgence. As always, he was overwhelmed by her presence. 'Yes!' she made up his mind for him, disappeared through a bead curtain and Father Michael could hear a fridge door open and shut.

Dorcas was a formidable woman. She had built the house herself and cultivated the soil with manure that she carried up the hill from the municipal corral. At night she ran a shebeen that was the most respectable establishment in town and had the tacit approval of the Constable, who dropped by for a sedate beer when his busy schedule allowed.

Nothing escaped her. She knew everyone in town and listened attentively to the conversations of her customers at night. She knew about every scandal and every tragedy before it became public knowledge. She attended every wedding, every christening, every funeral, offered valued advice to her customers on matters ranging from finances to unrequited love, shared their triumphs and sorrows, and scolded them if they drank too much.

Without ceremony, Morgan dragged him into the Children's Ward filled with AIDS patients. He found himself standing next to a bed where a dying mother was holding her child's hand. The woman refused to leave the boy and spent her nights sitting on a chair, sleeping with her torso resting on the child's bed, holding his hand.

'So, Father,' Morgan had said when they left. 'Who would you say should die first, the mother or the baby?'

'That,' Father Michael had answered, 'is God's will.'

'You are assuming that God cares,' Morgan pointed out.

Father Michael found himself looking into Morgan's flinty eyes that had lost every trace of softness. For a moment they stood under the trees in the hospital garden.

Then Morgan said: 'Come on, Father, let me give you a lift home. It is almost daybreak.'

Morgan's question had bothered Father Michael ever since, and he still hadn't resolved it.

'Father Michael,' Dorcas' voice interrupted his thoughts. 'I know you better than that. Something is bothering you.'

Overhead the sun relentlessly continued its journey across the afternoon sky, and a ray of light fell through the open window onto his bald forehead. Suddenly an uncomfortable glare from the rims of his spectacles shone into his eyes.

Dorcas got up and leaned across him to draw the curtain. For a moment, Father Michael was confronted by her surprisingly firm breasts.

He relented and told her about Morgan's question.

Dorcas laughed.

'Morgan,' she said, 'has no finesse.'

In his mind's eye, Father Michael again saw the dying mother, holding the child's hand.

The silence in the room was only broken by the sound of the chain of a bicycle being pedaled up the hill. Dorcas rested her chin in her hand, and Father Michael found himself staring at her profile in the reflected light from the garden.

Suddenly she got up and stood framed in the open doorway, looking out into the street.

Father Michael was uncomfortably aware of her shapely thighs, visible through the thin fabric of her dress. He took off his glasses and concentrated on cleaning them.

'It is not the question itself that is bothering you, Father,' she said, turning away from the door.

Father Michael stopped cleaning his glasses.

'What is bothering you is why anyone should find it necessary to ask such a question.'

MORGAN WROTE DOWN a list of instructions in a patient's file.

'I have this girl,' he told Thomson who was sitting opposite him at the desk in the nurses' office. It was cluttered with patient files, discharge summaries, laboratory reports, an ancient telephone directory, two telephones and a cowbell that was used to signal the end of visiting hours.

'She was thrown to the dogs because she was thought to have AIDS. Bastards sent her for home-based care. She weighs just twenty-nine kilograms.'

Thomson scratched his beard and filled out a laboratory form without lifting his head.

'So what does she have, to make her weigh only twenty-nine kilograms?' he asked.

'She is pouring pus out of her loin from a dead kidney. And her AIDS test is negative; I have done it myself.'

'Lucky girl,' Thomson said, and both of them ignored the phone as it started ringing. 'So what are you going to do with her?'

'Fatten her up first,' said Morgan. He reached for the phone, then changed his mind.

Violet came rushing in and picked up the receiver. 'Hold

on,' she said and put her hand over the mouthpiece.

'I will murder the two of you,' she said, moving her gaze from Morgan to Thomson.

'It's for you.' She handed the receiver to Thomson. Thomson laughed. 'Yes?' he said.

At that moment there was an overwhelming sound of plates and cups rattling as the food trolley negotiated the corrugations of the porch outside the ward.

'Wait,' Thomson said, and shut his eyes.

'Someone should design a proper suspension for that thing,' Morgan said.

The sound abated. Through the open door Morgan saw the food trolley being pushed into the passage by a stout woman wearing a white headscarf.

Thomson resumed his conversation. 'All right,' he said, 'send him over here.'

Violet stopped in her tracks. 'You are not admitting any more patients today!' she told him.

'I will only be talking to the man,' Thomson reassured her.

'Just look at that!' she said and pointed into the passage where the afternoon's admissions were waiting for her patiently; some were standing, some sitting on the few available chairs, and one scrawny man slouched on the floor. 'Where do you find all these patients?'

'We don't find them,' said Morgan. 'They find us.' He stood up and removed a diet sheet from the bulletin board.

'Have you cooled off?' she wanted to know from Morgan. She turned to Thomson, 'You should have seen him this morning. He nearly bit my head off about that girl. As if it was me who was responsible. And she came from another hospital!'

'Is this the girl you were telling me about?'

Morgan nodded. He was writing a letter to the cook.

Violet stood in the middle of the room and stared at the back of Morgan's head.

'And you,' she said to Morgan, 'owe me an apology.'
'Never explain yourself; never ever apologize,' said Morgan.
He looked up and handed her the note to the cook.
'This man,' she told Thomson, 'is incorrigible.'

7

The girl who forgot her name

THERE WAS NOTHING unusual about the emaciated girl who had been discovered in Morgan's ward. Dying patients often arrived under the cover of darkness. They came from all over, sometimes from other overcrowded hospitals, accompanied by men who respectfully held their hats in calloused hands and women wearing thin, much-worn dresses.

Everyone had become used to anxious, elderly mothers sitting on the floor next to the bedside. They would stay for the duration of the illness, silent observers watching from the sideline, rejoicing about temporary reprieves and stoically accepting the worst.

Afterwards, the mothers could be found at the entrance of the mortuary, gathered around the inevitable pick-up truck, accompanied by their men, who again held their hats in their hands, singing a hymn whilst the body was loaded on the back.

The night sister could be forgiven for not notifying the doctor on duty. In the file was a note, recording the fact that the girl had been brought by relatives at five o'clock. The sister had put up a drip and even recorded the girl's weight.

Morgan saw the girl in the course of his morning round. At first he thought he was dealing with another inevitable death. She was obviously dying. Her clavicles stuck out like flagpoles, every single rib was visible, her pelvic brim was covered by skin only, her withered hamstrings barely separated bone from skin, and her head was attached to her torso by neck muscles that looked as if they were going to snap. Foul-smelling pus drained from a hole in her left loin and she wasn't looking at him or anyone else; she was staring at the floor. Above her head, the bulb of the bed lamp hung precariously from its socket. He reinserted it, fiddled until it stayed in its socket and switched it on to see if it was working.

Returning to the foot of the bed, he took the battered clinic notes and started paging through them.

Slowly he put the story together: how she became ill during pregnancy, how she developed a perinephric abscess that was inadequately treated, how she delivered a live baby, was referred for an opinion and diagnosed as an AIDS patient without an AIDS test, and how she was discharged for home-based care.

At first he swore softly, under his breath. Then he swore a bit louder and eventually exploded like a powder keg.

Violet tried to pacify him but he ignored her. She put her fingers in her ears and the other women in the ward stared straight ahead of them.

The girl was twenty-three years old and she was at the end of the road. Ready to die. She was staring at the floor and wasn't speaking to anybody. Even Morgan's loud swearing didn't make any obvious impression on her.

Afterwards in the duty room, Violet told Morgan that he had intimidated the girl and that was why she consented to an AIDS test. 'She has made up her mind to die,' he said, 'so why would she be scared of me?'

He took the blood sample to the laboratory and watched as the technician drew up the serum with an air of impartiality, like a referee at a tennis match. They both waited as the control turned red and her test stayed negative.

'Miracles do happen,' said the technician as he wrote the

result in his book where almost all the results were recorded in red.

Morgan was not optimistic. 'It only means she is not going to die of AIDS,' he said.

For the next two days he expected to find an empty bed when he did his morning rounds, but somehow she managed to stay alive. She refused to eat; she refused to talk, and he wondered if she had even moved since the day she had been brought in.

On the third morning Morgan interrupted his ward round, drove to the mall, and found the baker in front of his shop feeding breadcrumbs to the noisy crows. They took off from the rooftops, glided into the mall, banked, turned above the baker's head, landed next to him and devoured his offerings.

Morgan strode past and walked into the shop.

He took all the ice cream out of the fridge, together with a dozen eggs, stacked it all on the counter and paid the baker's assistant.

He walked out past the baker who was still feeding the crows. The baker raised his eyebrows in surprise. 'What are you doing with all that ice cream, Morgan?' he asked.

'I'm having a party.'

In the ward he calculated a 3,000-calorie diet using ice cream, eggs, and protein powder and divided it into two-hourly portions. The other women were all sitting on their beds, watching him. Morgan paused, realizing that two-hourly feeds were going to be a problem since the nurses were already overworked. As he recommended writing, the answer to his problem occurred to him. Why not enlist the help of the others? At least it would give them something to do.

He straightened his back, faced the women who were all watching him and asked: 'Do you think you can help this girl?' They didn't know what he had in mind, but all of them nodded their heads affirmatively. 'Can you see she is very sick?' he asked, standing in the middle of the floor like a sergeant major. Yes, they nodded solemnly. 'Can you feed her every two hours?' he asked. Yes, of course, they nodded.

He paused and asked, 'Do you think I am crazy?'

'Yes!' they all said in a chorus and smiled their broadest smiles.

The irony was not lost on Morgan. All the women had terminal AIDS; they looked like scarecrows themselves and most of them were dying, but they were happy to help. It would take their minds off the business of dying.

Morgan also enlisted the help of the cook to make her omelets and smuggle ice cream into the ward.

Charles, the big, jovial, moustached cook often made him breakfast when Morgan sneaked into the back door of the kitchen after a long night, when he didn't have time to go home. Charles served his food and tea on a tray and didn't mind that Morgan smoked in his kitchen.

'It is very difficult now to give special diets,' he told Morgan, raising his voice above the din in the kitchen. 'But I will try'.

He raised his cap and mopped the sweat from his brow.

'That round man,' he said, meaning Holmes, 'comes here every day.'

Afterwards, whenever Morgan went to the ward, there was someone sitting next to the girl, who tentatively sucked milkshakes through a straw and seemed exhausted by this small effort. Even Mary was pushed to the girl's bedside in a wheelchair and sat there holding her hand.

At first, the girl seemed oblivious to all the attention and Morgan was dismayed by her lack of response. Her temperature chart looked like a drawing of high alpine peaks, her white blood cell count stayed high, which told him he wasn't controlling her infection.

He carefully chose the least damaging antibiotics to make

sure he didn't damage her other kidney.

Morgan sat down next to her bed, intercepted her gaze and said: 'I know what your name is, but I want you to tell me yourself.'

Her eyes seemed to stare straight through him. There was complete silence in the ward.

It seemed that she had forgotten her name, but just when Morgan was about to give up, her lips moved. He heard her speak for the first time in a barely audible whisper: 'Naledi.' And Janet, the woman with the Kaposi sarcoma, said: 'It means star.'

'How can you forget a name like that?' Morgan asked. He took his pen and drew a star on the bed sheet. Violet scolded him.

'Just so that everyone can remember,' he said.

IN FRONT OF Violet's office stood a familiar figure: the original, proverbial scarecrow, wearing a patched, dusty anorak in spite of the overwhelming heat.

'And you?' asked Violet. 'What are you doing here?'

'Let me introduce you to my friend,' Morgan mocked her.

'I know your friend only too well,' she said. 'And why on earth is he wearing an anorak in this weather?'

Johnson, the scarecrow, smiled and showed off his uneven teeth.

'I can't leave it in my house,' he said. 'There is no lock on the door.'

In his hand he carried a tattered copy of *Gorky Park*.

Violet laughed. 'Why *Gorky Park*?' she asked.

'Because all the snow and ice makes him forget the heat,' said Morgan. 'It counteracts the anorak.'

Maybe he should be reading the *Gulag Archipelago*, on

account of all the people we are burying, he thought.

Johnson was one of the regulars. He was weakened by the 'big disease', unable to work, and unable to feed himself properly. Morgan fattened him up, discharged him, and readmitted him when he reverted to scarecrow status.

On the floor was the usual plastic fertilizer bag containing Johnson's earthly belongings. Morgan spotted the end of a spirit level, Johnson's most treasured possession. It was the only link to his past as a bricklayer and it accompanied him wherever he went.

'You never know', he had told Morgan before. He might find a cure for his problem and, when that happened, he wanted to be ready.

Morgan sat down at the desk in the duty room with Violet opposite him and started filling in an admission form. Johnson stood in the middle of the floor with his plastic bag next to him and tried to make idle conversation.

Morgan sniggered as he heard Johnson say, 'The rain is conspicuously absent this year.'

Johnson could swear as badly as Morgan, but he had a healthy respect for Violet who had threatened to wash out his mouth with disinfectant if she ever heard him swearing again. In her presence he tried to impress her with his command of the English language and always got himself into trouble.

'In my village it is very dry indeed,' Johnson tried again.

Violet looked at him with smoldering eyes. 'If you don't become inconspicuous immediately, you will be very sorry indeed. Come on, you know the ward; go and get your clothes and get into the bath!' she dismissed him.

'And the reason for the admission, Dr. Morgan?' she asked with both her eyebrows raised.

'Tender loving care, sister,' Morgan said innocently. 'He is my friend after all.'

'You and your friends,' she sighed and then remembered.

'She waited for you for two afternoons. You disappointed her.'

'What do you mean?' asked Morgan and then realized. For two days he had been too busy to keep his afternoon appointment with Mary.

He found himself looking into Violet's unfathomable black eyes.

'You mean a lot to her,' she said. 'Personally, I don't know what she sees in such a scruffy character, but there you have it.'

'Oh my God,' said Morgan, his cynical smile wiped off his face and replaced by genuine remorse. 'I will have to make it up to her.'

'You had better,' said Violet. 'Two days is a big chunk out of her life.'

'AND WHERE HAVE you been, Oumar?' Rebecca briefly interrupted her conversation.

Oumar did not tell her about the morbid start to his day. Instead, he picked up a pack of files from the desk and started paging through them. He felt like a man rereading the same book. A repetition of symptoms recorded by nurses from familiar clinics. He could recognize each nurse by her handwriting as he read about tales of woe from clinics scattered through the countryside: loss of weight, night sweats, coughing, diarrhea, swollen glands, fever, and breathlessness; restless, sleepless nights and tiresome, dreary days.

He glanced through the window and correlated the notes with the scrawny figures waiting outside. I can make the diagnosis from here, he thought. All I can't do, is name them. Apart from that, they are all the same.

Diagonally opposite Rebecca sat a pretty girl. Her breasts were shaped like avocados and her nipples were clearly defined under her thin blouse.

He was interrupting the end of a post-test counseling session, Oumar realized. He did not leave the office since this one, surprisingly, had a happy outcome. The AIDS test was negative and the girl was ecstatic.

'And are you taking precautions, my girl?' Rebecca's manner was protective, almost conspiratorial. She was a pillar of strength in the fight against unwanted babies, randy young men, and runaway viruses.

Coyly, the girl assured her that she was.

'And are you working?' Rebecca asked her all-important question.

The girl turned out to be a messenger.

'And why only a messenger?' Rebecca was indignant. 'A clever, pretty girl like you?'

The girl was a school dropout, and Rebecca gave her a lecture on the importance of an education, as she did with every other uneducated woman. It was her mission in life.

Oumar stopped paging through the files and watched Rebecca admonishing the girl with the gravity of a concerned great-aunt.

'An education,' she told the girl, 'gives you a choice. Without an education, sooner or later you are going to share a bed you don't want to share.'

Oumar returned to the notes and found unexpected light entertainment. Two men had overturned a donkey-cart. An obsessive policeman insisted that they be tested for drunken driving. The apologetic note from the nurse bore the previous day's date. He glanced out of the window and saw the men sitting next to each other. They were the only healthy-looking people in the crowd and by now were predictably sober.

Rebecca's indignant tone had made way for a motherly one.

'You must do something about your education, my girl,' she was saying. 'Not tomorrow. Today. You owe it to yourself.'

The girl nodded in agreement.

'You must give yourself a choice,' Rebecca concluded. 'Otherwise, men are going to use you.'

At the end of the interview the girl got up and slung a trendy canvas bag over her shoulder. Her breasts bounced under the blouse, a thin leather belt accentuated her well-proportioned hips, and her thighs inside her tight-fitting jeans were perfectly shaped.

You are far too pretty for your own good, Oumar thought as he watched her walk through the door. He remembered a cynical colleague who told him about a place where he had once worked. It was no use, the man had said. All the good looking women were either pregnant or had venereal disease. The pressure of natural selection, was Oumar's comment at the time. Now, with AIDS rampant everywhere, he started wondering if there was an evolutionary advantage in being ugly.

'You make it sound as if all women run the risk of becoming prostitutes,' he told Rebecca.

'In a manner of speaking, they do.' She switched back to her indignant tone: 'If they don't have a job, no money, no roof over their heads and no food in their bellies, then what do you think they sell?'

8

Death of a child

AFTER TRYING TO sustain a breath rate of forty-five breaths per minute for a week, the child died just before six o'clock, with flaring nostrils and wide-open eyes. A weeklong marathon, thought Morgan, and wondered whether he shouldn't have ventilated the little boy after all, despite the fact that he had no prognosis.

Short of ventilation, he had given the child everything he could, and had gone back every night to see him and to continue his futile battle.

One night when he was struggling to reinsert a drip, he had been tempted to give up. He turned his gaze away from the boy and looked into the face of the exhausted mother. She didn't say anything, but her eyes scrutinized his face, trying to find out what he was thinking.

Do you really think I am doing you or your child any good? I am prolonging his agony; I put in drips that hurt him; I give him drugs that are not helping; my boss tells me I am wasting resources; and I pretend that I am trying to save his life. And, for what?

'Your responsibility becomes greater when you treat these people.' Old Jenkins' words came back to Morgan. 'They trust you absolutely, and they have no one else to turn to. They only have you.'

He had become aware again of the feeble cry of the boy, shook off the tiredness that hung over him like a cloak and continued until he managed to insert a cannula into a tiny vein. The mother gave him a faint smile.

She kept up her vigil for twenty-four hours a day right until the end, and thanked Morgan for his efforts when she realized the child was dead. Only after the boy's body had been shrouded did she allow the nurses to take her to the side ward where she fell asleep instantly.

'What are the mother's chances?,' Father Michael asked Morgan later that morning when he found him standing in front of the nurses' tearoom drinking a cup of strong, black coffee.

Morgan didn't answer immediately.

'You remember the question I asked you the other night?' he said, after taking another sip.

Father Michael merely nodded.

'Just imagine,' Morgan said, 'if she had died first and the child died without a mother to hold his hand.'

'It is a blessing in disguise,' Father Michael said.

Morgan drained his cup. 'So there is a God after all,' he said. 'The mother will not survive for long,' he added. 'In fact, I think it was only the child who kept her alive.'

Morgan's anger surrounded him like an electric field.

'We must learn to accept,' Father Michael tried to pacify him.

Morgan fixed him with an ice cold stare.

'You sound like Tesfai,' he said. Father Michael's face showed genuine surprise. 'Tesfai?' he enquired.

'A friend of mine,' Morgan said, but did not elaborate.

We must learn to accept, thought Morgan. That's what Tesfai had told him more than once. Tesfai—mountaineer, war veteran, and guide—who had lost most of his relatives in a bloody war and reputedly helped a fair number of the opposition to their untimely deaths.

Morgan, torn between his love for Africa and his

disillusionment with it, had met Tesfai on his travels through northeast Africa. He had been amazed by Tesfai's total lack of anger after all that had happened to him and his family. Tesfai, his friend and guide during their long sojourn in the mountains.

Tesfai's face lit up by a single remaining flame amongst the embers of their fire, around them the ruins of a village, a pale slice of moon above the towering peaks. Tesfai's eyes like two black slits in an orange mask, and his soft voice hardly breaking the silence: 'You must learn to accept; you have too much anger and it is not good for you.'

Morgan inspected the inside of his cup and cursed.

Around them was the usual early morning flurry of nurses changing shift, the noisy kitchen trolley being pushed down the passage, patients being wheeled to theater, and the cleaners conducting a cheerful conversation with the porters.

Morgan half-heartedly returned their greetings. Father Michael said: 'Cheer up, my friend; you have done your best.'

That's what everyone says, thought Morgan. The battle cry of people fighting futile battles with inadequate tools. We have done our best. But we knew the battle was doomed right from the start. And we know what the problem is, but we do nothing about it.

Father Michael made his way down the passage as Morgan drank another cup of coffee to fortify himself.

LIGHT FLOWED IN through the high window in the Children's Ward and fell on the table where the small children were sitting having their breakfast.

Children's voices filled the room. Laughter and giggles floated up towards the window, and Violet displayed her soft, just-for-children eyes.

Against the wall, in cots, were the not-so-lucky AIDS children. Blankets were spread neatly on the floor between the cots for anxious mothers to sleep on. During the day they sat on chairs holding their sick children's hands.

An inherited curse, thought Morgan as he looked at the mothers with heads a half a size too small, and eyes a half a size too big. They watched him as he examined their children, detecting the slightest change of expression on his face, studying his body language and peering straight into his eyes, trying to look past the irises into his mind, waiting for an unguarded moment.

He looked at X-rays with ominous signs and examined children who should have been running around spreading their joy and laughter. Instead, they were lying in bed like small forest animals caught in snares, looking at him with unaccusing eyes that humbled him.

He wrote up treatment with clenched jaws, keeping his face straight and shuttering his eyes so nobody could see what he was thinking.

Yvonne, a two-year-old with an old woman's face and shadows under her eyes, was sitting upright in her bed.

The day before, he had removed the drain from her chest after the pus in her pleural cavity had mercifully cleared up.

She eyed him suspiciously. The mother looked pleased.

'Come on Yvonne, give me a smile,' Morgan said. The girl looked at her mother and chose to ignore him.

'Does she ever smile?' he asked the mother, who looked surprisingly well.

The woman laughed. 'Sometimes,' she said. 'But she is a serious girl.'

'And the dress?' Morgan asked. On the day Yvonne had been admitted she had worn a pretty white dress and Morgan had spilled blood on it when he took a sample from her arm.

The woman reached into the locker and produced a snow-white dress, neatly ironed.

'I managed,' she said.

Yvonne stared at the dress without any sign of joy.

Morgan sighed, and took money out of his pocket. 'Please buy her some sweets, will you?'

He held up the chest X-ray and was happy to see the lung had re-expanded completely.

Near the door was the empty cot of the baby who had died during the night. Next to it was an angle-poise lamp, the only evidence of his nightlong battle.

IN FEMALE WARD Janet welcomed him with her usual exuberant smile. Next to her, ready to be inserted, was the drip with Vincristine. Morgan asked her to open her mouth and inspected the tumor. It wasn't getting any smaller; in fact, it was now invading her soft palate. But Janet believed in the Vincristine with religious conviction. When he inserted the needle and started the infusion, her gratitude was written all over her face. She lay on her back and watched the clear fluid trickle into her, almost counting the drops. He lingered on the veranda until the infusion was complete, then took a short cut across the lawn where a cow grazed peacefully.

Smirnoff was in Casualty, his tall frame swaying to and fro, wearing his coat as usual. The coat was for the sole purpose of carrying his most prized possessions. A bloodstained handkerchief was tied around his head. He was walking with a wide-based, staggering gait, unable to decide whether he wanted to sit down in a chair or on the floor with his back against the wall. After some deliberation, he chose the latter option. Leaning against the wall, he started sliding downwards. Rebecca tapped against the glass and shouted his name as she rose indignantly from her chair.

He arrested his downward slide, stood precariously and

regained his balance. Then he focused his eyes on the sound of Rebecca's voice, saw her outline behind the glass partition and managed a grotesque salute.

He owed his nickname to the label on a bottle of precious fluid that had disappeared from Mr. Georgiou's shop and was later found in his possession.

When caught, Smirnoff held the view that the bottle was half full, and regarded that as a mitigating factor. The Constable held the opposite, more pessimistic view. In court, the bottle—half full and half empty—earned Smirnoff a brief spell of rather secure accommodation with a regular set menu and no alcoholic beverages.

Rebecca's stout figure was framed by the doorway. 'Come here!' she shouted, and returned to her desk.

Smirnoff made his way across the floor and appeared in the doorway of the office. He rested his shoulder against the doorpost and steadied himself. Rebecca stared at him impassively. Smirnoff repeated his salute and almost fell over. He smelt of cheap alcohol, stale sweat, and pure wood smoke.

'Why are you so drunk so early in the morning?' asked Rebecca.

Smirnoff removed the handkerchief, bent down his head and displayed his latest war wound. He had been hit over the head with a beer bottle, he informed Rebecca, but stressed the fact that the bottle was empty.

'There are only three reasons for fighting in this town,' said Morgan, 'money, women and liquor.'

Rebecca stuck her hand into Smirnoff's coat pocket and retrieved a near-empty brandy bottle. 'The last in this case,' she said.

Smirnoff voiced his most immediate concern. He had cash flow problems and needed bridging capital to tide him through the day. To be paid back of course, he added generously.

'You stay here until you're sober,' said Rebecca. 'And where were you for your appointment?'

Smirnoff chose to answer one question with another.

'But my dog?' He raised an unsteady arm and pointed at the outside door. A black and white mutt was patiently waiting for him.

'We will make a plan,' said Rebecca. 'I'm surprised that dog hasn't run away from you yet.' She wrote out an appointment card and stuck it to the bulletin board, then called a nurse to take him away and shave his head. 'And give him a bath as well,' she told the nurse as Smirnoff was led away.

OUMAR WAS SITTING on a chair at the far end of Rebecca's desk, his face partly obscured by the usual early morning pile of patient files. He sat with his legs stretched out in front of him, his fingers intertwined in front of his chest and his eyes closed, seemingly oblivious to the disturbance. After Smirnoff had gone, he opened his eyes and glanced at his watch.

Meditating are we?' said Rebecca, and started sorting the files.

They were arranged in order of urgency. Very sick people first, then sick people, then not-so-sick people. Malingerers were last or not at all. Drunks received a tongue-lashing and were sent on their way, except if they were injured—then they received a tongue-lashing and treatment. Those who tried to jump the queue were sent back and fitted in after the malingerers.

'Now, Morgan,' Rebecca remembered suddenly. 'What happened to your dead cat?'

Morgan had almost forgotten about the vanished cat. 'I haven't heard a thing,' he said.

'Just imagine,' she told Oumar. 'This man here sends a

dead cat to the vet in his own blue cool-box and it disappears off the face of the earth.'

Oumar got up from his chair and stretched his arms upwards. 'I can think of better uses for a cool-box,' he said yawning.

'That cat is going to haunt you, Morgan,' she said. 'You'd better hope our highly respected superintendent doesn't find out about it.'

'The hell do I care,' said Morgan. Rebecca pointed at a protocol on the management of rabies on the bulletin board.

It bore Holmes' signature. It was his first official communication with the staff, written within a week of his arrival at the hospital, stressing the importance of the correct handling of potential rabies victims. Everyone had been perplexed. Had he not noticed the multitude of scrawny AIDS patients? Surely there were more urgent problems?

The reason for Holmes' distorted vision became apparent during one of the earlier doctors' meetings. He had once written a dissertation on rabies and considered himself an expert on the topic. In the process he had become almost paranoid about stray dogs and cats. 'You cannot be too careful,' the newly arrived city dweller told the bush veterans. 'In a place like this, after a prolonged dry season, it is a very real risk.'

'If your boss hears about the cat, he is going to take it out on you and me,' Rebecca said as she handed them each a handful of files. 'Now come on you two; who do you think is going to do the work?'

At noon the town surrendered to the simmering heat. Yellowbilled Kites circled in the thermals, surveying backyards in the hope of finding a stray chicken. The customers at Mr. Chiremba's bar moved their chairs onto the veranda. Dogs lay panting in the shade of trees, and stray cows grazed on the hospital lawn.

'I THOUGHT YOU had deserted me,' Mary said.

She was a small, solitary presence on a huge veranda, waiting for him. For a brief moment Morgan was reminded of the wastefulness of Africa. Here was a bright young girl with a college education wasting away on a veranda, like a withered plant, discarded and forgotten.

Morgan fumbled in his shirt pocket and produced a crumpled cigarette packet. From inside it he retrieved a small red rose.

Mary's laughter was infectious. 'The rose is a miracle,' said Morgan. 'It survived the cows, the gardener and the budget.'

He held it by its stem and handed it to her. For a moment he felt himself mesmerized by the perfect shape of her eyes, and he held onto the rose a little longer than necessary.

She took the rose, brought it up to her face, inhaled, and again burst out laughing.

'It smells of tobacco.'

'It's the idea that counts,' Morgan told her.

Admiring it, she said: 'I can understand why the Little Prince loved his rose so much. Just look at its perfect shape. I cannot imagine that such a beautiful thing could grow in such a scruffy garden.'

'Pity that I had to pick it,' said Morgan, 'but otherwise the cows would have eaten it, I'm sure. You shouldn't pick flowers; you should only enjoy them as they are.'

Suddenly she grabbed his hand, and he was surprised by the strength of her grip.

'Thank you,' she said. 'I will look after it and later when it wilts, I will put it between the pages of a book. That way it will be preserved forever.'

He noted her careful phrasing: 'It will be preserved forever,' and not, 'I will preserve it forever.'

Through the open window drifted the evening noises of

the ward: the rattling food trolley, the cheerful call of the kitchen assistant, the bathroom door slamming, taps running and, finally, Mary's name being called. A nurse appeared at the door.

'It's dinner time,' she announced.

'Take care,' Morgan said and jumped off the veranda.

AT HOME HE stood on the lawn, watched the starlings settle into a camel-thorn tree and listened to cheerful voices floating in the windless evening air. There was not a suggestion of a breeze.

Morgan decided he was too tired for an evening run. He felt relieved that the battle with the child was over. Lately, almost all his marathon battles had ended in defeat and his anger was always lurking just beneath the surface. The nursing staff and his colleagues had become used to it; the youngsters were scared of him and avoided him.

He shrugged his shoulders, went into the house, warmed up the leftovers of his previous night's dinner and ate at the table in the middle of the living room. There was no sign of Oscar.

He washed his plate, turned on the tape deck, and listened to the familiar sounds of Rodrigo's *Concierto de Aranjuez*.

He idly flipped through a much-used sketchbook, a chronicle of memories from his trip through northeast Africa that had inspired several half-finished paintings that remained stacked in his bedroom.

There were line sketches drawn in a hurry in the bus on the long dusty Asmara road, and more detailed sketches of places where he had stayed over: women roasting corn cobs on fires; horse-drawn Gharies; wild-looking men from the desert walking next to camels carrying salt blocks on their backs; women carrying clay pots on their heads; marketplaces and mosques.

He paused at a sketch of Tigrean women sitting on the ground, underneath makeshift shelters.

A vivid memory jolted him. Not shown in the sketch was the bridge over the river that was blown up during the war and the blockhouse, pock-marked by hundreds of bullets. Standing near the water's edge, Morgan had tried to imagine the sound of guns and shells and screams, with the smoke and dust and blood and sweat and fear and pain that make up a battle. From inside the blockhouse came the cheerful sound of children's voices. In front of it was a washing line with clothes that moved ever so slightly, like streamers, in the faint breeze.

The folly of war, he had thought. The heroes with their high ideas fight their destructive battles and move on. Women and children unconcernedly move into bullet-ridden blockhouses and put up washing lines.

He turned the page and found Tesfai's face staring up at him: stern, symmetrical and sharp featured. It was a hurried sketch made when he was sitting in the bar with Tesfai and Mohammed, pretending to take notes. Tesfai had a perfectly straight mouth, like a slit in his face. There were deep lines around it. Sometime later Morgan was looking at a pre-war photograph and was struck by Tesfai's youthful appearance. He had a different face then, happy and carefree. Deep post-war lines came later, creating a shadow at the corners of the nose. Delicate nostrils that flared as he spoke. A soft voice, he noted with surprise, as Tesfai explained about the route, sliding his finger across the map on the table. The map was held down by three beer mugs with bubbles that glittered like floating pearls in the late afternoon light.

Lines below level eyes, a hint of tiredness and vulnerability about them. Dark square cheeks that looked as if they were carved out of ebony.

Not a painting, Morgan decided. He wanted to retain the

apparent hurriedness of the sketch that started as concentric lines and gradually firmed until the outline of the face emerged.

He took rough watercolor paper and broke off a piece of charcoal, trying to recreate Tesfai as he had looked on that cold afternoon as he explained the logistics of their trip.

Four pack mules, two muleteers, and a scout with a Kalashnikov to keep the Shiftas at bay. Morgan had laughed about the hired gun and Tesfai was at pains to explain. 'Just in case,' he said, 'but I am sure they won't bother us.'

Morgan started drawing, almost absent-mindedly, noting the angles in Tesfai's face.

He gently rubbed the charcoal into the darker parts of the face. He held up the sketch and looked at the outlines of the eyes, measuring the distance of the pupils from the mid-line with a pencil.

Tesfai's eyes could be somber when he thought no one was looking—sometimes inexplicably tired, sometimes unfathomable, now and again a sparkle of slow, dry humor and, when he laughed about something, they were like lights suddenly turned on in a darkened house.

Morgan reminded himself not to draw the nose or mouth, but to draw the shade around them. He darkened the lines around Tesfai's post-war mouth, shaded the area around the nostrils and finished up with the hawk-like face as he remembered it. A hawk with a soft voice who had tried to teach him to accept things that couldn't be changed.

The music had stopped but Morgan didn't notice. He picked up the fixative, held the sketch at arm's length and fixed it. The smell of the fixative made him sneeze.

'So tell me, Tesfai,' he said aloud, looking at the sketch. 'When does one decide that something can't be changed?'

9

Holmes in action

THE KENYAN DISCOVERED three crates on the veranda of the office block. He climbed the stairs, sliding his hand along the rail, walked along the wooden floor, and inspected the contents. He instantly recognized old Jenkins' journals, carelessly flung into the crates: a torn blue cover of *The Journal of the Royal College of Surgeons of Edinburgh* lay protectively across copies of the *North American Clinics of Surgery*, *New England Journal of Medicine*, *The Lancet*, and *The Journal of Trauma*.

The Kenyan shook his head, glanced at his watch, leaned against the rail of the veranda, and waited for his colleagues to arrive.

'Come over here!' he shouted across the lawn when he saw Thomson and Oumar emerging from the side entrance between Male Ward and the kitchen.

He watched them as they jumped across an untidy flowerbed and made their way amongst the trees.

'Recognize these?' he asked when they were standing next to the crates.

Oumar, wearing his habitual starched white coat, surveyed the crates with the severity of a pathologist conducting a post-mortem.

Thomson felt like someone seeing shipwrecked cargo washed up on a beach. He clenched his jaw muscles underneath his beard, extracted a cigarette from the top pocket of his shirt and swore.

'No need to speculate about who did this,' he growled and exhaled the smoke through his nose. The smoke lingered in his beard, and the Kenyan laughed. 'You're not accusing our respected superintendent?'

'I am not accusing him; I just know it. He probably needs space for the minutes of all these goddamned meetings.'

It was five to seven and the sun was already above the rusted corrugated iron roof of the hospital with the sparrows' nests in its gutters and the row of pigeons sitting at the top away from the prowling cats. Thomson wiped his brow. The heat seemed to rise up from the ground and seep between the floorboards of the veranda.

'This,' Thomson said and flung his cigarette butt over the rail, 'won't do. After the meeting let's take these down to the nurses' tearoom. I will find some planks and make shelves.'

A car drove slowly along the potholed driveway and parked in the one and only dilapidated parking shelter, marked 'Superintendent'. They watched as Holmes extricated his overfed body from the car, then reached back with some difficulty for his briefcase on the passenger seat. For a long moment his broad backside was pointed at the side entrance from which the night nurses emerged, wearing capes in spite of the heat. Finally he stepped out from underneath the roof and the sun glistened on his bald scalp, like a signal that the dreaded morning meeting was about to start.

'Now don't argue with the man,' the Kenyan told Thomson. 'Say nothing; let him talk and don't get too upset. That way the meeting will be short.'

'We'll see about that,' said Thomson.

Two of the youngsters came striding rapidly across the lawn and Oumar spoke for the first time.

'If I were a magician,' he said, 'I would bring old Jenkins back.'

THE MORNING MEETING was a ritual. First, they entered the tired looking room with its worn-out, government regulation curtains and precarious sash windows that sometimes caused a welcome interruption when one of them slid down like the blade of a guillotine.

Then they took their places around the table, everyone always in the same place. The Kenyan collected three teapots, lifted the lid of the urn to make sure the water was boiling and filled them.

Everyone reached for a cup and the Kenyan poured the tea. The light-hearted banter was exchanged for an air of studied indifference the moment they heard Holmes' familiar voice saying good morning to Thunderbird, followed by the hollow echo of their footsteps on the wooden floor.

Holmes always greeted them twice. The first greeting came as soon as he entered the door, a jovial 'Good morning gentlemen.' His unconvincing air of camaraderie was canceled out by the lack of response. The youngsters grudgingly returned his greeting, the Kenyan merely nodded; Oumar and Thomson ignored the greeting completely.

Then, just before he sat down, Holmes opened his dreaded briefcase and uttered a curt 'Good morning', more befitting the mood of the meeting.

What followed was a long, melodramatic treatise, complete with hand gestures, changing body language, and altering facial expressions that depicted every emotion except genuine pleasure. It was delivered in a voice that traveled up and down the tone ladder like an inexpert violinist practicing scales.

The meeting concluded with the hand-over report from the man coming off night duty, followed by Holmes' ill-judged advice.

Thomson watched as Holmes removed the auditor's report from his briefcase, and glanced at Thunderbird for moral support. The meeting only included a very limited number of topics, but he managed to announce them with the conviction of Archimedes jumping from his bath—a Eureka moment, a groundbreaking revelation.

Holmes started talking. For a short while Thomson concentrated on the man's body language, trying not to listen to what he was saying. But the sound of Holmes' pretentious voice soon irritated him.

He remembered Morgan's dictum: 'A smooth talker always has something to hide . . . always.'

Holmes was whining about the kitchen and high-protein diets.

No one showed any sign of interest. The Kenyan got up and put the lid back on the urn, which was adding steam to the already humid air.

Holmes paused, exhaled through his nose, and appeared deep in thought. 'Do we really have to prescribe so many high-protein diets?' His tone resurrected Thomson's anger.

'We really do have so many AIDS patients who look like skeletons,' he imitated Holmes' voice.

There was a brief pause and for a moment their eyes met. Holmes instantly shifted his gaze away from Thomson's dark, unwavering eyes.

'I know,' he continued, allowing the angry moment to pass. 'The number of patients is another matter; we will discuss that later.'

Thomson cut him short. 'Why not right now?'

Holmes dithered. 'What I am saying,' he said, playing out the act of a reasonable man, 'is that we can't afford to have everyone in some wards on high-protein diets.'

Thomson scratched his beard. 'In some of the wards everyone has AIDS. What would you suggest we do?'

Holmes tried a different tack. 'We can send them for home-based care, can't we?' he said. 'It's no use keeping them here. We can't save everyone, can we?'

He delivered these words as though he were content in the knowledge that he had done everything humanly possible, but sadly had to arrive at an unsatisfactory conclusion.

Thomson's dark eyes turned black. 'You couldn't give a shit could you?' he said without raising his voice. One of the youngsters coughed. Thunderbird shifted in his chair. Oumar smiled a frosty smile, and the Kenyan folded his arms.

Holmes paused, looked around the table for support and found none. His voice rose half an octave.

'What I am saying,' he said, 'is we can at least try to conserve our resources.'

'So how do we fatten up skeletons without food?' Thomson growled. 'Or are you telling us we must send all of them home?'

The veins on Holmes' nose turned red and he paused before he answered. His shoulders moved sideways to and fro, and for a moment he looked like a fat chameleon balancing on a twig.

'I did not mean it like that at all,' he said and kept his voice even. 'I know it is difficult for you, but you must understand my position. I must contain costs.'

The electric fan overhead sliced chunks in the humid air. Thomson started saying something but thought better of it, shrugged his shoulders and allowed Holmes to continue his monolog.

He produced figures of expenditure and occupancy, and Thomson wondered where the occupancy figures came from. No matter how overcrowded the hospital was, according to Holmes' figures, it was always only sixty percent full, even if patients were sleeping on the floor. No one could tell how he arrived at the figures, certainly not Lawrence the hospital administrator who was supposed to compile them.

The magic figure of sixty percent allowed Holmes to freeze

nursing posts and not fill positions vacated by disgruntled nurses who left and went overseas.

Thomson placed his elbows on the table and rested his face in his hands like a chess player contemplating a move. He shoved his index fingers firmly into his ears and was pleased with the result.

It was like watching television with the sound turned off. He observed Holmes' body language. The eyes never changed; like those of a puppet, they were cut off from the movement.

Holmes' hands rose and stopped abruptly, like a conductor indicating a pause. His mouth gaped, the lips pouted like the open end of a balloon. The hands went down and then came smoothly up again, this time holding a pen between them. Legato.

The Kenyan's massive framed stirred, and Thomson saw him talking. He removed his fingers from his ears. The Kenyan had a problem. His prescriptions for intravenous antibiotics were being returned, to be countersigned by Holmes.

The response was predictably smooth and reassuring. The Kenyan must please not see it as interference from management's part, but we must think, gentlemen; before we prescribe, we must think. Who are 'we'? wondered Thomson. Does 'we' include you? I don't think so. You are screwing the people we are trying to help.

The Kenyan, who never lost his temper and spoke with the sobriety of a supreme court judge, was not placated. 'Even if I have a sensitivity report?'

Holmes' chair creaked as he shifted his weight. 'We must always look for the cheapest alternative.' Again he said 'we' as if he really cared about the patients.

'We' again, thought Thomson . . . fuck!

Everyone knew about the Kenyan's problem; they had all experienced the same frustration ever since a bespectacled auditor started prowling around the hospital and Holmes, as usual, made new rules without consulting anyone.

Morgan had no problem with the new rule. He walked into the pharmacy and raised so much hell that his scripts were issued regardless. Holmes knew about it and did nothing. The pharmacist knew that Holmes knew and did nothing, so Morgan continued to write out prescriptions as he pleased.

The meeting dragged on and Thomson followed the Kenyan's advice. He said nothing and allowed Holmes to ramble on. 'It is all a matter of management,' he heard Holmes say.

Behind Holmes, against the wall, was a framed, blown-up photograph of old Jenkins, put there by the Kenyan in defiance of what he called 'the new era'.

It showed old Jenkins standing on a landing strip in the bush, his hair blown sideways by the wind. Behind him villagers were admiring his trusty old Cessna.

The old man never talked about management, thought Thomson. 'Patient care' was all that mattered to him. It started and ended there. There were no fancy stories about structures that had to be in place, or outputs that had to be measured or targets that had to be set. Heaven help anyone who neglected a patient. Fat lot it helped you though, he told Jenkins' photograph. Maybe you should have been more diplomatic. As for what's happening now, you don't want to know.

Holmes never went into the bush. He knew nothing about the living conditions, and nor could he care. He had never bothered to dirty his shoes, and take a walk around dilapidated villages where people were thankful for body bags to contain the smell of the rotting corpses; where children played on floors contaminated with the excrement of dying AIDS patients; where funerals were expedited because of the rapid decay of bodies in the sweltering heat; where overworked nurses often had no transport, and people lived in one-room shacks with no running water and often very little food.

Holmes continued bickering about the costs and reminded them about the policy for home-based care.

He made it sound so easy and logical—sending people home to die, or to go home only to return to the hospital on the brink of death.

Thomson shoved his fingers back into his ears and watched Holmes' mouth moving like a flutter valve. The meetings were boring without Morgan; when Morgan had attended, these meetings had been fun. He interrupted and ridiculed Holmes, and generally caused havoc. 'I congratulate the profession,' he once said after listening to Holmes' treatise on shortening hospital stay, home-based care and referring all serious cases to the referral hospital, 'for producing the perfect hospital superintendent, completely devoid of compassion.'

But Morgan had stopped attending any hospital meetings, and no longer cared whether or not he was disciplined for insubordination. And, for his part, Holmes was no doubt relieved that he didn't have to face Morgan every day.

Suddenly, Holmes stopped talking. His shoulders slumped, his head dropped forward and he sat exhausted, with an air of utter dejection. Thomson considered it safe to remove his fingers from his ears, but he was mistaken.

'And now, gentlemen,' the voice hovered around middle C, 'a very serious matter.'

He paused for effect, and then said: 'We have a man on a ventilator.'

He managed to convey the incredulity of someone who had just discovered his wife in bed with the Bishop.

'This man has been on a ventilator for a week.' His voice jumped three tones up the scale. 'We simply can't allow this. Do any of you have any idea what this costs?'

'That happens to be the correct management of a flail chest,' Thomson told Holmes. 'Or can you think of another way?'

The urn hissed and boiled over, but no one noticed.

Holmes leaned his arms on the table. 'I know, I know,' he said. 'But we can't possibly carry the cost of ventilating a man for such a long time. We are working as a team, gentlemen, and I think I should be consulted before we get into situations like this.'

Thomson had had enough of Holmes' bickering. 'Do you want a surgeon to ask your advice before he operates?' Thomson kept his voice calm and matter-of-fact.

Holmes realized he was treading on thin ice, and he hated to be reminded that there were people on his staff who were better qualified than himself.

His smile vanished. 'But we can transfer him to the referral hospital, can't we? That could be easily arranged.'

The Kenyan's soft, restrained voice came to Thomson's aid. 'In the back of an ambulance, on a ventilator, to a hospital more than two hundred kilometers away? Will you accept the responsibility?' he asked, facing Holmes with an air of incredulity. 'Would you really?'

Holmes put his arms on the table and his cufflinks made a scraping sound. He persisted against his better judgment. 'Perhaps we could send him by air,' he suggested.

'And what about the cost of a mercy flight?' Thomson mocked him.

Holmes was stumped. To hide his embarrassment he turned to Thunderbird. 'Will you,' he asked, 'take up this matter with Morgan, so we can get a clear policy about matters such as this?'

'Also,' he added, 'we must get a clear policy on admitting AIDS patients into High Care.'

Thunderbird shifted uneasily in his chair and muttered

yes. He mistrusted Holmes ever since the day he had had his altercation with Morgan. Surely, Holmes had known how Morgan was going to react, he had thought afterwards, and since then he scrutinized Holmes' instructions a little more carefully.

Thomson sniggered, looked out the window and saw the gardener resurrecting a sprinkler that had been trampled by a cow. So we are passing the buck, he thought.

Oumar got up and poured himself another cup of tea. The others stared in front of them and wished Holmes would get up and go.

Outside on the lawn, a cat was stalking two unwary doves. Thunderbird dozed off and his head bent forward. Between his closely cropped grey hair that stood out like porcupine quills, his scalp was visible and was just as red as his polycythemic face. He woke with a start and stared at Thomson with eyes that looked like frosted glass. At a quarter to eight Holmes realized that nobody was listening.

He looked at his watch and asked: 'Who was on call last night?'

The Kenyan read his list of admissions: two chronically ill women with pneumonia, a man with a strangulated inguinal hernia operated on by Morgan in the early hours of the morning, two dehydrated children with gastroenteritis, a child with meningitis, a Caesarean section done at five in the morning. The Kenyan had had a busy night.

Mercifully Holmes had no advice to offer. He glanced at his watch. 'Today,' he announced dismissively, 'I will be out of the office for most of the day.' With that, the meeting was over.

10

Just another day

THE AILING AIR conditioners exhaled their stale breath into the alley between Male Ward and the kitchen.

From deep inside the belly of the building came the disgruntled rattling of water pipes. A discarded bathtub precariously straddled a storm ditch. Amorous doves carelessly pranced on rusted roof-plates. Desperate mops drowned themselves in buckets of dirty water. A row of balding brooms leaned against the mildewed wall. Flakes of paint fell onto a fractured concrete slab.

Morgan crouched next to a drainpipe, stalking an unwary kitten.

'You scoundrel!' The Kenyan's massive hand came down on his shoulder. 'We spend all morning defending you, and here you are playing with kittens.'

Morgan extricated himself from the Kenyan's grip. 'You chased it away,' he accused him, and at the same time saw Thomson and Oumar coming out of the side entrance.

'Cats are sensible creatures,' Morgan told the Kenyan. 'Why do you waste your time listening to Holmes?'

They clustered around Morgan like schoolboys spoiling for a fight.

He faced each of them in turn. 'You want to tell me something?' he asked with feigned innocence.

'We have an axe to grind with you,' Thomson said.
Morgan folded his arms in front of his chest.

Thomson put out his hand and removed the small pouch of tobacco from Morgan's shirt pocket. 'You,' he said, 'are making life difficult for us. We take most of the flak you are supposed to get, yet you are never at the meetings.'

'I have more important things to do,' Morgan replied.

'Like catching kittens?' the Kenyan laughed.

Thomson started rolling a cigarette and relayed Holmes' message. 'You are putting unnecessary strain on the nursing staff; you waste resources; you're not supposed to ventilate patients; and you are blowing the budget.'

'What does he want me to do, kill the guy?' asked Morgan disinterestedly.

'No,' said Thomson. 'He wants you to send him away.'

'He is going nowhere.'

'Holmes told Thunderbird to discuss it with you.'

'He won't,' said Morgan. 'He'll send me a memo. So what else did the oracle tell you this morning?'

The Kenyan laughed. 'We are a team,' he said. 'Before we do anything rash, like treating patients, we should discuss it with our leader.'

'Tell him he is not my leader,' said Morgan. 'He is not even in my team.'

He surveyed his three comrades: Thomson with his hairy arms and scruffy beard, the massive, benign-looking Kenyan, and the unflappable Oumar.

They had been thrown together in a sinking boat by random events.

Oumar with his greying temples, symmetrical face and starched white coat was the only real gentleman among them. An accomplished surgeon, he had been carried away by the currents of life and washed onto foreign shores. The enigmatic Nigerian never spoke about himself. The Kenyan now and again reminded them about the shores of Lake Victoria, the beauty of the tea plantations at Nyeri and the majestic outline of Mount Kenya. His life's ambition was to return there some day in the distant future. Thomson, like Morgan, was a rootless nomad.

IT WAS TIME to start the ward round, but they lingered. They always lingered, trying to postpone the inevitable, depressing start of the day. Thomson lit his cigarette and inhaled the smoke appreciatively.

'I hate going into that ward,' Morgan said. 'I hate seeing those patients and watching them die.'

'But we are not supposed to keep all these patients here,' Oumar mocked him. 'We are supposed to send them home.'

'And what happens to them?' Morgan asked.

'That, our leader tells us, is not really our concern. We are not a benevolent organization, and we have only so much money.'

'What one needs in this world is a big fat arse, eyes that do not see, ears that do not hear, a total lack of balls and a smooth voice,' said Morgan. 'Those are the requirements of the ideal modern manager.'

Oumar smiled his sardonic smile and taunted him. 'And if there is really not enough money?' he asked.

Morgan didn't answer immediately. He moved closer to the drainpipe and talked to Oumar over his shoulder. 'It's not only about a lack of money. It's about a total lack of imagination. One day when this continent has gone to the devil, Holmes and his friends will pout their greasy lips, wring their puffy little hands and say there was really nothing they could do.' Morgan imitated Holmes, clasping his hands in front of an imaginary belly and tilting his head sideways.

'Morgan, Morgan,' Oumar tried to soothe him.

'Do you know the joke about General Franco?' Morgan asked.

'The dictator?'

Turning to face Oumar, he nodded. 'General Franco is lying on his deathbed, and he hears a commotion outside the window. He struggles up against the pillows and asks: 'What's that noise?'

'Calm down, my dear, invincible general,' his aide tells him. 'It is only the people gathering in the street; they have come to say goodbye.'

Franco sits up. 'Where are they going?' he asks.

Oumar laughed, and patted Morgan on the arm. 'You think our leaders are like that?'

'Our venerable leaders live in a world of their own,' Morgan said. 'This time the people are really going, and they are not even saying goodbye.'

'You're a pessimist Morgan,' said Oumar.

'Get me antiretroviral drugs and I will become an optimist,' Morgan said and stalked the opening of the gutter. With a deft movement he bent down and grabbed the kitten.

It was charcoal-grey with light-blue eyes.

He held it by its scruff and the kitten hung motionless with its paws dangling.

'The gene pool of the alley cat, gentlemen,' Morgan said. 'Even if you tried you couldn't breed such a beauty. If I had any intention of renewing my contract with this unhappy hospital, I would have kept you,' he told the kitten.

Thomson flung his cigarette butt away into the drain. 'Come on, Morgan,' he said. 'Let's go and do some work.'

Morgan released the kitten and it promptly disappeared into the drainpipe again.

'I'm surprised Holmes hasn't declared a vendetta against the cats yet, or sent an auditor to collect rent from them.'

THE FORTY-FOUR GALLON drum man was awake and had learnt how to breathe with the ventilator.

'Mr. Bernard,' the staff called him, using his first name because he had a long complicated surname.

Ever since Holmes had reduced the number of oxygen cylinders in the oxygen bank without telling anyone, nearly killing one of Morgan's patients in the process, Morgan slept badly when he had someone on a ventilator. He had visited the man at midnight, just to make sure he was all right, until the night sister chased him away and told him to trust her.

Mr. Bernard was doing surprisingly well, in spite of his ribs that looked like broken matchsticks, his big laparotomy scar, his shattered pelvis and his femur that was in traction. Morgan classified complications according to the post-operative day on which they were supposed to occur. He looked out for them and was worried when nothing happened.

He gave the man subcutaneous Heparin and feared that he was going to develop a massive pulmonary embolus, but so far nothing had happened. He dreaded the possibility of pneumonia, but so far had cultured nothing out of the man's secretions, and, while he looked for signs of wound sepsis, the wound was healing perfectly. He lingered in High Care, trying to postpone his ward round, until Violet caught up with him.

'I have been waiting for you,' she said.

Morgan gave an exaggerated sigh and followed her into the heart of darkness, which was not dark at all. The bright morning light poured through the windows of Female Ward.

Women sat on neatly made beds. They all looked at him as he walked in and he was suddenly impressed by the deceptive cheerfulness of the room. Almost all the women were smiling. They were usually smiling, thought Morgan, in contrast with some of his private patients who had nothing wrong with them and were miserable.

Sometimes he had a whole ward full of patients who could hardly lift up their heads, lying on their sides, barely able to speak to him. Some of them stayed for a long time, some died, some got better and went home, only to come back again. In the end, they always died.

Through the windows he could see the lawn shaded by thorn trees. Weavers flew frantically amongst the branches with a sense of urgency, as if they had a deadline to meet. Morgan often watched the weavers, sometimes together with the patients, and sniggered when a female rejected a carefully prepared nest. 'Trust a woman,' he would say, and Violet reminded him that he was outnumbered and should be careful.

A mood of optimism pervaded the ward and he tried to find some explanation for it. Superficially, everything looked like it had the day before, and the day before that. But the stick-like figures were all a bit perkier, their body language more buoyant, their smiles more cheerful and their eyes a bit brighter.

Naledi's foster mothers were making a fuss around her, in their efforts to feed her. Naledi herself was no worse and no better. She was sucking a milkshake through a straw amidst sounds of enthusiastic encouragement and flattery. The melodious quality of the voices came as a surprise.

Even the girl in the middle bed, who weighed only slightly more than Naledi, was sitting up precariously. Morgan listened to the soft, barely audible voice telling him that she was feeling better, except for the TB drugs that made her nauseous. Flies circled around the protein food standing on her bedside locker. He noted her thin arms, and realized that she did not possess the energy to chase them away.

Janet was sitting on her bed quietly watching Morgan. She congratulated him on his cleanly shaven face.

'Most unusual for him,' Violet said, and all the women laughed.

'Thank you,' he said. Then he noticed the glass with high-protein food with a straw standing next to Janet's bed. So it's that bad, he thought. He asked her to open her mouth and inspected the tumor that was relentlessly growing bigger in spite of Janet's faith in the Vincristine. He could hear the slight nasal quality of her speech.

Janet appeared unperturbed and outwardly showed no sign that she was worried about it. But she must know, Morgan thought. He had met her bright-eyed, ten-year-old son with his wide, exuberant smile who visited her occasionally, leaving her pensive, absentminded, with a somber look on her face for a few days after his visit. 'Do you have pain?' he asked.

Janet shook her head and declined painkillers. She seemed more worried about Naledi.

It was the first time Morgan had seen Janet sucking her meals through a straw. 'Since when?' he asked and pointed at the glass.

'Since yesterday.' Violet showed him the intake and output chart. He insisted that all of his patients should have at least 3,000 calories per day, despite Holmes' protestations. 'Tell the cook to make more milkshakes for her. Use some of Naledi's ice cream,' Morgan said.

Kitso, the girl who had almost died from pneumonia, was smiling at him. She was the only one in the ward who warranted a cautious measure of hopefulness.

She had started off in High Care, gasping for breath, responded to Morgan's energetic treatment, and then slowly improved against his expectations.

He received a nocturnal visit from her two brothers who had made their own diagnosis, which turned out to be correct, and asked Morgan if he couldn't start her on AIDS drugs.

They were rugged, down-to-earth men, and between them had managed to scrape together enough money for the cheapest drug combination.

It was a tenuous arrangement at best, and they made it clear that as soon as she was fit to work she would have to pay one-third of the cost.

Morgan was reluctant at first. 'What will happen if you

can't pay anymore?' he asked.

They were adamant. They had steady jobs and as long as she could get back to work, they would manage, they told him.

'All right then,' Morgan had said. 'Your plan is certainly better than doing nothing.'

Morgan's duty was to help her to get back to work as soon as possible.

The arrangement pleased Morgan because she had a chance; it embarrassed him because all the other women knew about it and didn't seem to mind, and it infuriated him because he couldn't do anything for the others.

'For God's sake,' he told Thomson. 'These drugs work and they are available. So why the hell write off all these people simply because they can't pay?'

Kitso was still slightly unsteady after her brush with death, much better than she had been, but not ready for work yet. 'Another week or so,' he told her. 'Then we can send you out.'

IN THE CORNER next to the window was Mary. Morgan's voice lost its harsh character, the lines around his mouth became less defined and his eyes softened. Violet noticed his change of demeanor whenever he came to Mary's bed. Sometimes she teased him about it, always out of earshot, always gently, and Morgan smiled and allowed her to tease him.

Mary was lying on her back, fast asleep, a pink and blue towel wrapped around her head. Her face was serene and beautiful with a faint smile on her lips. Morgan looked at the wasted temples, the prominent cheekbones and the thin, wasted body with the ribcage sticking out through the blue hospital dress. He marveled at her undiminished beauty, in spite of the lymphoma in her belly that was slowly destroying her and which she ignored. He didn't have the heart to wake her up, and paged through the notes that he knew only too well. She didn't have much time left, he realized with sudden clarity, a few weeks at the most.

Morgan glanced back at her face, saw the perfect shape of her jaw and her long eyelashes and resisted the temptation to stroke her cheek. On the locker next to the bed was the rose, its short stem dangling in a specimen bottle. Next to it were the books that he had given her. Morgan smiled.

It was a love affair with a difference, he thought. A truly platonic love affair.

Morgan looked around the ward and tried to think how many of the women would be alive in six months. Probably Kitso only, he thought, if the brothers could keep up the payments. The others? Regrettably, no chance, except for some unforeseen and highly unlikely miracle. They would be taken away by deadly pneumonias, exotic tumors, various kinds of meningitis, diarrhea, or whatever other surprise package the virus had in store.

Naledi? Looking at the withered body flanked by foster mothers, he decided to give her an outside chance.

In the side ward stood the dead child's mother. No trace of optimism here, he thought. Since her child had died she had been hovering on the brink of death.

She faced Morgan and he saw her thin clavicles, her accelerated breathing and the rapid carotid pulse. Her lips were slightly parted, and he noted the paleness of her tongue, the narrowness of her face, and the feverish brightness of her eyes.

Her dress dangled from her shoulders to cover a body that had lost its curves. He was surprised she was standing at all.

'I want to go and bury my child,' she told him.

Morgan was at a loss for words.

'All right,' he said after a while. 'We will give you your

medicine to take with you.' Then he added, 'When the funeral is over, come back please.'

He knew he would probably never see her again.

In the corridor he cursed under his breath.

'Compassion has a price, nowadays,' he told Violet. 'I am doctoring people who have already been written off.'

IN MALE WARD three men had died in as many days. A post-battle silence hung over the room. The vacated beds were already occupied by scrawny newcomers. Nobody ever spoke about the deaths. It was an unwritten rule. Everyone wordlessly watched the final desperate days of fellow inmates. Afterwards, when their beds were empty, they were erased from the collective memory.

Morgan often wondered what they thought, and he cursed as he treated complications and re-admissions until they died.

A man was folding up a stretcher next to the bed of his brother. He slept on the stretcher every night, fed his brother, and nursed him during the day. Violet allowed him to, since it meant one patient less to be cared for by the staff.

As always, there was the inevitable artist in the ward: a cheerful man who made elaborate, naïve drawings of animals and people. But even he was subdued today. Johnson was his usual scrawny self and was devouring high protein food. On the back pages of his dog-eared copy of *Gorky Park*, he was keeping a meticulous tally of how many plates of food and high-protein mixture he had consumed so far. He had picked up one kilogram. Therefore, he told Morgan, so many meals equates to one kilogram.

According to his calculations, he declared, he should reach his target weight in twenty-one days exactly. He spoke with the conviction of an astronomer predicting the return of a comet.

Morgan didn't ask him if he had factored the virus into his calculations. Instead, he allowed Johnson to continue.

'I must find a job,' Johnson told him. Morgan saw his clavicles protruding above the pale blue hospital shirt and said, 'You must first reach your target weight, my friend.'

Johnson's innocent eyes probed Morgan's face. 'If I have a job, I can feed myself properly,' he said.

A job, thought Morgan, the difference between life and death.

'Let's try and make you better first,' he said as convincingly as possible.

The madman was on his way to the mental hospital, packed and ready. Next to him on the floor was a plastic bag containing his belongings. With his right hand he drew a comb through his beard. His left eye, below the laceration, was still swollen shut.

As always, he was in no mood for conversation and ignored Violet's pep talk. She told him to behave, take his medicines and not to disgrace himself.

The Constable, it seemed, had managed to withdraw all charges against the madman.

He had said nothing about Mr. Chiremba's response.

MORGAN HATED HIS ward rounds. He felt like an actor who pretended to be a doctor. He rejoiced about small victories and carried a mask of cheerfulness, but when he was out of sight of his patients he swore about his crushing defeats. His private patients both pleased and angered him. He saw several of them get better, so much so that you wouldn't even think they had AIDS, but the ward for the paupers was doomed. He had lost track of how many people he had known who had died.

When he walked in the street, he could pick out the tell-tale signs of the disease without difficulty. It depressed him to be able to make a diagnosis by merely looking at someone's face. It depressed him even more when he did this at Casualty and found that he was almost always right.

He dreaded his private consultations. Lately his booking lists had shown every sign of a conspiracy. All the most irritating people seemed to want to visit him on the same day.

The idea of spending a day in his office depressed him, and he walked to Casualty, hoping there would be an emergency to save him from a boring day.

Outpatients were sitting under the shelters outside, waiting to be promoted to the waiting room.

On the floor stood a single electric fan turning to and fro without making a dent in the heat. The stream of patients seemed never-ending.

On chairs and wooden benches sat women from the north, wearing fancy headscarves and long dresses, farmers with dusty, sandblasted shoes and faded trousers, old ladies in their Sunday best, young women holding small babies who looked like dolls, and old men who wore jackets in spite of the heat.

All of them were looking towards Casualty, like spectators at a soccer match, waiting for their names to be called.

He found Rebecca in her office, drinking a glass of ice cold water.

She put down the glass and wiped off the condensation with her handkerchief.

'This crowd is driving me crazy, Morgan,' she said. 'And how is our man?' she added without breaking her sentence.

'He's doing well,' Morgan said, 'in spite of our efforts.'

'Tough man that one,' said Rebecca. 'You're not here today?'

'I am seeing privates.'

Rebecca laughed. She shook her head and the shaking continued down her spine, like a dog shaking water off its coat.

'You make me feel better,' she said. 'I'd rather see this lot even if they drive me crazy. At least they are sick...and my little girl?' Rebecca looked at him over her glasses. She was referring to Mary.

'As well as can be,' said Morgan.

He returned to his room and subjected himself to twenty-minute portions of torture until noon, at which point he was granted a reprieve: his last patient of the morning failed to show.

The heat was worse than ever, and in the afternoon Mr. Chiremba's beerhall received a record number of patrons who moved their chairs around the trees to keep up with the shade and looked up for signs of rain; but saw only a clear sky.

In his office Morgan saw his last patient of the afternoon, a six month-old baby, the product of a teacher who wanted a child without the encumbrance of a husband and had spent a month's leave in the Capital with a willing, unattached man.

The shameless honesty of the mother and the cheerfulness of the baby lifted his spirits, and he did his afternoon round with a smile on his face. He listened to Mr. Bernard's belly and was pleased to hear the presence of bowel sounds.

IT WAS ALMOST dusk. Mary was on the veranda, a red ribbon in her hair. In her lap was the bird book.

'The bird woman of Alcatraz,' Morgan said.

Mary laughed. 'Am I your prisoner?'

'No,' said Morgan. 'I am a fellow prisoner.'

'Alcatraz is in the mind, my fellow prisoner,' she said. 'We can choose to be free, no matter what.'

'That's a comforting thought,' said Morgan.

Her dark eyes were looking straight at him. 'It is our expectations that trap us.'

Most people don't come to realize that in a lifetime, Morgan thought.

'That's more or less what the Buddha said,' he told her. 'Are you a Buddhist?'

'No,' replied Mary. 'I don't know anything about Buddhism.'

'Well,' said Morgan. 'I think you have discovered it for yourself.'

Somewhere he had seen reproductions of paintings of the Buddha in the various stages of his life, renouncing the material life and progressing from prince to Enlightened One.

Fate had destroyed all Mary's illusions, Morgan realized.

'I have lost everything,' she said. 'It made me free.' She said it without a hint of self-pity. Her calm, unwavering eyes mesmerized him.

'You are the richest woman in the world,' he told her.

'Not many people would agree with you,' she laughed. 'The richest woman in the world is a scrawny little girl in a hospital in Africa and she owns nothing,' she said. 'Who is the richest woman anyway?'

'Who cares?' asked Morgan.

She rested her chin in her hand and said, 'Being rich is not to want anything.'

'The paradoxes of life,' said Morgan. 'If you want power, you must relinquish it completely; if you want to be rich, you must spurn wealth. Strength is admitting your weakness.'

Mary broke the spell. 'It's going to rain soon,' she said.

Morgan laughed 'How can you tell?'

'I feel as light as a feather today.'

'What has that got to do with rain?' he asked.

'It's the air,' she explained to him. 'It's different. I know it's going to rain.'

'Female intuition,' he said.

'I just know I am going to see it . . .' she interrupted her sentence and put her hand in front of her mouth.

In his mind, Morgan completed the broken sentence: 'for one last time.'

An awkward silence hung between them.

She laughed at the expression on his face and told him not to look so serious.

Morgan smiled. 'I will go and see the witchdoctor,' he said, 'and tell him to make it rain, just for you.'

'You think I am a witch?'

'A very beautiful one,' said Morgan.

'Watch out,' she said. 'I will cast a spell on you.'

'You already have,' replied Morgan.

She was sitting in a wheelchair, and managed to look like a princess in spite of the dreary hospital gown.

'Shall I take you inside?' he asked.

'No,' said Mary. 'I am waiting for the owl. It always sits on that treetop over there.'

Morgan had discovered the nest of a Barn Owl in an empty water-tank mounted on a tower, and was waiting for the little owls to hatch. Jake, the stableman, had warned him against taking photographs of the owls, saying it would bring bad luck or even death.

Morgan had a sudden wish to show the little owls to Mary, but realized it would be impossible. There was no way she could climb up the side of a water-tower. She might even be gone by the time they hatch, he realized, and violently suppressed the thought.

'Owls are my favorite birds,' he told her.

'This one,' she said, 'is an Eagle Owl.' She softly imitated the call of an Eagle Owl and almost instantly, as if from nowhere, the owl appeared on outstretched wings and perched on top of the tree.

'You are a witch,' Morgan whispered, 'calling owls.'

She ignored his comment and pointed at the owl.

'Look at his ears,' she said.

Morgan saw the silhouette of the owl. It was too dark to see its eyes.

They watched in silence. The owl contemplated its surroundings, and then took off on silent wings.

As usual, the clattering of plates on the food trolley brought an end to their conversation. Someone called her name.

'All good things come to an end,' she said.

'Good night, madam.' Morgan blew her a kiss and walked away.

IN SPITE OF the heat, he put on his running shoes and jogged out of town along the bush road. He ran in the dark, amongst tall trees where nightjars flew up noiselessly ahead of him. Once he saw a dim flash of lightning, but only once, and later he thought he had imagined it. He reached the turning point of his run and heard the sound of jackals calling, then headed back towards town until he reached the stables. Amongst the pepper trees hung the smell of kerosene, and he stopped when he saw the orange square of light that was the window of Jake's hut.

Jake was sitting outside and his dogs were lying in the sandy road as if they were dead.

'Evening,' said Jake.

Morgan sat down opposite him, leaning his back against a tree and resting his elbows on his knees.

Jake spoke his own brand of English.

'You must come ride Sultan,' he said. 'He getting wild.'

'You're spoiling him, that's why,' said Morgan.

In the dim light he could see the flash of Jake's teeth.

'He want riding,' said Jake.

'Come,' said Morgan. 'Let's have a look at him.'

Sultan was standing in his pen, stamping his feet. Even

in the dim light, Morgan could see the shine of his coat. He went inside and put his hand under Sultan's mane, then slid it down until he could feel the shoulder muscles twitch. Sultan nudged him with his head and Morgan laughed.

'He best horse for this stable,' said Jake.

They watched the horse as it pranced around in the pen. Sultan was a bundle of muscle and nerves, ready to explode. A bomb, thought Morgan. A delicious, mane-flying, nostril-flaring, hoof-thundering bomb.

'I will come and ride him,' Morgan said, 'as soon as I can.' The door of Jake's hut was open. Inside he could see a kerosene lamp standing on the table with moths circling it, and he could imagine the heat in the room.

Outside it was bearable and in the semi-darkness Morgan imagined the grass growing under the trees again.

'Rain is coming,' said Jake, 'coming soon.'

'Why?'

'Lighting,' said Jake, leaving out the 'n', and pointed towards the sky.

'I will believe it when I see it,' Morgan said, and gave Sultan a pat on his rump.

He walked back towards the road and Jake stayed with Sultan. The dogs were still asleep.

'Your dogs are not much good,' he shouted over his shoulder.

'They knowing you,' Jake replied.

On the way home, Morgan remembered the message that Violet had left on his desk. Rastodika was back in town.

11

Rastodika

MOST MEN SPEND their lifetime acquiring money and possessions, and end up being enslaved to their ambitions. Few men seem to realize this before they are weighed down by mortgages, wives, children, brand new cars, swimming pools, in-laws, taxes, school tuition fees, insurance policies, overdrafts and French poodles.

They struggle on, looking forward to retirement, buy a cottage next to the beach, discover they have forgotten how to live, then die of a heart attack, cancer, or boredom, are briefly mourned by inheritance-flushed widows and children who squabble over their possessions, and are then forgotten.

Rastodika had pondered these issues while he stood on the wall of a corral. He watched as his herd of cattle poured in through the gate, aided by the cries of herd boys competing with the sounds of clanging cowbells and the bellowing of cows momentarily separated from their calves. He was a tall, lean man, with the strong, sinewy legs of a warrior. He gazed down at the milling mass of cattle that churned the dry manure into dust. Slowly he walked along the top of the wall and counted the number of calves. He was very satisfied with the condition of the cows.

He calculated the value of his herd and found that the money meant nothing to him. Rastodika stopped, stood with his legs slightly apart, lifted his gaze, and watched the sun as it sank below the horizon. He saw the shapes of thorn trees that stood like sentinels on the plain. Smoke from wood fires lingered amongst the huts and the laughter of children and the chatter of women floated on the faint evening breeze.

He absent-mindedly waved at the herd boys as they shut the gate. Then he turned, jumped down from the wall and walked away. A week later he had sold his herd and given away most of his possessions.

What do I need all these things for? he had asked himself. They just tie me down. From now on I will just live. He said goodbye to the villagers and left his relatives to squabble over what he had left behind.

THE STORY OF Rastodika's sudden strange behavior was discussed for years afterwards in Mr. Chiremba's beerhall. The explanations given had a direct bearing on the amount of beer consumed. Some said it was because of a woman; others blamed it on temporary insanity, or temporary insanity because of a woman, or even permanent insanity because of a woman.

Rastodika walked across the plain, then followed a dry river bed for a week. He set snares and caught rabbits and —sometimes—small antelope, and at night he slept under the stars.

After ten days he saw a small hill and climbed it to get a view of his surroundings. In front of him he saw a vast lake, which was almost empty. In the middle of it was a small pool of water from which animal footpaths fanned like the spokes of a wheel.

He was impressed by the vastness of the lake, and the silence that was only disturbed by the cries of a pair of eagles.

'This is where I will stay,' he said to himself, and built a shelter from branches and grass next to the lake. He was a free man, unencumbered by possessions. For the first time in his life he didn't desire anything more than he had. The landscape showed no sign of any human being, and he studied the tracks of the animals and their habits.

He stayed until the start of the rainy season. At night he listened to the raindrops falling on the roof of his shelter, and watched as the lake filled up and water birds came and nested. As he stood on top of the hill and looked across the lake and saw rain pouring out of clouds far in the distance, he started feeling restless. One morning he broke up camp and headed further north.

He skirted lakes, crossed streams and walked across another vast plain for ten days without seeing any human beings. He walked past herds of antelope, recognized the tracks of lions in the sand, and then worried about the lack of trees until he decided that the lions must have enough antelope to feed on. At night he could sometimes hear them roar, and during the day he saw vultures soaring above the leftovers of the lions' kills.

Unexpectedly, when he almost thought that he had left civilization behind forever, he heard the engine of a truck far away and later smelt the smoke of a wood fire. The villagers welcomed him and for the first time in months he had company. He found himself tongue-tied because he wasn't used to speaking any more. The people were surprised that he looked so well after crossing the plain on foot.

Rastodika stayed for a few days, then got a lift on a truck that headed further north, until he found himself in forest country with deep, fast-flowing rivers in which lurked fiery tiger fish, elusive bream, ancient malicious crocodiles and spiteful hippos. Under a sky filled with the cries of Fish Eagles, scantily dressed women defied the crocodiles, walked into the deep water and caught fish with baskets made of papyrus.

'There,' the truck driver told him, pointing towards

massive trees growing on a riverbank. 'Talk to the man who lives there; he needs someone to help him.' Rastodika followed a narrow footpath that led into the shade of the trees and found himself in a clearing amongst huge, ancient tree trunks. On the far side of the clearing he saw papyrus brightly lit by the sun and a battered aluminum boat moored at the riverside.

The shade was so dark, he almost didn't notice the man next to a wooden shelter amongst the trees. He was sitting on a grass mat with his legs crossed and his hands in his lap. His chest was bare, his heavy features appeared to be cast in stone, and he had grey hair. His powerful chest muscles belied his age. He stared impassively at Rastodika from underneath bushy, black eyebrows.

'So you have come,' he said, as if he had been expecting him. Before Rastodika could answer, he got up and walked towards a tarpaulin, which he pulled back with a rapid movement of his powerful arms.

'We load the boat,' he said, and Rastodika helped him carry flour, sugar, tobacco, kerosene, bars of soap, matches, candles, ladies' underwear, sandals, a bag of cement, and tinned food into the boat. Sam was the man's name, and he traded with his boat between the islands. Sam spoke mostly in monosyllables and knew every side-channel, every island, every lagoon, the breeding grounds of the bream, every hippo, and every herd of waterbuck.

He taught Rastodika to handle the dugout canoes and how to negotiate the side-channels that wove around small islands like roads. They traveled between the islands where people lived, oblivious to the trappings of civilization. With time, Rastodika came to know the river people, their habits, and their villages.

'The river,' Sam told him once, 'is like a mother. She provides everything you may need.'

Rastodika thought: this is all I need; what more can any man want?

Over the years Rastodika occasionally returned to town. His old friends recognized him and paid for his drinks at the beerhall, urging him to find a woman and settle down. He never stayed for long, preferring the uncomplicated life of his friends in the north. He always took the same route back and visited the lake where he had first lived alone.

Once, he arrived there after sunset and was surprised to see the light of a fire on the edge of the lake. He carefully stalked it and stopped behind a shrub from where he saw a tall, lean, unshaven man roasting meat on the fire. Behind him, Rastodika made out the shape of a well-used pickup truck. He watched the man for some time, since it was the first time he had encountered anyone at the lake. As he moved away, a thorn caught the sleeve of his shirt, causing a small twig to snap. The man looked up and saw the movement behind the bush.

'Yes?' he said in the local tongue, and his voice sounded unruffled. Rastodika stepped into the light of the fire, and the stranger calmly inspected him without saying a word. He took a packet of cigarettes out of his shirt pocket, offered him one, and invited him to sit down next to the fire. The man looked at Rastodika's dark-skinned legs that were covered with dust.

'Have you traveled far?' he asked.

He laughed when he realized that Rastodika had visited the town. 'I could have given you a lift,' he said. 'It would have saved you a lot of walking.'

They sat next to the fire and the man shared his meat with Rastodika, then walked over to the truck and came back with two cans of beer. 'They are not very cold,' he said and handed one to Rastodika. They sipped their beer and neither of them felt it was necessary to speak.

When the fire was almost burnt out, the man took his bedroll, spread it next to the fire and went to sleep. He seemed perfectly at home in the bush and treated Rastodika without any sign of suspicion. For a while, Rastodika sat and watched him, wondering how long the man had known about the lake. The face seemed vaguely familiar to him, but he couldn't be sure whether he had actually seen the man before.

At daybreak they drank coffee and sat next to the remains of the fire. Then the man stood up abruptly and beckoned Rastodika to follow him. He moved through the bush with ease and made no noise. Suddenly he stopped and pointed at something in the distance.

Rastodika saw a nest made of dry branches atop a tall tree and caught a glimpse of a baby eagle. The stranger waited patiently, now and again scanning the sky with a small pair of binoculars. After about half an hour, a huge Martial Eagle swooped down on the nest, carrying a luckless mongoose in its talons. The man handed the binoculars to Rastodika and they took turns to watch the magnificent bird.

'I love eagles,' the man said later as they were walking back.

Rastodika liked the man. There was a wildness about him that seemed to lie just underneath the surface.

'I might as well give you a lift,' he said when he heard Rastodika was on his way to the north. 'I am on leave.'

When they reached the gravel road, the man stopped the truck, cut a branch off a tree and obliterated his tracks well into the bush. 'I don't want too many people to discover this lake,' he said.

Towards midday they were waved down by two pale city dwellers standing next to a brand-new, four-wheel-drive vehicle, weighed down by every imaginable piece of equipment.

The men wanted to know the way to the lake they had

seen on the map. Rastodika listened with growing surprise as his companion carefully gave the men directions that would lead them onto a treacherous road through a riverbed that was impassable, even to four-wheel-drive vehicles, due to slippery mud under an apparently dry surface. They waited as the men drove off.

Rastodika's companion swore and cursed the drivers of trendy four-wheel-drives and civilization in general, and lamented the fact that it had become fashionable and possible for idiots to travel in the bush. 'Suburbians!' he exclaimed. 'May they get stuck for seven days and seven nights and have ample opportunity to use their high-lift-jack, their spade, their winch, their compressor, their sunscreen, their tent, their spotlights, and their deck-chairs, and may they wear out their batteries.'

For a while they drove in silence.

'I have a theory,' the man said, 'that the price of a four-wheel drive is inversely proportional to the size of the owner's dick.'

Rastodika laughed. 'Aren't you worried that they might get lost?'

'I am protecting them from themselves,' the man said. 'They won't be able to get past that river, and there is a village nearby. The villagers will pull them out and make money out of them. That is what I call economic empowerment.'

They traveled along dirt roads for the rest of the day and arrived at Sam's shelter just after dark. Rastodika wanted to introduce his friend and realized he didn't know his name.

'Morgan,' said the man and shook Sam's hand.

The old man and Morgan conducted an animated conversation, using Rastodika as an interpreter. They were astonished to hear that he was a doctor.

'You?' Rastodika exclaimed. 'You don't look like a doctor! You look like a mechanic.'

'What's the difference?' Morgan asked.

Several times that evening Rastodika looked at Morgan and burst out laughing.

'You wear old clothes and you drive an old truck,' he laughed. 'How can you be a doctor?'

Morgan stayed for two days and they traveled a long way in Sam's boat between the lagoons and followed side-channels, landed on islands and talked to the villagers. He sat in the front of the boat and watched the plants on the bottom recede from view as the boat moved forward into the deep, dark waters of the channels.

They poled the boat through heaps of papyrus dumped in the channels by elephants.

'Elephants are a bloody nuisance,' said Morgan.

'They belong here,' said the enigmatic Sam.

They cut the engine in the mainstream, hung out bait and the boat rotated lazily as they drifted down in the swift-flowing current and caught several bream. Sam cursed when the propeller got stuck in the papyrus obstructing a channel, and Morgan reminded him that the elephants belonged there. 'Come and help me,' Sam laughed and pulled up the engine.

They grilled the bream on the fire, and Morgan lay in his sleeping bag that night listening to the guttural ranting of the hippos. Once he heard the cough of a leopard. Twice in the night he heard Sam get up to put more wood on the fire. Morgan slipped out of his sleeping bag and climbed onto the roof of his truck. In the pale light of the moon he could see out over the papyrus. A cluster of trees seemed to be suspended in the night sky. Near him, a fish jumped out of the water.

What a life, thought Morgan. These men have discovered the secret of living. They don't take anything more than they need, and they don't need much. What do you need in life? A boat, a fishing rod, a few pots and pans, and some shelter.

That's all they had.

You don't even need a boat, a dugout canoe would do.

'I envy the two of you,' he said when he left the next day. 'I wish I could live like this.'

'Why don't you?' Rastodika interpreted for Sam, and Morgan looked into Sam's eyes that seemed as dark as the deepest pools in the river. For the first time, Morgan noticed the carving of the river god hanging around his neck.

Rastodika said, 'You can come back any time you want, Morgan.' Morgan committed the picture of Sam and Rastodika standing next to their boat firmly into his memory. He promised himself he would return there one day soon, but somehow never managed. Often, in an unexpected quiet moment, his mind wandered to the two of them and he felt a restlessness stir inside him.

MORGAN AND RASTODIKA'S next meeting was determined by fate. Prompted by Rastodika's request for headache pills the morning after a rowdy reunion with friends, a fastidious clinic nurse had insisted on referring him to the doctor after taking his blood pressure and testing his urine.

'Now I believe you!' Rastodika said, and was overjoyed to meet Morgan again. 'You said you would come back,' he said.

'There's too much work nowadays,' Morgan replied.

Rastodika was in hospital for quite a while. Morgan referred him to Thomson, who discovered Rastodika had a rare kidney disease.

'Why,' asked Morgan, 'does a man like that have to end up with such a curse?'

'Life is a random event,' Thomson said. Morgan felt a foreboding of a tragedy that was just starting to unfold, and forcibly drove the thought from his mind. Suddenly, in startling detail, he recalled the clearing where he had stayed with Sam and Rastodika.

'How much time?' he enquired from Thomson. Thomson shrugged his shoulders.

'Who can tell?' he said. 'A year, two years, five years maybe. But he is sitting on a time bomb.'

Morgan treated Rastodika's blood pressure and advised him to adopt a less strenuous lifestyle. Rastodika refused. 'If I must die, I must die,' he said. Morgan could sympathize with Rastodika since they shared the same philosophy of life. They agreed that Rastodika would come for regular follow-ups and, to Morgan's surprise, Rastodika reappeared at the hospital as scheduled. Morgan tried to forget that the disease was progressive, and that at some point in the future Rastodika would go into renal failure. He decided to mention it to Rastodika only when the time was right.

For a year or so the disease didn't interfere too much with Rastodika's lifestyle. He became a regular visitor to the ward and always insisted on staying in the room at the end of the passage. Each time he was discharged, Morgan said to himself: another few months of grace, so far so good. But his premonition returned with disconcerting regularity. Time, Morgan decided, is the most precious commodity.

The Matron liked Rastodika and treated him as a mother would her favorite black sheep of the family. She turned a blind eye when he disobeyed the hospital rules. Morgan thought he saw a sparkle in her eyes whenever she spoke about Rastodika, but maybe it was just the way the light fell on her glasses.

Rastodika's behavior exasperated the Assistant Matron. 'How can a rich man just give up everything he has and live like a pauper?' she once asked Morgan. 'He doesn't even have a house.'

'Who wants a house?' was Morgan's response. 'A house

just ties you down.'

'And a wife,' she carried on. 'He had so many women and he never married any of them.'

Morgan expressed his envy and admiration and said, 'Who wants a wife and a mother-in-law and children and the full catastrophe anyway?'

Rastodika is a free spirit, he warned her. Let him be.

She decided to ignore the warning and do something about Rastodika's soul before it was too late. For a short while she had considered doing something about Morgan's soul as well, but she was intimidated by him and understood him even less than she understood Rastodika.

She secretly arranged for a lay preacher to visit Rastodika during one of his admissions. Rastodika showed his appreciation by taking him to Mr. Chiremba's beerhall. But, the preacher discovered too late that he couldn't hold his liquor as well as Rastodika. This had unfortunate consequences, because Mr. Chiremba despised people who couldn't hold their liquor.

He called the Constable who took the preacher, locked him up, and charged him with drunk-and-disorderly conduct. Then the Constable took Rastodika back to the hospital. Since that incident, the Assistant Matron had handled Rastodika with caution and a grudging respect. She only enquired about his medical problems and left his spiritual well-being in the hands of providence.

VIOLET CALLED MORGAN at Casualty to tell him that his friend was back at the ward. He found Rastodika still dressed in his dust-covered clothes and wearing the same pair of sandals.

He noted the wear and tear on the tip of Rastodika's walking stick. There was something different about him. His head was shaven and the creases across his high cheekbones deepened when he saw Morgan, but it was not his usual exuberant smile.

For the first time since Morgan had known him, Rastodika looked tired.

'I have come back, and this time you must cure me,' he said, and his gravelly voice seemed to fill the room. Morgan momentarily had a vision of a free spirit trapped in a failing body, and Rastodika saw the shadow crossing his friend's face.

For a while they both avoided the question of Rastodika's kidneys, and talked about the river and his journey. Rastodika was convinced that it was going to rain. He had seen a flock of flamingos circle high above a dry lake, and flying ants after a few drops of rain as he walked across the plains. In a small village he had met a witchdoctor who said it was soon going to start raining for weeks on end. He informed Morgan that the eagles were nesting in the same place.

'I know,' said Morgan. 'I was there two weeks ago.'

'And how is Sam?' Morgan asked. Rastodika smiled.

'Sam is well,' he said. 'You must come to the north with me; we will show you a place where you can catch as many tiger fish as you want.'

Violet told them to stop talking.

'And you always say women talk too much,' she scolded Morgan.

Rastodika took off his shirt and hung it over a chair. His stomach muscles covered his abdomen like a shield. Morgan looked at the lean, tough body and hoped that the tiredness was due to the long journey. A man like this shouldn't get sick, he thought.

Rastodika lay down on the bed so Morgan could examine him, and stared at the roof while Morgan inflated the cuff to take his blood pressure. The blood pressure was raised and

Morgan tried to hide his concern.

Rastodika had taken his medicine religiously, he knew.

'Do you eat salt?' Morgan asked.

'Of course he eats salt,' Violet said before Rastodika had time to answer. 'He eats what people give him to eat.'

She wrote 'Salt-free diet' in big letters in her order book.

Morgan washed his hands at the basin and took longer than necessary. He met Rastodika's eyes in the mirror above the washbasin and said: 'It will only be for a couple of days,' and hoped his suspicions were unfounded.

NALEDI WAS SLIPPING away in spite of the diligent efforts of her foster mothers, who were taking turns to sit next to her bed and feed her according to Morgan's instructions. At the foot of her bed, Morgan discovered a neatly folded, week-old newspaper.

'And this?' he asked.

He was told that the women, or at least some of them, were reading to her, so she could keep up with political, social and financial events. Violet pointed out that the news was in itself not as important as the fact that she was being talked to and getting attention.

'They had better read her something else,' Morgan told her afterwards when they were standing in her cluttered office, dodging the broom of an enthusiastic cleaner. 'The news will depress the hell out of anyone. I will try to find her a decent book.'

He had taken more cultures and more blood samples while the other women watched, sitting upright on their beds, as attentive as hunting dogs. 'Tell the laboratory to hurry up,' he told Violet. 'I need to know what I am treating.'

Violet reminded him that bacteria did not grow instantly, and that nobody could make them grow faster.

MARY'S BED WAS empty and Morgan followed Violet onto the veranda where they found her sitting in her wheelchair.

'The angel in our midst,' was how Violet referred to her. Morgan thought the name couldn't be more appropriate when he saw her that morning, staring up at the sky, looking for her favorite pair of Yellowbilled Kites.

By this time Mary could identify the inhabitants of the garden's trees, shrubs and hedges at a glance, knew their habits and everything about their migratory patterns. She admired all the raptors with their huge wings and pointed out to Morgan that their primaries moved like ailerons as they watched them soar in the thermals above the town.

One day, confined in her wheelchair, she witnessed a raid carried out on the weavers' nests by a brazen Pale Chanting Goshawk. She watched him as he hung upside down and set about his business, unconcerned by the frantic cries of the weavers. She was torn between her admiration for the arrogant gracefulness of the raptor and her love for the industrious, noisy weavers.

Morgan consoled her by saying that it was the law of nature. Goshawks are programmed to do just that. They can fly between dense shrubs by folding their wings and dive through gaps in hot pursuit of small birds.

'What about the weavers?' she asked.

'That's why there are not too many of them,' Morgan said. 'The goshawk keeps their numbers in check.'

She pondered the issue for a day and then told Morgan that cruelty is part of nature and that maybe God uses viruses to keep the human race in check. Morgan could not refute her logic and felt a pang of remorse for having defended the goshawk, but Mary's face was serene as always. She had completely accepted her place in the bigger scheme.

'This,' she told him, waving a graceful hand at her wasted legs, 'is only a body; it is not important.'

PART II

12

Rachel

MR. GEORGIOU CAREFULLY adjusted his tie in front of the mirror and then drew a comb through the fringe of hair surrounding his bald head. Behind him, in a pool of light from the bed lamp, lay Rachel. Completely unembarrassed by her nakedness, she lay propped up against the pillows with her arms folded behind her head.

Mr. Georgiou finished grooming himself and turned around. He was momentarily unsettled by the perfect shape of her breasts. But he was a methodical man who planned everything in his life with care, even his clandestine lovemaking with this highclass whore.

Besides, he reasoned, the alarm clock on the bed table told him that it was already five minutes to five, and within half an hour the vendors would be on the streets. From the pocket of his jacket he took a small parcel. Rachel laughed and Mr. Georgiou found himself once again under the spell of the deep, musical quality of her voice.

'You don't have to bring me gifts,' she said.

Mr. Georgiou regained his composure. 'I am an old-fashioned lover,' he declared and opened the parcel himself. He took out a small diamond pendant and hung it around her neck. Rachel caught the diamond in the palm of her hand and held it up against the light from the bed lamp. She reached up and kissed him on his forehead. He was rewarded with a view of the shiny diamond as it settled between her dark breasts, and sighed, 'You are the most beautiful woman I know.'

'Why do you have to leave so early?' Rachel asked.

Mr. Georgiou consulted the alarm clock again. It was now past five. He stood up, parted the curtain slightly and surveyed the street in the pale, early morning light. There was no movement. Even the roosters were quiet. He hesitated.

Rachel smiled and reflected on the habits of her lovers. Mr. Georgiou always left before dawn. Mr. B couldn't care who saw him entering her house, and his petite, Ghanaian wife knew about it and was thankful that someone shared the burden of his voracious sexual appetite. The Mayor always arrived in a hurry, made love in a hurry, and ran off like a pickpocket caught in the act.

'Just sit and talk to me, please,' Rachel commanded, and Mr. Georgiou obediently sat down on the bed and took her hand, but he was unable to think of anything to say. Rachel squeezed his hand. 'Just tell me anything that comes into your mind,' she encouraged him.

Mr. Georgiou smiled as he remembered something. 'Morgan is looking for money again,' he said, and got an instant response.

Rachel's eyes softened, and she stretched herself like a cat.

'What for?' She couldn't suppress a giggle.

'A back operation on a small girl.'

Rachel turned on her side and the diamond shifted and settled on her right breast.

'Who is he stinging this time?' she asked, and Mr. Georgiou found it impossible to fathom the expression in her eyes.

'Round Table,' he said, 'and it is going to cost a lot of money.'

'Robin Hood Morgan,' said Rachel and laughed. 'Extorting money from the rich.'

'More like Captain Morgan,' said Mr. Georgiou.

'No,' said Rachel. 'He is a nice man and I like him a lot.'

Mr. Georgiou suppressed a pang of jealousy 'He is a wild man, that one,' he said, stood up, then bent forward and kissed her neck.

'You are a very good woman,' he said with sudden clarity. 'One day you must find yourself a decent man and marry him.' Mr. Georgiou peeked through the curtain again.

'Your wife is not in town,' he heard Rachel's voice from the bed and at the same time saw the first vendor walking up the street. 'Why don't you stay for breakfast?' she asked.

Suddenly Mr. Georgiou appeared to be in a hurry. 'I must go now,' he said and kissed her on the forehead as if she were his daughter. He lingered for a moment longer. A rooster called, and made up his mind for him.

When he opened the front door, Rachel called from the bedroom: 'It's Saturday!' and her laughter followed him into the street.

13

The dead cat returns

'NO,' SMIRNOFF TOLD Rebecca, 'I won't have the test because I don't want to know.'

For three months, since he had been discharged from the TB Ward, she had been trying to persuade him to have an AIDS test. He surprised her by turning up for his check-up appointment. Even more surprising, he was sober. A new job, he told her. A weekly income and booze only over weekends. He couldn't risk getting fired. A man needs a steady income and food in his belly.

Rebecca congratulated him, in spite of the fact that she had heard the same story before. Smirnoff never held a job for more than six months. She scrutinized his face. True, he had picked up a little bit of weight, his cheeks had filled out somewhat. But his temples were wasted and his eyes seemed anxious. She had no illusions about the cause.

'I think,' she said, 'you must reconsider.'

Smirnoff's tattered coat was folded in his lap and he looked almost respectable.

'What difference will it make?' he asked.

Rebecca didn't answer. Smirnoff had asked her the same question before, when he was still admitted. He couldn't face having TB and AIDS, he had told her. Better to know just about the one disease. He wasn't sure he could face two diseases at the same time. But now, thought Rebecca, we have cured your TB. Now let's talk about the other problem.

'It's not only about you,' she reminded him. 'You might

put other people at risk. Your partner, for instance.' Smirnoff shrugged. Lately he had had no steady girlfriend. His drinking tended to interfere with his love life. Nowadays he only slept with the prostitutes at the whorehouse near the bus station, and only when he had money. It was a sensible arrangement; no recriminations about his drinking habits; pay as you go.

Smirnoff took the question in his stride. 'If they make money out of men,' he told Rebecca, 'then they must run the risk.'

Rebecca shook her head and didn't even try to refute his warped logic.

'Have you ever thought about why they became prostitutes in the first place?' she asked, and at the same time reached across the table and took a handful of condoms out of a box. She handed them to Smirnoff. 'Next time you go to the prostitutes, use one of these,' she said, stifling her anger.

Smirnoff took the condoms and hid them inside one of the pockets of his jacket. 'I am not going to have that test,' he said with an air of finality.

Rebecca saw no reason to continue. 'All right,' she sighed. 'If you change your mind, come and see me again.'

Smirnoff closed the door behind him. Rebecca's shoulders slumped, and she let out her breath with an explosive 'Ohh!' She watched him through the window as he walked out. As usual, his dog was waiting for him at the entrance. It was a well-kept animal, in spite of Smirnoff's erratic ways. The dog gave him a warm welcome and jumped up against him when he crossed the threshold.

Smirnoff briefly paused to put on his coat, and when he resumed walking, the dog followed in his shadow.

THE WAITING ROOM on the other side of the window had filled up in the time it had taken for her to have her fruitless conversation. The morning had not started well and showed every sign of getting worse. Already she could pick out the AIDS cases with their prematurely aged frames and sagging shoulders. Oumar, who was on duty, had rushed to theater with a bled-out woman with an ectopic pregnancy.

In the same dust-covered ambulance, which had come from one hundred kilometers away, was a parcel for Morgan, a blue cool-box containing his errant dead cat. Rebecca stood up and placed the box in the corner of the room. Just then, she saw Morgan and the Kenyan strolling past. She rapped her knuckles on the window to attract their attention.

'Come on you two,' she said when they opened the door, 'help me clear out this place until Oumar comes back.' Morgan looked past her and immediately recognized the cool-box in the corner. He picked it up from the floor and placed it on the desk. 'First things first,' he said and opened the letter that was stuck onto it with tape.

He sniggered when he read it. 'Serves you right,' he said. There had been a small mistake, the veterinary surgeon wrote; somehow the cool-box containing his beer was replaced by the one occupied by Morgan's dead cat. A mutual inconvenience, the veterinary surgeon concluded.

'Now don't tell me,' said the Kenyan, 'you have ordered us some refreshment?' He smiled and the creases around his nose extended onto his chin. 'And it even has your name and address on it?'

'You are not the only one to make that mistake,' Morgan replied.

Rebecca snorted. 'Some refreshment,' she said.

'So what is in the box?' asked the Kenyan.

Morgan tossed the letter into the waste-paper basket and smiled. 'Do you know anything about quantum physics?' he asked innocently.

The Kenyan seemed genuinely surprised. 'What does quantum

physics have to do with it?' he asked.

'It has to do with Schrodinger's cat,' Morgan said. 'The cat that couldn't be dead and alive at the same time. Only, in this case the cat is definitely dead. Or so it seems.'

'A cat?' asked the Kenyan incredulously.

Rebecca's mouth twitched as she tried to retain a deadpan face. With a deliberate movement she took off her glasses and cleaned them.

'Do you know about Schrodinger?' Morgan needled the Kenyan.

The Kenyan only shook his head.

Morgan explained Schrodinger's thought experiment: a cat placed in a box together with a vial of poison that will break or not break, dependent on the decay of an atom. If the atom decays, the cat dies.

The Kenyan was nonplussed. 'But how do you know whether the cat is alive or dead?' he asked.

Morgan congratulated him. 'That is exactly what bothered Schrodinger. You can't know unless you open the box.' With a flourish he broke the seal and opened the box. Inside, in a plastic bag, was the formalin-preserved body of the cat. 'See,' Morgan said with the air of a magician. 'Reality is what we perceive.'

The Kenyan shook his head in disbelief and disappointment.

'The uncertainty in this case,' said Morgan, 'was not whether the cat was dead or not, but whether the cool-box contained beer or not.'

'Morgan,' said the Kenyan, 'there's a dead cat in your cool-box. You missed out on the beer.'

'Not me,' said Morgan, 'the veterinary surgeon. Imagine, you're hot and thirsty, you want to pour yourself a sundowner, and what do you get? A dead cat!'

The Kenyan was sorting the files on Rebecca's desk. 'Now that,' he said, 'is a serious matter.'

'It adds a whole new dimension to quantum physics,' said Morgan.

'Morgan, you are a crazy man!' The Kenyan picked up a bunch of files from the desk. 'Let me go and see those patients; they are far less complicated.'

'Come on, Morgan,' Rebecca hurried him along. 'Let's not waste time. The whole town is here today!'

She helped him to readdress the cool-box. Morgan scratched out the veterinary surgeon's address, then wrote a letter to the State Veterinarian in the Capital, placed it in a big envelope, wrote the new address on it with a marker pen and stuck it onto the top of the cool-box with tape. 'If that envelope falls off, the cat is going to come back to you again,' Rebecca said.

He had written the sender's address on both sides, and marked it *Rabies* when he first sent it to the veterinary surgeon. But, now there was no more room.

'We can leave it here for now,' he said. 'I will take it to the station-master myself; I am sure he will take decent care of it.'

Smirnoff's presence still lingered in the room: a faint smell of wood smoke.

'I am disgusted with men,' Rebecca said.

'So what's new?' Morgan asked.

She told him about her conversation. 'Denial is a defense mechanism,' Morgan said.

'It's not the denial that bothers me so much,' Rebecca said. 'It's what men think about women. They think women are just a commodity.'

'The virus,' said Morgan as he stuck more tape to the envelope, 'thrives on the morality of humans; or the lack of it.'

As he replaced the box in the corner, he thought about something. 'This epidemic is behaving like a magnifying glass, you know. 'It amplifies every defect in humankind as well as most of the fuck-ups of our apathetic leaders.'

'Your language, Morgan! A gentleman doesn't speak like that!'

'Whatever made you think I'm a gentleman?' Morgan asked.

AT NOON THE men in Male Ward were gathered around the kitchen trolley, waiting their turn. The stout, ample-breasted kitchen assistant cheerfully dished out the food amidst encouragement from all sides.

'A little bit more sauce, mother!'

'Do you like that man more than me, mother?'

'Did I do something to make you angry, mother?'

'This plate can take more than that, mother!' She complied generously and returned their light-hearted banter. All eyes were fixed on the overcooked meat submerged in a fatty sauce in which floated onions and sliced carrots. Next to it, in a large bowl, were boiled potatoes.

Johnson watched the queue and tried to gauge how many helpings remained. No cause for concern, he thought. There were only three men ahead of him and there was still enough of everything. He relaxed and enjoyed the smell of the food. From where he stood, he tried to assess the quality of the potatoes.

At last his turn came, and he watched the ladle as it went into the fatty stew. He was eyeing a particularly appetizing piece of meat. He saw the ladle disappear into the sauce and then watched its rim as it reappeared, encircling his prize. The ladle seemed to take forever to come out of the stew but then, thankfully, the precious piece of meat landed in his plate. The woman gave him a conspiratorial wink. She put the potatoes on his plate and covered everything with a liberal helping of sauce. Then, as an afterthought, she put another potato on his plate. 'You're spoiling him, mother!' came a benign chorus of dissent.

'Keep quiet, you lot,' she scolded them. 'Can't you see how thin he is?'

Johnson thanked her and ignored the cries of mock indignation from his friends.

He walked through the ward, carrying his plate like a trophy and went outside. Today he didn't want company. He needed a quiet, undisturbed lunch.

He walked until he was out of earshot and found a large concrete brick next to the stem of a tree. Sitting down on it, he rested his back against the tree and placed the plate on his lap.

He ate slowly, cherishing each mouthful, savoring the taste of the meat, which he cut into small squares with his pocketknife. He took great care not to waste the sauce. With the precision of a surgeon, he sized the pieces of meat and dipped them in the sauce, making sure it was divided evenly between the potatoes and the meat. He saved the potatoes for the end, cutting them in half to make them last for as long as possible.

It was a moment in heaven; nothing else mattered. All too soon he rubbed the last slices of potato in the remaining sauce and let them linger in his mouth. The plate was spotlessly clean. Now that was good, he told himself as he stretched his legs and put the plate aside. His appetite satisfied, his thoughts turned to other things.

The past few months had been tough. The dry season was a difficult time for a jobless man. There was no money to buy food, and no crops in the fields. It was hard to depend on the generosity of others, especially in a village where everyone had the same problem. The memories of the desperation in the village were fresh in his mind. How many nights did he spend with nothing in his stomach? How many mornings with nothing to look forward to? How many days with only a scrap of food?

And the days when he was lucky enough to find someone who offered to share a meal with him? Not too many of those, he thought. What was there to eat? The worst were the hungry children feeding on leftovers that were normally left for the dogs.

True, the dry season was never easy, but it was becoming impossible. The breadwinners were almost all without work, and the sprawling, cheerful village had become a den of misery. Thin, wasted people sat outside their huts or lay on mats inside. His own body was like a mirror image of all the others. How many deaths? He had stopped counting. With a jolt he remembered the smell of rotting bodies. Who could pay for coffins?

People used whatever they could find. Just before he had left, there was a small improvement. The clinic nurse received a generous supply of bodybags that she issued whenever she saw someone on the brink of death. These helped to contain the smell, but not completely; still the burials had to be expedited. Afterwards, the smell lingered in the huts for days.

And the funerals. People in ragged clothes following the body, the wailing of women, the crying of children, the heat, the smell and the ever-present flies. A meager meal afterwards, bought with borrowed money. He had temporarily escaped from that cheerless place and he was lucky.

Don't go to just any hospital, a man had warned him when he first became sick. Go to the Old Man's hospital. At the other places, they will just kick you out again. As a precaution he always lied to the reception clerk about his home address. The man had warned him about that; they might complain if you come from another district.

A job. The thought surfaced in his mind like a cork popping out of water. If only he could become strong enough to hold down a job. But that was exactly the problem; you needed to be strong to be a bricklayer. And he was the best. He had never had a problem finding a job. But now? He couldn't even climb onto a scaffold. He had kept his tools, cherished them. Between the roof and the top of the wall of his hut he had carved a niche and hid his trowel, a four-pound hammer and small tools such as screwdrivers wrapped in a cloth.

The spirit level had been a gift from a contractor, and he carried it wherever he went. It was a reminder of better times, as well as a beacon of hope. He had asked Morgan about the price of the AIDS drugs. At first he thought he could scrape together the money, or get someone to lend him some. Then he realized the figure Morgan mentioned was the monthly cost.

Still, if he could get a good job, then maybe, just maybe. But how do you get a job if you look like a scarecrow? The contractors wouldn't even look at him. They wanted you to be fit and fast. He looked at his forearms and noted the wasting of his once powerful muscles.

Someone was calling his name. He looked up and saw Rastodika on the lawn. 'Come on here. Don't sit there like an old man!' Rastodika shouted. Johnson picked up his plate and answered Rastodika's jovial greeting.

14

A reluctant Samaritan

'THAT BASTARD,' SAID Dorcas, referring to Mr. B. 'All he thinks about is money.' She placed two beers on the kitchen table. 'And more money.'

Kitso's brothers nodded in solemn agreement, and sipped their beers. On the table lay a piece of paper, testimony to a fruitless budgeting exercise.

'Forget it,' said Dorcas. 'She must get her job back. Mr. B can't just fire her like that.'

She peeked through the bead curtain and silenced an unruly Bulgarian contractor who was nearing the limit of his drinking capacity.

'Quiet!' she told him. 'If you can't behave, get out.'

The man had a very limited English vocabulary, but her uncompromising eyes told him all he needed to know.

It was Friday night and all the chairs in her living room were occupied. A huge, bearded maize farmer with hands the size of an average spade and fingers that were as thick as bananas took the contractor by the shoulders and with exaggerated gentleness rearranged him in his plastic chair. 'Now you shut up!' he said amicably.

'Thank you,' said Dorcas and let go of the bead curtain.

She addressed the brothers: 'I think you must speak to Morgan. He is the only man I know who can stand up to Mr. B.'

The brothers nodded in agreement, sipped their beers and offered to pay. Dorcas pushed the money back across the table.

'Some other time,' she said.

At noon on Saturday they went to the hospital to speak to Morgan, but he had done his ward round and left. They proceeded to his house and found him fixing a leaking radiator hose. He was lying under his truck trying to retrieve a socket wrench that had fallen onto a cross member.

From where he was lying, Morgan observed two pairs of coarse, weather-beaten boots. He slid out from underneath the vehicle and for a moment remained on his back, staring at the two brothers. On his right cheek was a patch of sand glued to the skin by sweat. He wore a t-shirt of indeterminate color, which was decorated with oil stains, ventilated with perforations caused by battery acid, and a much-washed pair of jeans.

'What do you want?' Morgan asked. He stood up without bothering to brush the sand off his clothes.

'We have a problem,' said the elder brother, respectfully holding his hat in his hands.

Morgan took the hat and put it back on the man's head. 'So have I,' he said, and tightened the clamp around the radiator hose. 'So, what's your problem?'

'Our sister has been fired from her job,' the elder brother informed him.

Morgan stood up straight and banged his head against the hood. He brought up his hand to rub his head and cursed the drug companies, the medical profession, the business community and humanity in general.

'Whose idea was that?' he asked.

The man hesitated before he answered. 'Mr. B's,' he said after a while.

Morgan picked up a watering can, filled up the radiator, replaced the cap, and banged the hood down so hard both men jumped. He cursed loudly, releasing a string of obscenities that attracted the attention of an old man walking past. 'Don't worry, old man,' Morgan reassured him. 'I am not swearing at you!'

The brothers were embarrassed by the outburst. Morgan noted that the elder brother had again removed his hat. 'So, what are we going to do now?' he asked.

They had budgeted for her to contribute a third to the cost of the drugs. The brothers had no solution to the problem and neither had Morgan. He berated himself for not discharging her earlier. It would be difficult for her to find a job, and without a job she was going to go hungry, never mind the drugs.

Morgan was on his way to the bush; he badly needed the peace and quiet. He looked at the faces of the brothers, saw their anxiety, and cursed himself for not speaking to Mr. B earlier. So much for my trip then, he thought.

'All right,' he said, still rubbing his head. 'I will speak to Mr. B for what it's worth. Come with me.'

They followed him into his house and stood in the cluttered living room. He beckoned them to sit down and they sat on the very edge of the couch while he made two phone calls. The second time he heard the unmistakable voice of Mr. B, and held the phone a safe distance from his ear.

'Morgan! How are you?' bellowed Mr. B.

'I need to speak to you about something,' Morgan said, with the phone momentarily near his face.

'You can speak to me any time, Morgan!' Mr. B's booming voice overwhelmed the receiver, and Morgan held it an arm's length away. 'You know you can!' boomed Mr. B. 'What can I do for you?'

'I would like to come and see you,' Morgan said.

'Of course, of course you can see me whenever you want!'

Morgan held the phone away from his ear again. There was a short silence followed by Mr. B's booming voice inviting him to dinner.

'You have never visited me!' Mr. B accused Morgan. 'Why?

I ask you. You know I like you! Come tonight, we can talk.'

'Seven o'clock, okay!' Morgan shouted into the receiver to give Mr. B a taste of his own medicine.

'You are most welcome!' Mr. B shouted back.

Morgan put down the receiver and both men stood up. 'Sit down, sit down, relax,' Morgan told them. 'You heard what the man said. I will speak to him tonight.'

He offered them a beer, but they declined out of politeness. He didn't accept their refusal. 'Now, sit down,' he ordered and took three beers out of the fridge. They sat right at the very edge of the couch, holding their mugs in both hands, and sipped ever so carefully. When their mugs were empty, they carefully wiped off the condensation on the fabric of their trousers before putting the mugs on the table.

'For God's sake,' said Morgan, 'don't be so polite. It's only me!'

His bush trip was ruined, and in the afternoon he took the truck and drove along the diminished river until he found one of the few remaining pools where men were casting nets from dugout boats, totally unconcerned about the potential threat of crocodiles. He sat on the river's edge and watched them as they hauled in the nets full of fish that had nowhere to escape.

At sunset he drove past the Indian shop until the houses started to peter out, and he found himself on the outer fringe of town. He stopped at a huge house, which seemed to have been transplanted from the Moroccan coast, and knocked on an impressive wooden door.

For once, Morgan was clean-shaven and looking respectable. Mr. B was expecting him and opened the door himself. His bulk seemed to fill the whole doorway. He extended a huge hand, greeted Morgan like a long-lost friend, and his personality seemed to fill the whole house.

'Come!' he commanded. Morgan followed him into a

courtyard where a table stood underneath a giant bougainvillea. In spite of his bulk, Mr. B walked with the grace of a cat. The sleeves of his white silk shirt were left unfastened to accommodate his enormous wrists. 'Drink?' he enquired from Morgan and then called: 'Ishmael!'

A manservant appeared who gave a wide smile of recognition when he saw Morgan.

'Everyone in town knows you, Morgan!' laughed Mr. B. 'And, what are you drinking?' he asked in the same breath.

'Whiskey,' Morgan said.

'Soda?'

'Ice.'

Mr. B poured the drinks with a heavy hand. Morgan wondered where Mr. B's wife and children were. 'My wife is visiting her mother in Ghana,' Mr. B seemed to have read his thoughts. 'It is only Ishmael and me here; it is very quiet.'

They sat down facing each other across the table and Mr. B lifted his glass in a jovial toast. 'So?' he asked. 'Why do you only visit me now, Morgan?'

'Because I want something from you,' Morgan came straight to the point.

Mr. B put down his glass. When he spoke, his voice was cautious and there was no smile on his heavy-featured face. Morgan found himself facing the hard nosed businessman and renowned former cattle smuggler.

'And what is it that you want?' Mr. B's voice was soft and polite, but he looked at Morgan like a boxer sizing up his opponent.

'I have a problem with a girl,' Morgan said.

Mr. B's smile returned instantly. 'And you want to confide in me?' His laughter filled the courtyard. 'You need advice?'

'You fired her,' Morgan told him flatly.

Mr. B's laughter stopped abruptly, and he raised his eyebrows. 'And her name, please?' His voice was soft and polite again.

'Kitso,' said Morgan.

For a moment Mr. B seemed puzzled. Then he said, 'Oh, you mean the girl in the shop?' and crossed his legs. 'There is one thing that you must understand,' he said to Morgan. 'I have a business to run. That girl has been off work for more than a month.'

'She will be back,' said Morgan.

'And in the meantime I have to pay her for no work?'

'It won't be long, ten more days at the most. But she needs her job.'

'And what is wrong with her?' Mr. B wanted to know. He sat back in his chair and straightened the arm that held his drink. His big hand almost completely enveloped the glass.

'She will be better soon,' Morgan sidestepped the question.

Mr. B frowned and said nothing. Behind him at the other end of the courtyard stood Ishmael, like a statue, expressionless.

Mr. B folded his arms. 'If I do it for her,' he told Morgan, 'then I must do it for everyone. I can allow her only one month.' He put down his glass and put the palms of both his hands on the table to indicate a full stop.

Morgan stifled his anger and raised his glass in a mock toast. Mr. B looked up into his unsmiling eyes.

'To your conscience, then,' Morgan said. 'I will remind you about it when she dies.'

The silence was broken only by an ice cube that sank to the bottom of Morgan's glass.

Mr. B shifted his weight almost imperceptibly. He rested his elbows on the table and it creaked under his weight as he considered his options. Morgan put down his glass.

Mr. B thought aloud. 'True, I fired her. I cannot carry people unnecessarily.' He looked at Morgan closely. 'Why is she so important to you?'

Morgan paused before he answered. 'I have spent a lot of time getting her better. And I think she deserves a chance.'

'People talk about you, Morgan,' said Mr B. 'They say you take money from the rich to help the poor.' He smiled a faint smile. 'Are you doing it to me now?'

Morgan lit a cigarette. 'Not yet,' he said.

Mr. B started laughing and all of his joviality returned. 'Morgan!' he said. 'You are a scoundrel!'

He took Morgan's drink from him and filled it generously, his huge, dark, fleshy hand engulfing the glass. A hand is as big as a face, Morgan remembered from a drawing lesson. Morgan looked up and compared the size of the hand with the broad, heavily featured face. Big, ever-watchful eyes below bushy eyebrows and jaw muscles that slanted slightly outwards. A large mouth with strong, regular teeth. The face exuded boundless energy.

'All right,' said Mr. B. 'Since I trust you, I will keep the girl and pay her. Treat her until she's fit.'

He changed topics in mid-stride, indicating that the matter was settled. 'You have never been to my farm!' he accused Morgan. Their conversation thawed, helped along by Mr. B's generous tots of whiskey. Ishmael served them a hot curry that they washed down with still more whiskey.

From somewhere, Mr. B conjured up a bottle of peach brandy, which they drank neat out of small glasses, and the conversation thawed considerably more. Halfway through the evening Mr. B remembered about Rastodika.

'I hear he is back in town?' he posed it as a question. Morgan merely nodded.

'Rastodika is my oldest friend,' Mr. B said. For a moment his heavy features softened in memory of times long past. Mr. B seemed to have an unlimited capacity for drink, Morgan realized at four o'clock in the morning when they concluded their deliberations with two whiskey Dom Pedros that Mr. B insisted on preparing himself.

They were standing in the dining room. On the wall were framed pictures of Mr. B and his family. The photographs provided a chronicle of the growth of the family as well as the accumulation of a fortune. In the first picture was Mr. B's beautiful wife holding their first-born. A proud Mr. B stood next to her, dwarfing her. The photograph was taken in the backyard of a very modest dwelling. The second photo showed the couple with a toddler and a new baby in the garden of a somewhat more sophisticated home. The last photo showed two school-aged children together with a new baby and was taken in the courtyard of Mr. B's mansion.

Later, when the two men were standing in the driveway, supporting themselves against Morgan's truck, Mr. B repeated his invitation, 'You must come and help me shoot that troublesome leopard on the farm,' he said. His speech was slightly slurred.

Morgan reminded Mr. B that he actually liked leopards.

'But not this one,' declared Mr. B. 'This leopard is a delinquent.'

Late on the Sunday, Morgan woke up with a hangover that still accompanied him on his ward round Monday morning.

15

Naledi at midnight

AT SEVEN O'CLOCK, just before the doctors' meeting, Lawrence brought an urgent order for more oxygen cylinders. 'How much longer are they going to ventilate this man?' Holmes enquired from Thunderbird, who considered it safer not to venture an opinion.

'They have to realize that we can't practice First World medicine in a Third World hospital.' Holmes cursed old Jenkins' legacy. 'Why the hell did he build a High Care unit in the first place? It's an utter waste of money!'

The morning meeting only served to aggravate Holmes' already sour mood. He was faced with open rebellion. When he complained about the man on the ventilator, Thomson asked him if he was going to bill people for the air they breathed. When he complained about the crowded wards, Oumar asked him why he did not hire more nurses. Holmes only saw the trap after he had walked straight into it. He told Oumar that the average occupancy rate was sixty per cent and that's how the number of nurses was determined.

'But then you don't have a problem,' said Oumar. 'Then the hospital is only sixty per cent full.'

'But it is overcrowded all of a sudden!' Holmes shouted.

'It's always like that.' Oumar was emphatic.

Holmes managed to control his anger with difficulty. 'I have figures,' he told Oumar with exaggerated politeness, 'that tell me the average occupancy rate is sixty per cent.'

Oumar rested his arms on the table and answered with

equally affected politeness. 'And I am telling you that since I have been here this hospital has always been overflowing. I suggest you visit it more often.'

Holmes turned away from Oumar and asked the rest of the meeting to try to admit fewer patients.

'Why don't you,' the Kenyan asked him, 'go and stand at the gate and turn people away yourself?'

'THEY ARE TOTALLY out of line!' For the second time in as many minutes Holmes lifted his rotund figure out of his chair and negotiated the right-hand corner of his desk. He came to a halt roughly in the middle of the room and faced Thunderbird, who took a step backwards and found himself standing precariously on the edge of the worn carpet.

Holmes was fuming. Gone were both his joviality and smooth manner. Small beads of sweat coalesced on his forehead and his shirt looked slightly crumpled. Thunderbird was intimidated by the tirade that had started the moment he arrived in Holmes' office. Holmes turned away from Thunderbird and opened his briefcase.

'This is going to change,' he told him. He took out a circular from Head Office about over-prescribing, threw it on the table, and forcibly shut the briefcase. 'From now on, we are going to take a more active part in the patient care. And, I'm afraid, a few people are going to be disciplined.' He was raising his voice, as if to convince himself as well. 'They will have to realize just who is running this hospital.'

Thunderbird nodded his head in obligatory approval. 'You have a very difficult job,' he agreed.

Holmes was thirsty. He walked into the secretary's office and ordered two cups of tea.

'It will have to be black,' Rose told him unenthusiastically. 'There is no milk this morning.'

'All right, then,' said Holmes, and turned back towards Thunderbird in exasperation. Thunderbird was standing with his hands behind his back, contemplating the pattern of the mildewed patches on the ceiling. Holmes' exasperation gave way to anger. 'This morning, this very morning you go and find out from Morgan how long that patient is going to continue to be on the ventilator.'

Thunderbird woke up from his daydream with a visible jolt. He looked straight into Holmes' eyes and hurriedly agreed.

'Why don't they refer these goddamned trauma cases?' Holmes' voice reached a crescendo. 'Why do they always want to treat everything here?'

Rose brought the tea, placed it on his desk and walked out. Holmes drank his cup standing next to the window. Outside on the lawn, the ambulant patients were getting ready for the ward round. Some of them were extinguishing cigarettes, others waved at Morgan and Thomson who were making their way towards the side entrance.

'And why are they hanging on to all these AIDS cases?' Holmes addressed his question to the window. 'They are behaving like a bunch of missionaries.'

OUMAR AND THE Kenyan were not sharing Holmes' black mood. In fact, they seemed hardly affected by the acrimonious morning meeting. Morgan found them standing in front of a side ward, looking very pleased with themselves.

'Come and see this.' The Kenyan caught Morgan by the arm and dragged him towards the door. Inside the side ward was their prize patient.

Everyone knew about the man who had been shedding his skin and had asked to die in the privacy of a side ward. His request was granted, and he prepared himself for the inevitable, until Oumar managed to persuade his relatives to pay for antiretroviral drugs. That was just over a month before.

The Kenyan opened the door like a circus impresario. 'Just look at him now,' he said.

Morgan was astonished. The man's skin lesions were gone and he was even growing new nails. The patient was as pleased as his saviors. 'Tomorrow he is going home,' said the Kenyan. 'It is a miracle.'

No it's not, thought Morgan. It's a matter of money. And about someone who cared. 'Do the other patients know about this?' he asked the Kenyan when they were outside in the passage.

The Kenyan looked uncomfortable. They knew, and not only did they know, there was a constant trickle of visitors from the other wards to come witness the miracle.

Earlier in the morning, in Female Ward, Kitso had told Morgan that Mr. B had visited her the previous afternoon. 'Take your time,' Mr. B had told her. 'Your job is waiting for you.'

Morgan had forced a smile past his splitting headache and wondered how Mr. B coped with his hangover. He congratulated Kitso, but when he faced the other women he felt like a traitor.

'I can read your thoughts,' Oumar said. 'We also feel like that. Strange, to feel guilty about saving someone.'

Thunderbird appeared at the end of the passage like a bad omen. 'I know what this is about,' said the Kenyan.

Morgan smiled a faint smile. Thomson had told him about the morning meeting. They watched Thunderbird negotiating the passage with his robotic gait. He reached them and came to a halt. No one returned his greeting. Thunderbird faced three pairs of expressionless eyes in turn. Against his better judgment, he mustered enough courage to face Morgan. It was safer in a crowd, he reasoned, thankful that he wasn't encountering Morgan alone. 'How is the patient on the ventilator?' he asked. Three seconds ticked by, and Thunderbird felt like a man who had lit a fuse, but no explosion occurred.

'Very well,' Morgan said amiably. The Kenyan's eyes glinted behind his spectacles. Oumar's face wore no expression at all.

After an uncomfortable silence Thunderbird tried again, this time visibly unsure of himself. 'How much longer is he going to be ventilated?' he asked.

Morgan paused before he answered. His body stiffened, his jaws clenched and he fixed Thunderbird with an icy stare. 'Who can tell?' he said.

Thunderbird read the danger signals. He greeted them politely and made his way down the passage. They watched his ungainly figure as it turned the corner, then continued their conversation.

'What about the other patients?' Morgan asked. 'Do they really believe we are helping them?'

Oumar shrugged. 'Every morning I tell them the same story. The problem is, I don't even believe it myself.'

The phone rang. 'You are needed in Casualty,' Violet told them. 'Rebecca says it is very busy and where are you?'

Morgan said, 'Tell her to send everyone home.'

Violet laughed. 'They will be coming soon,' she told Rebecca.

RASTODIKA WAS SITTING outside under his favorite tree. Inside his room, under the bed, stood the twenty-four hour specimen bottle for assessing his creatinine clearance rate. He had complained bitterly about the inconvenience of collecting twenty-four hours' worth of urine. Morgan took a syringe and two tubes and moved towards the door.

Violet scolded him about his patients who were scattered all over. 'I am not doing ward rounds under the trees,' she told him flatly. He ignored her, took the syringe and tubes and strode across the lawn on his own.

'It is going to rain,' Rastodika informed him. Rastodika's tiredness was gone; his eyes were bright and mischievous as usual. Probably it was the long trip after all, Morgan hoped. He followed his friend's gaze to the top branches of the tree. They were moving ever so slightly, and for the first time Morgan noticed the wind. 'It is blowing just right,' Rastodika said, holding out his hands as if guiding it. The wind was coming from the northeast.

'Let everyone wait for a while,' Morgan said and sat down next to Rastodika. The bright light reflecting from the walls hurt Morgan's eyes, and he rubbed his temples to rid himself of his headache. On the lawn, the ambulant patients with their stick-like figures fanned out in search of shade. They saw him sitting next to Rastodika, and kept their distance.

Rastodika greeted them with his usual exuberance, and Morgan again relived the memory from long before, of Rastodika and Sam standing in the shade of tall trees next to the boat, silhouetted against the papyrus on the opposite bank of the river. He turned his head sideways and looked at Rastodika. For a moment his friend appeared to be lost in thought, then he looked up at the weavers hanging upside-down from their nests.

'Morgan, you must come with me for some time, so I can show you the river properly,' he said suddenly.

'I have just been thinking about the same thing,' Morgan said. 'I hope you can go soon, then I can try to take a few days off.'

Don't disappoint me, Morgan thought. I am fighting enough futile battles. He looked at Rastodika's vigorous face.

It will be all right he told himself. It must be all right.

'Let me take your blood,' he told Rastodika. Rastodika rolled up his sleeve and used it as a tourniquet.

'You,' said Morgan with sudden conviction, 'have discovered the secret of life. To live exactly as you please.'

Rastodika bent his arm over the cotton wool swab and looked up into Morgan's face. 'Nobody is stopping you,' he said.

High above them were small wispy clouds, the first in months. 'Maybe you are right,' Morgan said. 'Maybe we are going to get some rain.'

'It will come,' Rastodika said without a trace of doubt.

CASUALTY WAS OVERFLOWING. Rebecca had lost all confidence in the electric fans and was fanning herself with a patient's file. In front of Casualty sat a dog with scars across its nose, patiently waiting for its owner, unfazed by passersby. The dogs never failed to impress Morgan. They sometimes waited for a whole day and they never came inside. The dog was panting.

'Please, could someone give the dog some water?' Morgan asked.

'What?' said Rebecca. 'We hardly have time for the people.'

Outside, under the shelters, people were arriving on foot, by bus, by bicycle, by ambulance, on the back of pickup trucks, by taxi, by donkey cart and some on horseback, leaving their horses to graze on the sidewalk.

'It's a carnival with a difference,' said Morgan.

'If we don't start now, we will never get through the day!' Rebecca said and handed him a pack of files.

Morgan shrugged and felt like a bullfighter entering an arena. Oumar and the Kenyan were there already. Nurses brought patients into cubicles, took histories, told people to undress, sent them to X-rays, translated, collected blood samples, shared jokes and sympathized with their stories of disasters.

At eleven o'clock Morgan heard a nurse call from the outside door. Rebecca was already standing in the doorway. An ancient Toyota was reversing towards the Casualty entrance, carrying the dust-covered body of a small boy.

'He's dead,' Rebecca said, but the boy surprised her by opening his eyes as they stepped outside into the glaring sunshine. Morgan and the Kenyan jumped onto the truck, knelt down next to the boy and felt his fast, thready pulse. The boy was as pale as death. Morgan ripped open his cotton shirt and noted the distended belly with a bruise mark running across it.

He heard Rebecca shouting for a drip followed by the clattering of the wheels of a trolley on an uneven surface. The Kenyan found a vein and inserted a cannula. A nurse stood next to him, holding the drip aloft like the Statue of Liberty. From two tough-looking men wearing leather hats with brims that ran exactly parallel to their eyebrows, Rebecca established that the boy had been injured in a donkey cart accident and that it had taken three hours to get him to the hospital.

They carefully lifted the boy onto a trolley and took him inside. Morgan infused the fluid rapidly, ordered blood, and felt the pulse grow stronger. The boy spoke for the first time. 'Your clothes are full of dust,' he told Morgan with the lucidness that precedes death.

'Let's take him to theater,' said Morgan. It took slightly longer than an hour to anesthetize the boy, open his belly and remove his shattered spleen. Morgan's mood improved considerably. 'At least we have accomplished something today,' he told the Kenyan. He saw the two men with faded overalls standing at the door with their hats in their hands.

'Come on in!' he shouted and they walked into High Care on tiptoe in their creaking boots, as if crossing a minefield. Morgan laughed. 'You can relax,' he told them. 'The boy is going to be fine.'

Rebecca called them back to Casualty, and through lunch-hour they battled to sort the sick and the very sick from the not so sick. By late afternoon the flood had slowed to a trickle and Morgan noticed that the dog had gone. He walked down to High Care to look at the boy. Good foot pulses and pink toes he observed, a sign of a successful operation.

The boy was awake, looking out of place with his hard, cracked foot soles on clean linen amongst monitors and drip lines. Mr. Bernard was breathing easily and the ventilator setting was down to six breaths per minute. He was watching Morgan and lifted his hand in greeting.

'Tell him I will get him off this ventilator soon,' Morgan told the nurse. Mr. Bernard seemed happy with the news. Morgan glanced at his watch, walked through Female Ward and found Mary in her usual place, sitting in a wheelchair on the veranda.

She was well, thank you; she never said she was anything but well. She told him about the Yellowbilled Kites. One of them had caught something that morning; she couldn't see exactly what it was. It swooped down and came up with something in its talons.

He looked at her thin arm and saw the veins that didn't stand out but coursed like furrows under the skin. He watched the way she moved her hands as she talked. She always talked with her hands, and he made a point of not teasing her about it because he loved their gracious movements, like the heads of swans on long necks.

'The rain is almost here,' she told him. The afternoon light was subdued due to a high, milky layer of cloud that covered the whole sky.

'Rastodika said so this morning,' Morgan told her. 'He predicted it according to the wind.'

If you really want to know what someone is like, he thought, you watch them when they are ill. He had read this somewhere, but his headache wouldn't allow him to retrieve the full quote from his memory. He tried not to think about how little time she had left, and suppressed a sudden burst of anger. Why does someone like her have to die? Why not some crazy dictator, or a demented old woman? Or a fat politician? Or an irritating, neurotic, suburban cow?

He pushed the wheelchair right to the edge of the veranda so she could see a bigger portion of the sky. He leaned against a pillar, studied her face and tried to memorize the angles between her jaw and cheekbones, the shape of her eyes and her long eyelashes. Her braided hair hung straight down and slightly increased the angularity of her face.

The women in the ward managed to look well-kept even if they wore only faded, shapeless hospital dresses. They paid particular attention to Mary's appearance. Morgan had been making a sketch of Mary's face at home, drawn from memory. Every day he noticed a different feature. The lines around her mouth became firmer and her lips became thinner when she was serious, her eyes slanted upwards ever so slightly, her nostrils flared when she spoke; she wrinkled her nose when she laughed; and when she was in pain she clenched her jaws and the lines around her mouth became deeper.

'Why are you staring at me?' she asked.

'I want to engrave your face in my memory,' Morgan said.

Mary laughed. 'My face was much nicer before I became sick.'

'I never knew that face,' Morgan said. 'But I will settle for this one.'

He didn't tell her about the sketch. Maybe if it's good I will show it to her sometime, he thought, then realized that 'sometime' in Female Ward was always in the all-too-near future. He banished the thought from his mind. She lifted a thin arm and pointed with her hand. Below the cloud an eagle soared effortlessly, and Morgan noticed the short, pencil-stub tail. 'Bateleur,' she said. Morgan congratulated her.

'I wish I could fly like an eagle,' Mary said. 'See how he dips his wings.'

Morgan looked at her finely chiseled face. 'You would make a fine eagle,' he said. A benign, soft-spoken eagle, he thought.

'And you?' she asked. 'Would you like to fly like that?' Morgan was surprised by the sudden urgency in her voice. From inside the ward someone called her name. She didn't answer at first. 'Maybe they will think I have run away,' she joked, putting her hands on the sides of the wheelchair.

Morgan lifted her hand and gave it a kiss. 'Good night, madam,' he said. 'Thanks for your company.'

'You didn't answer my question,' she laughed.

'Which question?' Morgan mocked her.

'The question about flying like an eagle.'

'If I could fly like an eagle,' Morgan said, 'I would fly away and never come back.'

ON HIS EVENING run the wind had freshened, and when the moon rose, it was a red smudge in the sky.

At home, Morgan observed the unfinished canvases standing on the trestle table in his bedroom, and wondered when he was ever going to have enough daylight hours to complete them. He switched on the reading lamp and paged through his sketchbook.

He stopped at a page where a figure had been cut out of a sketch of a marketplace. That was after he and Tesfai had come back from the mountains. Tesfai sat opposite him in a small café as Morgan glanced out over the marketplace and drew figures of people, the outline of a mosque and the shapes of horses.

'How can you draw people?' Tesfai had asked.

'I don't draw them,' Morgan answered. 'I draw the space around them. In fact, I draw the dent they make in space.'

He explained to Tesfai about negative space, then took out his razor-sharp pocketknife, cut out the figure of a man in the foreground and showed Tesfai the page with the excised shape in it. 'You see,' he said. 'I don't draw the hole; I draw the edges.'

'You'd better put that man back,' Tesfai had said.

A sudden gust of wind shook the roof of the house. Morgan stared at the gap in the page. Tesfai would hate to know how many cut-outs I have in my life, he thought, and I can never put them back.

He paged on until he got to his memory sketch of Mary, closed his eyes and recalled the shape of her jawbone. Gently he redrew the face with a soft pencil, changing the shape of the forehead and slightly tilting the eyes. He wondered what she had looked like before she became ill.

AT MIDNIGHT MORGAN was called by the night sister who was worried about Naledi's temperature. It was higher than ever. Would he come and see her, please? Morgan had left instructions that he should be called even if he was not on duty. If there was bad news, he wanted to know about it first.

He found Naledi propped up on a pillow, lying on her side, burning with fever, her skin hot under his hand. Surprisingly, she was more alert than before. In her folder were the culture reports and a full blood count delivered in the late afternoon. The white cell count was even higher than before, and Morgan found himself both dismayed and impressed.

At least the bone marrow was functioning as it should, he thought, pouring out white cells like an army stemming an invasion. A major war was being waged inside a skeleton.

Maybe that's why she was more alert, he thought. She might be starting to fight back. Or was it the final flicker of light from a dying flame? Probably the latter. The night sister seemed to read his thoughts. He saw a faint, almost imperceptible shake of her head.

The culture results from the pus swab depressed him. Powerful bacteria were launching their final assault. They were gram-negative organisms as expected. He scanned the sensitivity report and found the least damaging potent antibiotic. It was comparatively new and very expensive. To hell with the expense, he thought. I am not going to mess up that other kidney with standard drugs.

He wrote the drug on the chart and gave it to the night sister. There wasn't any in the ward, she informed him. 'Then call the pharmacist at home and ask him to get us some,' he said.

'It's very late,' the night sister reminded him.

'I don't bloody care!' he roared. 'Just get it!'

The night sister shrugged, took the drug chart and disappeared. Far down the passage he could hear her voice as she made the call. He left the ward for a while and strolled to High Care. The little boy was asleep, at peace with the world. Someone had rubbed emulsifying ointment on his feet. He checked the boy's pulse. It was strong and unhurried.

Mr. Bernard was awake, happily breathing between ventilator breaths. Morgan resisted reducing the rate. Better to leave that for the daytime, he thought. The night sister found him sitting in the tearoom reading a pamphlet about malaria. She waited for the kettle to boil, made two cups of tea and sat down across the table. They drank their tea in silence.

She was a true creature of the night, having done night

duty for more years than she could remember. For almost two decades, she had seen buildings rising out of the ground and growing bigger night after night, without seeing anybody actually building them. All she had seen were sleepy workers arriving on the sites in the early morning as she went home.

She preferred nights; the hospital was more ordered at night. The passages were empty; the patients were mostly asleep and she could look after the really sick ones, walking from ward to ward like Florence Nightingale minus a lamp.

Sometimes it was chaos, with badly injured patients going to theater, and sometimes being flown out in the early hours of the morning. And, of course, there were the babies arriving through the night. She loved the maternity ward and couldn't understand why Morgan hated obstetrics. 'Wait until you become a father,' she once said to him. 'It will change your life.'

'God forbid,' Morgan told her. 'I have enough problems already.'

Her children were all grown up and married. She carried photographs of her grandchildren in her handbag and every so often showed him a new addition or a school photograph.

As they sat opposite each other sipping their tea, Morgan wondered what it was like to live most of your life at night, spending one month a year on holiday in broad daylight. Did the sunlight hurt her eyes? Or did she go out only at night even then? The nightlife didn't seem to bother her; she was a cheerful, well-informed soul.

The sounds of the two monitors in High Care came floating through the door. Two pulses at a different rate, coinciding now again like converging lanes on a highway.

'That man is doing very well,' the night sister said, meaning Mr. Bernard. She sounded almost disappointed about missing the action.

The bespectacled, tracksuit-clad pharmacist made a hasty entrance. He didn't want tea, thank you very much, and no coffee either. It would ruin his sleep, he said. Didn't they know that? He handed the vials, still in their boxes, complete with package inserts to Morgan. 'For your new skeleton, I believe,' he said. 'Is she eating her ice cream?'

'She prefers this for now,' Morgan said, holding up the vials.

The pharmacist laughed and turned towards the door. 'She has expensive tastes, hasn't she? Your bosses will be pleased.'

'To hell with my bosses,' Morgan said as they parted in the passage.

He helped the night sister to put up the first vial and adjusted the drip. Naledi was asleep as were most of the other women. Mary and Janet were still awake and he could make out their eyes and a faint outline of their faces in the dim light. He caught Mary's eye and waved at her. The rest of the ward was dark. Only Naledi's bedside light was on. Like a Rembrandt painting, thought Morgan.

He stood next to Naledi for a long time. Once he put his hand on her chest and felt the pounding of her heart, like a bird trying to escape from a cage. He wondered how long it could keep beating as fast as that before it gave up. He went through the drug list. She was getting everything he could give her. She would have to fight this battle by herself. He walked down the passage convinced she was not going to be there in the morning.

The wind was still blowing when he drove home. Thick clouds obliterated the stars. Dust and paper bags were picked up by the wind. In the shanty town Smirnoff's tall, gaunt figure crossed the road, his coat flapping in the wind. The mongrel dog ran next to him like a shadow. On the horizon were flashes of lightning. Maybe Rastodika was right after all.

THE LIGHTNING AND thunder were part of Morgan's dream, and he woke up with raindrops falling onto his face through the open window. The wind blew into the room and carried the smell of damp earth. Above the sound of the wind, he could hear the raindrops splatter on the roof as it rained harder and harder until it was just one continuous roar. He got up and shut the window, then walked through the house and pushed open the door to the veranda.

Gusts of wind swept the rain underneath the roof. Morgan stood still, admiring the storm as the raindrops blew into his face. Flashes of lightning accompanied by instantaneous thunder revealed spray and wind and flying leaves. The wind drove the spray onto the rooftops, and stripped branches off the trees; a weaver's nest flew through the air and bounced as it hit the ground.

He stood there for a long time, watching the storm until the wind died down and only the rain remained. At three o'clock he felt Oscar jump onto the bed, his fur wet from the rain. Morgan pushed the cat to the far corner of the bed. He woke up again at six, and found the cat nestling against his chest.

He had expected a phone call from the night sister to inform him of Naledi's death. She sometimes neglected to tell Morgan about serious problems she experienced with the living, but she always phoned when someone passed on to the hereafter. She considered it her solemn duty, even when it was obvious that there was nothing more to be done.

Morgan lifted up the phone and heard a dial tone. He couldn't decide whether the girl was still alive or if the night sister had, for once, forgotten to phone.

16

Walking in the rain

RASTODIKA LEFT THE ward just after daybreak and wandered through the streets.

The rain was torrential and soaked him to the skin, but he didn't mind. It invigorated him, and soon he had forgotten about the lethargy he had felt in the previous couple of days.

There were lots of people on the streets, rejoicing about the rain. Some carried umbrellas, others held plastic bags over their heads and jumped over the puddles, while children shrieked with delight and ran through the puddles.

This is better than lying in a hospital bed, he thought. He walked up the hill and was satisfied that there were clouds as far as he could see. The river had already swollen somewhat and there was no sign that the rain was going to let up. The people in the shacks near the bank all seemed to be outside their houses, and he saw men digging a trench around a small house to keep the water away from the front door. Music from a ghetto-blaster floated up the hill, dogs barked, and naked, skinny little boys played in a ditch next to the road. At the top of the hill the clouds seemed to be hanging only a few feet above his head.

An old man came past wearing a suit. He was barefoot and carried his shoes in one hand and an umbrella in the other.

'Where are you going, old man?' asked Rastodika.

The old man looked over his shoulder. 'To the station!' he shouted and hurried along.

'Don't rush, old man!' Rastodika said. 'I'm sure the lines were washed away last night.'

I could just carry on walking and not go back, he thought, and realized he was still wearing his hospital clothes. He suddenly felt like an escaped prisoner in his blue clothes, and slowly he started walking down the hill. He returned to the ward just before seven and incurred the wrath of the night sister who was just going off duty. 'Just look at you!' she said. 'You are sure to get pneumonia. How long have you been in the rain?'

'Mind your own business, woman,' Rastodika said.

The night sister called a nurse to bring him some dry clothes and scolded, 'You know it's against the rules to walk around town in your hospital clothes.'

'Rules are made to be broken,' Rastodika laughed.

The night sister tapped him on the chest with the palm of her hand. 'Rastodika, if I didn't like you so much I would report you to the Matron.'

Rastodika felt a sudden foreboding together with the return of his headache. 'Are you threatening a condemned man?' he asked.

'Be serious for once, Rastodika,' the night sister said as she left. 'And stay indoors,' she added as an afterthought.

He changed clothes in the bathroom and went outside to the veranda where most of the patients were sitting. They were cheerful this morning and watched the rain with the attention usually reserved for soccer matches.

They saw Morgan park his truck and then observed him as he came running towards them. The heavy drops of water falling from the trees soaked his shirt. Morgan reached the veranda and climbed the stairs.

'So, what did I tell you?' asked Rastodika.

Morgan stopped and looked at the smiling faces. He wiped the water off his face with the sleeve of his shirt. 'Make it rain for another week or so, Rastodika,' he said. 'I like this cool weather.'

The creases over Rastodika's high cheekbones deepened. 'You think I am a witchdoctor?' he asked.

'I have my suspicions,' Morgan said.

Some of the men were enjoying a joke of their own. Morgan turned around and followed their eyes. Thunderbird was making his way towards his office, carrying an umbrella. He tried to walk fast but his bulk didn't allow him to. The rain hit him from behind and his wet trousers tightened around his thick legs. 'Hippo,' one of the men said and everyone laughed.

Morgan smiled a faint smile. He certainly is thick-skinned enough, he thought. In fact, he probably doesn't need an umbrella. He walked through Male Ward and found almost all the beds empty. Through the window he saw the men from behind, still looking out over the lawn. Thunderbird had disappeared and a continuous stream of water fell over the eaves.

He crossed the divide between Male and Female Ward like a soldier crossing no man's land, expecting to see a death certificate on the table. The table was empty, except for Violet's marker pen and her handbag hanging over a chair. From far away he heard Violet's voice. She was laughing. Naledi was sitting upright surrounded by Violet and her foster mothers.

For the first time she looked into his eyes and said, 'Morning.'

Morgan was astounded. He returned her greeting and looked at her temperature chart. Her temperature had plummeted straight down. He took her wrist and felt the slowed pulse.

Outside, the rain fell with renewed vigor and almost drowned Violet's voice. 'Don't look so surprised, Doctor,' she mocked him. 'She has already finished this,' she pointed at an empty glass standing on the locker next to the bed. 'Just so you know that we are following your instructions.'

The women were washing Naledi and changing her sweat-soaked linen. Morgan watched as they combed her hair and rubbed moisturizer into her skin. Morgan noticed a movement at the door and saw the Matron surveying the scene. Above her left breast pocket she wore a white rose.

'And?' she asked, with her eyes invisible behind the reflection of her glasses.

'A celebration,' Morgan said with a straight face. 'Do come in.'

The Matron removed the rose from her dress and pinned it in Naledi's hair with the air of a general decorating a soldier. Naledi's lips parted and her eyes widened slightly. 'So,' said the Matron. 'From now on I want to see you smile every day. When my red roses are ready,' she told Naledi in the tone of a benign grandmother to her granddaughter at her birthday, 'I will bring you a dozen.'

Naledi's foster mothers clapped their hands. Then they dressed her in a faded hospital dress and covered her bony frame. They propped her up with pillows and she looked like a wilted flower that had been partly revived by the rain.

She had a pretty face, Morgan noticed for the first time.

The rain on the roof fell harder like an amplifier turned louder, and Matron walked over to Mary's bed. She greeted her by grasping her hand.

Mary was her normal, cheerful, death-defying self, and she answered Matron's enquiries with a smile on her face. She was fine thank you, and very happy about the rain. Beautiful rain. Her last rainy season in this world.

Morgan was acutely aware of that fact, and so was Mary, but she accepted it with grace. There was always something to be happy about, he noticed. Small things like weavers building their nests, or the sound of rain on the roof, or Naledi's attempt at a smile.

Small things matter, he decided. Big things are too complicated.

ON THE WAY to his office he stopped at the laboratory to pick up the blood results. The technician, the pretty girl behind the microscope, and the assistant were standing with their backs towards him, looking out the window. The gardener was balanced precariously on a ladder, held casually in position by the handyman who was looking away to keep the rain out of his eyes. The gardener scooped a sparrow's nest out of the gutter and threw it down, narrowly missing the handyman. He wore a plastic cape and a stream of water poured down in front of his face like a curtain.

'Those two are an accident waiting to happen,' Morgan said, wondering who was on Casualty duty. On the table were the ward reports, kept for him as usual. Rastodika's lay on top of the pile. The smile on Morgan's face vanished as he reread the name at the top of the page, hoping he had made a mistake. The impartial figures confirmed his worst fears. Time was running out.

He was glad he had only seen them now. Suddenly his happiness evaporated; Rastodika was in big trouble. He didn't hear the uncharacteristically jovial greeting of the technician and had already forgotten about the pretty girl as he turned around and left.

He found Thomson on the porch between the wards. He was admiring the rain, small droplets of water in his beard, still wearing an anorak, his pitch-black sailor's beard wrapped around thirty-two shiny white teeth.

'What was going on in Female Ward?' he wanted to know. 'You having a party? You must watch out, that shapely sister is going to hook you!'

Morgan answered his greeting with a curt 'Morning,' and

handed him Rastodika's report. Thomson read it without saying a word, his dark eyes rapidly scanning the results, and he shook his head.

'How long since we did the biopsy?' He lifted his eyes and stood with his back towards Morgan, looking out towards the rain.

'A year.'

'He needs a transplant.'

'Fat chance.'

'I know.'

'I suppose we could try and make the government pay.'

'I can tell you now they won't.'

'I will try anyway.'

'Trouble is, he will soon need dialysis, and we can only do peritoneal dialysis.' A gust of wind blew the rain into their faces but they hardly noticed.

Morgan swore softly. 'Not today,' he said. 'I'm not telling him about this today. Let him enjoy the rain.'

THE RAIN REJUVENATED the town. People who hardly knew each other stopped on the streets and talked. Dogs used to lying wearily in the shadows of trees got up, lifted their tails, trotted down the street and briskly cocked their legs against lamp-posts. New vendors appeared at the mall and it turned into a permanent carnival. Farmers in mud-splattered trucks found an excuse to drive into town.

The soil around the houses was dug up and patches of mealies and vegetables rose out of the ground. At night, hundreds of springhares sat eating the soft, green grass growing next to the main road. The Yellowbilled Kites stopped chasing the chickens in town and hung around the road, feeding on snakes and rabbits run over by cars.

Cows grazed the fresh new shoots on the hospital lawn

until they found that there were fresh shoots everywhere. Sorghum grew in the fields and people started brewing beer. The shebeens did good business under the watchful eye of the Constable.

The first Saturday after the rain, a party started outside the beerhall. It didn't actually start, but broke out like a benign rash and spread to the mall, and then across the street into the township and when the sun set, it moved to the soccer field and stayed there. It carried on right through the night and the town reverberated with the music pouring out of huge loudspeakers on the back of a pick-up truck.

Someone complained about the noise. The police went to investigate, and joined the party.

Casualty was quiet for the first week or so after the rains, because people had to plough the fields. Nobody at the hospital complained. 'Only the really sick people will come now,' said Rebecca, and took a week's leave. She spent the time with her daughter and granddaughter in the Capital.

THE MADMAN ESCAPED death by a hair's breadth when one of his fellow patients at the mental hospital set the ward alight after locking the door.

He got out by breaking a window with his one and only hand, and then came back like a homing pigeon, walking part of the two hundred kilometers before finally getting a lift into town. He arrived at the hospital with half his beard burnt away and a wound on his arm where he had been cut by the glass. He refused point-blank to go back to the mental hospital. 'There are too many mad people there,' he declared, put his belongings in his locker and settled into being the only madman in the ward.

On an afternoon when there were no patients sitting in front of his office door, Morgan drove out to the stables, saddled Sultan and set off across the plain. On the east-west road he unleashed Sultan's power by loosening the reins completely. The magnificent horse did not disappoint him. They flew across the wide, empty space that carried no other sound than that of Sultan's thundering hooves. He rode casually, on the verge of total carelessness, standing up in the saddle and laughed into the wind that rushed through the horse's mane and up into his face.

The horse was spurred on by his wild, defiant laugh and propelled them forward in a reckless gallop until the world consisted of an image of Sultan's flying mane, and a perfectly straight sandy road with shrubs next to it that seemed to uproot themselves and hurtle past them.

The German who lived on the plain in the middle of nowhere, in a house that doubled as a pub, heard the familiar sound of Sultan's hooves and stood in the door and waved, his admiring call unheard.

A huge Bouvier terrier detached itself from the wall of the house and started its habitual, unsuccessful chase, only to be outclassed by Sultan in a fraction of a second. The dog sat down in the damp sand as if he was waiting for a bus and was rewarded by a view of Sultan's long tail flying straight in a speed-induced gale.

They reached the end of the plain and Morgan briefly tightened the reins, slowed down to an easy canter, felt the wind in his face slack off, turned into the bush road and watched the huge trees slip by as they made their way along the curving road.

When they rounded a corner, they saw a pick-up truck ahead of them. In his adrenaline-flushed state Sultan surged forward in hot pursuit and Morgan did nothing to stop him. They squeezed past the truck, hemmed in on both sides by trees right next to the road and a branch swooped over Morgan's head with an audible swoosh.

He became aware of the loud cheering and laughing of people on the back of the truck who knew Sultan and called his name. The unbridled power of the horse wound up the curving road like a rope. Near the end of their run, alongside the far fence of the grazing field, Sultan astonished him with a display of his inherited Arab endurance, gathering energy from a seemingly unlimited supply, and carried them along in a final, exuberant sprint. He was almost surprised to find the horse respond to the tightened reins and his spoken command.

The world returned with disappointing familiarity. The sound of birdsong reappeared, the voices of people walking in the road floated in the late afternoon breeze and, far away, the engine of a truck complained about unexpected deep mud under benign-looking sand.

Morgan arrived back in town just before the shops closed. He entered the Indian shop, an ancient version of a supermarket that sold everything from fertilizer to headache pills. There was an almost military logic in his shopping. He started at one end of the shop, walked past bags with fertilizer, shook his head at mops with hair like rap stars, turned one hundred eighty degrees when he reached the end of the shelf, and continued past sad-looking toilet brushes. He stopped for a moment to stroke a friendly shifting spanner, rescued a bottle of turpentine from amongst lethal insecticide sprays, turned again and continued his scanning pattern. He walked rapidly past fragile, trendy ladies' underwear, turned a blind eye to the men's toiletries, collected butter from a fridge, and casually threw a cabbage, onions, carrots for Sultan, potatoes and a loaf of bread into the shopping basket.

'Hello, hello.' Two women carrying shopping baskets greeted him with flirtatious smiles and he waved his hand at them. They laughed about his dirty riding boots.

He ignored kettles with electric cords like lemurs' tails,

resignedly picked up a bottle of dishwashing liquid, and stopped abruptly at a glass cabinet at the front of the shop.

Amongst cigarette lighters, wallets, bracelets and watches stood a small pair of binoculars. Morgan scrutinized the binoculars. They were small, like opera glasses. Light enough for Mary to hold.

The old, stooped, white-haired Indian got up from his chair, shuffled towards Morgan and greeted him like a long-lost friend.

'The binoculars.' Morgan tapped on the glass.

'Very good quality,' said the Indian.

Morgan laughed. 'Let me see for myself,' he said.

The old man unhitched a key ring with a dozen keys from his belt and unlocked the cabinet. Morgan took the binoculars outside and tested them.

'All right,' he said to the Indian. 'How much?'

'I will give you a very good price,' said the man.

'You'd better,' said Morgan. 'I am one of your best customers.'

He paid for the binoculars and the groceries and asked the Indian to gift-wrap the binoculars. The Indian looked at him with a knowing smile. 'For someone special?' he laughed with his old man's voice.

'Very special,' said Morgan.

There was still enough light left for Mary to test her gift. He drove through the back entrance and stopped right outside the ward. Mary was sitting in her wheelchair with Violet standing next to her. They were just about to go into the ward.

'Just look at you,' said Violet. 'I hope you're not coming for a ward round.'

Morgan laughed like a schoolboy. 'I have been out riding Sultan,' he said.

'I didn't know you ride horses,' Mary said, looking at his riding boots.

'Everyone knows about Sultan,' said Violet, 'and about the

wild riding habits of his master.'

Morgan handed the parcel to Mary. 'Please open this,' he said, 'before it gets dark.' She struggled with the wrapping and Morgan helped her.

'My, oh my,' said Violet. 'Only Morgan would think of buying a pair of binoculars for a lady.'

'It is a beautiful gift,' said Mary emphatically. She trained the binoculars on the pigeons sitting on the roof and was satisfied with what she saw.

'Tomorrow,' she said, 'I will watch the kites. They are circling over the road now.'

She wanted to know about Sultan.

Violet was standing behind Mary, ready to wheel her back to the ward. She caught Morgan's eye and tilted her head sideways, gesturing in the direction of the stables. Morgan understood immediately. 'Do you want to meet Sultan?' he asked.

'Why not?' said Violet. 'We can take you there on one of my off days.'

Morgan looked at Mary's smile and marveled at the joy small things can bring: a pair of binoculars and the prospect of a visit to a horse.

17

A night out

'UP THERE,' he said to Thomson. 'That's where she lives.' The empty water-tank stood on a steel tower that was higher than the treetops. Thomson switched off the headlights and they sat in the truck, waiting for their eyes to become accustomed to the dark.

'Let's get out,' Thomson said after a while and opened the door on his side. Morgan spotted the Barn Owl taking off. Her wings moved in slow motion, hoisting her up into the sky and silently slicing through the evening air.

'I'm sure there are baby owls in there,' Morgan said. He handed the big torch to Thomson, took the camera and attached the flash. They climbed up the vertical ladder onto the platform. Morgan hung a penlight torch around his neck, made sure it couldn't fall off and climbed up the side of the tank. On top was a circular hole just big enough for the camera and the flash. He switched on the penlight and peered through the hole.

Six small Barn Owls, with round, white faces and round, black eyes sat in a half-circle on the far side of the drum, the white slightly overhanging at the bottom, like napkins. They stared up at him and started hissing in unison, creating a racket. Sssssssss! It was a reception committee with a difference.

'What's going on up there?' asked Thomson. 'It sounds like a snake pit.'

'Six babies,' said Morgan.

He focused the camera using one hand, then took the penlight out of his mouth for a moment and said, 'Just look out for the mother. I don't want her to gouge out my eyes.'

'Are you scared of an owl?' Thomson asked. Morgan didn't reply; he switched on the flash and listened to the high-pitched whine as it charged, and the indicator light came on. Then he focused by the light of the penlight held in his mouth and started shooting, bracketing the exposure.

Flash, flash, flash and flash.

The hissing reached fever pitch.

Morgan turned off the penlight and the flash. 'Okay, that's enough. Thank you, ladies and gentlemen,' he said, and climbed down the side of the tank. Thomson took the torch and climbed up for a quick look. Morgan stood on the platform and listened, scanning the night sky for the mother. Above him the hissing started again. Thomson laughed. 'I think they're trying to tell us something.'

'Let's get out of here,' said Morgan. 'The mother is going to get worried.'

'Remember to send her a photograph,' said Thomson. 'She can hang it on the wall.'

'Mind she doesn't rip into you,' Morgan said. 'I don't think she likes us, wherever she is.'

'You are paranoid,' said Thomson.

'You can't hear an owl fly,' Morgan said, and told him about the book called *An Eye for a Bird*. The photographer had had one of his eyes ripped out by an owl that sneaked up behind him after he had taken a photograph of the nest.

'It's a beautiful book, but I would prefer to keep both my eyes for now.'

Owls are perfectly adapted for nightlife, he told Thomson. They have high-powered eyes and wings designed for noiseless flight, sharp beaks and claws for hunting prey. Beautiful birds. Sinister and mysterious. Morgan wished he could fly like an owl, silently scanning the bush at night, able to see even grass blades and mice running for cover.

'Let's go,' he said. 'The mother must be anxious. She's probably watching us from somewhere.'

THOMSON AND MORGAN were having one of their occasional night prowls around the bush, peering in under a cloak of darkness, listening, looking, enjoying the mystery. Morgan loved it. The dark shapes of owls moving silently across the night sky; the starlight undimmed by town's lights; the snort of a startled antelope crashing through the undergrowth; a hesitant duiker caught in the beam of a headlamp; delicate heart-shaped tracks in the sand; the soft call of a nightjar penetrating the bush like a polite question; the obscene calls of jackals unexpectedly shattering the peace.

Thomson was looking for snakes. He loved snakes and was an expert on them and all other reptiles. He handled both venomous and non-venomous snakes with confidence, wrote papers on them, gave lectures on them, took photographs of them and, if he could have, would have kept them inside his house as pets. To this, however, his wife would probably object and besides he had children; married men should at least act responsibly.

They went a long way along the bush road without any luck and then turned onto the main road to look for dead snakes. The dead snakes gave Thomson an idea of the species around the town. They found a dead puff adder, and Thomson lifted it up by its tail to measure it. 'What a waste,' he said sadly and laid it down next to the road.

Thomson wasn't sure whether he wanted to find a dead spitting cobra or not. 'Better a live one in the bush,' he said. They left the main road and drove back into the bush. A startled buck stood in the road for a moment, then fled. Thomson switched on the flashlight and shone it into the trees. An awkward and clumsy-looking Bearded Vulture sat motionless on the top of a tree. It didn't fly away as the light caught its solemn face. 'That thing doesn't have a night rating,' Morgan said. 'Visual flight rules only.'

Thomson turned off the light. They drove onto the long, straight, sandy road across the plain, stopped the truck and got out, walking along the road by the light of a thin slice of moon, shining the torch occasionally. Far across the plain were the lights of the town.

Two jackals were calling to one another and Morgan wondered if they were the same pair he heard on his evening runs. Africa, he thought, is a land of extreme moods, swinging back and forth like the pendulum of a grandfather clock: war and uneasy peace; drought and floods; feast and famine; breath-taking beauty and indescribable ugliness. Here the two of us are enjoying a beautiful African night, but tomorrow we step back into that hellhole.

'How far are we with Rastodika?' Thomson asked suddenly.

'The same,' said Morgan. 'He's holding his own. Just. They are expecting the Chief Physician back in about a week. Then we will hear.'

They turned around and started walking back. Nothing stirred. Rastodika had been in the ward for weeks. Morgan was surprised that he stayed. He probably realized he couldn't go home. We should have brought him along, thought Morgan. He could teach us a thing or two about the bush.

'In the meantime,' said Morgan, 'I'm going to start begging for money.'

'At the rate you are going, you will eventually bankrupt this town,' said Thomson.

They got back to the truck and Thomson took two beers

out of the cool-box at the back.

'Cheers!' he said, passing one to Morgan. They sipped their beers in silence.

'You have been leading a very stable life for a while,' said Thomson. 'When are you going on one of your trips again?'

'Soon, I hope,' said Morgan. 'My contract is expiring shortly.'

'You not renewing it?'

'Don't know,' said Morgan. 'Depends.'

'Depends on what?'

Morgan didn't answer. Suddenly he thought of Tesfai and wondered if he was still alive. Another war had come and gone. If he can survive a long war, thought Morgan, he can survive a short one. Maybe I should go and visit him again. Just after a war was a good time to visit a country: no tourists.

'Rastodika is going to miss you,' Thomson interrupted his thoughts.

'I will see him through,' Morgan said. 'One way or another.' He crushed the empty beer can in his hand. 'Come, let's go!' he said. 'Your wife is going to think a python got hold of you.'

They drove back on a dirt road as a rabbit ran in front of the truck, moving erratically: left, right, left, right, left and off the road.

18

A vendetta against all cats

HOLMES' MONTHLY HOSPITAL inspection was always a source of irritation, merriment, incredulity, anger, mystification, and frustration. It was dubbed the Fools' Parade by Morgan when he first saw the slow procession moving straight down the passage with Holmes leading, clutching a notebook in his hand: then followed Thunderbird, who was supposed to be followed by the Matron who had previously been warned by Rose, the secretary, just in time to find an excuse not to attend; then the Assistant Matron who had not received advance warning from Rose; and finally Lawrence, the hospital administrator who always disappeared after ten minutes, and had stopped attending lately.

The decisions taken after these inspection rounds baffled and angered everyone from the doctors to the cook to the cleaners for months to come. It took more than a month at a time to undo the ill-conceived and erratic decisions; consequently the effect of Holmes' bungling was cumulative. There was a brief period of sanity when Holmes went on leave, but he had always returned well rested, and resumed his path of destruction with renewed vigor.

Once the rainy season had started Holmes became increasingly uncomfortable, both physically and mentally. Because of the humidity he had to change his shirt every day at midday. He couldn't sleep at night since his wife was less affected by the heat and complained about the noise of the air conditioner. They ended up sleeping in separate rooms and he had a sneaking suspicion she preferred it that way.

He became preoccupied with the state of the budget. Rumors had reached his ears that the doctors were ignoring his orders and were prescribing drugs as they felt fit. The kitchen as usual was over budget, and he was amazed at how much the scrawny patients could eat. Drastic action was required, he told himself as he walked into Thunderbird's office and announced firmly: 'We must do a thorough inspection this month.'

The procession made a false start when Holmes stepped into a puddle of water caused by the leaking roof and nearly fell. He wanted to know why the floor in the passage was so dirty and was reminded that he had retrenched two more cleaners and that the remaining ones doubled up as orderlies. He wanted to know why High Care was full, and was bluntly told by the staff that the patients were sick.

Between the cots in Children's Ward mothers were sleeping on the floor on folded blankets. He rightly assumed that they were eating in the ward and told Thunderbird to look into the matter. The nursing staff received them with a contemptuous silence and refused to answer questions, busying themselves elsewhere. In Female Ward he paged through Naledi's file and frowned at the expensive antibiotics. He took a pen out of his pocket and drew a question mark.

He showed the prescription to Thunderbird who frowned in sympathy. He stopped at Mary's bed and paged through her notes, lifted his eyes, looked at her fragile figure and didn't bother to greet her. He stepped around the puddle of water next to the washbasin, caused by a leaking tap, taking great care not to wet his shiny shoes. As he moved along the passage past High Care into Male Ward and beyond, he ignored rattling water-pipes with airlocks, leaking geysers, non-functioning air conditioners, defective monitors, unsafe electrical fittings, the stench of urine, and inadequate oxygen piping.

Instead, he congratulated himself for stalling the order for a new ventilator. Then he stepped into the alley between surgical ward and the kitchen and focused on the cats that were living in the gutters. 'We must do something about these cats,' he told Thunderbird. 'They pose a serious health risk.'

Thunderbird congratulated him on his ability to see past the obvious. 'Few people see cats that way,' he said. Holmes wasn't sure if he was trying to make a joke. He slackened his pace and allowed Thunderbird to catch up with him and noticed that Thunderbird's face was as deadpan as ever.

Holmes spent an uncomfortable afternoon in his office with all his problems surging through his mind at once. The budget bothered him; there was every sign that the doctors were ignoring his efforts to cut spending. The Regional Superintendent had congratulated him on his efforts but the doctors hated him. The overcrowded wards were a source of irritation. What did these people think they were doing? Did they think they were curing these AIDS patients? Why were they spending money on expensive antibiotics? Their reckless spending could cost him his promotion.

He wasn't going to stay in this little hospital forever. Of course, it was just a stepping stone. But why did everyone seem to conspire against him? Even the cook ignored his instructions. Did he not see with his own eyes the ice cream and yoghurt in the fridge in Female Ward? And Morgan? Morgan blatantly prescribed the most expensive antibiotics for that dying girl. The nurses sniggered when they thought he wasn't looking. Still, he told himself, in spite of everything, he had almost managed to balance the budget.

The radiographer complained that the X-ray machine was nearing the end of its life. But it still works, he told her, so why do we need a new one? You have been warned, she told him. We will wait and see, he said. There are more important matters right now. People think they can just spend money, he thought. No one realizes the importance of the budget. He wasn't going to end up like Jenkins.

The cautery machine in Casualty had been condemned, Rebecca had told him. We will order it on next year's budget, he said. And he had almost forgotten about Morgan's rabid, dead cat that had disappeared. The State Veterinarian wasn't pleased, he could tell. The Veterinary Department had received a letter informing them about the impending arrival of the dead cat, but the body of the cat had eluded them. Holmes knew nothing about the cat and didn't know if the contacts had been vaccinated. The State Veterinarian wasn't very complimentary and reminded Holmes of the risks. He promised that he would immediately look into the matter and enquired everywhere about Morgan's whereabouts, except in theater where Morgan was doing a laparotomy.

And what about the hospital cats? he thought. Multiplying right under my nose? Something has to be done. How could we dispose of them? Gas them out with carbon monoxide or teargas? Poison them? Flush them out with water? Set traps for them? Lure them with bait and catch them with nets? Hunt them down with terriers?

He needed a cup of tea, but even his secretary seemed to be ignoring him. He had asked for it half an hour ago. So where was it? The urn takes half an hour to boil, didn't he know that? Rose told him without looking up from her desk. I will write out an agenda for tomorrow's meeting. I will make sure I make myself very clear. He suddenly felt in control. 'Get me Morgan on the line,' he said, peering into Rose's office.

'You are wasting your time,' she told him. 'Morgan unplugs his phone when he consults.'

I will write my agenda then, and a memo to Morgan. He will have to realize who runs this hospital. Am I not in charge?

THE NEXT MORNING everything conspired against Holmes after he had made his grand entrance at the meeting. The sun had already burned off the early morning drizzle, and there was no breeze to freshen the stale, humid air in the room. The overhead fan had stopped working for no apparent reason, and when he started to speak he was interrupted by the screeching from the wheel of a wheelbarrow outside.

Everyone around the table laughed when they heard about Morgan's stray cat. They laughed even more when Holmes announced the vendetta against the hospital cats. As usual, Morgan wasn't at the meeting, but his colleagues had become almost as difficult to handle, Holmes discovered. When he vowed to arrange a rabies vaccination campaign, he was told that it had already been started.

Oumar rapped his knuckles on the table and asked if there was anything more important to discuss than dead cats. Holmes paused to wipe the condensation from his glasses; sweat soaked his shirt where it touched the fat roll above his belt.

'Now, this girl in Female Ward,' he asked. 'What exactly are we trying to achieve? Surely she is going to die? Why are we spending all this money on intravenous antibiotics?' He pushed his glasses back and rested his arms on the table.

He looked at the bored faces around the table, and suddenly their ill-disguised contempt irritated him. 'I am asking you all a question, gentlemen,' he said and his perpetual grin vanished for once.

'She's getting better,' Thomson said. 'We are controlling her infection.'

'But at what cost?' Holmes asked.

Thomson was astounded. 'What do you mean?' he asked. 'Do you want us to let her die?'

Patches of sweat darkened Holmes' shirt higher up on his belly. 'I know, gentlemen. I know we are here to save lives but we have to select our patients. What chance does this HIV-positive girl have?'

Thomson smiled grimly. 'But she's HIV-negative. Didn't you read her notes?'

Small droplets of perspiration collected on the rims of Holmes' glasses, and he shifted in his chair. 'So what exactly is wrong with this girl?'

'Some people at another hospital also judged her at face value,' Thomson needled him. 'However, what she has, is a neglected perinephric abscess.'

Holmes realized he was being made to look a fool. Opposite him, the Kenyan gently drummed his fingers on the table and smiled. 'Surely, she should be referred?' Holmes tried his favorite remedy.

'Morgan is a surgeon; he should be able to handle her.' Oumar's voice had an air of finality in it.

Everyone smiled, for once enjoying the meeting. Holmes looked down at the paper in front of him and pursued his agenda against his better judgment.

'The girl in the corner of Female Ward?' he let the question hang in the air.

Thomson smiled again. You touch that girl and you will regret it, he thought. 'AIDS and lymphoma,' he told Holmes in an innocent voice. 'You are talking about the girl with the lymphoma, aren't you?'

Holmes was unsure; to him one AIDS patient looked like another, and he didn't know if Thomson was luring him into a trap.

'That girl doesn't seem to have any prognosis at all,' he said without conviction, trying not to show his ignorance.

'You are most probably right,' Thomson reassured him. 'I don't think there is much we can do for her.'

Holmes couldn't read Thomson's smile. 'Can't she be sent for home-based care?' he asked.

'Sure,' said Thomson. 'But she is Morgan's patient.'

'This meeting seems to be all about Morgan's patients,' said Holmes.

'Maybe we should ask him to attend more often,' Thomson said.

Holmes wasn't sure if Thomson was serious.

'Am I to understand,' the Kenyan deadpanned, 'that we have to refer every patient or send them for home-based care?'

'You know I don't mean that,' snapped Holmes, and the veins on his nose turned red again.

The Kenyan's voice when he spoke again was soft, barely audible. 'But that's what you keep telling us.'

Holmes took a deep breath. 'What I am saying is that we are not a hospice, and we have to keep within our budget.'

'Budget, budget...all the time, budget,' the Kenyan almost whispered. 'Patients are human beings, you know.'

Holmes felt the animosity around the table. He pursed his lips and wrinkled his chin. 'I will discuss it with Morgan,' he said.

Thomson scratched his beard. Just go ahead, he thought to himself. Just you go ahead.

MORGAN COMPLETED HIS ward round unaware of Holmes' misgivings over his patients, his dead cat, his alleged lack of respect for potential rabies victims, and the problem of the promiscuous hospital cats.

He was satisfied that Naledi was getting better. The pus had stopped draining from her loin, and her temperature had come down to normal and stayed there. She told him she was feeling better. Janet nursed her like her own daughter and seemed totally unconcerned about her own problems.

He continued the intravenous antibiotics. Violet warned

him that Holmes had paid the ward a visit and complained about the expense. On Naledi's chart he noticed the question mark in red next to the prescription. 'I love a touch of color,' he commented. 'Tell him to use a green pen next time.'

He found Rastodika in the company of the madman who sometimes slept on the veranda on rainless nights. The madman was sitting on the rail of the veranda, drying himself with his clothes on, like a cormorant, with arms outstretched. Rastodika was laughing at him, and the cheerfulness of his laughter and his warrior's figure disguised his illness completely.

Their newfound friendship greatly disturbed the Assistant Matron. She made it her business to keep an eye on them. She even knew about Rastodika's early morning walks, which took him to the top of the hill from where he could look out over the river, past the tall, dark trees that stood on its banks in the hazy distance.

She had warned the Matron that no good could come out of the liaison between Rastodika and the madman. They were both wild men and didn't she know about the episode with the lay preacher? The Matron smiled and said Rastodika was a good influence on the madman—it had been some time since he created havoc. But the Assistant Matron wasn't convinced and she continued to observe them suspiciously, especially when they were standing under the big tree at the bottom of the garden, smoking cigarettes supplied by Morgan.

Rastodika stoically accepted his prolonged stay in hospital. His unconditional trust disturbed Morgan, who sometimes woke up at night and sat in the dark in his living room, pondering the question of the divide between the haves and the have-nots.

He had told Rastodika nothing about his fruitless negotiations with a pompous little physician who didn't give a damn, and hid behind policies that allowed him to classify Rastodika as beyond repair. There was no money for dialysis and there wasn't even a dialysis machine in the country, he told Morgan with the air of a man who had better things to do.

Morgan had held his temper, and tried to find the Chief Physician, but he was out of the country. In the meantime, he tried not to show his concern, and wondered how he was ever going to arrange a renal transplant without some kind of miracle.

Across the lawn, still glistening from the early morning rain, came the brigade of scrawny patients in their blue, ill-fitting hospital fatigues and footwear that ranged from boots to shoes to sandals to nothing. Their thin frames bent forward as they ascended the stairs. and some of them gasped with the little effort required to climb onto the veranda.

'Come on, you lot, hurry up!' Rastodika mocked them, and their thin faces wrinkled as they smiled. Morgan looked into Rastodika's face. He saw the slight tiredness in his smile and the lines on his face that were deeper than before.

FRAMED IN THE doorway, Mary sat in her wheelchair with Violet standing behind her. The ambulant occupants of Female Ward were gathered on the veranda, with smiles on their bony faces and merriment in their sunken eyes. Mary wore a clean, white dress that hung loosely around her withered body. Her hair was neatly tied with a white ribbon. Morgan climbed the stairs amidst much laughter, excitement, and chattering of melodious voices in two different languages.

'When are you taking us?' they asked in a chorus and laughed.

'What!' said Morgan. 'How can I drive through the bush

with a whole truckload of women?'

They fussed over Mary and helped her down the stairs into Morgan's truck, and scolded him because it wasn't washed. They laughed when he said he never washed it because it would bring bad luck. Morgan took the wheelchair, folded it and placed it in the back. They stood on the veranda and waved as Morgan drove off with Mary sandwiched between him and Violet.

Soon, after they had crossed the cattle grid on the edge of the town, Mary asked Morgan to stop. She was scanning the treetops with her binoculars. Morgan burst out laughing. 'You look like the captain of a pirate ship,' he said.

'I will warn you if we spot our quarry,' she mocked him and handed him the binoculars. On the top of a tree sat a Lilac-Breasted Roller.

'Those birds,' Morgan said, 'are easy prey for the Bateleurs. They always sit on the very tops of the trees, so the Bateleur can just swoop down and catch them.' Mary thought it was sacrilege to kill such a beautiful bird, and had difficulty in reconciling the grace of the raptors with their merciless eating habits. She let the binoculars dangle from her thin neck. Morgan started the truck and drove on. Alongside the road, yellow and white flowers were growing amidst the grass.

'Stop,' said Violet, and she and Morgan got out to pick a big bunch of flowers.

'At this rate,' said Morgan, 'we are going to take all afternoon.' Violet scolded him, and told him he handled the flowers too roughly. From the truck they could hear Mary laugh. Violet made the flowers into a tidy bouquet and handed it to Morgan. 'Now give it to her like a gentleman,' she told him.

He bowed at the door of the truck and presented the bouquet to Mary with one hand held behind his back. Mary nodded her head gracefully, pressed the flowers against her face and inhaled. 'They will make you cough,' said Morgan, and both of them told him he was being an insensitive male.

Mary sat with her hands in her lap, holding the bunch of flowers. She marveled at the green grass, the shapes of the trees, the hornbills that flew up clumsily in front of the truck, the clear blue sky amongst the clouds, and the clean, red dirt of the road.

She's like a prisoner who has briefly escaped from jail, thought Morgan. I drive along this road, I chase down it on Sultan's back, I run along it at night and I take it for granted.

He slowed down on the bumpy sections because she looked so fragile. He was scared she might bounce off the seat. When they drove through puddles, water splashed onto the windscreen, and she laughed like a child.

JAKE WAS SMITTEN by Mary's smile and handled her like a VIP. He insisted on pushing the wheelchair himself.

He introduced her to Sultan who cocked his ears and sniffed the air, and ever so gently accepted a carrot from Mary's outstretched hand, allowing her to stroke his nose. Morgan was astounded because Sultan was usually very suspicious of strangers.

Jake elaborated upon Sultan's great qualities and switched to the local tongue to make himself better understood. The horse stood sideways in the pen, watching them with his intelligent eyes and moving his ears. 'He knows we are talking about him,' Mary laughed.

Jake brought Violet a chair and Morgan sat on the ground with his back resting against a tree. Jake made coffee on his kerosene stove, which he served in tin mugs. They drank it slowly. At sunset Jake started to lead the other horses out into the field. Morgan helped Mary out of the wheelchair and Jake held Sultan by the halter. The horse stood still as Mary stroked his mane and his powerful shoulder muscles.

In the semi-darkness Morgan could just make out her face. She was silent as she felt the warmth under Sultan's mane, and felt the ripple of muscles under her hand. She nestled her cheek against the horse's neck and said, 'I love his smell.' Morgan filed away the memory of the thin wisp of a girl who was barely more than a breathing skeleton standing next to the massive horse. They watched as Jake led him into the field and Sultan pranced playfully before galloping away.

19

Prescriptions, memos and dead cats

It has come to my attention that the instructions regarding expensive antibiotics are not being observed, notably in Female Ward where I saw a woman receiving highly expensive intravenous antibiotics.

MORGAN REREAD the memo, then handed a bunch of other memos to Oumar. 'You also receive these?' he asked.

'Not as many as you,' Oumar said, and started reading through them.

'I hope you find it entertaining,' Morgan said. He started writing a memo of his own. Next to him lay a photocopy of Naledi's culture and sensitivity report.

Oumar smirked when he read about the saga of the dead cat. 'Holmes is not pleased,' Oumar told Morgan. 'He told us you were being irresponsible.'

'What did he expect me to do—send the cat with an armed escort?' Morgan attached the laboratory report to his memo and took an envelope out of the drawer. The desk was cluttered. On the wall above it was a notice: 'Do not tidy this desk'. It was written in Morgan's handwriting in both official languages. The dustbin was filled to the brim with torn-up ads from drug companies. Papers were scattered all over the desk. On a shelf below the notice were several glass containers displaying dead snakes in formalin.

'You should tidy up this desk.' Oumar was sitting sideways on Morgan's examination couch.

'I know where everything is.' Morgan leaned over and opened the curtain.

'Let me see what you have written,' Oumar said and held out his hand. Morgan had asked Holmes to advise him which antibiotics to use, bearing in mind that the patient only had one functioning kidney.

'He is not going to be amused, I can tell you that.' Oumar handed the memo back to Morgan.

'I'm being democratic,' he told Oumar. 'I'm inviting our leader to share the burden of clinical decision-making.' There was a brief knock on the door and Thomson came in.

'The two of you are working late?'

'I'm protecting our friend from himself,' Oumar said, and made room for Thomson, handing the memos to him to read. Morgan sat back in his chair and put his feet on the table. The phone was unplugged as always.

Thomson finished reading and handed the memos back to Morgan. 'Ideally, you're supposed to have sent only the head or the brain, not the whole cat. That's probably why it can't come to rest.'

Morgan leaned back in his chair. 'What difference does it make? Besides, I wasn't going to decapitate the poor cat, not on a Sunday afternoon.'

He had spent the whole afternoon reading his mail and making fruitless telephone calls. 'I am getting nowhere with Rastodika,' Morgan voiced the thought uppermost in his mind. 'I only manage to get through to a pigheaded little physician who keeps telling me that I can forget about dialysis or a transplant.'

A shaft of light fell obliquely against the wall and lit up the side of Thomson's face. 'You should speak to the Chief Physician,' he said. 'You will get nowhere with anyone else.'

'The Chief Physician is out of the country. He will be back the day after tomorrow.'

Thomson stood up and looked out of the window. The madman was lying on the lawn, fast asleep, with a plastic detergent bottle under his head as a pillow.

'Look at that,' he said.

'The secret of life,' Morgan said, 'is not to crave anything. That man is perfectly happy.'

Thomson put his hand on top of the filing cabinet and drummed his fingers. 'You know,' he said. 'Sometimes we need to realize that we are beaten. The chances of saving Rastodika are slim, very slim, and you know it, Morgan.'

Morgan uncrossed his legs, stood up and faced Thomson. 'We can't just throw him to the dogs; we've got to do something.'

For a moment the sun shone directly into Thomson's eyes and he stepped out of the light. 'All right,' he said. 'But we will need money, lots of it, and it's not going to be possible to find it in any conventional way.'

'Morgan, you're a stubborn man,' said Oumar and got up from the couch.

Morgan picked up his keys from the desk. 'I will find an unconventional way,' he said. 'Let's get the hell out of here, gentlemen. I have had enough trouble for one day.'

JANET SAT OUTSIDE on the bare cement floor of the porch. In the late afternoon, she'd had a wake-up call from the tumor in her mouth. It's only a slight bleed, nothing much, she told herself. But it was more than before. Last time, Violet had given her iced water to rinse her mouth. Gently. This afternoon, she didn't want anyone in the ward to know about it. She found tissue paper and left the ward. She made her way to the kitchen and asked Charles for ice.

He gave it to her with a question mark on his face. She thanked him without explaining herself and carried it to the porch. It was already time for the evening visiting hour. From where she was sitting she could hear the drone of voices.

It was an hour filled with mixed feelings. Relatives brought food and sometimes flowers. The mood around each bedside reflected the condition of the patient. Each bed became a little island. Cheerful conversation around one bed, hushed deferential conversation around another, and almost total silence around another.

She herself had no visitors except her cheerful young son who occasionally came by bus. He carried money in an envelope together with a letter from her mother. She cherished the short walk to the ramshackle café down the road, he in his school uniform and she in her tatty hospital dress. They would stand in front of the café, drink cooldrinks, and talk about the people in her village and about his teachers at school.

Then, at four o'clock, he had to take his leave and get back on the bus. She always kept a brave face when they parted. She stood next to the road and watched him as he walked down the hill towards the bus station. Then she would walk up the hill alone with an infinite sadness in her heart. It was dark outside. From the town came the sound of a donkey braying and the laughter of children.

She gently folded her tongue around the tumor. It had stopped bleeding. She had been careless, she told herself. At lunch-time she had taken a piece of meat instead of sticking to her liquid diet. Careful, she admonished herself. She smiled at the irony: careful of what you eat, don't talk too much, guard your tongue. It was advice that would usually be given to a traveler in a strange place or a child going to a new school.

Don't disturb the animal that is growing inside your mouth. It might kill you. It was killing her already, she realized. Her son had noticed how much weight she had lost. Was it the tumor or the virus? Looking at the other occupants of the ward, it could well be the virus.

At some time or another, all of them had received the bad news; a polite, compassionate death sentence wrapped in the soft words of an AIDS counselor. And in the ward, they had become used to the hard reality of it. Naledi was the only one who had escaped the curse. Naledi, she thought, who was getting better every day and had become her pride and joy, the daughter she never had. Naledi was also a blessing in disguise. Looking after her took Janet's mind off her own problems. Feeding the girl and caring for her took up most of her time. Some days she almost forgot about the relentless growth of the tumor.

In that ward, you could never forget completely. Even when she herself had a good day, there was almost always someone on the brink of death. When the inevitable happened, there was a temporary hush. All the patients were reminded about their own, not-too-distant fate. They furtively looked at each other, wondering who was going to be next. Death was inevitable, they all understood that. The only question was when. At night, when the lights were off, the ward became quiet, and each of them pondered the same question.

Even during the day, in unguarded moments during cheerful conversation, it surfaced again. What was going to happen to the people who were left behind? Who was going to look after their children? They hid their concern under a layer of cheerfulness. In the early morning, Janet lay with her eyes closed and listened to the voices of the other women talking. It sounded almost like a normal household. There were cheerful greetings. How are you? Did you sleep well? There were the sounds of lockers opening and people going to the bathroom, the jovial voices of the cleaners, the rattling of the breakfast plates. But when she opened her eyes she saw the emaciated figures in their faded blue gowns, the drip stands, someone with an oxygen mask, the white uniforms of the nurses, and the medicine trolley.

The sound of a cowbell came from deep inside the ward. A few minutes later Janet heard people walking into the passage and their voices fading away. Visiting hour was over. She stood up and slowly walked back to the ward. The main lights had been switched off and only the bed lamps were on. No one was deadly sick, so everyone could look forward to an undisturbed night with no midnight interventions by the nurses and the doctor on duty.

Cheerful banter filled the room. One woman was looking forward to going home in the morning. News from the visitors was circulated. In the world outside, life carried on as always. The crops were growing. The rain had revived the countryside, rivers were flowing. All was well.

Janet sat on her bed and smiled her usual cheerful smile. She tried to talk as little as possible, even when Naledi asked where she had been. She rationed the words, making up for it with her body language. How many times a day did her tongue touch the tumor, she wondered.

In the corner, Mary was reading a book. Next to her, Naledi was sitting upright, talking to the woman across the aisle. Janet turned on her side and shut her eyes. Gradually the conversations petered out and the lights were switched off.

She slept fitfully, dreaming about her son, talking in her sleep. Long past midnight she woke up and found Naledi's thin figure next to her bed.

'Is something wrong, my mother?' asked Naledi.

20

Phone calls and creatures of the night

MORGAN CURSED VIOLENTLY.
'I hope you're not swearing at me,' a voice said from the other side of the line.

Morgan laughed. 'I've been waiting so long, I thought the receptionist had cut me off.'

Jowitt, the Chief Physician, chuckled and said, 'The man we spoke about yesterday; I gave it some thought.'

Morgan pricked up his ears. 'Yes?'

'We have done it once before, as I told you. We sent a patient across the border. Unfortunately, I couldn't find the man in charge on the other side. But I did find the records from our end.'

'And?' said Morgan.

'It's a costly exercise, as you can imagine. Don't forget about the immuno-suppressive drugs.'

Morgan smiled. 'Most of my patients are immuno-suppressed.'

Jowitt laughed, 'I didn't mean like that.'

'So we have to find money,' said Morgan.

'Last time the government paid,' the physician said, 'but you realize that transplants have become a luxury with all the other problems we are facing. I can only try.' He didn't sound very hopeful.

Morgan said, 'I will see what I can do.'

'You realize there will be no hemodialysis,' Jowitt said. 'It will all be very difficult to arrange. Better a live donor. So, if you can get an HLA-typing and do a full work-up, including HIV-testing, it might just be possible to persuade them to take him. I will send you all the details and a copy of the bill. I am sure that will sober you up.'

Morgan remarked: 'You're not very optimistic are you?'

'No,' said Jowitt. 'It won't be easy.'

THOMSON WAS IN Casualty, swearing away through his unkempt beard. 'Bloody hell,' he said. 'That youngster Mark sent a patient home yesterday with a roaring pneumonia.' In the cubicle Morgan saw a man with a drip.

'How could he have missed it?' ranted Thomson. 'It's a straightforward pneumonia; stands out like a dog's testicles.'

Morgan was uncharacteristically lenient. 'The youngsters are under too much pressure,' he said, 'and no one teaches them anything.'

Thomson snorted. 'But this is medical school stuff,' he said. 'I would fail a fourth year student who couldn't pick up a pneumonia.'

'The lads are under too much pressure,' repeated Morgan. 'They're not supposed to work as hard as they do; all of us are barely keeping our heads above water.'

Rebecca commented, 'It's most unusual to hear you taking their side, Morgan. Normally you swear and Thomson takes their side.'

'Fair is fair,' he replied, and tried to change the topic. 'The physician says we may or may not be able to help Rastodika. It will be touch and go.'

'You are not telling me anything new,' growled Thomson. 'Let me sort this man out, and if you see young Mark, tell him he's in trouble.'

THE OLD INDIAN was as good as his word. Just after four o'clock he personally delivered a packet of prints to Morgan's office. Morgan was embarrassed. 'You only needed to phone me,' he said.

The frail old man with his untidy, grey hair laughed. 'You're one of my valued customers,' he said. 'My son went to the Capital on business, so he took the films with him. The slides will be ready next week.'

Morgan thanked and paid him, then watched as the old man walked down the passage as fast as his stiff hips would allow. Thomson and the Kenyan were in Casualty clearing up the last patients. A thin, wasted man clutched his folder under his arm and the Kenyan directed him to the ward.

Thomson had told Rebecca about the continuing saga of the dead cat and she couldn't contain her mirth. 'I warned you, Morgan! It got separated from the letter!'

As she laughed, her huge torso shook and her glasses fogged up. She took them off, cleaned them and said: 'That cat is going to haunt all of us. Matron tells me that Holmes wants to flush the cats out of the sewers. Imagine flushing them out! With what?'

'Just tell me when my cat comes back,' Morgan said. 'I've become rather attached to it.' He glanced around the almost empty Casualty and asked: 'Why is it so quiet?'

Almost immediately, Rebecca's huge right hand came down on the wooden tabletop. 'Don't say it, Morgan!' she shouted. 'We need a bit of peace and quiet now and then.'

The Kenyan was on call and was hoping for a quiet night. 'Don't tempt fate, Morgan,' he said.

'Come,' Morgan said to Thomson. 'I've got the photographs of the owls. Do you want to see them?'

'Morgan!' Rebecca said. 'You're doing all the wrong things. Don't you know that owls bring bad luck? Take those photographs out of here!'

Morgan looked at her sitting behind her desk. With her big glasses and round face she looked just like an owl herself, a wise old owl. 'You're just superstitious,' he said.

'Out of here, you two!' Rebecca shouted. 'You are going to attract trouble.'

He walked down the passage and Thomson followed him. Morgan continued walking. Thomson asked, 'Where are you going?'

'To Female Ward,' answered Morgan. 'I want to show the photos to Mary.'

'Do you think it's a good idea to take them to Female Ward?' Thomson asked. 'We have enough trouble there already.'

Morgan laughed. 'Don't tell me you are becoming superstitious.'

They walked past Violet's desk into the ward. 'What are you two doing here?' Violet wanted to know.

'Just a social visit,' said Morgan.

Mary was sitting outside as usual. In her lap were the binoculars and the field guide. Morgan noted the slight pallor of her face. Maybe it's the reflection from her dress, he told himself, but he was disturbed by how frail she looked. She cheered up when she saw them. Her smile was the same as always.

For a moment Morgan hesitated before he took the photographs out of his pocket. He had told Mary about the Barn Owls and she was expecting to see the photos. He gave a faint shrug and handed her the envelope. She opened it and fanned out the photographs like a hand of cards. Morgan and Thomson stood behind her and peered over her shoulder.

Six little Barn Owls were arranged in a semicircle at the bottom of the tank. They were staring at the camera, their white heart-shaped faces turned upwards. Small eyes, just a hint of the reflection from the flashlight.

Mary stared at the photographs. 'They already look like wise old men,' she said.

'They were not pleased to see me,' Morgan said.

'It's because you were messing up their night vision with your flash,' said Thomson.

Morgan took the two best photographs and put them in the field guide, next to the section on owls. 'There you are,' he said and handed the guide back to her. 'Our very own Barn Owls.'

'I wish I could get a photograph of my owl,' she said, 'but he is too elusive. He never sits still for long enough and he doesn't come close.'

'What kind of owl is this?' asked Thomson.

Mary shifted in her chair and turned her head towards Thomson. 'A most beautiful Eagle Owl,' she said. 'He is so striking, you can't imagine.'

'Are you also into owls, like my friend Morgan?' Thomson mocked her, but his voice was gentle. Morgan smiled. Mary was casting a spell on Thomson, he noticed.

'Only at night,' Mary jested.

'And during the day?'

'The kites. I love the way they soar.'

'I can understand that,' Thomson said. 'Sometimes I wish I could fly like that.'

Morgan said nothing. He listened to Mary's pure voice and saw the clearness of her eyes. She was grasping every day with both hands. The birds had become her passion. She saw beauty in things that most people didn't even notice. With sudden certainty Morgan realized that she was not destined to stay in the world much longer; she was far above the banality of everyday life. Like the Little Prince. An advanced human being.

Somewhere in the field guide was a drawing she had made, painstakingly done on a page of an exercise book, showing the shape of the wings of a kite with the extended primaries. The head was only a curve, an aerodynamic foil. When Morgan explained the principles of flight to her, he drew the cross-section of an aircraft wing and explained Bernoulli's law: how the air accelerates along the top of the wing and produces lift.

'Birds are just like aircraft,' Morgan said. 'Some are designed for fast, unstable flight, like swallows with their swept-back wings; others are designed to soar like gliders and some are heavy duty, like pelicans.' He showed her a picture of a pelican and said: 'They look like freight planes when they fly.'

Then she pointed out that birds' heads are shaped in exactly the same way, not only their wings. Since that day, whenever he saw a bird, he looked at the shape of its head and the curve along its back and marveled at the design.

On another day he found Mary paging through her field-guide, comparing wing shapes and relating them to function. 'They are all so different and they are all perfect,' she said, and added, 'But they are better than aircraft, and more beautiful.'

Now she was telling Thomson about the dainty little waxbills that lived in the hedge. 'I didn't even know they were here,' Thomson said.

It was time to go. Mary thanked Morgan for the photographs, and he gently tapped her on the shoulder.

'I'll speak to you again soon,' said Thomson.

IN THE OLDEST part of town stood a decaying colonial mansion that hid its secrets behind moss-covered walls and stared accusingly at the river through shattered windowpanes. Next to it leaned an ancient, seedy hotel that appeared to be leaning on a crutch. It bore the distinction of landmark, restaurant, drinking place, guesthouse and whorehouse.

An uneven row of pillars bravely supported the drooping roof of the veranda. Below the decomposing roof-plates, in stuffy rooms with sagging ceilings, resided tired beds with battered mattresses. On the ground floor a bar opened onto the scruffy veranda.

Just across the narrow, potholed street was the bus station. Through the open doors of the bar came the sound of diesel engines, energetic voices of truck drivers and passengers, bleating goats, manhandled roosters, and blaring horns. Inside the bar glasses rattled, beer cans hissed, chairs creaked, women giggled, and men shouted rude remarks. A wobbly fan under the ceiling methodically blended the smells of diesel fumes, cigarette smoke, beer, cooking oil, and cheap perfume.

Smirnoff sat at a small table with neglected beer stains and cigarette burns on its vinyl top. Directly opposite him wound an unstable, spiral staircase with worn, concave steps. He surveyed the room and observed the noisy crowd. He could recognize the truck drivers at a glance: stocky, with muscular arms, jovial voices and protruding potato-shaped bellies. On their way north as far as the Congo or south as far as Cape Town. Here tonight, gone tomorrow, and back again next week.

The regulars from town were sponging from the truck drivers. Other travelers, too well dressed for the occasion, stood out like sore thumbs. There was the inevitable backpacker, unaware of the reputation of the establishment. The only women present were the prostitutes: young, firm-breasted ones with tantalizing legs and thin, transparent dresses that clung to their bodies like cling wrap; jolly barmaids who doubled as prostitutes; and the veterans, unable to hide their premature decay, cheated out of their youth with breasts like shrunken lemons, gazing at the scene with cheerless smiles and unresponsive eyes.

Prices were determined by market forces and the quality of the stock. You get what you pay for, and sometimes you get what you didn't bargain for—like a dose of the clap. Then you went to Rebecca who scolded you and told you that it might only be the tip of the iceberg, so to speak. Far worse things might be happening to you.

Smirnoff sipped his beer and reflected on his last conversation with Rebecca. She suspected what he already knew. He had been in hospital long enough to confirm his own worries. And he saw what the end was going to be like. That's what bothered him the most. He could feel the disease in his joints, in his tired muscles and in his belly. He could see the reflection of his face in the shop mirrors and could gauge the course of the disease by the changes in his face.

His eyes had changed. Somehow they looked more intense than before and seemed to grow larger as his head assumed a conical shape. It was narrow at the top, slightly wider at the bottom—but only just. His face had become thinner and the conical shape more angular. That's what everyone else in that ward looked like, and they had only one disease.

He had watched them dying and, as he lay in hospital, he considered his options. His resolve grew as he watched the carnage around him. He was not going to die like that, and he was not going to die in that place. How many people died when he was there? Waiting their turn, seeing their friends die, wondering who was going to be next. And for what? In the end they were not living even if they were still alive. They were living, battered corpses. Life is there to be lived. If you end up like that, then you might as well be dead. With time, his choice had become clearer, like a lens shifting into focus.

So, he thought, I will live as well as possible, while I still can. If I can't anymore, then...then what? Then...I will make a decision.

A woman came down the staircase and paused for a moment to adjust the shoulder straps of her dress, which somehow seemed to flaunt her nakedness rather than conceal it. She reached the bottom of the stairs and smoothed the creases of the dress with deliberate movements, caressing her hips and thighs like a cat grooming itself. Then she walked towards his table and carelessly flung her legs over the barstool opposite him.

She rested her arms on the table, leaned forward and brought her face closer to his. Her light-brown irises were almost transparent. Under the cheap make-up her face looked tired. She contrived a mirthless smile. 'Buy me a drink?'

Her dress gaped at the top and he caught a glimpse of her breasts.

Why not? he thought. The privileges of a condemned man.

21

Father Michael carries a message

MORGAN WALKED BENEATH a bougainvillea with water dripping from its leaves, along a path paved with stones unable to contain shoots of unruly kikuyu grass awakened by the rain.

He bent his head slightly to pass underneath the branch of a peach tree, climbed up the stairs of a veranda with potted plants hanging from the beams and knocked on the door. Father Michael raised his eyebrows above the rims of his spectacles.

'You have come to confess, my son?' he asked with mock sincerity.

Morgan laughed. 'I won't bother you with my confession.'

'It would be a lengthy business,' Father Michael said. 'A full day at least.'

Morgan shook Father Michael's hand and said, 'I'm afraid we won't have time for that tonight.'

Father Michael let out a sigh. 'Can I offer you a beer instead?'

'Please, Father.' Morgan waited for Father Michael to return from the kitchen.

They sat down next to a coffee table. It was stacked with books and had a chessboard in the middle of it. Morgan relaxed and rolled a cigarette.

'I love the smell of the tobacco,' said Father Michael.

'You're not the only one.' Morgan offered him the pack. Father Michael expertly rolled a cigarette. Morgan struck a match and held the flame in front of the priest's face.

'Mmm,' said Father Michael and inhaled the smoke like a true connoisseur.

'The pleasures of the flesh,' said Morgan.

'One of the lesser ones,' Father Michael exhaled.

Morgan poured his beer and raised it in a toast. 'To our premature demise,' he said.

'Speak for yourself.' Father Michael raised his glass and took his first sip. Morgan wiped the foam from his moustache, put his glass on the table and watched the reflection of the light from the reading lamp in the bubbles. 'So,' Father Michael said, 'I take it this is not a purely religious visit.'

'You can rest assured,' said Morgan. Father Michael tapped the ash off the tip of his cigarette and carefully arranged the pieces on the chessboard. 'Care for a game?'

'My turn to play white,' Morgan said.

Father Michael sighed and turned the white pieces towards Morgan.

The sound of the rain on the roof showed no sign of abating. 'Place is going to wash away,' Morgan said and advanced his king's pawn. Without hesitation Father Michael played his queen's bishop's pawn.

'Sicilian Defense, no less,' observed Morgan. 'You feel like a fight, Father?'

Father Michael said nothing. Morgan moved his knight and they rapidly played the first six moves.

Morgan sat back in his chair, lifted his glass and caught Father Michael's eye. 'Do you know a man called Rastodika?'

A faint amusement crept into Father Michael's eyes. 'The man who drank the lay preacher under the table?'

'Not much escapes your notice, Father.'

'I know about most of the sins in this town, including some of yours,' said Father Michael.

Morgan raised his eyebrows ever so slightly, and moved his bishop.

There was a brief lull in the rain. Chess is an aggressive game, Morgan reminded himself as Father Michael exchanged two pieces to give himself room to breathe. The game was almost level. Morgan only had a slight advantage left.

'Rastodika used to be an acquaintance of Mr. B's in the early days,' Father Michael said, pondering his next move. He took care not to say anything about cattle smuggling. Morgan feigned surprise, and took a long sip of his beer. He made a careless move and Father Michael rapidly wiped him off the board.

'You are too impulsive,' Father Michael smiled benevolently, and helped himself to another cigarette.

'You are a devious man, Father,' Morgan laughed and declined another game. 'Let me lick my wounds first.'

Father Michael got up and opened a window. 'You wanted to tell me about Rastodika,' he said.

'The man is in trouble,' Morgan said. 'He is going to need a kidney transplant sometime soon.'

'And it's going to cost a lot of money?' Father Michael addressed his question to the black night outside the window.

'Compassion has a price nowadays.' Morgan drained his glass and put it down on the table.

'I know that only too well,' said Father Michael turning away from the open window. 'You will need to find someone with a lot of money, or at least someone who can support some kind of fundraising.'

'I've already depleted the Round Table's money,' Morgan said.

'Then,' said Father Michael, 'I can think of only one person with enough money.' He didn't elaborate.

'So can I.'

Father Michael sat down and replaced the pieces on the chessboard. 'You will have to involve the whole town,' he said, and advanced his king's pawn.

They played in silence and Morgan concentrated, battling for control of the center. He remembered that if you see a good move there is always a better one. It was a merciless contest that saw Father Michael demolishing Morgan's supply of tobacco. Morgan won by the skin of his teeth.

'Now that,' smiled Father Michael, 'is what I call a decent game.'

'Shall we call it a night?' asked Morgan.

Father Michael was adamant. 'Best of three. Shall I get you another beer?'

Close to midnight there was a brief lull in the rain and Morgan conceded defeat.

'Serves me right for underestimating you,' he said. 'You will not forget about Rastodika,' he reminded Father Michael as he stepped outside.

Father Michael stood framed in the light of his doorway. 'I will do my best.'

DORCAS WOKE UP to a grey and humid dawn, parted the curtains of her bedroom window, walked barefoot through the house and felt the dampness of the floor. She lit the stove, opened all the doors, and sat down in the darkened living room to wait for the coffee to boil. She listened to the water dripping steadily from the eaves.

There was not the faintest suggestion of a breeze and the stale air in the house surrounded her like a blanket. She poured herself a cup of coffee, drew up a chair, sat at the front door contemplating the wet garden, and planned her day. When she had finished her coffee she got up abruptly. Still barefoot, she started cleaning the house, dispelling the early morning gloom with her vigorous movements.

For more than an hour she swept the floor, washed the dishes and shook out the bed-sheets, polished the furniture, swept spiders off the wall with the aid of a duster, cleaned the small carpet in the living room, leveled the portraits of her children and late husband, waged a war against the sugar ants and cleaned the windows of the kitchen.

Then she stepped into a pair of gumboots standing in the living room, went out into the garden and saw the vendors wearing fertilizer bags as raincoats making their way to the mall. Their cheerful greetings lifted her spirits and she collected a tray of tomato seedlings and started planting them in a freshly dug bed. She heard the first cars making their way up the hill along the slippery road, the voices of children going to school, the belated sound of roosters, the shouting of the builders at the building sites, and the cheerful voices of women on their way to the mall.

She worked methodically, making symmetrical holes with a steel blade and planting the seedlings firmly in the wet soil. Near the end of the bed she looked up and found Father Michael standing in front of her, holding an umbrella and wearing his ancient raincoat. She stared at him in surprise. 'It's only eight o'clock Father,' she said, looking down the hill to where she could see the clock on the church tower.

A sudden heavy downpour forced them to retreat into the house. 'Just a moment, Father,' she excused herself and disappeared into the bedroom. Father Michael stood in the middle of the living room, unable to decide what to do with his raincoat.

The bedroom door opened, and she reappeared wearing dry clothes. He marveled at the speed of her transformation. 'Your coat, Father,' she commanded and took it from him.

They exchanged pleasantries about the rain, and Father Michael contemplated the mud on his shoes while Dorcas made coffee in the kitchen. 'So what brings you here so early in the morning?' she asked as she handed him his cup.

Father Michael didn't answer immediately. He tested the temperature of the coffee and put the spoon in the saucer. 'Morgan spoke to me last night,' he said.

Dorcas smiled. 'I hope he minded his language.'

Father Michael stretched his legs. 'It was about a man called Rastodika. I believe you know him.'

She laughed out loud. 'Rastodika. What has he been up to?' A sudden gust of wind parted the curtains and she stood up to close the window.

'Rastodika is a very sick man,' Father Michael informed her. Dorcas turned her head. 'That rascal?' she enquired. 'I thought he was indestructible.'

'Morgan tells me he will need a kidney transplant.'

'I can't believe it,' she said. 'He was a wild man when he was younger,' her eyes brightened. 'Both him and Mr. B.'

'So I understand.' Father Michael put down his cup and carefully polished his glasses. 'What does Morgan want?' Dorcas asked.

'Money,' Father Michael said vaguely. 'The operation can't be done in this country.'

'Morgan is going to bankrupt this town.' Dorcas stood up and again leveled the portrait of one of her daughters. 'So where does he think he is going to get it from?'

'A fund-raising of some sort, I think.'

She returned to her chair. 'Mr. B,' she said almost immediately. 'Why not? He and Rastodika were the best of friends after all.' Father Michael didn't answer.

'The problem is,' Dorcas said, 'how to make him do it?'

She stood up and opened the front door. A car was coming up the hill and Father Michael saw the brown, muddy water churned up by the wheels. Dorcas' figure was framed in the open doorway; she had her hands on her hips. Father Michael contemplated her silhouette and tried to calculate her age.

'That man,' Dorcas said, meaning Mr. B, 'has so much money he doesn't even know what to do with it.' She turned towards Father Michael and rested her back against the doorpost. She had known Mr. B for most of her life. He was wild, huge, jovial, ruthless. Sometimes generous, but only when it suited him. Unassailable? No. Every man has a weakness. A smile crossed her face. There was someone Mr. B couldn't resist. And it was not his Ghanaian wife.

With a sudden movement she pushed herself away from the doorpost, shut the door and faced Father Michael. She folded her arms below her breasts, placed her legs slightly apart and said: 'There is something that never fails. A weakness. Every man has the same weakness. It has always been like that.'

It was not difficult for Father Michael to figure out what she had in mind. He knew about all the weaknesses and sins and scandals in the town. He noticed the thin fabric of her dress, the firmness of her figure and the perfect shape of her mouth.

For a moment there was only the sound of the rain on the roof. Father Michael pocketed his handkerchief and shifted in his chair, very aware of her powerful presence.

'You mean,' he asked tentatively, 'the pleasures of the flesh?'

Dorcas smiled faintly and nodded her head.

Father Michael gave a sardonic smile and suppressed a pang of guilt.

'Do you think,' he asked, 'the end justifies the means?'

'We live in troubled times, Father.'

The wind freshened and drove the rain against the side of the house. Raindrops hit the windowpanes like bullets. Father Michael glanced at his watch. 'No,' said Dorcas. 'You can't walk home in this rain.' She took him by the arm, led him into the kitchen and made him breakfast, which he ate at the table by the light of an electric lamp suspended from the ceiling, covered by a shade that hung at the level of his eyes.

He was surprised by his big appetite and ate slowly, enjoying the meal. She sat opposite him, her arms on the tabletop. Father Michael looked up into her inscrutable black eyes. 'You deserve to be spoiled now and again,' she said.

At eleven o'clock there was a brief respite in the rain and Dorcas accompanied him to the gate. They walked through the water-soaked garden and she thrust a bag with a selection of vegetables into his hands despite his protestations.

The rain had slowed down to a drizzle when Father Michael stopped at his usual resting place and looked down on the river. It had spilled its banks. The shacks closest to the road had been flooded. They were being demolished and carried to higher ground.

From where he stood, Father Michael could hear the voices of people carrying their meager pieces of furniture. He watched as two men rescued a bed, complete with mattress and bedclothes. Behind them, he saw dead trees floating in the brown swirling water, while above the river, snow-white egrets flew against the wind.

22

Conversations with Mary

MARY OBSERVED THE laparotomy scar on her belly while Violet was washing her. The daily bath had become their morning ritual ever since Mary had become too weak to wash herself.

Inside her belly the lymphoma grew unabated. When she rubbed her hand over it she could feel its outline. She had become accustomed to the monster growing inside her, and monitored its progress, wondering when exactly it was going to kill her.

She looked at her thin arms and legs that seemed to belong to someone else and found with surprise that she had difficulty remembering them as they were before the start of her illness. It's the tumor, she told herself, that's sucking me dry. She looked down and saw the vestiges of her once-ample breasts. She suddenly realized there was not much left of her for the tumor to devour.

If the tumor doesn't kill me, the virus will. The virus caused the tumor—that's what Morgan had said. She smiled faintly. And I got the virus from someone I once loved and who has since died. I have known all along that I am dying, but now I know that it is near. I'm not afraid. I'm more concerned about the people I'm leaving behind. She looked at herself again. What is this? she thought. This is just a perishable body.

'You must tell my mother to look after my child well when I am gone,' she said when Violet was washing her arms. She stopped and looked into Mary's eyes. This was the first time Mary had talked about her impending death. She put down the soap and gently dried Mary's skin.

'I will tell her,' she said. 'I promise you. Don't worry about that.' Violet finished dressing her and then put her in a wheelchair and pushed her onto the veranda, where Morgan found her later when he came on his ward round. He was pleased with Naledi's progress. She had picked up another kilogram and her foster mothers proudly showed him the weight, written down on her temperature card.

Morgan laughed. 'You lot are all going to get your nursing diplomas,' he said.

He noticed the empty bed. 'Mary's outside,' Janet said before he could ask.

She was watching the faint drizzle and the low hanging clouds with her chin resting in her hand. 'I like it when it's like this,' she said, 'just when it starts to rain.'

Morgan drew up a chair and sat down next to her. 'Everyone else can wait for a bit,' he said. 'I am taking a break.'

Mary laughed. 'That is one of the privileges of dying,' she said. 'I can sit and enjoy this all day; nobody's going to call me.'

She turned her head and faced him. Morgan noted the shape of her eyes. 'I wish you didn't have to go.' He said it simply, as if she had a choice in the matter.

Mary put her hands on the sides of the wheelchair. 'You know,' she said, 'I think I am privileged.' She shifted her thin frame in the chair.

Morgan turned his head and looked out over the lawn. 'Why?' he asked.

'Because,' she paused, 'I can prepare myself for it properly. In fact, I can almost predict the exact time.'

Morgan thought about it. How long was it going to be? A few weeks? Maybe even less, he thought.

'Are you scared of dying?' he asked her.

'No,' said Mary. 'I have learnt to appreciate every moment.'

'A mountain guide once told me more or less the same thing,' Morgan said. 'He said that the proximity of death sharpens our senses.'

'I have never climbed a mountain,' she said.

Morgan smiled. 'In our next life, I will take you up a mountain.'

Mary laughed. 'I will make you keep your promise. Tell me about the mountains,' she said with sudden urgency.

'What about them?' Morgan asked.

'The most important things only, please.' She was looking at him intently and he saw her perfect eyebrows, her slanting eyes and her thin, delicate nose with a slight flaring of the nostrils. Morgan laughed. 'I wish you could see yourself,' he said. 'You are looking more and more like a hawk.' And soon you will fly away, he thought.

She smiled fleetingly. 'Tell me, please.' It again struck Morgan that she was trying to cram all the images of a lifetime into a few precious weeks.

'My favorite people live in the mountains,' he said.

'And more?' she demanded.

'If you stand on a mountain top, you can believe in God.'

'Do you believe in him?'

'Not down here,' said Morgan, and she laughed.

'And?'

'The wind,' said Morgan. 'Sometimes it is playful and just tugs at your windbreaker, sometimes it howls and blows the snow off the peaks so you can see a plume of white snow from many miles away.'

'I wish I could see that,' she said.

'Not from close by,' Morgan said. 'It can blow so hard that you can hardly stand up.'

Mary was constructing a picture in her mind. She narrowed

her eyes and a slight furrow appeared between her eyebrows. 'And more?' she prodded him.

For a moment he did not know what to say. 'You realize how small you are,' he said. 'We are all really very insignificant.'

23

A soccer match

THE PREPARATIONS FOR the soccer match coincided with the rabies vaccination campaign sparked off by Morgan's dead cat.

Shebeen queens were replenishing their stocks, the beerhall was packed, unfamiliar trucks were driving in the streets, people from the country poured out of overcrowded buses, women carrying shopping bags stood chatting at the mall, people danced to the music from ghetto-blasters under the trees, new friendships were struck up and old friendships were reinforced at Mr. Chiremba's beerhall.

Dogs with red blotches of paint on their foreheads as evidence of their rabies vaccination barked enthusiastically at passersby. Horsemen rode into town; their hobbled horses grazed next to the streets and were chased out of gardens by skinny little boys.

Holmes and Thunderbird declared war on the cats living in the sewers of the hospital. For reasons best known to themselves, they decided to flood the sewers with water and catch the cats as they emerged. They hired men from the town council who blocked most of the entrances and guarded others with nets. They did not take into account the fall of the land, the size of the underground maze, or the leakages, and did not even find all the openings. They proceeded to flood the sewers with water from the fire hydrants. The pressure of the hydrants was predictably inadequate to fill the sewers.

The cats were mildly irritated. Some moved to higher

ground while others didn't even bother to find out what was going on. The remaining cats waded through belly-deep water and found men waiting for them with nets. They retreated and escaped unseen through an unguarded opening next to the maternity wing, fanned out across the lawn and climbed up the trees where they sat grooming themselves and observing the activity around the drainpipes with interest.

Morgan laughed when the Kenyan told him about the abortive vendetta.

'What were they going to do with the cats if they caught them?' the Kenyan wanted to know.

Morgan said, 'Knowing Holmes, he would probably feed them through a roller and fax them to the Regional Superintendent's office.'

'Morgan! Only you could imagine faxing a cat!'

'Faxed cats for fat cats,' said Morgan. 'It sounds like a motto.'

'What was that man's name again?' asked the Kenyan.

'Oh you mean Schrodinger?' said Morgan. The Kenyan nodded. 'That,' said Morgan, 'would add an interesting perspective to quantum physics. Imagine, the cat can't be in the fax line unless it comes out on the other end. The only way to know it is in the line is to see it coming out the other end. Then it becomes reality. But is it? What about the real, flattened dead cat on the sender's side? What is the relationship between the dead flat cat and the flat faxed cat? Imagine the image of a cat hurtling down a fiber optic cable. How does it reassemble itself? What if its whiskers get stuck somewhere?'

'Enough, Morgan!' said the Kenyan. 'I'm sorry I told you about the cats.'

'Maybe,' said Morgan, 'I should consult a book on quantum physics.'

'Maybe you should take a holiday,' said the Kenyan.

'Now you're talking,' Morgan replied.

ON SUNDAY EVENING Rebecca had a premonition. She was walking home from church when she felt a cold gust of wind between her shoulders, as if someone had opened a door on a cold winter's day. But there was no wind. The leaves of the camel-thorns did not move at all. It was a hot, windless summer night.

'Something bad is going to happen,' she told Morgan and Oumar on Monday morning.

'You are a superstitious woman,' Morgan told her. 'Do you think things can get any worse than they already are?'

Rebecca looked at him over the rims of her spectacles. 'Wait and see, Morgan,' she said.

On Tuesday morning Morgan drove past the soccer field on his way to work. He saw the builders raising the wall that started as a fence, which they would then cover with black plastic sheeting to hide the game from non-paying spectators, and then build a wall over which people could barely see if they were standing on their toes. They will have to chop down the trees, he thought. Some people will watch from the trees, thorns or no thorns.

Exactly at noon a drunken man misjudged the speed of a car as he was crossing the road. He was picked up from the pavement and taken to the mortuary, where the Constable noticed he was still breathing. He brought him to Casualty in the back of the police van. Three hours later he had windows in both temples, his spleen had been removed, a piece of small bowel had been resected, his bladder sutured, and the fracture of his right leg cleaned and splinted.

Oumar contemplated the bruised brain from which he had removed a subdural hematoma on each side. 'Keep hyperventilating him,' he said. 'We want to shrink the volume of the brain.'

'PCO_2 is twenty-eight,' Thomson read from a strip of paper handed to him by the nurse.

'Good,' said Oumar, glancing at the monitor. 'Seems to be holding his own.'

It was his first positive statement of the afternoon. Nobody had expected the man to survive. He'd arrived in Casualty with a slow, bounding pulse and a widely dilated right pupil that appeared to be staring into the beyond. Morgan, Rebecca, the Kenyan, Thomson, Oumar and all the nurses in Casualty battled to keep him alive.

They expected him to die on his way to theater, they expected him to die as they were shaving his head, then they expected him to die as he was being draped; but he surprised them and stayed alive.

Unknown Male was written in the name space of his folder.

Rebecca promoted him to *Unknown Male No.1* since it was near month end and because of the soccer match. 'There may be more coming,' she said. 'We don't want to mix up the unknowns.'

Morgan couldn't decide whether she was being optimistic or pessimistic. Optimistic in believing that the man was going to survive, or pessimistic in expecting more trouble. 'Is this your premonition?' he asked during a lull in the proceedings. Rebecca shook her head.

'No,' she said emphatically. The man's passage from Casualty certainly hadn't been a smooth one. He had had the misfortune to be met by Holmes and Thunderbird, who'd found themselves in Casualty on the insistence of Rebecca who'd had enough of the overcrowded and understaffed place. The doctor for the day was called away to the wards and she was left with two nurses and almost a hundred patients.

Holmes and Thunderbird observed the new arrival through eyes that reminded her of the eyes of the dead fish in the baskets of the fishmongers at the mall. When she urged them to do something, they didn't know where to start. She thrust a laryngoscope and a tube into Holmes' hands and at the same time yelled at a nurse to call Morgan and the Kenyan. Holmes handled the laryngoscope like someone who had picked up a live hand grenade.

At that moment, Morgan and the Kenyan arrived. Morgan pushed Holmes aside and relieved him of the laryngoscope. Between him, Rebecca, the nurses and the Kenyan, the man was kept alive.

Holmes regained his composure and started venturing unwanted opinions. Nobody paid any attention to him, and he started raising his voice above the din in the resuscitation room. 'Call the referral hospital!' he shouted at Rebecca who turned her back on him.

He grabbed the phone and asked the receptionist to put him through to the referral hospital. Miraculously she got through straight away. Above the din in Casualty they could hear him speak to the Regional Superintendent. He rang off and inserted himself between Rebecca and the Kenyan. 'I have arranged a transfer,' he said triumphantly as Morgan was adjusting the ventilator.

Morgan observed the patient's dilated pupil, felt the slowing pulse, saw the rapidly distending belly, and didn't bother to answer.

'We are transferring this man,' Holmes said, emboldened by Morgan's silence.

Morgan paid no attention until he had adjusted the ventilator to his satisfaction, then he turned towards Holmes. He took Holmes' silk tie between his fingers and gently pulled him closer until their faces were six inches apart. 'Fuck off,' he whispered and pulled Holmes closer until their noses were touching.

'FUCK OFF!' he yelled at the top of his voice and turned back to the patient.

Holmes and Thunderbird retreated, and from then everything proceeded rapidly. When the man's head was finally draped and ready for surgery, Oumar said, 'They should have left him at the mortuary, he is probably going to end up there anyway.' Then he exposed the skull in his methodical fashion, and started drilling the first hole.

Morgan stood behind him waiting for the abdomen to be draped and watched the crater made by the trephine. He waited until it pierced the inner layer of the skull.

'You carry on with the abdomen,' Oumar said as he picked up the burr. 'I don't need help for now.' Later, as he was tying off the pedicle of the spleen, Morgan heard him say 'Massive subdural.'

He heard the sound of the bone forceps as Oumar started chipping away the temporal bone. Morgan could feel the vessels pulsating between his fingers, and the pulse was returning to normal. They worked in silence for a while. Morgan removed a piece of small bowel and sutured the tear in the bladder. Then he rinsed the abdomen with lukewarm saline. As Morgan was closing the abdomen, Oumar drilled a hole in the opposite side of the skull. Morgan changed gloves and started cleaning the leg.

'Damn, more blood,' he heard Oumar say as he entered the other side. 'Damn' was the worst swear word Oumar ever used.

'I gave him antibiotics,' Thomson's voice came from the top of the table, 'since he is still with us.'

Morgan waited for the plaster to harden and suddenly found himself with nothing more to do. He took off his gloves, stood behind Oumar, looked over his shoulder and watched him as he enlarged the window in the temporal bone, sucked out the hematoma and cauterized bleeders, working without hurry until he was satisfied. Below the raw edges of the bone lay the brain like a bruised and exposed secret.

Oumar started to close the dura. 'Well, it's up to him now,' he said philosophically. 'We've done our bit.'

'Get the bed from High Care,' said Thomson. 'I didn't expect him to get off the table alive.'

Two rows of relatives were standing in the passage outside High Care. They made way for the bed to pass, standing on tiptoe, backs against the wall, craning their necks to see into the bed. A frail, frightened old lady with arms like twigs was standing amongst them.

Next to the door stood the Constable with a clipboard under his arm.

The night shift was coming on duty. Relatives peered into the room as the nurses connected the man to the ventilator, untangled the drip lines and drainage tubes, attached monitor leads and sorted out flow rates, tidal volumes and alarm limits.

Morgan supervised the chaos until he was satisfied that the nurses knew what they were doing.

'Come,' he said to Thomson. 'Let's go and have a smoke while this lot sort themselves out.'

They stood just outside the door on the veranda. The afternoon was gone—swallowed up by theater and replaced by a benevolent slice of moon that hung above the trees, overseeing the merriment beyond the hospital fence. Disembodied voices of men and women singing, loud music, the cries and laughter of children and the barking of dogs hung in the thick evening air. The piercing sound of the monitor came through the door in metered portions, ninety times a minute, regular. 'Pulse is a bit fast,' said Thomson.

'*Unknown Male No.1*' now had a name and even an address.

'Wild Man' the staff called him.

The night staff knew him anyway. He was a regular shebeen customer and veteran of many fights as evidenced by the scars Morgan had noted on his head as they were shaving him. One shebeen too many today, Morgan thought, as he wrote out the treatment and observations. Thomson said goodbye. 'I will think about you when I sip my beer,' he said.

At midnight Morgan returned home. He stood outside on the veranda and smoked a cigarette. The town was asleep except for a single dog keeping watch, barking dutifully at the moon.

VIOLET WAS NOT in the duty room. He found her standing next to Mary's bed. The night sister had inserted a drip since Mary wasn't eating and had been vomiting the previous night. The fluid had revived her somewhat, but her eyes looked tired.

Why didn't they tell me? he wanted to ask. The night sister probably thought he was too busy to attend to such a small matter. Damn, thought Morgan, I could have come and greeted her at least.

He remembered the afternoon with Thomson on the veranda, Mary's slight pallor and the almost imperceptible change in her demeanor. He had blamed her pallor on the reflection of light. Sometimes, he thought, you only see what you want to see.

Mary was talking to Violet, her voice as pure as ever, telling her she was feeling better. Morgan watched her thin right hand move as she talked. The left hand was immobilized by the drip. 'Do you have pain?' he asked.

'No,' said Mary. 'I just feel weak.'

He examined her, felt the size of the tumor and wondered what kept her alive. Mary smiled and said, 'It is growing like a baby.'

Morgan avoided her eyes and wrote up a prescription for

intravenous fluids. As Mary began to doze off, he watched her peaceful face and remembered Rebecca's premonition.

Suddenly she opened her eyes and looked at him. 'You look tired,' she said, and drifted off to sleep.

THE EXCITEMENT IN the town had spread into Male Ward. Everyone was feeling better. As usual, Morgan ended the round at Rastodika's room. Rastodika was sitting on his bed in high spirits. 'We need to talk to you,' he said. 'Let's go outside.'

Morgan wondered just who 'we' referred to until he looked into the passage. Several men—the not-too-bedridden—were waiting in benign ambush with Rastodika as their spokesman. Morgan could guess what was coming, but he let Rastodika say it anyway. 'We want to go to the soccer match,' said Rastodika.

Morgan scrutinized the faces in front of him. Eager, pleading eyes, some sunken in their sockets, thin, bony frames, clavicles sticking out above V-shaped necks in coarse, blue shirts. There were seven men, including the madman, staring at him, begging wordlessly.

Violet was about to say something, but thought better of it. Morgan ignored her, and thought about the many potential repercussions. The madman offered interesting possibilities. Maybe I should warn the Constable, he thought. The match was three days away. He would definitely see him before then. The Constable was an understanding man; he wouldn't spoil the fun unnecessarily.

'Okay,' said Morgan at last. 'Soccer match only. No shebeens, no beerhall, no drink, no fights. No black eyes. I don't want to sew up any cuts, understand?'

There were happy smiles, heads nodding in agreement, shoulders pulled back, spines straightened by magic energy from somewhere. And an unhappy sister.

'You spoil them rotten,' Violet said.

'We only live once, sister. Let them have their match,' said Morgan and left her standing in the passage.

Casualty was less crowded than usual. 'Only the sick people are here,' said Rebecca. 'The hypochondriacs have more important things to do. They will bring their hangovers next Monday.'

'SO, THAT'S AS much as I know,' said Dorcas. 'According to Father Michael, there isn't too much time to waste.' She was sitting opposite Rachel at a table in the overcrowded café at the mall. Workers stood in a queue and waited for their take out orders. From across the mall they could hear the music and loud voices at Mr. Chiremba's beerhall.

Rachel sipped her drink and ignored the admiring stares of the men in the queue. A man nearing the register couldn't keep his eyes off her and failed to notice when his turn came. 'Come on, wake up!' said the cashier, and the other men in the queue laughed boisterously.

Rachel was wearing a white summer dress with thin shoulder straps that hardly broke the line of her exquisite shoulders. 'You are as beautiful as ever,' said Dorcas, without feeling the slightest pang of jealousy.

Rachel ignored the compliment and said: 'I can remember Rastodika from when I was a girl. He used to be a wild man.' Dorcas said: 'He was Mr. B's friend; they were both rather wild.'

Rachel took a sip of her cooldrink and looked at Dorcas over the brim of the glass. 'And Morgan?' she asked. 'He wants to save Rastodika, and for that he needs money?' She started to laugh. 'I like that man.'

'He needs a wife, I tell you.' Dorcas took out her purse and laid it on the table.

'I will volunteer,' Rachel said.

Dorcas laughed. 'You will have to tame him first.' She took money out of her purse but Rachel stopped her.

'I will pay,' she said.

24

The notice on Morgan's door

T HE MEMO CAME in a sealed envelope with Morgan's name on it. At the morning meeting each of them had received a copy of the referral policy written by Holmes. Holmes handed Morgan's copy to the Kenyan, judging him to be the least defiant.

It was a grocery list of conditions that had to be sent to the referral hospital. Ventilation only to 'stabilize' patients. Stabilize. A nice term to hide behind, thought Thomson. It could also be translated as passing the buck.

'AIDS patients to be stabilized and referred for home-based care.' How do you stabilize an AIDS patient? he wondered. It would be a medical breakthrough.

He heard Holmes' voice. 'I will not be insulted again, like last week. From now on we will follow procedure.'

Oumar smiled. So it's an ego thing is it? Morgan made a fool of you all right.

Thomson carefully read through the policy. Holmes sat pompously at the top of the table, his face without expression. Next to him sat the inscrutable Thunderbird. On the wall above them hung the photograph of Jenkins. The youngsters all sat on the one side of the table, like spectators. Young Simon was watching Oumar with interest, expecting another scene.

Thomson finished reading and pushed away the policy with a gesture of contempt. 'I will use my own judgment, thank you,' he said with a faint smile.

Holmes' cheeks became only slightly puffier. His face

showed as much expression as that of a bullfrog. He is an evil man, thought Thomson.

Oumar moved in his chair and flicked the document across the table using his middle finger. Holmes stiffened almost imperceptibly. Oumar's voice was soft. 'Does this policy reflect your level of competence or ours?' he asked.

Holmes didn't stir.

'Just for the record,' Oumar continued. 'There are people on your staff who are much better qualified than you.' He paused. 'I will not take orders from you.'

It was quiet in the room. Outside, the gardener was conducting a cheerful conversation with someone walking past in the street. Oumar and Thomson pushed back their chairs almost simultaneously and walked out, leaving their copies of the referral policy on the table.

THE KENYAN FOUND Morgan in his office, reading his mail. 'You are sitting here all by yourself, Morgan, and we have to face all the trouble.'

'Why,' asked Morgan, 'do you even bother listening to that creep?' He crumpled a drug ad and threw it into the dustbin. The Kenyan handed him the envelope and Morgan surprised him by opening it carefully with a pocket knife. As he slowly read through the policy, the Kenyan waited for the explosion; but Morgan disappointed him. He carefully laid it down on the table and read the attached memo out loud.

'I have to point out to you once again that neurosurgery and major trauma surgery are best carried out at the referral hospital. That, I have to remind you, is official hospital policy; you seem to have a total disregard for the cost of ventilating a patient.'

'What exactly is the moron trying to tell me?' Morgan seemed to be talking to himself. 'He's crazy, the man would have snuffed it long before he even got to the referral hospital.'

He laughed aloud when he read the next sentence: *Your insubordinate behavior and the use of foul language in front of the nursing staff is, to say the least, deplorable.*

'As if he cares a hoot about the nursing staff. It's his own fat ego he's worried about.'

'You humiliated him, Morgan,' said the Kenyan. 'You should have been more diplomatic.'

'You shouldn't waste diplomacy on idiots,' said Morgan. 'They should be treated like idiots.' He read the last sentence: *May I remind you that I am your senior and that any such behavior in future will lead to disciplinary action.*

'Well, well, well,' said Morgan. 'Why wait? Why doesn't he discipline me right now?'

He stood up and took a dictionary from the bookshelf.

'Insubordination,' he read, 'disobedient, rebellious.'

'Do you think I am a rebel?' he asked the Kenyan.

'That would be an understatement.'

To resist authority or control, to refuse to obey, to protest strongly, Morgan read under the entry, 'rebel'.

He opened the top drawer of his untidy desk and rummaged around until he found a red ballpoint pen and six push pins. At the bottom of the memo he printed: 'Obedience is at the root of all atrocities.' He took the policy and the memo and carefully pinned them on the outside of his door, the memo at the top.

'You are mad,' said the Kenyan.

'Think so?' Morgan came back into the room and closed the door behind him.

'It is a confidential hospital document,' said the Kenyan. 'Everyone who walks past will read it.'

'That's the intention,' said Morgan. 'If we screw people in confidence, we might as well start screwing them openly. Come to think of it, we should put it up at the gate outside.'

'Morgan, you must watch out for Holmes. He's a bad man,

very bad, I tell you. I can see it in his eyes.'

'Think I'm scared of him?'

The Kenyan shrugged his massive shoulders with an air of resignation.

Morgan was standing at the window with his back towards the Kenyan. Outside on the lawn the ambulant AIDS patients were waiting for the morning round. Their backs were bent forward, as if they were bracing themselves against the wind.

'That's what obedience does for you,' said Morgan. 'Look at the poor bastards. Our noble profession obediently sends them to their deaths. We know that the drugs are available, but we don't have the balls to make waves.'

'Where is the money going to come from?' asked the Kenyan.

'The only reason there is a lack of money is because no one raises hell.'

'Morgan, Morgan!' The Kenyan shook his head and sighed.

Morgan was suddenly angry. 'How many people do you think know what's going on behind the walls of this hospital?' With a sudden movement he shut the curtain, turned around and faced the Kenyan. 'Even if they had all the money in the world, Holmes and his mates would fuck it up through sheer incompetence.'

MARY WAS SITTING in her bed, propped up by pillows. Her hair was tied with the same white ribbon she had worn when he took her to visit Sultan.

The room was redolent with the smells of clean pillows, fresh bed sheets, and bath soap. Violet was facing him from the head of the bed with her spotless white uniform and watchful eyes.

'A picture of cleanliness, the two of you,' Morgan said.

'We can't return the compliment,' Violet said.

Mary laughed. Morgan scrutinized her face. Her smile was back; not quite the same, he noted. The lines around her mouth were slightly deeper. If you paint a face, he remembered, you must be careful of jaw lines and lines around the mouth. They must be subtle, just a suggestion of a line, or no line at all. He saw that lines had crept into Mary's face, around her mouth and under her eyes; aging her almost imperceptibly.

He was surprised she had survived the weekend. He had expected a phone call at any moment. Several times he drove to the hospital, and found evidence of Rebecca's visits. A whole repertoire of soups: chicken, vegetable, pumpkin, beef and mushroom. They had certainly helped to achieve a temporary revival. The drip was gone. Her hands were moving as she talked. They were a little slower than usual, but as graceful as always.

'I recognize that ribbon,' he said. How long ago was it since they had visited the stables? It seemed like years ago.

'Sultan?' she asked. 'How is he?'

'I haven't seen him for some time,' Morgan said.

'You must not neglect him,' she reproached him. 'You must send him my regards.' Morgan looked out through the window. A patch of sunlight fell onto the veranda.

'Violet is taking me outside just now,' she said.

SOMETIMES A FAINT breeze catches the edges of a lace curtain, parts it slightly and allows a brief glimpse of the inside of a room. Rastodika's pupils widened briefly and for a moment Morgan had the feeling that he was peering straight into his mind.

'You want my relatives?' he asked. 'Why?'

He was sitting on the ground, arms resting on his bent knees, looking up into Morgan's face. Around them were the mealie plants that Rastodika had planted in the far corner of the hospital garden with the explicit approval of the gardener. Morgan was surprised to see how quickly the plants were growing.

'We are thinking of sending you for a kidney transplant,' he broke the news. Rastodika said nothing; he put out his hand, caught a locust crawling up the stem of one of the plants and flung it over the wall.

'But why do you want my relatives?'

'We want to see if one of them can give you a kidney.'

'What will happen if you don't do it?' he asked.

'Your kidneys are failing, Rastodika.' Morgan avoided a direct answer.

Rastodika was silent for a long time and then he said: 'You are telling me I am going to die.'

'I am telling you I want to help you.'

The idea of a transplant was strange to Rastodika. He thought for a little while and said: 'You want to take one of their kidneys and put it inside me and make it grow?'

'If we can, yes.'

For a long while he said nothing, staring at the black fertile soil. Then he shook his head. 'I will call them.' Rastodika looked past Morgan at the AIDS patients sitting under the trees. Three men were sitting on the bench under Rastodika's tree, bent forward as always, their femurs disproportionately long. The cheerful sound of their voices floated lazily in the humid air. Rastodika reached out his hand, pulled out a tuft of grass and said: 'All of us are dying, not so Morgan?'

25

An empty veranda

REBECCA WAS WALKING down the passage, carrying a small bowl of chicken soup.

'For my daughter,' she told Morgan before he had time to ask.

'Let me go with you,' said Morgan. 'The rest of them can wait a while.'

They walked down the passage that smelt of food, disinfectant, washing powder, floor polish, and excrement, past the nurses' desk, sidestepped the empty food trolley with its rattling plates, acknowledged the kitchen assistant's jovial greeting, and entered Female Ward.

Everyone seemed to be speaking in hushed voices. Violet was standing with her back towards them, adjusting the drip. The bedclothes were almost unruffled. Mary was lying very still with her eyes closed. Violet spoke in a stage whisper: 'She asked for painkillers; it's the first time ever.'

Rebecca put the bowl of soup on the bedside locker. Very gently she stroked the side of Mary's face. She didn't wake up. Her hands were on her chest with her delicate fingers intertwined and she smiled in her painless, morphine-assisted dream.

Rebecca clasped her hands in front of her belly, her head sagged forward, her features softened and her broad shoulders slumped. The reflection of the dim light on her glasses obscured her eyes.

Morgan stepped out onto the veranda. It was raining

softly, the clouds were hanging low. The kites were nowhere to be seen and the weavers were subdued. A solitary pigeon sat on the edge of the gutter of the opposite roof.

Bad day for flying, he thought. All flight operations suspended until further notice.

He went back to Mary's bedside. 'Don't wake her up,' he said to Violet. 'I will come to see her later.'

A nurse called Rebecca to the telephone; all hell had broken loose in Casualty. Her exit was delayed somewhat by a procession of scarecrows making their way towards the door. Naledi was in the middle. Two equally frail women supported her. All of them moved with unequal, poorly coordinated steps, swaying to and fro like reeds in the wind.

Morgan expected the three of them to collapse in a heap of tangled, bony limbs. They spoke softly in deference to Mary, and whispered their words of encouragement. Janet was sitting on her bed, watching the spectacle, sucking her breakfast through a straw. They reached the door and turned around.

No curves in their figures, he observed. The blue hospital dresses hung straight down. If I had to draw them, he thought, I would only draw angles and straight lines, except for their heads of course. But even their heads were angular, with their cheekbones sticking out below the flattening of their temples where the temporal muscles used to be.

Their staring eyes were filled with concentration. Naledi's eyes were fixed on the floor. They reached the safety of Naledi's bed. She turned around laboriously and collapsed on the mattress. Her two helpers sat down on the edge. All of them were breathless.

'She's getting better,' Janet told him with motherly pride. Naledi managed a faint smile. Violet touched his arm. Her voice was unusually soft. 'Let's start the round,' she said. Morgan started his round feeling like a sleepwalker on the edge of a cliff. He looked into face after face that wore a death-defying smile.

A separate reality, he thought, where dying scarecrows treat death with contempt and grasp life to the very last day. Running the marathon right up to the finish line with wasted muscles and creaking joints.

In the passage in front of High Care stood a dumbfounded police officer. It had been a case of mistaken identity, a mixing up of names. The officer thought Thomson's new patient was the same man who had been killed in the previous night's car accident. At first he thought he was witnessing a resurrection. He suppressed a curse, tore his report from a clipboard and crumpled it. Thomson came out of High Care, arranging a mercy flight for a man with a broken neck—phoning the man's employer to get guarantee of payment, phoning his relatives, phoning a neurosurgeon, phoning med-rescue, phoning the airport and customs. He had been at it since five in the morning.

'This bloody phone has been barred,' he said. 'It can only take incoming calls all of a sudden.'

'Cost-cutting,' said Morgan. 'They probably decided it at one of those infernal meetings we don't attend.'

'Bloody circus!' Thomson's beard was pointing in all directions and his voice sounded hoarse.

'Are they flying in this weather?' Morgan enquired.

'I spoke to Mike and he's going to try flying in under the clouds.'

'Clouds are pretty low.'

Thomson turned back towards the door. 'Let me sort this man out, in case Mike makes it.'

VIOLET WAS HOLDING the ward diary in front of her chest, hugging it. She started walking towards the duty room, then remembered something and turned back towards Morgan. She said: 'Our nurse was buried over the weekend, the one you diagnosed with the Virus when she came in with pneumonia.'

The Virus, he thought. A capital letter Virus. He didn't know she had died.

'She went back to her family near the end,' he heard Violet say. 'She died at home.'

Morgan remembered the last time he had seen her. It was towards the end of winter, on a cold, windy evening at the mall. He had waved at her and caught her eye as she was walking through the crowd.

Across a crowded room.

Across a crowded, windy, dusty African mall.

There had been a smile of recognition on her face, a secret shared. He remembered stopping and watching her as she left the mall and walked towards her little house near the Indian shop. Tall, thin, slightly stooped, her loneliness hanging around her like a cloak, still wearing her nurse's uniform, working at the clinic and caring for her child, with a lifetime's love to give in a few measured months.

Was there anybody she could talk to near the end? he wondered. What was she thinking about when she lay awake in the small hours of the night? Was there anybody she could cuddle up to and get a hug from? No, Morgan thought, probably not.

'Violet,' he said, 'one day you must give me some good news and tell me about something nice. Even if you make it up.' She was facing him. Dark, satin-smooth skin. Perfectly regular features. Black, imponderable eyes. Firm, sensitive lips with a touch of red. Morgan tried to translate the face into a painting.

Gauguin, he thought. Gauguin would have painted that face. A faint amusement crept into her eyes. She gave him a carefully measured smile.

'I will think about it,' she promised.

The madman walked past them and Violet smelt the smoke on him. 'How many cigarettes have you had today?' she asked in her sternest voice.

The madman held up his one and only hand, spread five fingers and then subtracted one by bending down his pinkie. 'Does that mean four?' asked Violet.

The madman nodded.

'You should ask him when he's had seven,' Morgan said. 'I want to see what he does.'

ABOVE THE MONOTONOUS sound of the compressor, the hissing of the ventilator, the shrill sound of monitors and the obscene noise of suction tubes, Thomson heard a smooth, unwelcome voice.

Holmes was standing next to the Wild Man's bed. His portly figure looked out of place amongst all the activity. The High Care nurses walked past him as if he was just another obstacle in the crowded space. Thomson noticed his shiny shoes, meticulously pressed shirt and the maroon silk tie. He turned around and faced Holmes without greeting him.

'This man,' Holmes said with exaggerated politeness, 'is still being ventilated.'

'This man' had been the cause of the most discordant doctors' meeting ever held. The previous morning, Holmes, still humiliated after his encounter with Morgan, had accused them of undermining him.

'The man should have been transferred, you all know that,' he said. There was no trace of his usual smoothness. He was the master talking to his serfs. Morgan was not present as usual. The ever-polite Oumar surprised everyone by telling Holmes to get stuffed. Just like that. Then he got up, walked out, and slammed the door behind him.

Thomson looked into the dead eyes behind the gold-rimmed spectacles and suppressed his irritation. 'He's doing well,' he said amiably. Thomson noticed the fat, flabby cheeks and saw the jaw muscles contract slightly. It came as a surprise; he tended to think that Holmes consisted of fat only.

Holmes' attempt at a smile turned into a grimace. 'How much longer?' he asked.

Why the hell do I have to explain myself to you, you fat, flabby bastard? Thomson thought. He tilted his head, lifted his shoulders slightly and said: 'It depends.'

The radiographer was removing the mobile X-ray machine and asked Holmes to move out of the way. He stepped sideways, keeping his eyes on Thomson.

'Depends on what?' he asked.

'On the condition of his chest.' Thomson pointed at the viewing box where the radiographer had just put up the latest X-ray. There were two X-rays, one of a broken neck and the Wild Man's chest X-ray.

'The one on the right,' he said, as if Holmes wouldn't have noticed the difference.

Holmes' nose turned red. 'What I am actually asking,' he said with contained anger, 'is why don't we fly him out as well? I believe you are flying this man out.' He pointed at the man with the broken neck.

Thomson shook his head, gave a wistful smile and replied in the measured tone of an airport official announcing a delayed flight. 'Unfortunately, it is only a single-engined aircraft.'

Holmes persisted. 'What has that got to do with it? Surely they can make room for two?'

'Why don't you ask Morgan?' Thomson suggested helpfully. 'He knows something about aircraft.'

There was a sudden commotion at the entrance. A small

boy attached to a drip was wheeled into the room. Holmes had to give way as they came past. He nearly tripped over the wheels of the drip stand.

'And this?' he asked.

'Insecticide poisoning,' said Thomson. 'Two brothers, the other one is still in Casualty, waiting for this bed.' He pointed at the man with the broken neck.

Holmes started to say something but the sound of his voice was obliterated by the noise of an aircraft engine. It seemed to come straight out of the ceiling.

Thomson glanced out of the window and saw the Cessna skimming the treetops.

The pitch of the engine changed as it prepared for its final approach.

His face lit up with a radiant smile. 'There's Mike!' he said.

Holmes followed the direction of his gaze. 'Mike?' he asked.

'Mike,' said Thomson, 'is the pilot.' He turned away from Holmes, snatched the man's X-rays from the screen and put them in an envelope. 'The aircraft has arrived,' he told the man. 'They will be here just now,' he said and patted his shoulder.

Holmes' figure was obscured for a moment by a businesslike nurse fetching something from the drug cupboard. The nurse moved away and they were facing each other again. 'Busy day!' Thomson said cheerfully, and gave Holmes his broadest smile.

He glanced at his watch and attracted the attention of the staff: 'They will be here any minute now, will someone please call Morgan?'

THEY FOLLOWED THE ambulance to the airport in Thomson's car. The clouds started to clear and the puddles in the road shone like mercury. The heat returned; steam rose up from the uneven tarred road. The humid air came in through the open windows and they could smell it and taste it. It felt as if they were diving through lukewarm custard.

'That man's very lucky he's not a quadriplegic,' said Thomson. 'He was dragged out of the car. Nobody cared about his neck.'

Morgan laughed. 'The police officer thought he was dead.'

'The police officer didn't have a good night,' said Thomson.

He turned onto the dirt road leading to the airport and swerved to avoid the potholes. Suddenly he laughed. 'Holmes was in High Care this morning. He wanted me to fly out the man we operated on.'

Morgan shook his head. 'Bloody worm,' he said.

'You heard about the doctors' meeting?'

Morgan nodded. 'I heard Oumar told him to get stuffed. My sentiments exactly.'

'You and Oumar must watch out. Holmes is a vindictive bastard and he has connections.'

'The hell do I care,' said Morgan.

Next to the aircraft was a drum of fuel. Mike was standing on a ladder, refueling.

He wore sunglasses underneath bushy eyebrows, took them off and used them to point at the blue sky between the clouds. 'Now they open up,' he said. 'It's Murphy's law.'

The back seats of the Cessna had been removed, and they squeezed the stretcher in through the back door. The medical rescue man sat down next to the patient. The man complained about the collar around his neck. 'It feels as if it is choking me,' he said.

Thomson carefully swept his fingers around the brim of

the collar. 'It's all right,' he said. 'It's not too tight.'

Mike strained fuel out of the wing tanks. A small layer of water settled at the bottom of the strainer. 'Last time I refueled here there were flakes of paint in the fuel,' he said and emptied the strainer. He continued until he got fuel only. Finally he held the strainer to his nose. 'Avgas. Beautiful smell.' He held the strainer out to Morgan and allowed him a sniff.

He was suddenly in a hurry. 'Let's get the hell out of here,' he said, 'before those clouds change their minds.' He checked that the back door was shut and paused for a moment before he climbed into the cockpit.

'How can you guys live in this godforsaken place?' he asked.

'Beautiful sunsets,' said Thomson.

Mike laughed. 'Of all the excuses . . .'

He switched on the master switch. Morgan could hear the gyros spooling up. Mike waved his hand. 'Keep clear,' he shouted, and slammed the door shut. The engine started noisily at first and then ran smoothly. The aircraft started taxiing reluctantly, and there was a change of pitch as Mike did his engine checks on the run. The ailerons moved up and down, first the left and then the right as if the aircraft was waving politely goodbye.

At the end of the runway it turned around and there was a sudden burst of sound as Mike gave full power against the brakes. Plovers took off from the grass and flew erratically above the aircraft as it lurched forward, gathering speed. Three quarters of the way down the dirt runway it lifted its nose-wheel tentatively and flew up into the turbulent air.

They watched it bank slightly and then disappear. The sound of the aircraft was replaced by the excited voices of the plovers. Pink-white, rounded faces of clouds pushed their way through the haze on the horizon.

'Not a nice day for flying,' said Thomson.

They drove back slowly. On the tarred road a Yellowbilled Kite flew up from the remains of a dead rabbit. 'Mary's favorite bird,' Thomson said. 'How's she doing?'

'She's dying,' Morgan told him.

'Why do the nice people always have to die?' asked Thomson.

MORGAN PICKED UP his stethoscope in the ward and walked to Casualty. The Matron was standing in the passage in front of her office, and beckoned him to go inside.

She closed the door behind her and invited him to sit down. 'There has been a complaint,' she said. The reflection from her glasses was very bright for the time of day. She started to say something and took a handkerchief out of her dress pocket and pretended to sneeze, holding the handkerchief in front of her face.

She removed the handkerchief and put it back in her pocket. Her voice sounded muffled when she continued, and her cheeks seemed to balloon when she pursed her lips.

'The private wing,' she said, straightening her voice, 'couldn't serve ice cream and yoghurt on their menu last night.' Near the end of the sentence her voice deserted her. She sounded somewhat breathless.

Morgan raised his eyebrows in mock surprise. 'That is terrible,' he said innocently. 'Someone should investigate this.'

'Oh I have already,' said the Matron 'The ice cream went to your friends, your skeletons.'

Her voice regained its normal tone. Her lips were twitching, curving upwards.

Morgan feigned relief. 'At least there was enough for them then.'

'I know all about you and the cook,' the Matron said, covering her face with the handkerchief, turning her head away from him. Morgan made a mental note to tell Charles to be more careful. The cook was developing a Robin Hood syndrome. He had a sudden image of Charles hijacking all the food and starving the private wing.

Matron finished sneezing, and turned back to him, facing him. Her glasses were slightly fogged and she started taking them off, thought better of it, and pushed them back firmly. Her eyes seemed unusually bright. Her cheek muscles were twitching and she developed a sudden coughing fit.

'I have told the cook to be more careful,' she said, turning her head away from him and pretending to study the nurses' duty roster. 'So now I have spoken to you about it.'

Morgan smiled like a reprieved schoolboy in the headmaster's office. 'Thank you, Matron.' He heard her sneeze as he shut the door behind him.

THERE WAS NO one on the veranda. Morgan climbed the stairs and stepped into the ward. Mary opened her eyes as he moved closer. 'Hi,' said Morgan. 'You were sleeping this morning.'

Her smile returned briefly. 'Just a little pain,' she said.

'You must ask if you need something,' he said. How can I judge your pain? he thought. And I can do nothing about your loneliness.

With an effort she turned on her side and reached out with her hand. She pointed at the aviation textbook. It was at the bottom of a pile of books weighed down by a jar of water.

Morgan lifted the jar and took out the book. 'Open it,' she said. He paged through the book, found the sketch of the raptor's wings. In the middle was the rose, neatly pressed.

'It is a beautiful rose,' said Morgan.

Mary smiled. 'Tomorrow I will be better.' She pointed at a half empty glass of high-protein food. Rebecca's soup bowl was gone. 'Violet is feeding me your special mixture,' she said. The small effort had exhausted her and she drifted off to sleep.

26

You should have been dead

MORGAN LOOKED CLOSELY at the miracle sitting on the other side of his cluttered desk. Eighteen months earlier, on a morning round that started half an hour before the usual time, he had found an emaciated, dehydrated young man in a side ward, lying in a pool of excrement. Oblivious to his surroundings, he stared into space out of sunken eyes.

Morgan had felt for the young man's pulse and looked into his pupils to confirm that he was dead, then noted a faint flicker of a pulse. He ran intravenous fluid into the collapsed veins and later, while the nurses were changing the soiled sheets, he wrote up his treatment without much conviction, cynically wondering why he'd arrived half an hour early. He walked out of the room to find the young man's brother standing in the passage.

'Do something for this boy, please, Morgan,' the man had begged him.

'I am only a doctor,' he told him, 'not a miracle worker.' The man confronting Morgan wasn't taking no for an answer.

'That boy,' said the man, 'is my favorite brother. He has completed one year at university.'

Well, thought Morgan, that is going to be his only year. That morning Morgan found himself in the depths of gloom. He had spent a week of sleepless nights trying to save a man with AIDS-related pneumonia.

'I can pay,' he heard the man say. 'Do whatever it takes. I know you can, Morgan.'

The heavy-featured face in front of him exuded confidence. Damn, thought Morgan, your brother is a corpse. He is only alive because of a stroke of luck.

'Do you know what you are saying?' Morgan had asked. 'Do you know what those drugs cost?'

A nurse opened the door and let the smell into the passage. The man appeared not to notice. 'You know I'm a businessman,' he replied. 'I will pay whatever it costs.'

'Very well,' Morgan had said. 'Even so, I can't guarantee anything. Personally, I think he is too far gone.'

The man had grabbed Morgan by the arm. 'I trust you, Morgan,' he said.

'I think you're going to waste your money,' Morgan told him. 'Before we even think of giving him AIDS drugs, I will have to get him better.'

'Just try, Morgan,' the man said. 'God will help you.'

I am trying all the time, Morgan thought. And what do I have to show for my efforts? Nothing. As for God, I think he has forgotten about this place.

He rehydrated the boy, treated his diarrhea and opportunistic infections and, when he refused to eat, inserted a tube down his throat and force-fed him. The boy improved and, with his tongue firmly in his cheek, Morgan started him on antiretroviral drugs.

The brother paid diligently and Morgan was astonished. The boy went home and each month on his return visits he looked better. Every time Morgan saw him he was reminded of that morning when he had thought he was looking at a corpse. He remembered his reluctance to insert a drip when he felt the feeble pulse, and his irritation when he realized he was starting yet another hopeless battle.

Eighteen months later a healthy second-year law student sat on the other side of the desk. Morgan looked at the laboratory report in front of him. The boy had made an astonishing recovery.

I should be rejoicing, thought Morgan, but I am not. What about all the others that I am not able to treat? He looked up into the smiling eyes of the youngster. 'You should have been dead,' he told him flatly.

'You saved me.' The boy gave him a wide grin out of a face that bore no resemblance to the one Morgan had first seen in the ward.

'No,' Morgan said. 'Your brother saved you. You owe everything to him.' He wrote out a script and slid it across the table. 'Give my regards to your brother.'

Afterwards, he stood at the window of his office and gazed out over the lawn. Languishing under the trees, as usual, were his ambulant, scrawny scarecrows, whiling away the time, waiting for the inevitable. How many more people like them, he thought—twenty million, thirty million? Who cares?

It was going to make the Holocaust look like a Sunday-school picnic. A slight difference though, he thought. Instead of Nazi camp Kommandants, we have apathetic, smooth talking, ineffectual administrators, wearing suits, ties and Gucci shoes instead of uniforms. Apathy is nothing new, he reminded himself. It has been with us forever.

THE SMELL OVERPOWERED the efforts of the noisy, outdated air conditioners, the ineffectual fans and the aerosol sprays. Everyone in Casualty wore masks. On a trolley, in the middle of the room, lay a man with bandages around both his legs. At the head of the trolley stood the man's friend, a nurse from a bush clinic, and Rebecca.

Two nurses wearing gloves unwound the bandages and gradually released the odor into the stifling atmosphere. Morgan stood next to the open window. He had taken off his mask and was smoking a cigarette. For once, Rebecca didn't object.

As Thomson was inserting a drip, she scolded the man, his friend, as well as the nurse, and relayed the story to Morgan. An intimate little party around a fire ten days before; three motherless friends downing a bottle of brandy or two; a drunken shove and a man in the fire with brandy in his veins, fire in his pants, lead in his feet, and two friends too drunk to be of any use.

'How can anyone get so drunk?' Rebecca wanted to know.

'It's his democratic right,' Morgan told her.

She faced the man's friend, who had inexpertly tied a mask to his face so that it also covered his right eye. He brought up his hand to adjust the mask, but then decided he would rather receive Rebecca's icy stare with only one eye. Rebecca wanted to say something more, but the nurses simultaneously removed the last bandages and the stench became overwhelming.

Morgan threw his cigarette out of the window, put on his mask and inspected the festering burns. 'It will take all afternoon to clear up this mess,' Thomson said, looking at the man's legs.

'Better order some blood too,' Morgan said.

'And,' Morgan heard Rebecca say. 'Why did you only bring him now?'

The nurse from the clinic cringed under her gaze. Timidly she told Rebecca about the lack of transport, but Rebecca wasn't letting her off.

'Ten days!' she said. 'You mean you couldn't find transport for ten days?'

The nurses covered the legs with clean bandages but the smell permeated every corner of the room. Morgan wrote up his orders and treatment and booked theater for the afternoon. Through the open door came a continuous hum, like a beehive.

'We'd better start seeing that lot or we will be here forever,' said Rebecca.

'Okay,' said Thomson, 'send them in.'

'And this man?' Rebecca asked.

'He stays right here where I can see him,' said Morgan.

'And the smell?' asked Rebecca.

'They will just have to get used to it,' Morgan said.

'They are going to complain,' said Rebecca.

'Give them masks,' said Morgan. He grabbed the laboratory report a nurse held out to him. 'Call them in,' he said to Rebecca. 'And keep the drips running.'

The patients came in through the door and sniffed the air like hunting dogs. Amongst nurses running with files, blood specimens and urine samples, a woman was walking on tiptoe towards a cubicle as if scared of adding any more noise.

Morgan burst out laughing. 'You are not disturbing anyone,' he said. 'Relax.' The woman started walking on flat feet and gave him an uncertain smile.

Two hours later a semblance of order returned. The hospital was running on skeleton staff, Rebecca informed Morgan when lunchtime approached. She wore a faint, sardonic smile, and carefully scrutinized Morgan's face, awaiting his response. Morgan tilted his head sideways and waited for her to continue.

Holmes called it a workshop, she told him. It was all about cost effective management, presented by consultants from who knows where. It was going to last three days; everyone was going to get a chance to attend. 'And it's compulsory,' she told him, 'except of course for you.' Morgan was speechless.

'They know trouble when they see it,' she said.

'Fuck!' said Morgan.

Rebecca ignored the curse and told him not to despair. Thomson and Oumar were not attending. 'They are picking up all your bad habits,' she told him. 'And Oumar,' she added, 'disrupted the meeting this morning and took out two of the youngsters and three nurses. According to young Simon, he did it in such a gentlemanly way Holmes had no option but to release them. He couldn't afford a showdown in front of the management consultants.'

'Why don't I know anything about it?'

'It was intentional,' Rebecca told him with a smirk on her face. 'We decided to protect you from yourself, and save Holmes from grievous bodily harm.'

Young Simon came through the door, a smile on his rosy face.

'You see,' said Rebecca. 'Everything has been taken care of.'

'AND TO WHAT do we owe the honor?' Oumar found Smirnoff standing in the passage outside High Care, wearing his habitual tattered coat.

'I have been visiting my friend,' Smirnoff told him. 'The man from the accident.' Oumar realized he was talking about the Wild Man with the head injury. 'He is my best friend,' Smirnoff added helpfully.

'That figures,' said Oumar and sampled the air with his nose. There was no trace of the usual alcoholic vapor. Smirnoff appeared sober, but he was not well. Oumar noted the flaring of his nostrils and the slight wheeze of his breath. Smirnoff suppressed a productive cough.

'You are a sick man,' Oumar said. 'Let me have a look at you.'

Smirnoff backed away from him. 'I did not come for myself,' he said. 'I only came to visit my friend.'

'But,' said Oumar, 'I can see you are not well.'

Smirnoff was adamant, and Oumar remembered how much persuasion it had taken to admit him into TB Ward. He gently took Smirnoff by the arm and led him towards Violet's office. As they neared the door, Smirnoff jerked his arm free and retreated. 'I am not staying here,' he told Oumar with sudden vehemence. He turned around and rapidly walked away.

Oumar stood watching Smirnoff's receding figure and shook his head.

IN THEATER, CONSTANCE faced a small dilemma. She could speed up the procedure and get rid of the smell sooner, or she could rub Holmes' nose in his ill-considered meddling. After brief consideration, she decided on the latter option. After all, everyone would get used to the smell, and it would only add another twenty minutes or so to the procedure. She took a whole pack of the cheap, new scalpel blades that Holmes had forced her to buy.

Morgan was going to complain like hell; he used only one particular brand name. She smiled. She had a whole supply of Morgan's blades hidden away, out of sight. So there was no reason for concern. Why waste good blades on drunks with self-inflicted burns? Tomorrow she would take all the used blades to Holmes and give him tangible evidence of his folly. If you deal with fools, she told herself, you need to treat them like fools.

Her eyes wore no expression above the mask as she handed the scalpel to Morgan. He complained almost immediately. He held the scalpel sideways and cursed, threatening to drag Holmes out of the meeting to try and do the operation himself.

Constance let him into her secret. She told him it was all for a good cause. If Holmes realized how many blades they were using, he might revert to quality stock. Morgan gritted his teeth and hacked away, cursing under his breath.

Constance kept renewing the blades and collected them in a bowl.

Halfway through the operation Morgan straightened his back and asked: 'What on earth is this meeting about?'

Thomson adjusted the drip and looked at the monitor. 'Don't you know? Holmes has been on about this for weeks. Strategic planning. Our vision of the future. What do we want this place to be? Doctors are managers. Didn't you see the memo?'

Morgan swore.

'Your language, please,' Constance reprimanded him.

'There is no language that does justice to idiots,' Morgan said. He continued cutting away dead, burnt skin until the legs looked like those of a skinned animal. Thomson put up another unit of blood. The monitor measured out eighty heartbeats per minute.

'Holmes brought in some nondescript people from somewhere,' said Thomson. 'We are all going to be managers, you will be happy to know. All chiefs and no Indians. Everything hinges on cost effective management.'

'And fuck the patients?'

'Morgan!' said Constance.

'And why are you here, then?' Morgan asked.

'I am a fool like you,' Thomson said. 'Someone has to do the work, you know.'

They applied dressings and bandaged the legs. 'He should be back in theater in about ten days,' Morgan told Constance. 'And if you give me those blades again I will slit your throat!'

'You will need quite a few,' she reminded him. 'Don't find anyone else to operate on now; we need to fumigate this place.'

The meeting was still on. They walked along the back of the hospital. A huge solitary cloud was hanging over the town. From where they stood, they could see the silhouettes around the table in the tearoom. Someone was standing next to a flip chart.

'I pity our poor colleagues,' Morgan said. 'Why don't they just walk out?'

'Some of us have wives and children to feed,' said Thomson.

'Where do these people come from?' Morgan asked.

'God knows where Holmes found this lot.' He took a cigarette from Morgan's shirt pocket, and Morgan handed him the matches.

'Doesn't matter,' said Morgan. 'They are all exactly the same. They put structures in place; they measure outputs; they don't talk. They network; they create interfaces; they are committed to cost effective management. They see the big picture and they have as much compassion as a dead fish.'

'They manage, Morgan, they manage. It's the new buzzword.'

'They couldn't manage a whorehouse on a Saturday night!'

'Now that,' said Thomson, 'is a serious allegation.'

'Why,' asked Morgan, 'is everyone so hell-bent on making rules and protocols and more rules to explain other rules? Can't they just use their common sense and act like human beings?'

'It makes life easier,' said Thomson. 'Not to have to think for yourself. Just follow the rules.'

They found Oumar in the passage, carrying his white coat over his arm. 'The Wild Man is doing well, I see,' he said. Thomson had taken the man off the ventilator that morning and was rewarded by a string of curses as soon as the tube was removed from between the vocal cords.

'His speech center is intact,' he reassured Oumar.

'I don't think he will take a degree in higher mathematics.'

Oumar took the coat, folded it neatly and again hung it over his arm. 'He must have knocked off a lot of brain cells.'

'You should send him to that workshop; he would shine like a star,' Morgan said.

Oumar shuddered. 'I couldn't do that to the poor man, not even to him.'

They were walking back towards Casualty across a square of light that came in through an open side door. In the shadow just beyond it stood Charles the cook, between two food trolleys, wiping the sweat from his brow. He greeted them with his usual exuberance. 'Fat man is making lot of trouble for me, Morgan,' he said. 'Fat man says I cook too much food, far too much!'

'Take a break, Charles,' Morgan reassured him. 'The fat man is talking nonsense for three full days.'

'Fat man is always talking nonsense.' Charles' laughter filled the passage.

'Don't you sometimes pity Holmes?' Thomson asked. 'Poor man is just doing his job.'

Morgan snorted and made no reply.

JUST BEFORE SUNSET Morgan walked across the back lawn. On the veranda sat Mary, in her wheelchair as usual. He slowly climbed the stairs and blinked his eyes, as if he couldn't believe what he was seeing.

She smiled, and he was struck by the translucence of her skin. He noticed her frailty as if he saw it for the first time, and realized she was sitting outside by an effort of will, for the last time. 'Hi,' he said and kept his voice as neutral as possible.

'The cloud,' she said, 'see how beautiful it is.' There was a slightly hoarse quality in her voice. It had lost its music. Morgan looked up at the massive cloud caught in the last rays of the sun and suddenly remembered the feeling of taking off from an almost dark runway, pulling up the nose of the aircraft and flying into the light. I couldn't tell her about that, he thought. Not now. 'It must confuse the high-flying birds,' he said, 'flying up there and coming back to the dark earth.'

'I wish I could be up there,' she said, and he heard a note of finality in her voice.

That's where you belong, Morgan thought, soaring up there, unencumbered by a body and free of pain. Does death finally set one's spirit free?

'Look,' she said. He followed her gaze just in time to see the Eagle Owl flare and land on the top of a tree. 'He is early tonight,' she said. 'Usually he comes later.'

Morgan had a sudden premonition. Even in the poor light, he could make out the piercing eyes of the owl. It was looking straight at them. Mary seemed unaware of the superstition attached to owls. He looked at her face and realized she had no fear of death. Instead, she was embracing it and cutting her ties with the troubled earth.

The owl took off and flew away.

Neither of them spoke. High above them the light drained out of the cloud.

27

Mr. B takes the bait

'A BEERFEST!' Rachel shouted at the critical moment. She pushed the palms of her hands against Mr. B's massive chest.

'What are you talking about, woman?' Mr. B regained his breath.

'You're crushing me!' Rachel complained.

Mr. B shifted his weight and looked at her, 'So?' he enquired.

'If you sponsor a Beerfest, you can simply say the money is for the needy, or for charity or whatever. If you use it for Rastodika, nobody will question you.'

Mr. B stood up and wrapped a towel around his waist. They had been talking about Rastodika earlier in the night. He had told Rachel that he was a businessman, not a charity organization. If it became known that he had paid for a renal transplant, every benevolent organization would be on his doorstep. But he had been dreaming about Rastodika, and remembered the early days of their friendship, before Rastodika went mad and wandered off.

'Where do you get all these ideas from?' he asked. 'And, come to think of it, how do you know about Rastodika in the first place?' Rachel switched on the bed lamp, took the diamond pendant from the bedside table and sat up in bed. Mr. B laughed. 'Why does it concern you so much?' he asked.

'Everyone in this town knows about Rastodika,' she said.

'And Dorcas told me he is very sick.' She lay down again and turned on her side. Mr. B watched the diamond as it settled on her right breast. He sat down on the edge of the bed, rested his chin in his hand and considered his options, trying to calculate the cost. Georgiou could get a discount on just about anything. And he could find other sponsors as well. Even from other towns. It wasn't such a bad idea at all. No one in town would say no to a big party.

'What made you think of a Beerfest?' asked Mr. B.

Rachel laughed. 'People will always find money to buy liquor,' she said. 'Just look at Mr. Chiremba's bar.'

Mr. B was already thinking about a venue. The soccer field, he decided. It will have to be a big, big party. Finally he said: 'Rastodika was my friend after all. I will talk to Morgan and find out what it will cost. And I will talk to Georgiou and the Mayor. I am sure Georgiou can get a discount on large quantities of beer.'

All my lovers arranging a Beerfest, Rachel thought, and laughed.

'What's so funny?' asked Mr. B.

She stood up and put on a gown, then bent down and gave him a kiss on his forehead. 'I can see the whole town getting involved,' she said.

'What time is it?' asked Mr. B.

Rachel sighed, looked across his shoulder and consulted the alarm clock. 'Ten minutes to six,' she said. 'Now, don't tell me you want to run off unnoticed.'

'No,' said Mr B. 'I want to speak to a few people before I go out of town today.'

He ran a bath, aware of her smell that seemed to permeate every corner of the room.

When he had dressed, he found that she had prepared him an ample breakfast. Mr. B sat down at the kitchen table and Rachel sipped her coffee and watched him as he ate. This is what married people do, she thought. Somehow his presence in her kitchen seemed almost as intimate as him being in her bed.

Mr. B looked up. 'One day,' he said, 'you must find yourself a decent man and marry him.' Rachel laughed and wondered why two of her lovers suddenly wanted to marry her off. 'Why do you want to see me married?'

Mr. B drank his coffee in one gulp and put down the cup. 'Because you are a good woman.'

He looked through the window and saw the vendors walking in the street. 'I must go now,' he said.

'Will you tell me what's happening?'

'Of course I will let you know,' he said from the door. 'You talked me into it.'

He walked up the street and returned the greetings of the vendors.

The rain had stopped for the time being, and patches of clear sky showed between the clouds. He went to his office and watched the early morning light as it brightened up the room. Outside in the street the vendors had unpacked their wares and he could hear their loud voices.

He waited until he saw the shopkeepers arrive, then crossed the street and called on Mr. Georgiou. In the time he had spent in his office the heat had returned, and the stifling, humid air hung over the town like a blanket. Mr. Georgiou was sitting behind his table in his shirtsleeves. The fan rotating below the ceiling was unable to evaporate the beads of sweat on his bald head. He greeted Mr. B with excessive politeness, invited him to sit down and called for his secretary to bring two cups of tea.

'A Beerfest?' he said incredulously when Mr. B explained the reason for his visit.

'I want the best possible price,' Mr. B continued.

'Of course,' said Mr. Georgiou.

'And the money will be for charitable purposes.' Mr. B accepted his cup of tea from the secretary.

Mr. Georgiou mopped the sweat from his brow, shook his head and wondered if Mr. B had gone mad. 'You are not serious?'

'Come on, Georgiou.' Mr. B leaned his thick forearms on the table. 'We have made a lot of money in this town; don't you think it's time we put something back?'

Mr. Georgiou opened his diary and looked up. 'How much beer do you want?' he asked.

MORGAN FOUND MR. B sitting next to Rastodika under the tree. They stopped their conversation, and watched him as he approached across the lawn.

'What is this I hear, Morgan?' Mr. B took his hand and shook it. 'Rastodika tells me you are feeding him terrible food.'

Morgan reflected for a moment on the irony of having Rastodika on a low-protein diet whilst trying his level best to fatten up all his other patients.

'It's for his own good.' Morgan waved his finger at Rastodika. 'And he knows it.'

'Rastodika,' said Mr. B, 'When you get better, I will slaughter a cow for you.'

'Tell this man,' Rastodika said, and pointed at Morgan with his walking stick.

Morgan laughed. 'I will remind Mr. B,' he promised.

Mr. B said goodbye to Rastodika, using his joviality as a smoke screen. 'I will be back soon,' he said. 'And I will tell Morgan to look after you.'

He turned to Morgan. 'May I speak to you for a moment?' As they walked to the car park Mr. B laughed at the antics of the weavers. 'Look at them,' he said. 'They are building a whole town.'

He suddenly became serious and glanced back to where Rastodika was sitting out of earshot. 'So what is this I hear about a kidney transplant?'

Morgan waved at Charles who was standing at the back door of the kitchen to escape the heat. 'Rastodika is a very sick man,' Morgan confirmed.

Mr. B tilted his head. 'And the cost?' he enquired.

'A lot of money. I can't exactly say how much.'

Mr. B. stopped and faced Morgan. 'Could you find out how much, please?'

Morgan looked into Mr. B's face and tried to fathom his mood. 'I can find out,' he said.

Mr. B's huge hand folded around his shoulder and he dragged Morgan closer to him. 'We are going to have a Beerfest,' he announced. 'A huge Beerfest to pay for Rastodika's operation.'

He unlocked the door of his truck and said, 'And you must come and help me shoot that leopard.'

MORGAN WATCHED LAWRENCE'S dark face as he leafed through a file with Thomson peering over his shoulder. Outside, dark clouds gathered. Lawrence looked away from the file for a moment to switch on the reading lamp.

The light accentuated the lines around his firm lips and reflected from the reading glasses perched on his nose. The files containing Holmes' murky dealings lay in a pool of bright light, and the rest of the room receded into the late afternoon darkness. A few drops of rain fell on the roof.

Lawrence turned a page and then stopped triumphantly. 'Here! I told you I sent it. Look, there's even a date.' He tapped on the file with his pencil, as if to underline his words. 'There,' he pointed. 'See for yourself. I always do it; I've been caught before.'

'Bastard!' said Morgan. Thomson audibly exhaled through his nose.

Next to Lawrence's elbow lay another open file exposing Holmes' trail of deception. 'You see, everything is here, quotes, the lot. It has to be finally authorized by him. And it was sent. See here, it was taken to his office on this date.'

They found themselves peering into a devious mind. 'How many times has this happened?' Thomson spoke for the first time in ten minutes.

'Too many times for my liking, and people always blame me.'

'One monitor and one drip counter,' said Morgan. 'We will have to go through the whole bloody lot, then.'

Thomson cursed. 'I was surprised he was so lenient,' he said. Holmes had looked at the shopping list during the budget meeting, and approved it.

'Now,' said Morgan, 'what about that defibrillator?'

Lawrence paged on. 'Here it is.' He stopped. 'Same story, different date. So they couldn't have been lost in a single batch. They are deliberately being shelved.'

'But he blamed you,' Thomson said.

'Yes, he does. Usually people don't query delays because it takes forever anyway. If something doesn't turn up they either think it is still on its way or it has been blocked at Head Office. Or, he tells them he never received anything from me. By the time they realize there is a problem, the deadline for orders has already expired.'

'He's not going to get away with this,' Thomson said. He turned to Morgan. 'I will handle this my way.'

Morgan smiled grudgingly. 'I will give democracy a chance,' he said. 'How are you going to do it?'

Thomson switched on the photocopier in the corner of the room. 'Give me those papers,' he said. 'I will pick the right moment.'

Morgan returned to his office. The memo he had stuck on the door had been ripped off forcibly. Shreds of paper hung from the push pins.

IN THE LATE afternoon the rain returned, softly at first, then it started pelting down relentlessly until the streets were flooded. Morgan made his way to the mall and got soaked in the thirty seconds it took him to run from his truck to the shelter of the verandas that were crowded by vendors.

He made his way past wooden carvings standing on the ground, side-stepping dresses that hung on coat hangers suspended from the roof, and stopped at a table with second-hand books but found nothing to read.

Next to the table stood a girl selling scratch cards. 'Buy one?' she mocked him.

He took a coin out of his pocket, bought one and scratched off the surface to see the numbers. 'You're stealing my money.'

He bought another one, and won enough to buy another ticket, and then lost again. 'You're an evil woman,' he told her.

'Another ticket?' The girl laughed and her dark eyes danced with mirth. For a moment Morgan studied her perfect teeth. 'You're selling me all your bad tickets today,' he said.

'Just one more, Morgan,' she said. 'Then you win the big prize, and we go traveling together.'

'You are a wonderful saleswoman.' He played again and lost. 'It was not meant to be,' he declared.

'Pity,' laughed the girl. He returned her smile and waved at her as he walked away. She waved back with enthusiasm. 'Come again soon.' Her voice rose above the din of the market.

Father Michael came out of the bakery carrying a freshly

baked loaf of bread and a newspaper under his arm.

Morgan spread his arms and blocked his way. 'You can't live on bread alone, Father,' he said.

The priest laughed. 'It's about the only thing I can afford.'

They stood out of the way next to a pillar, and watched the water spilling over the eaves. The cool air coming from the square blew into their faces.

On the veranda on the other side of the courtyard, a woman was boiling mealies in a pot. She had managed to rescue her fire in a drum and her customers were standing around it, peeling the leaves off the cobs. She offered them salt from a small tin. Big drops of rain were pelting the square and a man using a plastic bag as an umbrella ran across it.

'I wonder why he bothers with the plastic bag,' said Father Michael.

'It's called faith, Father.'

The priest ignored the comment.

'So, we are having a Beerfest,' said Morgan.

Father Michael's face retained its expression. 'So I hear,' he said and watched the rain flooding the square.

'How did that come about?' Morgan asked.

Father Michael smiled. 'Who can tell?' he said. 'God works in mysterious ways.'

The vendors started packing away their wares and people began heading home. Father Michael raised his voice to match the renewed onslaught of the rain. 'You shouldn't ask too many questions, Morgan.'

He moved around a man pushing a wheelbarrow and they got separated in the throng of people. 'Thank you, Father!' Morgan shouted above the noise. The priest waved at him before he was swallowed in the crowd.

Morgan stopped at the woman with the mealies and bought two. She had silky black skin and eyes that registered everything around her. She smiled at him and displayed a wide gap between her front teeth. Her hand delved into a pocket of her apron and she rapidly counted his change. 'Next time, you ask for chimanga!' she shouted above the noise of the rain hitting the roof. 'That is what we call mealies in our language.'

'SHALL I GIVE her morphine?' the night sister was asking. Morgan pressed the telephone tightly against his ear.

'Is she in pain?' he asked.

'Yes,' said the night sister.

'Then give it,' Morgan said. 'I have written it on her chart.'

The night sister sounded apologetic. 'I just wanted to make sure,' she said.

He drove to the hospital. It drizzled just enough to force him to use his windscreen wipers. Mary seemed dwarfed by the size of the bed. He stood next to her and looked down at her sleeping face. 'At least she's free of pain,' whispered the night sister.

Mary opened her eyes and looked straight at Morgan. 'Don't look so worried,' she said, and drifted back to sleep.

28

A smile to remember

IN THE SHANTYTOWN next to the river, people stirred in their uneasy sleep, slowly becoming aware of a dog's incessant barking. Amongst the branches of a partly submerged tree lay the bloated body of Smirnoff, gently rocking to and fro in the current, guarded by his dog sitting on the bank.

The Kenyan was trapped in a never-ending sugar cane field. In his dream he heard his wife's voice calling him. He couldn't see her; his vision was obscured by dense cane leaves. She poked him in the ribs. 'Wake up!' she shouted. The Kenyan sat up in bed.

'It's still dark,' he said, bewildered. She turned the alarm clock towards him, jumped out of the bed, and parted the curtains. It was drizzling. Inside the bedroom the air was thick and humid.

'I was in the cane fields,' he remembered.

'What are you talking about, man?' She was getting dressed. 'You'd better hurry!'

DORCAS WOKE UP to the sound of breaking glass. In the living room, her husband's portrait lay in a shattered frame. The dampness seeped out of the walls. She picked up the portrait and carefully laid it down on the table.

'Are you trying to tell me something?' she asked and gently cleaned the glass fragments from the photograph that was fading at the edges. 'I will buy you a nice new frame,' she told him.

She walked back to the bedroom, opened a cupboard and found his suit. She held the sleeve against her face and inhaled the faint smell of soap, deodorant and tobacco, closing her eyes as she remembered his ready smile.

Rebecca left home at six thirty and walked along the dirt road past small dilapidated houses with smoke coming from their chimneys. Through open doors drifted the smell of coffee and spices. Pots rattled, mothers woke up their children, roosters cried belatedly. Dogs barked tentatively at her as she avoided puddles in the road.

She followed a footpath amongst tall trees and heard the sound of flapping wings directly above her head. Looking up, past the brim of her umbrella, she saw a black crow landing on a tree-top. Its beak opened and it gave a hoarse, taunting cry. For a moment it balanced precariously on a thin branch, then spread its wings and flew away.

Oumar recognized the Constable behind the wheel of the police Land-Rover and waved at him. Only then did he see the ambulance driving right behind it.

He found Rebecca standing in front of Casualty. 'I'm looking for Thomson,' she told him. A small boy had been bitten by a snake, and a man had run ten kilometers for help. The Constable had come to fetch the ambulance.

'I saw the Constable,' said Oumar.

'It's going to be a bad day,' said Rebecca. 'There's a curse on this town, and it's not going to lift soon.'

'Every day is a bad day.' Oumar felt the dampness settling in his joints. 'What makes this one so special?'

Rebecca looked at the ominous clouds swirling just above their heads. 'It's written in the sky,' she said.

MARY WAS LYING on her side. The drip had been reinserted. She said something incomprehensible in her sleep. Suddenly she turned on her back, opened her eyes and saw Morgan next to the bed. Holding up her left hand attached to the drip she said, 'I don't need this.' Her voice was hoarse, barely audible.

She drifted off to sleep again and, with a motion of his hand, Morgan indicated that the drip should be removed. Outside, huge clouds were moving in like ships. A nurse appeared at the door. 'Thomson needs your help,' she said.

Amidst the bedlam in the room off Casualty lay a solitary young boy, his grossly swollen arm resting on a pillow. A drip was attached to his leg. On a trolley was a tray containing a bloodstained scalpel blade, artery forceps and sutures. Decapitated anti-venom ampoules lay between the instruments like spent cartridges. The battered head of a dead snake protruded from a plastic bag on the fridge.

Like a dissipating whirlwind, the chaos receded and order returned to the room.

'Where were you?' Thomson asked. 'I had to do a cut-down by myself.' The boy stirred and bravely suppressed his tears. Rebecca leaned over him and engulfed him in her bosom.

'Damned nearly died, this boy,' Thomson said.

Morgan inspected the arm.

'Fasciotomy,' he said, raising his voice to make himself heard above the noise of the rain on the roof. 'As soon as possible.'

Thomson looked at the blood results. 'He needs red cells and platelets,' he said. 'This venom is a bastard!'

He walked over to the fridge and took the snake out of the fertilizer bag. The blow that killed it had flattened the back of the triangular head and forced open the snake's jaws. The hinged fangs protruded from the mouth—long, thin, curved and lethal. From the table Thomson took a wooden spatula and marked the distance between the fangs with his pen. He dropped the snake into the bag, and went back to the boy.

There were three bite marks.

'A lot of venom for such a small boy,' he said.

Rebecca turned towards them. She stood in front of Thomson with her hands on her hips and took a deep breath. 'Now that it's over, I have to inform you that we have used up all the anti-venom in the hospital.'

'Why didn't you tell us earlier?' Thomson asked incredulously.

'I only found out this morning; there was just enough for this boy.'

Morgan cursed. Thomson was speechless, but not for long. He reached for the phone and called the pharmacist. Morgan strolled to the boy's bedside and felt his pulse. The boy didn't understand a word of English.

'Better?' Morgan asked in the local tongue. The boy silently nodded his head and tried to lift his swollen arm.

Thomson was speaking to the pharmacist: 'What the hell is going on?'

Rebecca covered the boy with a clean sheet, and adjusted the drip.

'What!' shouted Thomson. 'Now, I understand. That's why we are running short of everything else. Do you have such a list? Yes, bring it over here!' Thomson slammed down the phone. 'Fucking imbeciles!' he shouted.

Rebecca admonished him. 'Don't use foul language in front of the child.' Morgan wanted to remind her that the child couldn't speak English, but thought better of it. Swearing is an international language. The boy probably knew a few choice words himself.

Thomson swallowed his anger and relayed the conversation. In the interests of rational practice, Holmes and Thunderbird, without consulting any other doctor, had taken it upon themselves to reduce the stock levels in the pharmacy, beginning with infrequently used items, and then generously extended their meddling to include almost every item on the shelves.

'A little knowledge is dangerous,' said Morgan. 'That's why we ran out of quinine last week.'

When the pharmacist arrived he was indignant. He took a glance at the boy and shuddered at the thought of a near disaster. 'Everyone is yelling at me!' he told Morgan.

'We're on your side,' Morgan said amiably.

Thomson looked at the list. 'Those are the items that are either out of stock already or just about to run out,' said the pharmacist. Thomson suppressed a curse and handed the list to Morgan.

The pharmacist said, 'They are in the pharmacy almost every day, those two.'

Morgan listened to the conversation with half an ear as he scrutinized the list. Soon even the most basic antibiotics were going to be out of stock.

'Antibiotics,' the pharmacist was saying. 'I showed him the consumption over two years and he said prescription patterns will have to change. Imagine, with all the pneumonias we're treating.'

JUST BEFORE LUNCH Thomson and Morgan found Holmes on the veranda of the office block.

He objected to Thomson's abrasive language and his impertinence. 'You don't understand,' Thomson told him. 'I am not asking your permission; I am telling you.'

The garden was obscured by a curtain of rain. A gust of wind blew onto the veranda. Small droplets of spray settled on Holmes' glasses, partially darkening his lifeless eyes. Next to Thomson stood Morgan, hands folded in front of his chest, observing Holmes with a detached, clinical air, like an entomologist classifying a specimen. His blue eyes showed no expression at all.

Holmes stirred. He inhaled the humid air and said, 'We will have to discuss this.'

Thomson held up the list. 'There will be no discussion. I have already told the pharmacist to order all of this. And I am sending Maxwell to fetch it.'

Morgan casually took a step closer. Holmes clenched his jaws, relaxed them, parted his lips, then thought better of it and shut his mouth tightly.

'You were going to say?' Morgan's voice was soft with an ominous edge to it.

Holmes rapidly changed his tack. 'There must be some problem at the pharmacy,' he suggested helpfully. 'There has been a delay with the placing of orders.' His voice was suddenly reasonable.

Morgan unfolded his arms and dropped them to his sides. Holmes stirred almost imperceptibly. They left him standing on the veranda.

'Son of a bitch,' Thomson said when they reached the passage.

REBECCA AND THE Kenyan were sharing a laugh. The Kenyan had sent a man into a cubicle and told him to undress. He found the man stark naked, sitting on the bed.

'What's your complaint?' the Kenyan asked.

'I have come to visit my brother,' the man informed him.

Rebecca was cleaning her glasses and regaining her breath. A man came through the door, using an ancient golf club as a crutch. She wordlessly waved him into a cubicle.

They operated on the little boy in the afternoon. Morgan

started the cut on the outside of the upper arm, S-shaped, exposing all the muscle compartments right down across the wrist into the palm of the hand. The knife went through blackened subcutaneous tissue then muscle sheaths. Muscle bellies jumped into view and turned pink as he watched.

He waited a while. All the muscles were still alive and twitching.

'Good!' said Thomson from the top of the table.

The arm looked like a burst sausage.

In High Care, Morgan watched as the little boy woke up, then drifted off to sleep again. His little feet, coarse from barefoot walking, looked out of place against the white linen. From a cupboard next to the window, the nurse took a bottle of emulsifying ointment and started rubbing it into the boy's feet.

'You are not doing him a favor,' said Morgan. 'He can't afford to have soft feet.'

The nurse pretended not to hear him and carefully rubbed the cream into the little cracked soles.

'The bush children are the most beautiful children in the world,' she said.

MARY WAS ASLEEP. The drip had been removed and Violet told him she had been sleeping for most of the afternoon. She breathed mechanically, as if breathing had become a burden to her. All the joy of life seemed to have left her.

Like a dying butterfly, thought Morgan. She has had far too short a life. He gently touched her face but she didn't stir. The rain had relented for a while and bright sunlight shone through a gap in the clouds.

On the lawn Rastodika sat in an old office chair that he had taken from somewhere. He sat in a shaft of light with his eyes closed and his hands folded in his lap. In the street, children were running on the pavement, catching flying ants with wings that shone like silver in the sun.

At eleven o'clock the night sister called Morgan at home. Mary was dying.

He found her lying very still, with closed eyes, and noted that the night sister had again put up a drip. Mary opened her eyes and saw him sitting next to her. A wasted arm appeared from underneath the sheet and reached out towards him. A shadow of her smile crept back onto her face and reassured him.

It's only death, she appeared to be saying. It's normal. Don't worry about it. It happens to everyone some time or other. Mary spoke softly and he hardly recognized her voice. 'Remember about the mountain,' he heard.

'I will come and fetch you,' he said, his voice hoarse with emotion.

Mary turned her head towards the locker. 'The books,' she said, almost inaudibly, 'You must take them back.'

Morgan squeezed her hand and said, 'Don't worry about them.'

He noticed her uneven breathing. The night sister wanted to draw the curtain around the bed but Mary shook her head. 'Don't!' she said, and the effort seemed to exhaust her. Morgan briefly cast his eye around the ward. All the women were in their beds and the room was completely silent.

He heard Mary catch her breath sharply. Her pulse wavered, slowed down and stopped. Morgan looked at her face. It still bore the trace of a smile.

The phone in the duty room tore open the silence with its harsh ring. The Kenyan wanted Morgan to operate on a man with an acute abdomen.

He arrived back at Female Ward at three o'clock. Mary's bed was empty and neatly made with clean white linen.

'She's gone,' the night sister said, not knowing what else to say.

Everyone was awake. Morgan looked at the quiet faces and wondered what they were thinking.

Janet said something in the local tongue. The night sister suppressed a smile.

'What was that?' asked Morgan.

'She says, Mary has left her smile behind and they want to keep it here.' A smile crept back onto the sister's face and spread wordlessly around the room.

29

Funeral in the rain

IT WAS A very pretty village. Jacaranda trees grew next to the streets. Small houses perched on rolling hillsides.

Morgan followed the directions written on a piece of paper. He stopped next to a church that was a simple oblong building with a cross on one side and a small tower with a bell on the other. He walked up the hill and found the house, surrounded by frangipani above steps that led up from the street.

So this is where she grew up, he thought, in this beautiful place. Her presence seemed to linger in the smell of the frangipani. He hesitated before he knocked on the door to pay his respects to her mother whom he found lying on a blanket spread on the floor, next to the coffin of her daughter, surrounded by mourners. There was no sign of Mary's young child.

She was glad Mary's ordeal was over, the mother told Morgan. It was a pity she couldn't be with her daughter near the end, but she herself was not well. The uncle had paid for a coffin. Morgan studied the features of the old woman and found himself looking at an older version of Mary. She had the same hand movements when she talked, the same eyes.

He stayed for dinner but not for the all-night wake. Instead, he spent an uneasy night in a shabby hotel with a creaky ceiling fan that inexplicably stopped after midnight.

The burial started at five o'clock in the morning with a viewing of the body. Morgan did not attend because he wanted to remember Mary the way he had known her.

He sat at the back of the church and listened to the singing, marveling at the way some people can sing in different voices and stay perfectly in tune. Next to the coffin stood some of the nurses wearing their capes. They held candles in their hands. He saw the smoke from the candles and the reflection of the early morning sun on the window panes, and wondered when last Mary had been in the very same church.

She must have been there often, he decided, since she had grown up there. He understood only snatches of the service because it was all in the local tongue, of which he only had a basic grasp. Towards the end of the service, the sun was suddenly subdued by clouds rolling in over the hills. A fresh downpour started.

They buried her in a cemetery surrounded by jacaranda trees at the bottom of a rolling hillside, walking past puddles of water in which fallen purple flowers floated. The bearers skidded in the mud around the graveside. An old man carrying a Bible under his arm led the congregation in song. He sang so enthusiastically and opened his mouth so wide that Morgan feared he might unhinge his jaw.

The rain did nothing to dampen the singing and it also did not subdue the preacher conducting the sermon. The undertaker stood next to him without an umbrella, seemingly oblivious to the rain that soaked his suit.

Mary would have smiled if she could have seen this, thought Morgan. How many rituals do we have in life? he thought. Birth, christening, confirmation, marriage and burial. All conducted according to tradition, and most of us do not have much of a choice.

But, Morgan told Mary in his mind, these people loved you and still love you and this is all they can do for you now. All I can do is to be here to remember you—and I don't think you are in that coffin anyway.

The coffin was lowered and soon he could hear the damp soil landing on it. Later the bearers compacted the soil and added more. Then they placed a simple shade-cloth covering over the grave and attached a metal plate with her name, date of birth and date of death.

On chairs next to the grave sat the elderly mother and Mary's six-year-old daughter who cried intermittently. Morgan looked up as another funeral procession came past. As he looked around he tried to count the fresh new graves, but there were too many.

This is a fitting resting place for her, he decided; except she wasn't there.

The congregation sang one last song. Goodbye, they sang, and slowly waved their hands to the words. Goodbye.

HE DROVE HOME immediately after the service. It took him most of the day, traveling in the rain.

When he arrived home he stood in his silent living room. The humidity depressed him. He threw his camping gear in the back of his truck, drove into the bush, camped next to a small lake and listened to the sound of hundreds of frogs.

The rain had stopped and through the swirling clouds, a half moon shone. He took dry wood out of a plastic bag he kept in the back of his truck and cooked a meal. A soft drizzle started again. He sat next to the embers of the fire and listened to the sound of raindrops falling into it.

The rain fell harder and put out the fire. He lay in his tent, listened to the rain and finally fell asleep. He woke up at daybreak and went for a walk underneath trees with blackened, water-soaked stems.

PART III

30

A food shortage

'SO IT HAS to be paid for?'
Oumar's good mood rapidly evaporated. All his patients were sicker than the day before, the weather depressed him, and his dietary instructions had not been carried out—or so he had thought until a junior nurse told him not to accuse her of things beyond her control.

Violet looked up from her desk. 'Or motivated for,' she replied. 'Those are our leader's instructions.'

'And the food?'

'That is another matter. Didn't you hear Morgan curse? He wants to murder Holmes, and this morning I'm not going to stop him.'

Oumar had observed the meager helpings of porridge, and the absence of high-protein diets. The patients had accepted the situation uncomplainingly like they accepted all their other misfortunes.

Is there any limit to the amount of punishment these people can endure? he wondered.

'Where is Morgan?' he asked wearily.

Morgan was at the pharmacy, holding four tins of protein food. The pharmacist was writing a receipt.

'You can motivate for it, of course,' explained the pharmacist.

'He said each case should be motivated for.'

'Do you know how many patients I have?' Morgan asked. 'It is simpler just to pay.'

He held the tins in front of the pharmacist's nose.

'Give me that receipt. I'm going to ram it down Holmes' throat!'

'No you're not,' said Oumar. 'We are first going to get all the facts.'

The pharmacist handed the receipt to Morgan. 'You are going to bankrupt yourself, Morgan,' he said. 'It's cheaper to write motivations.'

'Is there,' Oumar enquired from the pharmacist, 'anything in writing about this?'

The pharmacist squirmed, berating himself for not insisting on a written instruction. Holmes had come into the pharmacy late on Friday afternoon and told him to clamp down on protein powder.

'Relax,' said Morgan. 'We are not accusing you. You must be careful of that man. Make him put everything in writing.'

'I think someone must speak to that man,' said the pharmacist. 'He is interfering in things he knows nothing about.'

'My sentiments exactly!' Morgan pocketed the receipt.

CHARLES THE COOK was in a sullen mood. The kitchen was filthy. Stacks of unwashed plates stood next to the washbasin. One of his assistants was on sick leave; Holmes had retrenched the other one.

'I'm surprised we haven't had a salmonella outbreak yet,' said Oumar, surveying the scene.

'My friend tell me I must come work in hotel. Nice work, nice place. No of this nonsense,' Charles said in his West African accent.

'That's all we need,' said Morgan.

'This morning no omelets, no yoghurt, no even bread for your ward, nothing!'

Just then, the Kenyan arrived on his way to the kitchen. 'Don't bother,' said Morgan.

ROSE WAS WEARING a thin, low-cut dress and had put on a touch of make-up. Holmes was at the Regional Superintendent's office, she informed them cheerfully, and so was Thunderbird. Morgan glanced again at her dress. She is like a flower that only blossoms in Holmes' absence, he thought.

The Kenyan wanted to turn back. 'No,' said Morgan. 'Let's phone the bastard from his own phone. It is the only direct line left in this place.'

'Tea?' asked Rose. She offered with such good humor, neither could refuse.

Morgan handed the phone to Oumar. 'Let's try constructive engagement first,' he said. Oumar dialed the number, and had to pass the scrutiny of the Regional Superintendent's secretary. 'Yes it is urgent,' they heard Oumar say.

It took a while to get through to Holmes.

Morgan noticed a framed photograph on the desk: the inevitable family portrait. It showed a much younger Holmes with almost all his hair and only a slight hint of impending baldness. He was stocky but not fat, with just a hint of an advancing double chin.

His wife was smiling at the camera and two boys in school uniforms were standing in front of their parents. Somehow Morgan couldn't imagine Holmes as a young man. The two boys came as a complete surprise. He definitely couldn't imagine Holmes as a caring father.

He had met the wife once, briefly. Expensive clothes, expensive hairdo, expensive perfume; a city woman whose several layers of make-up were unable to mask her unhappiness. The boys must be grown up by now, he thought. There was no current photograph to show their maturing or Holmes' progression into complacent, bloated middle age.

Oumar sat with the receiver against his ear, staring at the desktop. Suddenly Holmes' voice came from the other side of the line. He sounded indignant. Oumar kept his voice even. From where he sat, Morgan could hear Holmes' voice faintly. The receiver gave it a metallic quality. Oumar said: 'But it is not even near the minimum required calories.'

Holmes' voice came back, louder this time. Morgan made out something about the budget. Rose put the tea tray on the table. Oumar gave her a faint smile and pressed the receiver closer to his ear.

'But it is completely unacceptable.' Oumar's shoulder muscles tightened.

There was a curt reply and the sound of a receiver being slammed down on the other end.

'And?' asked Morgan.

'Rationalization,' Oumar answered with a perplexed look on his face. 'Actually, I think he told me to piss off and mind my own business.'

'One can call an atrocity by any name,' said Morgan. 'But it remains an atrocity.' He reached across the table. 'Give me that damned phone!'

Oumar didn't object.

'Let's move up through the ranks.' Morgan dialed the number and asked to speak to the Regional Superintendent himself. The Regional Superintendent recognized his voice immediately. 'Hold on,' he said.

The sound was muffled by the man's hand placed over the mouthpiece, but Morgan could faintly hear him say: 'Get this man off my back, will you?' There was a brief incomprehensible conversation and then Holmes' voice came on the line. 'Yes?'

The voice was gruff, unfriendly. 'I am here with Oumar

and I am arranging a press interview for you,' Morgan said. 'What time would suit you?'

For a moment Holmes was dumbstruck. 'You can't do that,' he said. 'You're totally out of line.'

'You will be at the Regional Office all day, I take it?' Morgan said. 'Put on your make-up; do whatever else you need to do to make a good impression. I will make sure you get decent coverage.' Morgan replaced the receiver.

'You're not serious?' said Oumar.

The Kenyan laughed. 'Holmes will think you are crazy enough to do it.'

'He might be right.' Morgan stood up, drained his cup and placed it in the saucer.

'You must send your boss away more often,' he told Rose and thanked her for the tea.

During the course of the morning he received two messages to phone Holmes at the Regional Superintendent's office. On each occasion he declined. Let him stew in his own lies, he thought.

'We can issue the protein powder again,' the pharmacist told him, looking puzzled. 'I can't understand this sudden change of heart.'

HOLMES CLAIMED IT was all an unfortunate mistake. He blamed the hospital administrator for not placing an order, and denied that he had ever issued an instruction to cut the high-protein diets. There was nothing in writing, he claimed. So why was he blamed?

'I am afraid you overreacted, gentlemen,' he told Thomson and the Kenyan. 'The matter could have been solved amicably. There was no reason to go over my head.'

'You are lying to us,' Thomson said, and Holmes cringed like a thief caught in the act. 'You haven't said anything about the kitchen,' Thomson persisted.

'That matter is receiving attention.'

You can be glad Morgan is not here, Thomson thought. The Kenyan had persuaded Morgan not to attend the meeting for fear that he would cause too much havoc. Oumar was too disgusted even to talk to Holmes. 'I am taking a break from the meeting,' he told them. 'I can only listen to so many lies in one day.'

'We are a team, gentlemen. In my position I cannot possibly know about every problem; I need to be informed,' Holmes tried to soothe them.

Thomson took the photocopied orders from Lawrence's office out of his pocket and placed them in front of Holmes. 'You forgot to authorize these.'

Holmes blamed Lawrence for not sending the orders. 'Look at the dates,' Thomson said, 'in the top right corner.'

Holmes stared in front of him and didn't answer.

'So we can expect it soon?' asked Thomson.

'In his position,' said the Kenyan when they were outside, 'you cannot possibly know that people starve if you don't feed them.'

A truckload of food had arrived early in the morning. In the wards, the high-protein diets appeared again. In Female Ward, Janet was conducting a cheerful conversation with Naledi, who was getting better by the day. She sounded like a cheeky puppy. She wanted to go home, she told Janet, to see her baby. It was the first time she had spoken about the baby.

Mary's bed had a new occupant, but the women still called it Mary's bed. On the windowsill next to it was a single red rose in a jam bottle.

MORGAN RAN ALONG the bush road. Droplets were shining on the grass blades in the late afternoon sun from a shower earlier in the day, and he skirted puddles in the road. After five kilometers he reluctantly turned around and ran back towards town. A prematurely aged, noisy pick-up truck came rattling towards him. The driver flashed a row of perfectly white teeth, and the truck came to an abrupt halt. Morgan stopped and caught his breath.

'Hello, Morgan!' the driver greeted him like a long-lost friend. Morgan vaguely knew the man, but couldn't place him. The man lifted a tarpaulin on the back and produced a watermelon. With an exuberant smile, he handed it to him.

'From my farm, my friend,' he said. 'This is for you!'

Morgan had no choice. He took the proffered gift, thanked the man and watched as he got back in the truck. 'Goodbye!' the man shouted as he drove off.

Morgan stood next to the road and wondered how he was supposed to run with a watermelon tucked under his arm. He shrugged, took a short cut through the bush and started walking towards the stables.

In a clearing stood a kudu, its head held high, suspiciously sniffing the air. Morgan stood completely still and watched its ears moving to and fro. There was no wind to give his presence away. His fingers became numb from holding the watermelon and he hitched it onto his hip. The antelope jumped over a shrub in slow motion and Morgan saw its short white tail as it disappeared into the bush.

He found Jake grooming Sultan; the horse didn't want to stand still.

'He very naughty,' Jake said. 'You come riding?' Morgan held up the watermelon. 'Sultan no eat watermelon,' Jake said. 'He get colic from eating watermelon.'

'Come on, Jake,' said Morgan. 'Let's eat it ourselves, then. Get me a knife.'

Jake released the horse and they sat down in front of his hut. Morgan sliced up the watermelon and they enjoyed the cool, succulent fruit.

'The lady?' enquired Jake, using the local word for woman. It took Morgan a moment to realize he was asking about Mary.

'The lady is dead,' he said numbly.

31

Three weeks of rain

THE RAIN POURED down relentlessly; the river spilled its banks again and forced the squatters to move to higher ground. The streets became flooded. Two men had drowned when they tried to cross the river in a dugout canoe.

The wards filled up with emaciated patients who came from everywhere and from nowhere. They carried their belongings in plastic bags and sat in Casualty staring into space—anemic, breathless, and on the verge of dying.

The Children's Ward overflowed with scrawny babies suffering from diarrhea, malnutrition and pneumonia. Morgan and the Kenyan spent their nights putting drips into tiny veins. The drip lines blocked frequently because there weren't enough nurses to care for them. They got called back again and again to reinsert the drips.

Everyone was irritated due to overwork and lack of sleep. The madman felt claustrophobic because of the rain. He took to walking the streets and would come back drunk from the shebeens, and climb into his bed in his wet clothes.

Malaria cases came in relentlessly. They were admitted into beds; as they got better, they were promoted downwards onto blankets on the floor, and then finally promoted sideways out the door.

'If our leaders would get off their arses and make sure the mosquitoes were properly sprayed, then we wouldn't have all these malaria cases,' said Morgan.

'If Africa's leaders would get off their arses and do

something about poverty and women's rights, then we wouldn't have so many AIDS cases.' Violet adopted Morgan's language.

'What are the chances of that?' asked Morgan. 'They can't even handle the mosquitoes!'

No one really complained about the malaria cases. At least they responded to treatment and got better.

'WE MUST ADDRESS the problem at its source,' Holmes told Thunderbird after his abortive attempts to cut down on food and medicine. 'The real problem is that there are far too many patients.'

Thunderbird, as usual, had no opinion to offer. He waited for Holmes to enlighten him.

'We are going to do a daily ward round,' Holmes informed him. Thunderbird shifted uneasily in his chair, remembering his own abortive ward round in High Care.

'Not with the others,' Holmes seemed to read his concern. 'We'll do it on our own time.'

The nurses met the new initiative with a display of insolence expressed by their body language. Their legs straightened, their backs stiffened, their pupils widened, and they walked like cats about to enter a fight. They restricted their vocabulary to the absolute minimum and said 'yes' and 'no', deliberately omitting 'Doctor'.

Some, like Violet, openly showed their contempt and went out of their way to make fools of them. They stopped at every bed. Holmes paged through the file without looking at the patient and Thunderbird stared skyward, with his hands behind his back.

Holmes' questions again displayed his clinical incompetence. With a red pen, he made comments in the margins of the clinical notes, questioned decisions and the choice of drugs.

The doctors responded with comments of their own.

Holmes wrote: 'What is this man still doing here?' Someone replied: 'He's waiting for a bus.'

He found a very sick man, gasping for breath, and wrote: 'This man is obviously terminal. Why is he receiving all these intravenous drugs?'

Underneath was written: 'Who are you, the terminator?'

'I am being undermined,' he told the Regional Superintendent.

'Doctors,' scoffed the Regional Superintendent, 'know nothing about business management.' His comment made Holmes uncomfortable, occasioning a brief identity crisis. The Superintendent seemed oblivious to the fact that he and Holmes themselves were doctors, or at least had practiced as such at an earlier stage of their lives.

On the day after the debacle with the food, he managed to get hold of Morgan on the phone, and reminded him that they were colleagues after all.

'I regard that as an insult,' Morgan responded. 'My colleagues care about people; you don't deserve to call yourself a doctor.'

Violet complained to Morgan. 'He's just wasting our time,' she told him. 'And he wants to know what Rastodika is doing here.'

'If he touches Rastodika or any other of my patients, I will kill him,' Morgan said.

THE CARNAGE CONTINUED. Three of Morgan's regular patients in Male Ward died within a week. They were taken to the mortuary on a trolley with a canvas cover, pushed by nurses who had become used to this chore.

In the afternoons, the bodies were collected from the mortuary by relatives who gathered around the entrance and sang hymns, unconcerned about the pouring rain. Morgan recognized some of the relatives. Without exception they greeted him respectfully if he happened to walk past. Their blind trust made him feel like a traitor.

'Does anybody know what is going on here?' he demanded from the Kenyan one afternoon when they had unsuccessfully tried to resuscitate a baby who had finally died after a week of futile interventions.

'These are forgotten people,' the Kenyan said, looking down at the withered body of the child. He stripped off his gloves and threw them in the bin. 'And so are we,' he said, and walked into the passage to explain to the mother.

At night, women slept on the floor on blankets in the crowded Children's Ward. They watched over their babies and stood out of the way if someone had to come to put up a drip. Morgan taught them how to care for the drips, since he had grown tired of being woken up at night to come and reinsert them.

The mothers surprised him; they almost always understood what was expected of them and he congratulated them in the mornings when he found the drips still running. The women themselves were undernourished and he ordered protein powder for them.

The only child who had a new lease on life was the boy bitten by the snake. He had had a skin graft and was almost ready to go home.

The artist happily propelled himself along in a wheelchair and made elaborate drawings of animals, lakes and trees. Morgan bought him a set of crayons and taught him to draw people. 'You must draw exactly what you see,' Morgan told him, and gave him a quick drawing lesson every morning.

After two weeks he was presented with a reasonable likeness of himself and Thomson smoking cigarettes.

In the district, the walls of mud huts started collapsing from the rain and fell on small children and old women. Rebecca explained the extremes of age to Morgan and the

Kenyan. 'It's simple really, they can't move fast enough.' Morgan pictured people scrambling to safety, sidestepping crumbling walls and falling roof-plates.

In front of them on the trolley lay a small girl with an abdominal injury, damp soil still in her hair. The girl was looking at them with tearful eyes. Rebecca explained to the mother that her daughter needed to have an operation.

'You do realize that, according to Holmes' policy, we have to send her to the referral hospital?' the Kenyan said.

'Like hell we will!' Morgan picked up the phone and dialed theater.

THE NEXT MORNING, they were standing in High Care, brittle from lack of sleep. An extra bed was pushed in to accommodate a little baby with AIDS and pneumonia.

Holmes, Thunderbird and several men dressed in suits appeared at the door.

'Who the hell are they?' Morgan enquired from the Kenyan, and then recognized the Regional Superintendent, who nodded his head cautiously.

'An inspection tour,' the Kenyan informed Morgan.

'Fucking morons!' said Morgan.

'Shhhhhhh,' said the High Care sister. 'They can hear you.'

'I don't care,' said Morgan.

Holmes was standing in the passage, and Morgan could hear him clearly: 'This is a transit unit,' he informed his guests. 'From here we transfer to the referral hospital. We ventilate patients for forty-eight hours maximum.'

'You're lying again, you creep,' Morgan said loud enough to be heard in the passage.

'This way, gentlemen,' said Holmes, and walked straight down the middle of the passage, past Male and Female Wards without looking left or right.

'Five fat men with unseeing eyes,' Morgan said. 'Nothing good can come from it. They are cooking up some idiotic scheme; just wait and see.'

TESTING THE WATERS, Holmes tried to discharge one of the Kenyan's patients.

'After all, who is in charge of the hospital?' he asked Thunderbird as they walked back to his office at Thunderbird's snail's pace.

The Kenyan took all his patient files, walked into Holmes' office and laid the files on his desk. 'Please take over these patients,' he said calmly. 'I will tell the staff to call you at night.' The Kenyan's face was dark and angry; he declined Holmes' invitation to sit down.

'I was only making a suggestion,' Holmes said lamely.

'If you don't trust my judgment,' said the Kenyan, 'you must please treat all my patients and do all my night calls. Or fire me.' His voice was like an icy wind blowing from a mountaintop. Holmes reverted to writing comments only, but one morning, he misjudged his timing.

Oumar had asked Morgan to see a patient and they returned to the ward. Holmes was standing with his back towards them, complaining to Violet about the numbers of patients. He didn't hear them approach. Holmes was not speaking in his usual creepy, obsequious voice; he was barking at Violet who stood as straight as a ramrod, facing him with blazing eyes.

'Tell your doctors they must get rid of these patients!' Holmes ordered.

Morgan tapped Holmes gently on the shoulder. 'Why don't you just tell me?' he asked.

For a moment Holmes was speechless, then he made a

feeble attempt to assert himself. 'You really can't keep all these patients here, Morgan,' he said, but his voice faltered when he looked into Morgan's eyes.

Morgan pointed at the ward filled with a new crop of scrawny AIDS patients. 'Just look at them!' he shouted.

Holmes took a step backwards and balanced precariously against Violet's trolley.

Morgan placed his index finger under Holmes' chin, like the tip of a dagger pushing upwards. Holmes' head tilted backwards. 'Even if you and your cronies started dishing out AIDS drugs tomorrow, you would still have to explain why you allowed all these people to die,' Morgan hissed.

Holmes started to say something, but he almost lost his balance, leaning backwards against the trolley. Oumar saw Morgan's left hand clench into a fist. He grabbed Morgan's arm. 'Come on, Morgan,' he said. 'Let's go.'

'Move your fat arse out of here!' Morgan told Holmes.

'You can't treat your boss like that,' Oumar said after Holmes had made his retreat.

'He is not anybody's boss,' Morgan said, trembling with anger 'He's…the lowest form of life.'

'Come, come,' Oumar soothed him. 'Let's go and see the patient.'

He led Morgan into Female Ward and showed him a woman with a benign breast lump. She was a picture of health and was just being admitted. She stuck out amongst the AIDS patients like a sore thumb.

'I've booked her on the afternoon list for you,' Oumar said. 'She's on nil per mouth.'

Morgan didn't answer. He looked around Female Ward at each bed in succession until his eyes rested on Mary's bed, now occupied by a seamstress who had lost her job due to ill health and an atypical pneumonia. She had spent ten days hovering between life and death, and he had depleted the hospital's supply of intravenous cotrimoxazole to keep her alive. Holmes had complained about it at the doctors' meeting until Thomson asked him what else they were supposed to use.

Suddenly Morgan recalled Mary's calm eyes and angelic voice. You can be glad you are not here, he thought. Would you have been able to cope with this carnage? Certainly she would have; she could have coped with anything.

'Morgan!' It was Oumar's voice. 'I am talking to you.'

'All right,' said Morgan. 'This afternoon then.'

'Morgan, what is wrong with you?' Oumar asked as they made their way down the passage.

'I wish I could get out of this fucking hellhole,' Morgan replied.

'Won't do the patients a lot of good,' Oumar said.

At the entrance to Children's Ward, Oumar stopped to wave at Yvonne, the girl who never smiled. She was back with pneumonia.

'That girl must think life consists of pain only,' said Morgan.

'My God, but you are morbid this morning!'

Morgan shrugged. 'I'm trying to do something for her,' he said.

He had spoken to Father Michael two days before, and wondered if it would be possible to get someone to pay for antiretroviral drugs for her, just to give her some joy in life.

But he would have to treat the mother as well, otherwise what would happen if the mother died and she was orphaned? The mother worked as a barmaid and didn't even earn enough money to pay for half of the monthly cost of the drugs. Father Michael didn't have an answer.

AFTER THREE WEEKS the rain stopped and suddenly the hospital became quiet; a lull in the storm. Nobody could explain it.

'It should be the other way round,' said Rebecca. 'They should stay at home when it rains and become sick when it is hot and humid.' The ward rounds became manageable and for a while even the sick children seemed to be improving.

Yvonne rewarded Morgan with a faint smile one morning and he repaid her with raucous laughter. 'So you can smile after all,' he said, and gave Violet money to buy her a chocolate.

'Only for her?' Violet asked.

Morgan dug into his pocket and said: 'Buy all of them some sweets.'

Johnson had discovered there was no discernible correllation between his weight and the amount of food he consumed. His painstaking record showed a distinct plateau in spite of the fact that he chewed his food carefully and weighed himself on the same scale.

He reviewed his calculations and extended the target date. It must be some other factor, he told Morgan. Maybe something in the food?

Naledi was visibly putting on weight, and one morning Morgan found her sitting outside with the patients from TB Ward. It both pleased and worried him. Sooner or later I will have to go in and remove that kidney, he thought. That is going to be a hell of a job. I'd better talk to the professor, he decided.

The professor used to visit in old Jenkins' time and was now retired. The problem would be how to get him over here, thought Morgan. There was no way Holmes would pay for his flight to come and operate on a pauper. Janet was sinking slowly. On one of his rounds, when he was talking to Violet about another patient, Morgan saw her sitting on a chair with her arms resting on her bed.

Her face was somber and he detected the tightening of her jaw muscles. She was looking straight ahead, deep in thought. What would she be thinking about? wondered Morgan. She suddenly became aware that he was looking at her and looked up. Her usual smile returned, and she greeted him with feigned cheerfulness; but she knew he had seen her in an unguarded moment.

Morgan marveled at the resilience and resourcefulness of the women. They always put on a brave face, kept up appearances and helped each other. The hospital gowns they were wearing were nothing more than pieces of cloth and yet they always managed to look feminine.

He felt his anger stirring inside him again like a restless animal. 'What we are doing is immoral,' he had told the Kenyan the day before. The Kenyan was sitting outside on a bench under the trees, with his face resting on his hands.

'The drugs are available, we can see that they work and we keep them away from all these people.' Morgan pointed at the patients sitting in the shade.

The Kenyan briefly looked up and then stared at the ground again, but kept quiet. He shifted his weight and folded his arms. 'I am,' he said, 'studying those ants.' He pointed at the ground. 'And I am thinking about the futility of life.'

Morgan liked to listen to the Swahili lilt in the Kenyan's voice as he continued: 'Look at them hurrying along, rushing up and down, collecting food, but what can be more insignificant than a single ant? An individual doesn't count, whether it's an insect or a human.'

'So?' asked Morgan.

'So, if God looks at us, all he sees is a line of ants. Do you think he cares if some of them die?'

'Well,' said Morgan, 'if he doesn't do anything, he is going to see a lot of dead ants shortly.'

'But there are always going to be ants,' said the Kenyan. 'It doesn't matter if some of them die.'

Morgan laughed. 'Pretty ineffectual ants the two of us are, working our butts off and getting nowhere.'

'You and I don't count,' said the Kenyan.

RASTODIKA WAS GETTING restless. Playing the waiting game was foreign to his character.

'He walks the streets at night,' Violet told Morgan. 'I found him next to the river the other night.'

'Let him be,' said Morgan 'I will take him into the bush for a day, that's what he needs.'

On a Saturday morning, Morgan walked into the ward just after daybreak and signed him out. 'Come on,' he said to Rastodika. 'Let's get the hell out of here.' The night sister was astonished. Rastodika was standing next to Morgan and carried his walking stick and canvas bag.

'I take full responsibility,' Morgan said and took Rastodika by his arm.

'Come, Rastodika,' he said. 'Let's go before this woman calls the Constable.'

Morgan drove into the marshlands and the truck skidded in the mud. They drove through deep water that seeped in underneath the doors. Under tall mopani trees they drove into thick, black mud and got stuck. They spent an hour putting grass under the wheels and moved in five-yard increments until they reached firmer ground. Then they drove across the wet shore of a lake and Rastodika said: 'Follow the animal tracks; they know where the firm ground is.'

The truck skidded and once spun around completely and faced the way they had come. They laughed like naughty schoolboys. 'Do that again,' said Rastodika, and Morgan waited for a muddy patch and did it again, also managing to get them thoroughly stuck.

'Look at the truck,' Rastodika said when they stopped for lunch. 'You will never get it clean again.'

'Look at yourself,' Morgan said. Their legs were covered with black mud and white clay. 'Let's go for a walk,' said Morgan and took his binoculars.

They walked along the shore and stalked a large flock of storks, which flew up when they came near. The storks circled above them on outstretched wings, flapping them only now and again, ascending in a thermal like a slow whirlpool, their shadows moving over the ground.

Morgan and Rastodika stood still and watched the huge birds soaring like gliders. The storks floated on motionless wings, which sliced through the air with an audible 'swoosh'.

'You must get me out of that place, Morgan,' Rastodika said.

Morgan didn't answer. He kept looking at the storks and committed the moment to memory.

'I HAD FORGOTTEN all about them,' Violet said guiltily. From the locker underneath her desk she took three books and a small pair of binoculars.

Morgan absent-mindedly paged through *The Little Prince*. Two faint pencil lines drew his attention, both drawn in the margin of the same page. The Little Prince was addressing the roses: *'You are like my fox when I first met him. He was only a fox like a hundred thousand other foxes. But I have made him my friend, and now he is unique in all the world.'*

Further down the page was the simple secret of the fox. *'It is only with the heart that one can see rightly; what is essential is invisible to the eye.'*

In the aviation textbook, he found the photographs of the owls and the sketch of the kite's wings. In the middle of the book lay the fragile rose, carefully preserved.

32

A kidney for Rastodika

THE MADMAN WORE a shield over his left eye. On his forehead and cheeks were long, linear cuts, sustained whilst flying through the central windowpane of Mr. Chiremba's bar.

The cut ends of the sutures stood away from his face and with the shield on his eye, he looked like a whiskered pirate. Bright red, mercurochrome-painted abrasions on his elbows and shoulders indicated his abrupt acquaintance with the rough pavement outside the bar.

The madman was as tight-lipped as ever, but everyone knew the story even before the Constable dumped him at Casualty. 'He must have been mad,' the Matron said to Morgan as she cornered him in the passage between the wards. Morgan pointed out to her that madness was the reason for his admission. She pretended not to hear.

He leaned his back against the wall and allowed her the pleasure of telling him the story already told to him by the night nurse, the Constable and the pharmacist.

The madman had snuck away from the hospital and gone to the bar.

'He should not have been drinking,' the Matron was saying. 'Not in his state.' After a few beers he had started a fight with the biggest contractor in town.

'Have you ever seen this man?' the Matron was asking.

Morgan nodded yes. He knew the man, who was built like a tank. Six feet tall and six feet wide, all muscle, no fat.

Maybe I should change the madman's medication after all, he thought. He had displayed a definite lack of judgment. At first the man just brushed him off like a bothersome fly. This had infuriated the madman who felt he deserved more attention.

He used his good hand to knock over the big man's beer. The contractor, without getting up from his chair, took the madman, lifted him above his head, and flung him right across the room through the window, glass flying everywhere. Then he calmly ordered another beer.

'Mr. Chiremba is sitting in my office,' said the Matron. 'He wants to lay a charge against the madman. Drunk-and-disorderly, damage to property, creating a public disturbance and using foul language in public.'

'No chance,' said Morgan. 'The police won't take the case. They know he is mad.'

'So what shall I tell him?' asked the Matron.

'Tell him to put in bigger windows,' he said. 'And keep them open.'

The return of the sun had brought some cheerfulness into the ward. Or maybe it was due to the antics of the madman. Everyone was feeling better.

MR. B HAD paid a visit to Rastodika and told him about the leopard.

'I hope he never finds that leopard,' Morgan said. Rastodika laughed. 'That leopard is going to cause trouble,' he said. 'It needs to be shot.'

He got up and stood in front of the window. 'My relatives are coming tomorrow,' he informed Morgan.

'What kept them so long?'

'They had to discuss it first.'

Okay, Morgan thought. If we can get together a Beerfest,

a willing HIV-negative compatible donor, and be able to keep Rastodika alive for long enough, we have a fighting chance.

'Call me when they arrive,' he said.

Naledi's operation had been arranged. The professor was flying up in two weeks' time. Morgan had arranged it with Mike the pilot, who was flying the professor free of charge. Naledi was going home for a week to see her baby. Morgan wasn't happy about the arrangement, but Naledi was adamant. The nurses had collected money and bought her a suitcase. She was wearing a new dress, made by the other women in the ward. Morgan hardly recognized her.

Her foster mothers were fussing about as if they were preparing for a favorite daughter's wedding. Janet was having difficulty in swallowing her saliva and had lost a lot of weight. She held a handkerchief in her hand, and now and again wiped the corner of her mouth. With one hand she made final adjustments to Naledi's dress.

Naledi carried a bag of food for herself and the baby. Morgan dug into his pocket and gave her some cash. 'Tell her to buy something for the baby,' he said, took her hand and shook it. What do you buy for a baby? he wondered.

Naledi said goodbye. He watched her as she picked up the suitcase and the bag with food and walked down the passage. She was still thin but she walked briskly. At the far end of the passage she turned, put the suitcase down for a moment, and waved at them. The mothers were standing next to him, waving and cheering.

Naledi disappeared through the door. 'I just hope she comes back,' Morgan said to no one in particular.

'ARE YOU MAD?' Thomson held the quote in his hand and marveled at the amount.

'Where will you get the money?'

'A Beerfest,' said Morgan. They were sitting in Morgan's office. The telephone was off the hook as usual, the cord disappearing between books and papers scattered all over the desk.

'It will have to be one hell of a Beerfest,' Thomson said.

'I'm quite confident it will be,' Morgan said.

'And are you arranging it?'

'Not me,' Morgan said. 'It is already being arranged.' He had spoken to an enthusiastic Mr. B who had printed posters and was going to distribute them to every town in a two hundred kilometer radius. 'I have friends who can do these things,' he said, and laughed at the disbelief on Thomson's face. 'This quote is only valid if we can find our own donor,' he added.

'Make sure Rastodika's and the donor's passports are ready,' Thomson said.

'I still have to find the donor,' Morgan said.

'You don't give up easily, do you?' Thomson studied one of the specimens in Morgan's snake collection and said, 'I don't want to disappoint you, but this is a very long shot.'

'I know,' Morgan said, stood up and pulled open the curtain. He looked across the lawn to where the patients from Male Ward were sitting under the trees. 'Do you realize that not one of those people is going to be alive in six months' time?'

'You would do better to use the money to buy antiretroviral drugs for that lot,' Thomson said.

'The thought had crossed my mind,' Morgan said, and shut the curtain again.

There were four of Rastodika's relatives: two nieces, an aunt and a cousin, introduced to Morgan by Rastodika with Violet as an interpreter. One of the nieces withdrew as soon as she heard that she would actually have to lose a kidney. The other had refused an AIDS test, so Morgan was left with the aunt and the cousin.

The aunt was a prim and proper lady of forty. The cousin was a huge jovial man who didn't mind giving his kidney and didn't mind an AIDS test and, yes, he had a passport. Both their tests had turned out to be negative, so Morgan arranged with Mike to fly out fresh blood specimens in the morning.

The laboratory technologist was confident that the auditor wouldn't know what HLA-typing was and they were within their budget anyway, thanks to old Jenkins who taught his doctors to rely mostly on clinical judgment and not burden the laboratory with unnecessary investigations.

The posters for the Beerfest were put up and Morgan and Thomson kept quiet about the real purpose of the occasion.

'THE SOCCER FIELD,' the Mayor was saying to Rachel. 'Just imagine. Mr. B would settle for nothing less.'

Rachel sympathized with him, and the Mayor relaxed somewhat. They were sitting in her living room. The Mayor had parked his car several streets away, and had made sure he entered her house unseen. As always, he didn't have much time. In one-and-a-half hours' time he had to attend a ceremony at the school together with his wife. He wasn't looking forward to it. I have a bit more than an hour, he told himself. I will just stop by for a cup of coffee and be on my way.

'I had to reschedule a soccer match,' he said. 'Mr. B doesn't realize what an effort that was.'

The Mayor liked talking to Rachel. She always listened patiently as he unburdened himself, and he was more loyal to her than to his frigid, domineering wife.

'You are a fine woman,' he said to her. 'You deserve a decent husband,' he told her in a moment of inspiration.

There must be a conspiracy somewhere, Rachel thought.

All my lovers suddenly want to see me married. She sniggered, kicked off her shoes and walked towards the Mayor with her graceful, feline gait. The late afternoon light outlined her perfect figure through the thin dress. By the time she bent over him and he caught a glimpse of the pendant between her breasts, his resistance had already crumbled. He followed her to the bedroom where he made love to her urgently and hurriedly as always, falling into a deep sleep afterwards from which he woke with a start.

'What's the time?' he asked in a panic.

Rachel stretched her arm and turned the face of the alarm clock towards him. This must be the most consulted alarm clock in town, she thought to herself. It was a quarter to seven. The Mayor flew out of bed and jumped into his clothes.

'I'm already late!' he exclaimed, ran down the passage, realized he hadn't put his socks on, came running back, put on his socks and fastened his tie.

'Tell her you were held up by the Beerfest!' Rachel shouted after him, but he was already running down the street.

33

Naledi's reluctant return

MORGAN WAS LYING in his bath struggling to keep his eyes open. At the entrance to the bathroom lay his shirt, splattered with blood from a leaky transfusion set he had used at some point during the long night.

He had spent hours with a badly injured man whose unstable fracture of the spine added to his other misfortunes. The man was flown out just before dawn. It was a chaotic night with frantic calls to find donors, fruitless calls to the referral hospital, more fruitless calls to an official number that stayed busy and desperate calls to friends and relatives of the patient.

Nobody at the referral hospital could authorize a mercy flight. After midnight, in desperation, Morgan got the man's friends to break into his house to look for a medical insurance card. They ransacked the place and found one, carrying it back to the hospital like a trophy. Morgan thanked providence and arranged to have the man flown to a private hospital.

The plane landed just after four.

At five thirty, with the man ready for transport, strapped into a scoop stretcher, the lock of the ambulance jammed and they couldn't open the door. Morgan swore loudly, clearly and obscenely into the humid morning air and attracted the attention of the night watchman who came to investigate. He was dispatched to find a crowbar so they could break open the door, but there was no crowbar or any other instrument of destruction to be found.

The med-rescue man was philosophical about it. 'Just imagine the lock jamming with us inside,' he said.

The man was taken to the airport on the open back of a pickup truck. Morgan arrived home at half past six. A faint sound woke him from his slumber. Oscar was sitting on the edge of the bath, clawing the water with an outstretched paw.

'One day, my friend, you are going to slip and fall in,' he warned the cat.

He took the soap and started to wash himself. Oscar jumped onto the floor and lay down at the door, eyeing him. Afterwards Morgan threw the clothes into the bath and sprinkled soap powder over them, then fed the cat and stood outside, sipping his coffee.

A man on horseback came riding past. He rode bareback and sat easily, holding the reins lightly in his left hand. I must go and ride Sultan some time, Morgan thought. He looked at his watch. He was already late. He took two eggs out of the fridge, made himself an omelet, and wolfed it down.

A NEW SHEBEEN had opened, run by an unscrupulous shebeen queen who supplied liquor freely and didn't control her customers. The Kenyan was irritated by drunks who got into fights and had to be sutured in the early hours of the morning. He had spoken to the Constable. 'Why don't you put that damned woman away?

The Constable had been his usual unflappable self. 'We are waiting for her to make a mistake,' he said.

'It's that same shebeen again!' he complained to Rebecca, who was attempting to pacify him. 'Aren't shebeens illegal?'

'Strictly speaking, they are,' Rebecca said. 'But they also provide a necessary service.'

'Like whorehouses?'

'No, not like that,' she scolded him. 'They are nice meeting places. Like Dorcas' shebeen.'

The Kenyan frowned, 'Dorcas?'

'Are you new in town?' Rebecca was astonished.

'I'm a married man,' the Kenyan informed her.

Rebecca laughed. 'I will tell Morgan to take you there. Dorcas is a fine woman. She looks after the AIDS orphans.'

'But this other shebeen?' the Kenyan returned to his initial line of questioning. He had just sewn up two customers after an early morning brawl.

'It won't last long; the Constable will pounce on her soon. Wait and see.'

Rebecca was looking past him towards the entrance. The Kenyan turned around, expecting more trouble. At the entrance was a dog. It was looking straight at them.

'That's Smirnoff's dog,' said the Kenyan.

'He's been hanging around for days,' Rebecca said.

'He must be looking for Smirnoff,' said the Kenyan. 'They brought the body here.' He remembered the postmortem: death by drowning. A small container of sedatives was found in a trouser pocket and the toxicology report was pending.

'He's more intelligent than that,' said Rebecca. 'He knows Smirnoff got treated here.'

'So who's feeding the dog?' asked the Kenyan. Rebecca drummed her fingers on the tabletop and pointedly ignored the question.

TWO NURSES WERE tidying up in High Care. A huge bin was standing in the middle of the floor, rapidly filling with empty fluid containers.

Drugs were being replaced and a cleaner was washing the floor. The ventilator tubes were lying in a washbasin and the smell of disinfectant hung in the air. Order was returning after the chaos.

Morgan found his stethoscope hanging over a chair. The desk was tidy again. A piece of paper with telephone number in his handwriting was pinned to the bulletin board. He pocketed the stethoscope and waved at the nurses. 'Have fun,' he said and walked to the ward. Malaria cases were lying all over with their quinine drips. Two brothers lying next to each other were complaining of a ringing in their ears.

'It's the quinine,' he told them. 'It will go away again.'

The madman had been out for the night. 'Where were you?' asked Violet.

He surprised her by answering her question. 'Couldn't sleep!' he said. 'Too much noise.'

'I would have left too, if I had a choice,' said Morgan, wondering how many people had heard him swear about the ambulance door. Naledi wasn't back yet. He couldn't believe it had been a week since she left. 'I wonder if she's going to come back?' he said.

'Don't worry,' said Violet. 'The bus only arrives at twelve.'

'She'd better be here,' he said. 'Her operation is on Thursday.'

Rastodika wasn't in his room. While Violet called him in from outside, Morgan flipped through the blood results. He was dismayed by what he saw. Rastodika was going to need dialysis soon. Morgan turned and was already on his way out when Rastodika came in. He was in good spirits.

Morgan tried unsuccessfully to hide his concern from Rastodika.

'You mustn't worry,' said Rastodika. 'I am well.'

Morgan went through the treatment chart and tried to keep his voice normal. '

What's happening to his diet?' he asked.

'He's getting a low-protein diet,' said Violet.

'They are giving me terrible food,' added Rastodika.

Morgan tilted his head and said, 'I know, but we are trying

to help you.' He went through the ritual of taking blood, throwing his gloves into the bin and picking up the tubes.

Rastodika was watching him, sitting on the bed, squeezing the puncture wound in his arm. 'You are taking a lot of blood.' He said it in a quiet voice, making an impartial observation.

Morgan left the hidden question unanswered. He was suddenly in a hurry.

'I'm taking this to the laboratory,' he said to Violet.

Rastodika got up from the bed.

'You're not going outside,' she said to Rastodika.

Morgan stopped at the door and thought about it. 'It's okay sister, as long as he behaves himself.'

'No smoking,' she said.

Rastodika's usual smile returned briefly to his face and he said nothing. At lunchtime Morgan remembered about Naledi and walked down to the ward. There she was, looking so well he wished the operation weren't necessary. There was a rapid conversation in the local tongue between her and Violet of which he only understood snatches.

'She wants the operation done quickly so she can go back to her baby,' came Violet's translation.

Her blind faith made him feel uneasy. 'The professor is coming on Wednesday,' he said, and managed to smile.

He stopped at the laboratory and made sure there was going to be enough blood.

OUMAR WAS STANDING on the veranda, looking out over the lawn.

Morgan pushed open the door. 'Oumar?' he called. Oumar was observing the scarecrows from Male Ward. They had carried their lunch outside and were sitting under the trees. Around them sat five cats, in a semicircle, waiting for discarded bones and scraps.

'The problem with our patients,' Oumar said without turning around, 'is that they are on the wrong side of the breadline. They are simply not important enough.'

Morgan walked up to Oumar and stood next to him. The voices of the men came floating across the lawn. They were cheerful voices; there were jokes and laughter. It sounded normal, like the conversation of men sitting in a bar having a beer. But they were all dying. Dead men laughing, talking; living dead men.

'Can you imagine this happening in America?' Oumar asked. 'Scarecrows sitting under trees with no prospect of antiretroviral drugs? There would be a public outcry.'

'But we are in Africa,' said Morgan. 'Africans are expendable, don't you know that?'

Oumar nodded in silent agreement.

'What we are witnessing,' Morgan told Oumar, 'is genocide by omission.'

For a while they silently watched the men. 'Someone,' Oumar said, 'must write this down somewhere. Or put it on film. So no one can say they didn't know, or that it didn't happen.' Oumar's anger was like a volcano on the verge of erupting. The only outward signs were the straightness of his back and the occasional movement of his shoulders.

He had lost his favorite patient during the morning, after a long heroic standoff with the virus. 'That girl died this morning.' Oumar's voice was flat.

Morgan knew all about Oumar's girl and her thwarted ambition; her desperate race against time to complete her degree by correspondence. Some might say it was an unreasonable obsession. Seen in a different light, it was a true act of heroism. She had been defying all odds and treating her impending death with contempt.

'What makes people carry on living?' Oumar asked suddenly.

What do you do if you know you are going to die? Morgan asked himself. You can't die before you die. You do what those men on the lawn are doing. Live every day as it comes, just one day. Not tomorrow, not yesterday. Just today. Did they secretly hope for a miracle? They never spoke about it. But they must hope, he thought. And dream. Hopes and dreams keep people alive.

'Hope,' he told Oumar.

NALEDI WOKE UP just after midnight. The ward was quiet.

On the wall opposite, a single bed lamp was burning. In the pool of light lay a girl, staring straight ahead of her. Naledi could see her labored breathing, as if the girl were concentrating on each breath. The breathing was deliberate; the muscles in her neck contracted visibly every time she breathed. She appeared to be measuring each breath, carefully, as if the air in the room was rationed.

The girl was new in the ward; she had come in just before visiting hours and, later when the night sister wanted to switch off the light, she had refused. She spoke haltingly, catching her breath between words. 'Please…leave…it…on.'

The girl, it seemed, was scared she might fall asleep. Later, after the night sister had left, she had removed the oxygen mask. For a moment, Naledi watched the girl who reminded her of a frightened rabbit that had briefly escaped the attention of its hunters.

Everyone else was asleep. The hospital was at peace for once, except for the occasional sound of a nurse's footsteps in the passage. Naledi turned on her side, away from the light. Next to her, Janet was stirring in her sleep. In the dim light she could vaguely make out Janet's face. Her figure was an angular line starting at the base of her neck, straight up to the tip of her shoulder, obliquely down to her wasted hips, slightly up again then descending towards her slightly bent knee, and ending at her feet.

Her mother-away-from-home with her ever-present smile and gentle voice that seemed to become softer and more nasal by the day. Janet was her very first memory of the ward, from the night she came in. Not that she could remember much about it. Just a vague recollection of a gentle voice speaking to her on that first feverish night.

There were even more hazy memories preceding Janet's voice: pompous doctors wearing white coats, standing around her bed, talking to each other, not to her. She remembered one asking 'What else can it be?' and the others nodding their heads in solemn, subservient agreement. Soon after, her mother's indignant voice addressing a helpless nurse: 'How can they discharge my child? They are sending her to her death!'

Then a journey in the back of a truck: pain, dust, an ultramarine night sky with incandescent stars that blurred as the truck negotiated the potholes. That's all she remembered. She didn't even remember if there was someone with her, or to whom the vehicle belonged.

The next memory was of a man swearing at the top of his voice, an unkempt man who had switched on the lamp above her head even though it was broad daylight. She thought he might be an electrician. Naledi smiled to herself. She couldn't understand why an electrician should ask her to have an AIDS test, neither did she care.

Only later did she realize he was her doctor. Gradually the memories became clearer. She hated the food they forced down her throat. Eating and drinking milkshakes became the pivot of her life. Janet seemed to be there with a gentle voice and a smile every time Naledi surfaced from her perpetual slumber. Always talking to her, chiding her gently, congratulating her, soothing her.

Then, like a baby, learning to walk again. Getting out of bed by herself and eating normal food. Picking up weight and feeling better, being able to laugh again. Even in her blurred state of mind, she realized that the faces around her changed continuously. They came and went, managing to look both similar and different, like waves breaking on a beach.

One night she saw a shrouded body being taken away on a trolley with a coarse canvas cover and wondered if she was going to be next. Since then she had become used to the ritual, and watched the other women's carefully rehearsed indifference when the trolley picked up the remains of yet another trusted comrade. The old hands were battle-hardened veterans with melodious voices, gentle smiles and withered bodies. They treated death with the same contempt as soldiers who had received a no-retreat order.

The newcomers learned quickly, if they survived long enough. Naledi had graduated into the sisterhood where everyone shared everyone else's triumphs and woes, cherished good days and endured the bad days that always outnumbered the good ones.

Slowly she returned to her normal self—in contrast to her newly acquired mothers and sisters who, almost without exception, were visibly fading away.

She realized she had become the only one with any chance of escape. No one begrudged her the unforeseen opportunity; instead, she became the symbol of all their dreams. There was a brief period when the topic of a furtive conversation was suddenly changed when she approached; a slick, underhand exchange of money, clandestine dealings with Violet and one day, for undisclosed reasons, her measurements were taken in Violet's office.

And then, a new dress made by the foster mothers under the instruction of the emaciated seamstress who now occupied Mary's bed. After that, a temporary reprieve. Going home to her mother and the baby, riding in the bus like a normal person. On her own again, unsupervised. Remembering the voices of her foster mothers and the smell of that ward that seemed to cling to everything, including her new dress.

The baby had bonded with her mother, not with her. Holding it, she had the feeling she was holding someone else's child. She didn't want to return to the hospital, but her mother was adamant. 'You have come this far; you can't throw it all away. The baby will get used to you; there's a whole life ahead of you.'

And in two days' time, the long-awaited operation would happen. She suppressed a pang of fear. It will just have to be all right, she thought. All this effort can't be wasted.

Janet stirred restlessly, said something incomprehensible in her sleep, and cleared her throat. Naledi had watched Janet's decline, which seemed to accelerate every day. Now she lay in her bed most of the time, with her face sometimes turned towards the window and sometimes towards Naledi.

The previous afternoon Naledi had been sitting next to Janet's bed. She watched as she woke up. Janet didn't answer her greeting. Instead, she lifted a withered arm and extended her hand. Naledi had taken the hand and held it in her own. Its size seemed inconsistent with the thin arm. Almost like a puppy's paws, waiting to grow into them.

But Janet's body was dwindling away from her hand, a working woman's hand with square fingernails and just a trace of the former calluses on her palms. For a moment, Naledi had pressed the hand against her lips. Janet lifted her head and smiled. Then she gently extricated her hand and stroke Naledi's face, exploring its contours.

Naledi drifted back to sleep. Just before daybreak she surfaced briefly from a deep slumber. The curtains around the new girl's bed were drawn and she recognized the subdued voice of the night sister.

When she woke again at six o'clock, the new girl's bed was empty.

34

A well-traveled cat

'MORGAN, LOOK OVER there!' Thomson, the Kenyan and young Simon couldn't contain their mirth.

Coming through the Casualty entrance was the stationmaster, dressed in his sweat-stained uniform, carrying a blue cool-box.

Morgan was astonished: 'It came back! After all this time!'

'A well-traveled cat,' the stationmaster said and placed the box on the floor. The inscriptions in indelible ink looked like graffiti. *Rabies* written on each side, the local veterinarian's name obliterated, and replaced with Morgan's name and address.

It had spent all the time in the Capital. At some point on its journey, it had been soaked with rain and separated from its covering letter, as Rebecca had predicted. A week earlier it was finally noticed by a diligent clerk who returned it to its sender.

'I don't know how this happened,' the stationmaster said. 'It could only have been the rain, but still, someone should have put two and two together.'

'Anything is possible,' said Morgan. He broke the seal of the cool-box and inspected the contents. The cat was still safely in the plastic container of formalin, exactly as he remembered it. Morgan faced the Kenyan and said. 'Now this cat would have baffled Schrodinger.'

The Kenyan held up both of his hands and said: 'No Morgan! Please don't start again!'

The stationmaster was nonplussed. 'Who is Schrodinger?' he asked.

'You don't want to know,' said the Kenyan.

'Schrodinger was a man obsessed by cats in boxes,' Morgan told the stationmaster, who took off his cap and said: 'If this cat comes back again, I might have that same problem.'

'It is the uncertainty that did it for Schrodinger,' Morgan said innocently.

'Morgan!' said the Kenyan.

The stationmaster glanced at his watch. 'If you want to write a letter, I can wait,' he said to Morgan. He was interrupted by the sound of a low-flying aircraft. Morgan's face lit up with sudden inspiration. 'Thank you, but,' he pointed at the ceiling, 'I think from now on, this cat is traveling by air.'

OUMAR TOOK THE laboratory report from Violet and frowned. 'Are you sure?' he asked.

Violet nodded. The man had been in hospital for two weeks and never received visitors. 'So he must have picked it up here,' she said.

Oumar wasn't convinced. 'Someone could have given him something,' he said. 'Or he might have sneaked out and bought food from the café.'

Violet assured him it hadn't been the case. 'He has no money and he has never been well enough to go anywhere.'

'But still,' Oumar wondered aloud, 'you would expect an outbreak.' True, there were a few cases of diarrhea, but that's not unusual in an AIDS ward. This patient was the only one with salmonella. But maybe Violet was right to raise the alarm.

Oumar spoke to the man himself. He was lying in the ward attached to a drip put up by the night sister. He was adamant that he hadn't eaten anything but hospital food from the day he came in. Bad luck, thought Oumar, to have salmonella food poisoning added to your misfortune. 'It will get better,' he told the man. 'We have you on the right treatment.'

In the kitchen he found Charles amongst steaming pots, peeled potatoes and a pyramid of stale bread. He struggled to make himself heard above the combined noise of the extractor fan and an asthmatic air conditioner. Stacks of dirty plates stood in ramshackle pillars next to the washbasin. A cleaner wiped the tabletop with a dirty rag. A plastic bag with leftovers hung from a hook against the wall. Flies landed on the tabletop, took off and circled the leftovers.

Oil vapor coalesced on the ceiling and seeped down the walls. Water dripped from a leaking tap, the business end of a broom was wedged underneath a fridge door to keep it shut and a grimy thermometer on the wall registered thirty-six degrees centigrade. Charles wiped the sweat off his face and waved away the flies.

'This place no good,' he told Oumar. 'No enough people. I tell the fat man and all he say is carry on. Carry on how? No enough people to cook and clean. I think I must talk to my friend again. He say come to hotel; this place no good.'

Oumar told him he was going to send the Health Inspector to come and look at the place. 'Fat man's going to say it's my fault,' Charles protested.

'No,' said Oumar. 'I am going to talk to the fat man myself.'

Holmes was not in his office. He was collecting people at the airport, Rose told Oumar. Her depression had lifted the moment Holmes' car drove out of the gate, and she offered Oumar a cup of tea.

'When will he be back?' Oumar enquired. She was standing with her back to him, pouring tea from a white porcelain teapot—not the usual battered, government-regulation teapots in the doctors' room.

Holmes was going to be away all afternoon, she told him. First a business lunch, then a meeting about rationalization. The lunch, she understood, was not at the hospital. It was at one of the clubs, along with the meeting. They should have the lunch at the hospital, thought Oumar. Then they could all get a dose of salmonella and feel what it's like to become dehydrated in this heat.

'And who's paying for the lunch anyway?' he asked. Rose had no idea. It probably comes off the kitchen budget, he thought wryly.

'Give me a piece of paper will you?' he asked as he was sipping his tea. 'I want to write him a letter.'

'I wish I could communicate with him only by letter,' Rose said. 'Want an envelope? Better that way, otherwise he might think it's just another piece of paper. An envelope makes it look more official.'

Oumar wrote his letter telling Holmes about the salmonella outbreak and the condition of the kitchen. He informed him that he was reporting the matter to the Health Inspector.

'Enjoy your afternoon,' he greeted Rose.

'It feels like a holiday,' she told him.

AT THE AIRPORT Morgan found several important-looking men wearing suits in spite of the heat.

'Who are they?' he asked Mike who was refueling his aircraft.

'Some VIPs,' he said. 'Don't ask me what kind; they are here for a meeting and they are a pain. They arrived late and next time I think I should leave them on the runway.'

Morgan took a second look at the pompous parade. 'They look like the kind of people my boss would entertain,' he said. As he spoke, he saw Holmes' car negotiating the bumpy road.

'What did I tell you?' he told Mike. 'I can recognize them anywhere.'

Holmes greeted his visitors effusively. He saw Mike and Morgan standing next to the aircraft, but paid no attention to them, no nod of recognition. All his charm was reserved for his guests.

Mike snorted. 'It takes all kinds.'

'The world is ruled by faceless men carrying briefcases,' said Morgan.

He told Mike the story of the cat and handed him the cool-box. Mike laughed. 'I'm impressed,' he said. 'Nothing but the best for this cat.' He took the cool-box and carried it into the aircraft.

'Make this its final journey, please,' Morgan said as Mike came back to stand next to him. Mike took a handkerchief and wiped the sweat from his face. 'I will deliver it personally,' he said. 'I know where the office is.'

Morgan stood next to a propeller and ran his hand along the leading edge. There was a chip near the tip. 'Stones,' said Mike. 'There are too many dirt runways in this country.'

'You will remember about the professor?' asked Morgan.

'I will fly the professor any time,' Mike said. 'Rather than that lot; just look at them.' Holmes' passengers were trying to fit themselves and their shiny briefcases into the car.

THE KENYAN FOUND Rachel in front of his office door.

He led her into the room, sat her down in a chair, and opened her file. He wrote down a code number on a piece of paper and said, 'I will be right back.' He shut the office door behind him and Rachel prepared herself for the worst.

She knew from experience that the five minutes' wait felt like eternity. Once every six months, she put herself through this ordeal. The AIDS tests were done in batches once a week. She chose to come to the Kenyan with his fatherly figure and calm, unruffled voice. If it had to be bad news, she wanted it to be broken gently.

She arranged her appointments for Tuesdays, the tests were done on Wednesday and the results were out on Thursday. The real agony lasted from Tuesday until Thursday. The worst part of it was the five minutes it took the Kenyan to retrieve the results. By the time he reentered the office with the small sheet of paper, her pulse was racing uncontrollably. Gone was her self-assurance. She became a lonely, frightened, little girl sitting with her hands clasped in her lap, her shoulders taut, hoping the Kenyan wouldn't notice the pounding of her neck pulses. She felt at his mercy, waiting for him to pronounce her death sentence. And then came the reprieve.

Negative. Not guilty.

The post-test euphoria lasted two days. On the calendar, she marked the date of the next test and then forgot about it until the week before, when she would start worrying again. Were her precautions adequate? Were her lovers faithful to her? How could she expect them to be faithful to her if they were not faithful to their wives? What guarantee was there that they didn't sleep with other women? How many partners did they really have?

And, what if the test turned out to be positive? Would she tell her lovers about it then, or just carry on as always? How long could her luck last? Did she really want to carry on doing this? The last question was always on her mind. She knew exactly why she was doing it. It was all carefully planned, a strategy.

If you have to sell your body, she had told herself a long time ago, you have to sell at the top end of the market. There was no point in doing it like the girls at the station and the truck stops, that is, selling cheap. Her beauty and intelligence were her biggest assets. And she was lucky. Her lovers were all older men, fatherly almost. They took good care of her, almost as if she were their daughter.

Fathers, mentors and lovers: Mr. B, Mr. Georgiou, and the Mayor, with now and again a carefully selected newcomer. Men of the world who shared her body and expanded her vision. An intimate education using a bed as a lecture room. A cushioned, soft-mattressed university with ready information about the business world, its secrets, opportunities, do's and don'ts. Information to be filed but not forgotten. Most importantly, the habits of successful people: diligence, discipline, courage and a certain amount of ruthlessness.

She reflected on these matters in the small hours of the night, with a lover lying next to her in deep post-coital sleep. She wasn't wasting her time. Time was a precious commodity, the most precious commodity of all. And money? Money could buy only so much. It was a necessary evil, but useful to buy what she wanted most. And what she wanted more than anything was a decent education. She had completed her interrupted school career by correspondence. Then two computer courses in the Capital, one more to go.

She had become employable. For three days a week, she initiated Mr. Georgiou's employees into the mysteries of the computer world. And she studied and read every book she could lay her hands on. Soon she was going to have to make a change. Pass the last course, move to the Capital and find a job.

How much longer? Six months or possibly a year. One or maybe two more AIDS tests. And then escape from this trap, forever. With more than mixed feelings, no doubt. But that was the intention right from the beginning: to escape from a trap, to become herself.

The Kenyan entered, shut the door behind him and sat down at his desk. It felt as if her heart was going to jump right out of her chest. For reasons of confidentiality, the result was written on a small piece of paper, folded, with the ends stapled together. For the Kenyan's eyes only, and the laboratory technician's, of course. The verdict to be pronounced verbally and then filed away.

The staples had been removed, she noted, so the Kenyan knew the result already. So why did he not tell her as soon as he walked in through the door? Why did he have to sit down at his desk? Why did he have to inspect the paper again? To double check? To double check what? She clenched her fists, gritted her teeth and held her breath.

Why don't you say something? she wanted to scream. On the wall behind the Kenyan's back, a clock was ticking away. For a moment her eyes focused on the clock, and she appreciated the interminable length of one second.

She looked away from the clock and fixed her eyes on the Kenyan's huge fingers that spread out and straightened the paper on the desk. From far away, she heard his voice. The Kenyan was smiling at her when she looked up. 'It's negative,' he was saying.

Her shoulders slumped visibly and she let out her breath. From inside her rose an urge to laugh out loud. She suppressed it and smiled.

'Congratulations,' said the Kenyan. 'Keep it like that. We don't see too many negatives nowadays.'

Rachel felt like someone who had played Russian roulette and lived to tell the tale.

'What's wrong with the men in this town?' the Kenyan asked. 'Why is a beautiful girl like you still unmarried?'

Rachel observed his innocent face. The Kenyan's arms were resting on the table and he was smiling at her like a benevolent uncle.

Don't you know who I am? she thought. In this town everyone knows everything about everyone else. She thanked him and prepared to leave. 'See you in six months,' she said when she reached the door.

The Kenyan sat back in his chair. 'Stick to one partner,' he echoed the words on the poster in the passage.

Stick to one partner, she thought. You really don't know who I am, do you?

35

The professor pays a visit

MORGAN FOUND THE professor standing at the end of the runway, a pair of binoculars around his neck. He brought the binoculars to his eyes and scanned the sky above the horizon. Morgan walked up to him quietly, stood watching over his shoulder and saw the dark shapes of birds spiraling up a thermal. 'Marabou Storks,' Morgan said.

The professor turned around and said 'Oh' with a startled smile. He dropped the binoculars and extended his hand. 'I didn't hear you arrive.'

Morgan smiled and shook the old man's hand. The old man took a handkerchief out of his pocket and mopped his brow. 'I don't know how you manage in this heat,' he said.

'It's very humid now because of the rain,' said Morgan. The professor took a last look at the storks. 'Beautiful aren't they?' he said, talking past the binoculars. The storks were circling slowly, tracing out a funnel: a lazy tornado flying a holding pattern.

A notice to pilots. Storks congregating at runway so and so. Pilots to exercise caution on take-off and landing. Storks have right of way. Look out. A memo with a difference, to be crumpled and thrown into a dustbin at your own peril. To be remembered when a stork comes flying through the windscreen; too late for tears.

'It's a matter of perspective,' he said to the professor as they were walking back to the airport building. He collected the old man's bag from the airport attendant.

'How is that man of the other night?' asked the attendant.

'So far, so good,' said Morgan. 'Thanks again for your trouble.'

'No trouble,' he said, and laughed. 'Did they fix the ambulance?'

'I gave them a blast.'

'So, no more open-air deliveries?' asked the attendant.

Morgan laughed. 'Hopefully not.'

The professor was waiting at the truck. 'Do you want me to drop you at the house?' asked Morgan, putting the bags on the back of the truck.

'No,' said the professor. 'Let's go and see the patient first. I gather she is a very special patient.'

On the way, he made Morgan stop the car to look at a Yellowbilled Kite sitting on a telephone pole.

'You will see a lot of those; they are all over the place,' Morgan said, and wondered if it wasn't one of Mary's kites.

The old man was pleased. 'I love the birdlife in this place,' he said.

Naledi was sitting on her bed, waiting.

The professor greeted her with old world politeness. He examined her, looked at the X-rays and made her lie on her side to palpate the kidney. Then he looked at the blood results and seemed satisfied. He talked to her all the time even though she couldn't understand a word.

The professor was unaware that he was being observed from all sides—sized up, weighed and measured. Janet had woken up and lay on her side, watching him. She was too weak to wipe the saliva off her face. Violet took a paper towel and wiped her cheek. Naledi was taking a shine to the old man. He patted her on the shoulder.

'See you tomorrow, then,' he said.

She waved at them as they left. The old man returned the wave.

'That must have been a battle,' he said to Morgan when

they were walking down the passage. 'From twenty-nine kilos.'

'So far, so good,' Morgan said. He wasn't looking forward to the operation but said nothing. Morgan rang the bell at theater, and the staff all came to the door and greeted the old man like a long-lost friend. Constance brought the instrument tray and he checked the instruments, taking his time. Satisfied, he closed the pack and adjusted his glasses. 'This will be fine,' he said. 'I won't need more than this.'

'Seven o'clock tomorrow morning,' said Morgan as they left.

'We will be ready,' said Constance.

Morgan dropped the professor at Thomson's house and declined an invitation to dinner. He went home, cooked his own dinner and slept badly, waking up, dozing off and finally waking at five with the purring Oscar nestled on his chest. He opened his eyes to find a pair of green eyes looking into his. 'Why are you home so early?' he enquired. 'Did someone jilt you?'

He left Oscar lying on his chest and shut his eyes again but couldn't sleep. At twenty to six he grabbed Oscar in a bear hug, carried the cat to the kitchen and fed him. He took a bath, had breakfast but couldn't sit still.

At six thirty he picked up his keys. Oscar was lying on the couch, one front leg stretched out, bent at the joint, licking himself, the tongue moving down the leg and up the wrist, his head turning slightly from side to side. A hedonist luxuriating in a stretch and a lick. He stopped and looked at Morgan pensively, like a bank manager considering a loan.

'Keep your fingers crossed, will you?' Morgan said to Oscar as he opened the door.

THEY WERE STANDING in the recovery room when Naledi was wheeled in. The professor was happy to be out of the heat in an air-conditioned room. Naledi didn't say a word. At that moment she was the loneliest person in the world.

Morgan put up the first drip and strapped it to her wrist. 'We will put up the rest when she's asleep,' he said. It's better that way, he thought, looking at her face. He put up his hand and adjusted the theater light so it didn't shine into her eyes.

The old man nodded, took the pack of X-rays and put them on the screen. Then he took his glasses out of his pocket, put them on, stood back from the screen and scrutinized the X-rays once again. His forefinger traced the outline of the kidney that wasn't excreting any dye. 'We will go though the bed of the eleventh rib,' he said, counting the ribs and comparing it to the renal outline.

Thomson was ready to start. Morgan stood next to Naledi and squeezed her hand. He gave her a thumbs-up sign and she managed a faint smile that froze on her face as Thomson injected the Pentothal. He waited until she was intubated and then put up two more drips. 'Okay,' he said. 'Let's strap everything properly, and then we can turn her on her side.'

In case of trouble, there were six units of blood on the anesthetic table. 'I hope we won't need these,' said Thomson.

He took two units and gave them to a nurse to put in the blood warmer. The old man cleaned his spectacles again and put on a plastic apron. Morgan handed him a brush, took one for himself, and started scrubbing.

The old man hummed a tune as he washed his hands and then stood with their hands up as they waited to be gowned. Morgan lifted his gaze and saw the sister preparing to drape the fragile body on the table. The old man read his thoughts.

'You did well to get her this far,' he said.

'I am glad you are here,' Morgan replied.

The creases around the surgeon's eyes deepened above his mask, but he said nothing. Morgan suspected he knew how much anguish he felt.

'It will be all right,' said the old man. He waited for the nurse to tie up his gown and then walked into theater and took his place next to the table.

They waited for the cautery and the suction to be connected. Then, without further ado, the old man took the knife and cut through the skin. Morgan felt his tension unwinding as he watched the professor working away, and saw how gently he was handling the tissues. Unhurriedly, cauterizing every bleeder as he went along. The capsule of the kidney had been destroyed by the infection, making dissection difficult, but the old man was unfazed.

Morgan watched his fingers as he handled the tissues. They were knowing, careful fingers: sensors that handled instruments as if they were extensions of his hands, finding bloodless planes almost without looking. Much sooner than Morgan had anticipated, they were tying off the structures in the pedicle. Three shining clamps on three structures.

The old man removed the kidney unceremoniously, held it in the palm of his hand and briefly looked at the destroyed organ. 'She's better off without this,' he said, and handed it to the theater sister.

'For histology, please,' he said. They closed the wound from its depth. She hadn't lost much blood. Morgan watched the shiny tip of the needle holder, the needle curving effortlessly through the tissue, leaving evenly placed sutures as if they were placed by a machine.

Then they dressed the wound and it was all over.

'That didn't take long,' said Thomson.

The old man allowed himself a smile. Then he took off

his gloves and sat down with the folder on his lap, writing notes in his meticulous handwriting. Then, as he was about to leave, he stopped to take a final look at the X-rays on the screen.

The nurses in High Care were expecting her. Morgan hung around until Naledi was fully awake. There were no relatives. He felt her pulse. It was full and strong, and she was breathing easily.

It was almost too good to be true. Morgan tried to picture Naledi as she had been when she was first admitted but found he couldn't. At the back entrance of High Care, Morgan heard Violet using her mock-scolding voice.

In the passage next to the wall stood most of the occupants of Naledi's ward. Backs against the wall, heads turned towards the door, eyes alert. A row of spies without trenchcoats. They were listening; their ears cocked to pick out the sound of the monitor and gauge the heart rate. Naledi's remaining mothers. One not able to attend; Janet, fighting her last battle. Flat-breasted scarecrows with warm hearts. Five pairs of eyes saw his unguarded moment and he quickly turned back towards the door.

'Let them come and see her when she's settled,' he said to Violet over his shoulder.

AT LUNCHTIME THE old man allowed himself one beer, which he sipped slowly and appreciatively. They were sitting outside on the thatch-roofed veranda of the only restaurant in town. The old man was calm and relaxed. He was going birdwatching in the afternoon and he was looking forward to it. Next to him on the table was the case containing his binoculars and a book on birds.

'I enjoy coming out here,' he said. 'In spite of the heat.'

'You helped us a lot this morning,' said Morgan, feeling

very relieved that the operation was over.

'I'm sure the girl will be all right,' said the old man. 'There is no more active infection and there was no bleeding. Just mobilize her soon.'

He wanted to know all about the Martial Eagles. 'Next time they nest, you must let me know,' he said. 'I would like to take some photographs.'

Morgan told him the saga of Rastodika. The old man was silent for a while. He cleaned his glasses, then stared at them and rubbed them again.

Morgan looked up and saw calm, grey-blue eyes slightly magnified.

'Do you realize,' said the old man, 'that even if you are successful in getting a transplant, you are going to have to change his whole way of life?' He paused, taking a sip from his beer. 'It would be very difficult to monitor a man who lives in the bush.'

'Rastodika is a very intelligent man,' said Morgan, but he doubted that Rastodika would change his lifestyle.

'Should we prolong life at all costs?' asked the old man, almost as if asking the question to himself. 'Very difficult question, no easy answer,' he said.

IT WAS A quiet afternoon. Morgan had cancelled all his appointments in advance and kept the day free for Naledi. At home, he opened the door to the veranda, drew away the curtains and looked at his neglected garden. I must do something about that lawn, he thought.

On the table was a pile of mail. He had asked Violet to fetch it out of his office and had brought it home with him. He took the dustbin out of the kitchen and started opening the mail.

Included was a newspaper from across the border. He

idly paged through it, and the news was the same as always. Murder and mayhem, war and peace, money and the lack of money, floods and droughts, scandals, strikes, political rallies, famine, greed, religion and a crossword puzzle.

He turned to the sports page. A steroid-saturated, vitamin-popping, wide-smiling sports hero filled half a page. Some hero, thought Morgan.

I have lots of heroes, he told the sportsman. They wear blue hospital clothes or sandals or worn, buggered dresses mostly without bras because they have nothing to put in bras anymore. Some of them look like scarecrows; some look like skeletons. But they are all beautiful, I'll have you know. They can't afford toothpaste but their teeth are clean. I give them vitamins for a reason and steroids you can stick.

We operated on one this morning and took out her kidney. Now she has only one kidney and she is still my hero. In fact, she will always be my hero and tonight I'm going to drink a toast to her. God and accidents and other unforeseen natural and unnatural disasters permitting, I'm going to pour the beer with a big head on it and stick my moustache into it and drink the beer twice and toast her. Then toast all the others because they are all my heroes and they could lick you any time for being a hero with one or both hands tied behind their backs!

36

End of a shebeen

'DO YOU LOVE this woman?' asked the Constable.
'No,' the man said emphatically.

'Then why,' asked the Constable, 'did you beat her up?'

The Kenyan pondered the logic of the question. We are all tired, he decided. The Constable's question made no sense. Or maybe it was just the way in which it was asked, an unfortunate juxtaposition of questions.

The woman concerned was standing in front of the dressing room waiting for painkillers and a tetanus injection. Inside Rebecca's office was a huge cast-iron pot, exhibit number one, containing presumably poisoned food. The shebeen queen had made a mistake, according to the Constable.

On the table were exhibits numbers two and three; a sample of the contents of the pot and green leaves that were stirred into it by the shebeen queen, thinking that they were marogo, which they weren't. There was a subtle difference, evidenced by a dead old woman in the mortuary, one young woman in High Care on a ventilator, and several other people lying in the hospital, partly paralyzed but thankfully improving.

The shebeen queen was behind bars and the shebeen under lock and key. The man and the woman were the last customers. They ate no food; only took liquid refreshments and then had a difference of opinion. The Kenyan wrote up his notes. Thomson had just left. Through the window, the Kenyan saw the day nurses coming on duty, wearing their capes. How can they wear capes in this heat? he wondered.

Rebecca came in through the door. 'And this?' she asked, putting her bag on the floor. The Constable took the cast-iron pot and made for the door. 'Our shebeen,' said the Kenyan. 'This is the last of it.'

'Careful with that pot,' he told the Constable. 'I don't want any more trouble.'

'What's in the pot?' Rebecca asked.

'Poison,' said the Constable and saluted the Kenyan.

'So tell me all about it.' Rebecca folded her arms in front of her chest.

The Kenyan told Rebecca about the misfortunes of the night. There was mayhem before midnight and some more after midnight. Before midnight, the shebeen queen impassively observed the chaos from a chair in Casualty. No one saw her disappear. She went back to the shebeen and conducted business as usual, feeding more customers out of the same pot. At one in the morning they had a repetition of the same problem. The Constable took the shebeen queen and locked her up.

'There's a curse hanging over this town, like I told you before,' said Rebecca, 'and it is not lifting.'

'You and your premonitions,' said the Kenyan. 'Don't predict anything for at least a week; I need some sleep.'

NALEDI WAS SITTING up and smiling. The nurses were changing the dressing. 'The other dressing was too bulky,' said the sister.

Morgan looked at the clean, neat wound. 'That's fine,' he said. 'Just put on a light dressing; and make her walk. Naledi is in a hurry to go home.'

'Not long,' he reassured his patient, 'Ten days at the most.'

'She is one of our few happy endings,' he said to Violet

when they were in the passage.

'I'm very glad for her sake,' she said. 'Soon she will be with her baby.'

'I have never seen this baby,' said Morgan.

'The baby stays with her mother. They are too far away to come to visit.'

The women in Female Ward wore triumphant smiles. They had already paid a visit to High Care and were sitting on their beds talking quietly. Except for Janet. She was lying on her side, wasted, her one hand immobilized by a drip; unable to eat.

A pool of saliva and blood had collected on her pillow. She tried to push herself up onto her elbow. A thread of saliva hung from her cheek and she managed a lopsided, distorted smile. Bloody hell, thought Morgan.

He stood next to her bedside and she turned her face towards him. 'Naledi is fine, Janet,' he said. He didn't know what else to say. He noticed the dirty pillow and helped Violet to clean Janet's face. Outside in the passage Morgan cursed under his breath. 'A person like that shouldn't die,' he told Violet.

She looked at him and smiled an enigmatic smile. 'Do you really think anyone cares about these people?' she asked.

He suddenly remembered something old Jenkins had said after one of his meetings with the blinkered warriors around the mahogany table. 'Statistics and figures are all they can talk about!' he had fumed. 'A patient sitting in front of you is not a statistic. A patient is a human being!'

'No,' he told Violet. 'I don't think so.'

He found Thomson and Oumar outside High Care, recovering from the morning meeting. Oumar was angry. 'I should follow your example and stop going to those goddamned meetings,' he told Morgan.

Oumar's letter about the kitchen had not been well

received. How dare he report the kitchen to the Health Inspector? Holmes was indignant and told Oumar to stop interfering in matters that didn't concern him. From then on, Holmes did not have an easy ride. Everyone was sick of his pompous manner. Thomson invited him to take his own meals from the kitchen. Holmes wasn't amused. He defended his decision to cut down on the kitchen staff and called it an effective use of manpower. Oumar told him he called it deliberate sabotage.

'You should come to the meetings again,' Thomson told Morgan, 'They are becoming more and more interesting.'

'Thanks, but no thanks,' said Morgan. 'I have better things to do.'

Oumar was unconsoled. 'Do you know what that man told us?' he asked indignantly. 'He told us he is the one who sees the big picture. What bullshit!'

'Oumar, you're starting to talk like Morgan,' Thomson laughed, patting Oumar on the shoulder: 'Don't take it so personally. The man is a moron; we all know that.'

'If I meet Holmes in the bush, I'll drive over him with my truck,' said Morgan.

'He doesn't go to the bush,' said Thomson.

'Pity,' said Oumar. 'I'd buy myself a truck for just that purpose.'

'I see our girl is doing well,' Thomson changed the topic.

'At least we have one success story.'

'Good thing we are not putting a percentage to our successes,' said Morgan.

Oumar started walking towards the side entrance.

'Where are you going? Stay here and talk to us,' Morgan called after him.

Oumar shook his head. 'I am going to phone the Health Inspector again. That bastard is not going to get away with it.'

Just then, Holmes and Thunderbird appeared on the other side of the grounds, next to the administration building. Holmes was pacing the distance between the building and the parking lot.

'What are those two bunglers up to?' Morgan asked.

'You mean you don't know?' Thomson laughed. 'The administration building is going to be rebuilt and modernized; and we are getting a brand-new parking lot.'

'What?' said Morgan. 'We don't have medicine, we are saving on food, and those idiots build parking lots.'

'Management is what it is all about,' Thomson imitated Holmes.

'After all, how can we expect our leader to spend his time in such a ramshackle place? He deserves to work in decent surroundings. Unlike us; we are merely cannon-fodder.'

Morgan shook his head. 'Heaven help Africa. Who needs enemies with people like that in charge?'

'It's a matter of priorities,' said Thomson.

'Do you think,' said Morgan, 'those guys know how many people they are sending to their deaths?'

Thomson lit a cigarette and flung the match on the roof. 'They have rules and drug prices to hide behind. They couldn't care a damn.'

'Evil is a tangible thing,' Morgan said. 'It comes packaged in the bodies of idiots wearing expensive clothes.'

IN THE EVENING Morgan got to the ward at the end of visiting hours. The sister was standing in the passage in front of the reception desk. Behind the desk sat Oumar, waiting for a blood smear result.

'You still here?' asked Morgan. 'You must have had a hell of a day.'

'I'll be going just now,' said Oumar.

Visitors were clustered around each bed, and the many simultaneous conversations produced a continuous hum.

'It's like a beehive,' said the sister, 'but they only have a minute left.'

'Time to break up the hive,' Morgan said.

'No,' said Oumar. 'Give them the full minute. Sit down Morgan. Talk to me.'

'About what?' asked Morgan.

'Anything you like.'

The sister waited out the minute and then picked up an old, battered cowbell from the desk and started ringing it. At first the noise level increased and then the beehive poured into the passage. Old women in long dresses, grandfathers leaning on sticks, smartly dressed young men, women with children and trendy young women.

'That one, look!' the sister said, gesturing with her eyes. Morgan followed her gaze and saw a man wearing a string of beads around his neck. 'He is a witchdoctor,' she said.

'I wonder if he doesn't treat my patients,' said Morgan.

The sister put the bell on the table. 'You never can tell,' she said.

'I should refer a few patients to him,' said Oumar. Morgan said good night to Oumar and entered the ward. Around a table four men sat playing cards, concentrating on the game and hardly noticing the visitors as they left. It was a congregation of scarecrows. Their blue hospital shirts hung loosely from their bony frames. One man had ulcers on his lips and the man sitting opposite him had no temporal muscles left. His eyes looked like those of a praying mantis.

'See, you're changing this place into a gambling house,' the sister accused him.

Morgan greeted the men. 'Are you playing for money?' he asked, and they smiled their death-defying smiles.

'We are playing until it is time to sleep,' said the tall man at the head of the table.

'Where is Rastodika?'

'He doesn't play cards. He's outside.'

They carried on, absorbed in their game, a cartoon of living skeletons sitting around a table. He stopped at Rastodika's room and looked at the latest blood results. They were no better and no worse.

Outside the ward, music, loud singing, the sound of laughter and barking dogs came drifting in from the town. Morgan wondered what the occasion was and could not recall any unusual event. Rastodika was sitting under his favorite tree. The lights from the town bounced back from the clouds, and he could see Rastodika's profile as he sat down next to him. Rastodika was leaning forward on his stick, then sat back a little and with both hands used the stick to draw a line on the ground.

Morgan offered him a cigarette.

They sat smoking, and Morgan gently broached the subject of peritoneal dialysis, should he deteriorate before the Beerfest. Rastodika refused without hesitation. 'I am not going to walk around with tubes in my stomach,' he said.

In the dim light he could see Rastodika's eyes. His face looked as if it were carved from stone, like the statues the vendors sold at the mall. In the dim light Morgan could see his eyes glitter.

'I have had a good life,' said Rastodika. 'Maybe it is time for me to die.'

Morgan finished his cigarette and flicked the butt into the dark. He stood up and put his hand on Rastodika's shoulder. 'Let's not give up hope, Rastodika,' he said.

JANET WAS TAKEN to a side ward. Next to her, on the floor, sat an old lady whom Morgan had not seen before.

'Her mother,' the night sister introduced the woman.

Briefly, Morgan explained Janet's illness. Naledi had kept her alive, he thought. She stayed alive only for her sake. He wondered about her boy. Good thing he hasn't seen her like this, he thought. The old woman was looking at him without saying a word. He put his hand on Janet's shoulder, but she barely responded.

At three o'clock he was woken up by the ringing of the telephone. 'Janet passed away,' the night sister informed him.

'Thank you, sister,' Morgan said, and put down the phone.

He tried to go back to sleep. After a while, he got up and sat outside on the veranda. In the moonlight he saw Oscar sitting on the garden wall. The cat jumped down, walked across the lawn, jumped onto the veranda and rubbed himself against Morgan's legs.

37

Holmes chases another cat

TO: The Hospital Superintendent
FROM: The State Veterinarian

We have received the body of a cat, suspected to be rabid.

On examination of the brain, no Negri inclusion bodies could be found. However, some autolysis of the brain cells had taken place, and the result should be interpreted with caution.

We would advise you to vaccinate the contacts regardless.

TO: Dr John Morgan
FROM: The Superintendent's Office

I have received a report from the State Veterinarian about yet another cat sent to them by you.

I have not received any information about the contacts and whether they have been vaccinated or not.

As you know, all rabies cases have to be notified, and contacts have to be vaccinated in any case where rabies is suspected. Please furnish me with information about the contacts as soon as possible.

TO: The Superintendent
FROM: Dr John Morgan

The cat you refer to is the same one that I sent to the State Veterinarian earlier in the year.

For reasons beyond my control, it had a fairly prolonged journey.

The contacts, as I have pointed out to you earlier, have already been vaccinated.

I'd like to remind you of a case of salmonella food poisoning that was picked up in Male Ward. There were several cases of unexplained diarrhea but only one positive culture.

Since the patient had been in the ward for some time and had not taken, as far as Oumar could establish, any food from outside the hospital, we must assume that he picked it up from hospital food.

I have inspected the kitchen and found the hygiene to be far below standard and, as you know, Oumar has reported the matter to the Health Inspector.

TO: Dr John Morgan
FROM: The Superintendent's Office

You and Oumar must kindly refrain from taking matters into your own hands. The matter of the kitchen is receiving attention and I don't think that one case of salmonella is cause for undue concern. The Health Inspector receives instructions from me and should not be called upon unnecessarily.

TO: The Superintendent's Office
FROM: Dr John Morgan

I think the matter of the hospital kitchen is of extreme importance. I would advise you to go and have a look yourself instead of running around after dead cats.

NALEDI WENT HOME exactly ten days after her operation.

She had returned from High Care to find a new neighbor occupying Janet's bed. This time, the silent changeover was more difficult to get used to. Naledi's last memory of Janet was her voice—hoarse and somewhat slurred—that followed her as she was being pushed to theater: 'Goodbye my child!'

In the short time Naledi had spent in High Care, two new faces had appeared in the ward. She was welcomed back like a long-lost daughter. Even the newcomers knew her story.

On the ninth day the sutures were removed. While Violet was dressing the wound, Naledi observed the neat scar and suddenly thought of the gentle professor. With Violet's help, she dictated a letter. It was a sincere, naïve expression of thanks. Violet took care to translate it literally as Naledi dictated it. Then she gave the letter to Naledi to sign.

'If I were the professor, I would frame it and hang it on the wall,' Morgan said when Violet showed it to him. 'Maybe he won't,' he added as an afterthought. 'The professor is a humble man.'

On the last day Naledi again went through the ritual of being dressed meticulously, with everyone, including Violet, fussing about. On the bed was the suitcase, not the usual plastic bag or fertilizer bag, neatly packed and ready. Naledi was suddenly struck by the incongruity of cheerful voices of her fellow patients who were not much more than a bunch of skeletons. Didn't they realize they were never going to see each other again?

After all this time, all she had to do was pick up the suitcase and walk away from them. She was a free being, unencumbered by disease. The faces of the women were cheerful, without a touch of envy. They rejoiced in her good fortune. She greeted them one by one, trying to engrave their faces in her memory.

Then she followed Violet, carrying her suitcase. When they reached the end of the passage she turned and for the last time saw the scrawny figures of the women framed in the light of the outside door. The cheery sound of their voices followed her around the corner.

They found Morgan on the lawn next to Casualty, talking to Oumar and Thomson.

'And this?' he asked. 'Are you running away from us?'

He wanted to give her a formal handshake, but she ignored his hand, stepped forward and gave him a hug. For once he was embarrassed. Everyone laughed and then, suddenly, no one knew what to say.

She silently went up to Thomson and Oumar and shook their hands.

'Come, my girl,' Violet said. 'I will walk with you to the gate.'

'I didn't think you would pull it off,' Thomson said to Morgan. 'Remember the way she looked when she came in.'

Morgan watched her as she walked away from them, listing slightly to the right as she carried the suitcase in her hand. 'If it wasn't for the other women in that ward, she would not have made it,' Morgan said, thinking of Janet who had treated Naledi like her own daughter. He was irritable and short-tempered. Even Naledi's cure couldn't cheer him up.

The wards were again full of patients who had no hope of recovering. 'What the hell are we doing here?' he asked, talking to no one in particular.

'We are playing out an act,' said Thomson.

'A pretty macabre act,' Morgan replied. He turned towards Oumar. 'I take it you also had a memo about the kitchen?'

Oumar had his hands in his coat pockets. 'I am preparing a surprise for our friend,' he said. 'He is not going to have his way.'

'The sooner the better,' Morgan said. 'The kitchen is in a mess, and it's not getting any better.'

'YOU SHOULD HAVE castled earlier,' said Father Michael and wiped Morgan off the board.

Morgan had won the first game, but played carelessly in the second. Father Michael wasted no time in taking advantage of his mistakes. 'And how is our man?' asked Father Michael after Morgan had acknowledged defeat.

'Lingering on,' replied Morgan. 'Hopefully he will last until the Beerfest.'

'Not long to wait,' said Father Michael. 'The whole town is waiting for it.'

Indeed, the town was bursting at the seams in anticipation of the Beerfest. It was the main topic of discussion in the seedy, fly-infested little tearooms at the station, in the shebeens, around the tables of the vendors at the mall, at Mr Chiremba's beerhall, around open cooking fires on the dusty little streets of the squatter camp, in the queues at the government offices, at the building sites, and in hot and overcrowded cafés.

An exuberant Mr. B had told Morgan that the Beerfest

was going to be the biggest party the town had ever had. 'You wait and see,' he told Morgan. Father Michael stacked the pieces on the board again. Morgan protested.

'Best out of three,' Father Michael insisted, and helped himself to a cigarette. Morgan started carefully, but after a while he lost interest in the game and Father Michael thrashed him again.

'You are not concentrating,' he told Morgan. 'Too many things on your mind?'

Morgan sipped his beer. 'That ward is driving me crazy,' he said. 'I might as well not be there.' He put the glass on the table with some force and almost spilled his beer.

'The patients trust you.' Father Michael's voice was reassuring. 'That's the important thing.'

'That's exactly my problem,' said Morgan. 'They trust me and I am not doing anything for them.'

'You are doing what you can,' Father Michael said with an air of finality.

'But you and I know there's a lot more that could be done,' Morgan replied.

'You can only do what you can do, my friend. Some things are not in our hands.'

'Says who?'

'We are only human.' Father Michael scooped the chess pieces together with both hands and left them in the middle of the board, lying haphazardly, like bodies on a battlefield.

PART IV

38

A bad omen

DORCAS SPENT A difficult night drifting off to sleep and waking up almost every hour, aware of the rustling of leaves and the gentle whispering of the wind. She heard a soft spell of rain, sank back into sleep and dreamed of a lakeside, fishing boats with coarse, off-white sails and fishermen hauling in nets. The rain stopped and long past midnight she woke up to a bright moon.

She sat up in bed with the realization that she had been dreaming about her childhood. On the windowsill sat a pigeon with puffed feathers. She got out of bed, walked to the kitchen, made herself a cup of coffee and drank it in the darkness of the living room. A dense silence hung over the town, punctuated by the occasional drop of water falling from the eaves. A sudden gust of wind stirred the leaves of the banana tree. The clock in the bedroom ticked away, impartially rationing the night hours.

At last, in the small hours of the morning she fell into a fitful sleep from which she woke just after daybreak, aware of the braying of a donkey. She dressed, put on the gumboots that stood next to the front door and walked into the garden that smelt of rain and damp soil.

She carefully picked up an earthworm from the path between two patches of cauliflower and released it into cultivated soil. She walked amongst tall mealie plants, raising her arm in front of her face like someone blocking a blow. The leaves parted and made a scraping sound as they brushed against her clothes. She reached the end of the row and froze.

There, in the clearing in front of the house was a black cat. It stood completely still, its back slightly arched, its legs straight, its tail aloft. It stared at her with yellow, incandescent eyes. Nonchalantly it walked across the clearing and started crossing the road. It stopped halfway across the road and looked back. She again briefly saw the yellow flash of its eyes, and shuddered.

RASTODIKA LAY IN his bed. A faint breeze came through the open window. In the dim light of dawn he saw droplets of water on the overgrown grass. He lifted his gaze and saw the tall camel-thorn trees with pink-tinted clouds above them. From the passage, a rectangular patch of light fell onto the floor of the room.

Across the passage, in Male Ward, the lights were already on. He heard the measured footsteps of nurses, the sound of a drip stand being pushed along the passage, a toilet being flushed, the sleepy voices of the men, the door of a bedside locker being opened and the rattling of the water pipes.

He turned on his back, propping up his head with the pillows, and surveyed the familiar scene. Next to the bed nearest to the door, a man was saying his prayers. He was sitting on a chair, his back turned to the rest of the ward; arms resting on the bed, hands clasped together, eyes shut, lips moving in an earnest, early morning conversation with his maker.

Behind him, men were getting out of their beds, going through an early morning ritual, rummaging through lockers for soap, toothbrushes and towels. The usual morning greeting: 'How are you?' as if something could have changed during the night in which everyone knew what was happening to everyone else. In a space where they were so close together, they could share each other's dreams.

In the second bed lay a man attached to a drip with an oxygen mask on his face. Everyone had become accustomed to the hissing sound of the oxygen. Humidified air escaped from underneath the mask and condensed on the man's face like drops of dew. His eyes followed the activities in the room, but he was too breathless to partake in any conversation.

The madman was still asleep, a half-smoked, hand-rolled cigarette on the locker next to his bed.

Johnson came back from the duty room. He had weighed himself and found no change in his weight. He was philosophical about it. He wasn't getting better he told his neighbor, but he wasn't getting worse—purely from a nutritional point of view of course.

A man came back from the toilet pushing a drip stand, staring in front of him through eyes sunken into bony eye sockets. His shrunken frame took up only slightly more space than the flimsy drip stand.

Rastodika didn't get up. He lay in his bed with a blanket wrapped around his feet. A dull headache had disturbed his sleep. He was aware of his joints. They felt stiff and uncooperative. During the night he had seen the night sister walking past but didn't ask for painkillers. It will go away in the morning, he had told himself; it always does.

He was alone in the side ward; the most recent occupant of the other bed had died after a brief, breathless struggle with the virus. Rastodika had witnessed the short, fierce battle that seemed to take place mostly at night. The room was crowded for a few days with nurses and doctors engaging in futile interventions, and relatives sitting next to the bedside.

The kitchen trolley came down the porch and turned the corner. The loud rattling of plates sounded the morning reveille.

MR. B WAS OCCUPYING half of Rastodika's room. Rastodika was sitting on the bed, seemingly cheered up by Mr. B's booming voice.

'Morgan!' Mr. B grabbed Morgan's hand and dwarfed it with his own. 'We were just talking about you! I have been telling Rastodika to be patient,' Mr. B said. 'Soon he will be back on his river!' His laughter poured out into the passage. 'We have been saying,' Mr. B continued, and obscured the window with his massive frame, 'you have to come and help me shoot that leopard.'

Morgan examined Rastodika's laboratory results. He was going to need dialysis soon, whether he liked it or not. Time was running out fast.

'You know I don't like shooting animals,' Morgan told them. 'I would rather shoot one or two people I know.'

Mr. B laughed. 'You can get into trouble for that; better to take it out on the leopard.'

'It has done nothing to me,' Morgan said.

'But it is killing my calves, and one day it is going to hurt someone,' Mr. B reminded him.

From the bed came Rastodika's voice. 'Come on, Morgan. It would only be for the weekend. Don't worry about me; I'll be fine.' Morgan hesitated.

'Come, Morgan,' said Mr. B. 'You need a break.'

'I will have a look at the duty roster. And I won't be shooting the leopard. I will only come for the walk in the bush, and I hope we don't find him.'

Later, when he was sitting in his office, Mr. B phoned. 'Come, Morgan,' he heard the jovial voice. 'It will be a nice outing for you.'

'All right,' Morgan said. 'I'll come along.'

What could go wrong? he asked himself. Everything could go wrong, he answered his own question. He looked at the duty roster and was reassured. Young Simon was on call. If there is any trouble with Rastodika, he told young Simon, you can talk to the Kenyan; he will be in town.

39

The troublesome leopard

BY LATE AFTERNOON they had found the leopard's tracks, but they were at least a day old, according to Elijah.

'The wind is blowing the wrong way, in any case,' Mr. B said. Morgan was relieved. He was carrying the shotgun. 'For self defense, and to save your skin if you wound him,' he had told Mr. B when they started. 'And I hope we don't find him, as I told you before.'

Mr. B laughed and said, 'That's no way to start a hunt.' They had arrived the previous night and Morgan had met the trackers and Mr. B's dogs, which had fought with the leopard only a week before. The dogs had long, linear lacerations on their faces and flanks.

'See,' said Mr. B. 'See what he did to my dogs.'

'I hope we're not taking them along,' Morgan said.

'No,' Mr. B replied. 'They are having a rest.'

Elijah had been walking ahead of them for most of the day. He read the signs on their path like a book. Tall and sinewy, with a long-distance athlete's legs, wearing a sleeveless shirt and carrying a long stick, he walked effortlessly and pointed out tracks of antelope, jackals, hyena and guinea fowl. Now and again he signaled them to stop and pointed out an animal they would not have noticed by themselves.

They walked in silence for most of the time. In the early morning they stood and watched antelope grazing in a clearing in the forest. They skirted the clearing under cover of trees and the antelope belatedly picked up their scent, snorted and ran away. They surprised a kudu standing in tall grass. It lifted itself gracefully off the ground and they could hear it crashing through the undergrowth.

'You see,' Mr. B read Morgan's thoughts. 'I don't shoot everything on sight; only troublesome leopards and food for my people.'

At midday the wind changed. 'He will know we are coming,' Elijah said.

'Let's carry on a little longer,' Mr. B said.

Morgan enjoyed the walk. He scanned the trees with his binoculars and saw nests of eagles and vultures. I will come here in early spring when the eagles are nesting, he thought to himself. At four o'clock they turned back.

Mr. B said, 'I will set out bait and come and wait for him one night.' He took the rifle off his shoulder and exchanged it for the shotgun Morgan was carrying. 'I want to shoot something for Elijah's family.'

They walked in silence for a while. 'And how is Rastodika?' asked Mr. B.

Morgan shrugged. 'He's holding his own,' he said, and felt a pang of guilt.

'The Beerfest is in two weeks' time,' Mr. B said. 'A big, big Beerfest. Tell Rastodika not to worry.'

Towards sunset they were picking their way through marshland. Ibises and egrets flew overhead. Mr. B slackened his pace and looked up for a few minutes. They walked slowly on and Mr. B kept the shotgun ready, his gaze moving along the tree line and upwards.

A pair of Spurwinged Geese flew overhead. Mr. B took aim rapidly and shot the first bird. Morgan saw the second bird spread its wings, its tail feathers fanned out like air brakes. It turned and flew away in the opposite direction.

Mr. B followed through smoothly, almost casually, with

the barrel of the shotgun describing an arc. He squeezed the trigger and Morgan saw a cloud of feathers as the second bird plummeted to earth. 'I never miss,' said Mr. B as he broke the shotgun and expelled the spent cartridges.

40

Holmes swaps duties

AFTERWARDS, MORGAN WAS astonished that he had had no premonition whatsoever.

Nothing on that Monday morning alerted him to the tragedy. Not the polite, remote greeting of the Matron when he met her in the passage, nor the averted gaze of the night sister as she left the hospital, nor the subdued greetings of the scarecrows on the verandas.

He went straight to the laboratory, smelling the agar being prepared for cultures, and only came to a halt at the last bench where the technician was plating stool specimens for culture. 'Has the HLA-typing arrived?' Morgan enquired.

The technician silently heated a wire loop in the unruffled blue flame of a Bunsen burner. 'What would you want it for now?' he asked.

He saw the look of surprise on Morgan's face and asked, 'You don't know?'

'I've just arrived,' Morgan said. 'What's going on?'

'Rastodika is dead,' said the technician. 'Salmonella probably, 'he added laconically.

In the side ward, Rastodika's bed was empty and his walking stick and canvas bag were in the nurses' office. Morgan found a stone-faced Violet sitting behind the desk and extracted the story from her.

During the night, several patients had developed diarrhea, and Rastodika was vomiting all night. The night sister phoned Holmes, who had swapped duties with Simon that afternoon.

He refused to come to see Rastodika, and prescribed an anti-emetic over the phone.

On Saturday morning he did a cursory round and told the staff to give him oral fluids. During the day, Rastodika became more and more dehydrated. Violet had phoned Holmes who prescribed an anti-diarrheal drug, which was hopeless since Rastodika was still vomiting all the time. She put up a drip and at night the High Care nurse took a blood specimen and phoned Holmes because she was worried about the results.

He scolded her and gave her a lecture on the inappropriate use of resources. 'The man has terminal renal failure, sister,' he told her. 'What do you want me to come and do, a renal transplant?'

In desperation, in the early hours of Sunday morning, the night sister phoned the Kenyan, but when he arrived, Rastodika was dying and there was nothing that could be done to save him. Morgan asked softly, 'Is Holmes in his office?'

Violet saw his eyes and grabbed his arm. 'No, Morgan!' she exclaimed, 'Don't!' Morgan broke free from her grip as she tried to pacify him.

'The nurses have lodged an official complaint,' she told him.

'And who do you think is going to investigate the complaint?' asked Morgan. 'His great friend, the Regional Superintendent.'

Morgan swore. 'I have bloody well complained about the kitchen forever. I warned him this was going to happen! I cannot believe this!' he shouted. 'Is that man really a doctor?'

She tried again to grab Morgan's arm when he abruptly turned and left the office, but he was moving too fast. She ran into the passage and found the Kenyan in a side ward. 'Quick!' she shouted, 'Go after Morgan! He is going to do something terrible!'

The Kenyan didn't have to be told what Morgan was going to do. He started running towards Holmes' office just in time to see Morgan climbing the stairs, three at a time. He ran across the lawn, but realized he was going to be too late.

Morgan strode down the passage past workmen scraping paint from the wall, past Rose, and burst into Holmes' office. He shut the door behind him. Holmes started to say something, but his mouth remained half open once he looked into Morgan's blazing eyes. Morgan moved towards the desk and Holmes' face turned pale at his approach.

'You murdered my friend,' Morgan told him matter-of-factly.

Holmes sat behind his desk like a hypnotized rabbit. Morgan leaned over the table and grabbed him by the collar of his shirt. He hauled him out from behind the desk and shook him like a terrier shaking a rat. Holmes' face turned blue, his glasses slipped off and fell on the desk.

The Kenyan burst into the office. 'No Morgan…NO!' he shouted, and tried to restrain him.

Morgan shook him off, slid his hands underneath Holmes' tie, grabbed his shirt and ripped it off. He pushed him back into his chair, turned and walked out. The Kenyan was left to pacify Rose, laughing hysterically at at the sight of her boss with a tie around his bare neck and the remains of his shirt hanging around his waist like a skirt.

In Violet's office Morgan found Rastodika's uncompleted death certificate. 'Take this to Holmes,' he said, still shaking with rage. 'Tell him if he murders people, he should fill in the death certificates himself.'

THE NEXT DAY Morgan's anger still burned inside him like a cold, blue flame. He talked only as much as necessary. He stood under Rastodika's tree and smoked a cigarette before he started his round. He noticed a faint breeze, held up the cigarette and determined the direction of the wind. It came from the northeast. More rain, Rastodika would have said.

In Children's Ward, he found a baby with a bulging fontanelle who had been admitted only two hours before. There was no drip and the child was on insufficient oral antibiotics. 'Who saw this child?' he asked. The icy quality of his voice sent a shiver down Violet's spine. 'Was it Mark?' he demanded.

Reluctantly Violet nodded. Morgan looked at the nurse standing next to her on the other side of the bed. 'Call him,' he said. 'Call him, now!'

She scurried off like a frightened rabbit. Morgan did a lumbar puncture and had just finished putting up an intravenous line when young Mark arrived. Morgan picked up the test tube with milky cerebrospinal fluid, held it up to the light and tilted it for Mark to see. Morgan's eyes were as cold and blue as ice in a crevasse.

Mark stammered and broke off his sentence halfway. 'I didn't think...' he said.

'Next time,' Morgan said, 'take more care.'

He did his ward round mechanically. The patients were subdued and nobody talked unless they had to. He found himself standing in front of Johnson's bed. Johnson sat upright and supported himself with straight arms so that his bony chest seemed to hang from two thin clavicles. 'You must not feel bad about Rastodika,' Johnson said, 'God took him; it was his will.'

Morgan looked into the thin, bearded face and innocent eyes with their dark irises. An angel with a scruffy beard, he thought. The pupils dilated momentarily and exposed Johnson's soul. 'God has a lot to answer for,' said Morgan.

A faint smile crossed Johnson's face. 'You can't say that, Morgan,' he said. 'God gives and God takes; we can't change that.'

Morgan wasn't listening. He looked down at Johnson's notes and recalled a morning with Tesfai just before he had left. 'Come with me,' Tesfai had said and started walking up the road towards the high part of town.

'Where are we going?' Morgan asked.

'You will see.'

They crossed the road to the marketplace and weaved their way through the crowd, walking past donkeys and horses laden with bags of barley and garlic and men carrying the entrails of a freshly slaughtered goat wrapped in its skin.

Tesfai didn't pause for a chat as usual, but kept walking. They stopped in front of a house with mud walls that were painted blue. The door was open and the wooden windows were shut. Inside it was dark.

They were greeted by a man and his wife. After the bright light in the street, it took a while for their eyes to become accustomed to the dark. Against the opposite wall was a bed, and on it, under a rug, lay a small girl. Tesfai was talking to the parents. They all moved towards the bed. 'Come,' he said. 'We want you to look at this girl. Maybe you can help.'

The girl was paralyzed. The mother bent over her and gently removed the rug as if she was unveiling a shrine. When she pulled up the girl's dress Morgan noticed the angulated spine, bent forward like a broken stick. He saw an old scar where the father had, in desperation, drained a cold abscess in the left groin with a hunting knife heated in a fire. A tuberculous spine, concluded Morgan. He noted no bedsores, due to the constant vigilance of the mother.

Morgan had felt anger stirring inside him.

'It was during the war,' Tesfai explained.

It was quiet in the room. The child was studying the foreigner with her calm, impartial eyes, devoid of self pity. Morgan knelt next to the bed and wordlessly examined her. A beautiful child, he thought, broken in half. Four pairs of eyes were looking at him.

'She has never seen a doctor?'

Three adult heads indicated no. It was war; don't you understand? Sick children don't count; anguished mothers don't count; not in war. Don't you know?

There was an exercise book in the house, with a child's handwriting in it. He wanted to tear a page out of it, but that would have ruined it. Instead, he tore a page out of his sketch-book and wrote a letter to the regional hospital. It was all he could do.

The thankful mother covered the child up again, then offered them coffee, but they declined. In the bed, the child smiled and waved at him as he left with Tesfai.

They were back in the bright, dusty street; out of sight, out of earshot. Morgan stopped and swore vehemently.

'You don't understand,' said Tesfai. 'It was war.'

'I understand only too bloody well! . . . Fucking war!' he shouted, causing a horse carrying a load of garlic to shy and flatten its ears.

'I don't think you do understand,' said Tesfai. 'God decides these things.' He spoke in a quiet voice.

'God has stuff-all to do with it!' shouted Morgan. 'Or is God a crazy politician?' As he shouted louder people stopped and stared at him.

Tesfai laughed. 'You are funny,' he said. His eyes had the wisdom of the mountains; the knowledge of what can be changed and what cannot.

THE KENYAN FOUND Morgan in the passage. 'May I talk to you?' the Kenyan asked.

'Why not?' said Morgan.

At the doctors' meeting, the Kenyan told him, Holmes had announced that he intended to discipline the cook.

He was met by a wall of animosity. Everyone knew what had happened to Rastodika and reminded Holmes of their concern about the kitchen.

'I should have killed the bastard,' said Morgan.

In front of his office was a woman with a snot-nosed child. She was obviously a newcomer; freshly transplanted from suburbia into the heart of Africa, complete with lipstick and bangles, seeking an instant remedy for 'flu.

He listened to her high-pitched, panicky voice and resisted the urge to put his fingers in his ears. Through clenched teeth he told the woman to put the child onto the examination couch. The child screamed and the woman tried to bribe it with sweets. Morgan examined the child, wrote out a script and pushed it across the table without saying a word. When they had left he slammed the door so hard a piece of plaster dropped from the ceiling onto his desk.

The phone rang and Morgan recognized the voice of one of his hypochondriacs. He reached over and unplugged the phone at the wall. 'Why don't you all just fuck off!' he said. He waited a while, reinserted the plug and dialed Mr. B.

'I have heard,' Mr. B told him. 'But, we can't stop the Beerfest,' he said.

'I know,' said Morgan.

'We can use the money for something else,' Mr. B was saying. 'Something special,' he added.

Morgan looked out of the window and saw the scrawny crowd from Male Ward sitting under the trees. He remembered the conversation he had had with Thomson on the day he showed him the quote for the transplant.

'Maybe,' he said, 'you should speak to Father Michael.'

41

An afternoon with Sultan

HOLMES DID NOT press charges against Morgan. When he requested Morgan's file, he saw that his contract was due to expire in a few weeks' time. Then he afforded himself the pleasure of writing him a civil letter, telling him that unfortunately his contract would not be renewed.

Thunderbird congratulated Holmes on his hollow victory. 'Things will run a lot more smoothly, you'll see,' he said, relieved he wouldn't have to bear the brunt of Morgan's temper for much longer.

Technically Morgan was fired. He showed the letter to Oumar and Thomson, then threw it into a dustbin.

'That's not cast in stone,' said Thomson. 'I'm sure you could contest it.'

'It would amount to begging,' said Morgan. 'That's not my style. Besides, next time I might just strangle the bastard.'

'Morgan,' said Oumar, 'we need you here. You can't just go.'

'So what do you want me to do, go and beg for a contract?'

'If you wanted to, you could give Holmes a very rough ride,' said Thomson.

'And who would listen to me? His friends in Head Office?'

'You could at least try,' said Oumar.

'No,' said Morgan. 'Holmes and his friends make me sick. I think I'm better off without them.'

ON WEDNESDAY HOLMES announced that the cause of the salmonella outbreak was being investigated. He was met with silence. When the Kenyan discussed his night's work, everyone ignored Holmes completely.

On Thursday morning Morgan took a short cut to the wards. He walked across the lawn that was still wet from rain that had fallen during the night. A dilapidated pick-up truck was parked in front of the mortuary. Four men were sliding a cheap wooden coffin onto the back. He recognized Rastodika's relatives, walked over and greeted them.

'You did what you could,' the jovial would-be donor reassured Morgan. Morgan said nothing. He merely shook the man's hand goodbye.

He heard the engine start up as he reached the side entrance. On Violet's desk was another death certificate: a young man, the son of a woman well known to Morgan and well liked by him. Morgan had stood next to her for part of the night, as her son gasped for breath behind an oxygen mask, like a marathon runner nearing the finish line.

The mother had been quiet, serene and understanding. She tried to relieve her son's agony with her soft voice. Morgan, knowing what the end was going to be like, sent her home just before midnight, telling her to get some sleep. He called her back two hours later to tell her what she already knew.

He waited for her in the nurses' office. When he looked into her devastated face he did not know what to say. She closed the gap between them, hugged and thanked him. He stood rigid, not returning the hug.

'I want to see my son for the last time,' she said. A nurse pulled back the sheet and uncovered his face. The woman bent over, kissed the boy, and squeezed his lifeless hand. The nurses were still handing over, night to day staff, as Morgan walked through the ward.

A woman with pneumonia was in High Care. She too was

gasping for breath and there was nothing he could add to her treatment; she was terminal. In the Children's Ward was her daughter, with the same virus inherited from her mother. Like her mother, she was dying. The sins of the fathers, thought Morgan.

The little girl had had a drug reaction and her skin was covered with itchy, red blotches. He stood next to her, rested his arm on the side of the cot, then rested his face on his arm. He stared at the beautiful face that didn't match her withered little body. The child was too weak to lift up her head. She turned her eyes towards him and looked at him like a lethally wounded duiker.

Was there anybody anywhere who could give a damn? he thought. In spite of faxes and e-mail and cell phones and voice-mail and television and satellites and racing-pigeons and cleft sticks and runners, there seemed to be no one listening.

Who do you think could care anyway about babies born to mothers living in huts?

Why would anyone care about women who walked barefoot to a well to fetch water and carried firewood on their backs?

Tourists would notice, he thought bitterly. They would stop their air-conditioned 4x4s and look and breathe in the ambience; focus their telephoto lenses without realizing they were filming a tragedy.

They would tell their friends how exciting it was, how wild, how vast, how amazing. And the little children. How absolutely gorgeous.

So what are you doing here, John Morgan? he asked himself. Just tell me that. Tell me exactly where you think you fit into this gorgeous fuck-up? Do you think you are doing anything? Are you making a difference, or are you suffocating in the ambience? Nobody is keeping you here, Morgan. You are free to go. But you will always be here. No matter where you go.

THE SNAKE-BITE BOY and Mr. Bernard had been discharged and Rastodika's room was still empty. Morgan opened the back door and walked into the garden. Weeds were growing amongst Rastodika's mealies. Cobs were appearing between the leaves. The weavers were kicking up a racket. Mary's kites were soaring above the town.

He canceled his bookings and put in a day's leave. Then he wasted the morning wandering aimlessly around the mall, avoiding all conversation. At lunchtime he bought two mealies. He didn't return the woman's smile.

She looked at him closely. 'Why are you looking so angry today?' asked the woman as she pocketed his money.

'Because I bloody well am,' he said belligerently.

She laughed, picked up another mealie and gave it to him. 'To make you feel better.'

He felt embarrassed and wanted to give it back. Then he tried to pay for it.

'No, no!' she said. 'It is my gift to you,' and she held up her palms. 'Next time, you smile,' she said. 'Smiling is good for you.'

After lunch he fell asleep on the couch in his living room. At four o'clock he woke up, got into his riding boots, picked up the saddle and the bridle hanging over the back of a chair and drove to the stables.

Jake was delighted. 'Sultan very wild,' he said. 'He need fast riding.' The gap between his teeth showed.

'He will get it,' said Morgan, and put the saddle on the beam of Sultan's pen.

The horse stood with his ears cocked. His coat was shiny; every muscle showed. Morgan got into the pen and held out his hand. The horse moved his head forward and sniffed his hand. Morgan smiled. 'He thinks he is going to get carrots,' he said to Jake.

The horse reared his head when he saw the bridle. 'Come on,' said Morgan, and pushed Sultan into a corner. The horse was a bundle of muscle and nerves. Morgan put his hand on Sultan's shoulder and felt the muscles twitching underneath. 'You're just naughty,' he told him.

He saddled him and tightened the girth. The horse moved restlessly, stamping his feet. Jake was holding the reins and had difficulty keeping him still. Sultan almost crushed him against the wall of the pen. For a fleeting moment Morgan saw a vision of the same horse, standing motionless, allowing a fragile girl in a white dress to stroke him.

'Give him to me, Jake,' he said and held out his hand for the reins. He led Sultan out of the pen and turned to Jake. 'Don't wait for me, Jake; we will be going far.'

Jake grinned. 'Make him tired,' he said.

Morgan got into the saddle and the horse turned around excitedly. 'Wait until the bush road, Sultan,' he said, and allowed him only a trot, holding the reins tightly. The horse snorted and kept asking for more rein. As they came nearer to the bush road the horse sensed it. He lifted his feet high and demanded to go.

'Okay, horse,' Morgan said. 'Show me what you can do.' He let go the reins completely. Sultan shot forward like a rocket and the curves in the narrow track straightened as he gathered speed. Trees flashed past and Morgan had to duck under the low branches hanging over the path.

The great power of the horse exhilarated him and he squeezed its sides and urged Sultan to go faster. A thorn branch ripped his sleeve, drawing blood, but he didn't notice. They burst from amongst the trees and flew across an open stretch of veldt. Morgan stood straight up in the saddle.

'Come on, you mad horse, go for it!' he shouted, his voice carried away by the wind.

He saw the horse's ears move back for a brief moment and then forward again. Out of the corner of his eye he could see the powerful shoulders move even harder when the horse started to gallop as fast as he could. They careered down a slope; there was a brief break in the sound of the hooves as the horse jumped across the streambed at the bottom. They raced up the other side. 'I am not going to stop you!' he shouted wildly, recklessly, standing on his toes in the stirrups, leaning forward. 'Go on you, crazy bastard!'

The road turned south and dense bush grew alongside it, like a hedge. Sultan showed no sign of slowing down. He seemed to have boundless energy. As they came hurtling around a corner, a few guinea fowl flew up ahead of them. Morgan braced himself, but Sultan hardly missed a stride and carried on, running between the flying birds until they gained height and disappeared above the bush.

At last he could feel the pace slacken and he slowed the horse down to a canter. It was late afternoon. At the east-west road he reined in the horse and let him walk. They were both spent. He leaned back in the saddle and listened to the hard breathing of the horse. He put his hand on Sultan's neck and felt the warm sweat running between his fingers.

The muscles on the horse's shoulders were glistening like copper in the red evening light. There was a small village next to the road. Morgan could smell the wood fires and hear the sound of cowbells mingling with the laughter of women and children. Across the plain, the sun was setting. Its bottom widened as it touched the horizon where it hung like a drop of molten steel.

He looked across the plain as if he was seeing it for the first time. He slightly tightened the reins with his left hand and pushed his right hand under Sultan's mane, feeling the warmth of his neck, inhaling the smell of the horse's sweat mixed with that of the wood fires in front of the huts.

The wide flatness of the plain, the size and redness of the sun never failed to fill him with a sense of awe. 'I love Africa,' he told Sultan.

He was listening to the horse's breathing and the creaking of the saddle. The sun was sliced in half by the straight horizon. 'And I hate it!' he hissed under his breath.

The horse wanted to move again, but he tightened the reins and made him walk another few hundred yards. It was past sunset now and they were a long way from town.

He turned off onto a winding road running between the trees on the edge of the plain. There he loosened the reins and pushed the horse into a smooth canter. It was almost dark and he could barely make out the shapes of the trees as they slid past. He sat easily in the saddle with the sound of the hooves and the wind in his ears.

An Eagle Owl flew from the top of a tree. For a moment it hung suspended by its large wings as it turned in flight, then it vanished over the bush.

42

The party of the year

MR. B. WAS HAPPY. The Beerfest was bigger than even he could have predicted.

The night before he had observed the large crowds at the mall, the number of dilapidated cars driving around in the streets, the overwhelming sound of music from loudspeakers, the shrill notes of a lone trumpet, the excited barking of dogs, the giggling of women, the raucous laughter of men, the arrival of soldiers on weekend pass, a busload of teachers and the clanging of a church bell.

He discussed the issue with Mr. Georgiou, and they ordered several more truckloads of beer. These arrived in the nick of time since, in the end, almost everyone in town was inebriated, and afterwards there was no beer left.

The Beerfest had even received mention at a doctors' meeting where Holmes had expressed his concern, and condemned it since he felt it would promote promiscuity.

'If a man wants a screw,' the Kenyan said afterwards, 'he will get it—Beerfest or no Beerfest. It is on a Saturday night after all.'

He nevertheless conveyed the message to Morgan, who spoke to Father Michael, who remembered the condoms kept at Dorcas' shebeen and asked her to speak to Mr. B.

He placed an order for condoms that was so large it depleted the supply in the Capital. This pleased health officials and statisticians because it clearly showed that the national condom consumption was sharply on the increase.

At noon on the day of the Beerfest, an expectant silence hung over the town. At the soccer field, the skinned carcasses of oxen and sheep, impaled on steel rods, were rotated methodically over glowing coals by cheerful men who now and again chased away the stray dogs that caught the scent and came to investigate.

Mr. Chiremba's beerhall closed at eleven o'clock, and by noon the mall was almost deserted.

Women took all afternoon agonizing about what they should wear while their husbands tried to sleep through the humid post-lunch hours.

Mothers admonished their daughters, but nevertheless dressed them for maximum effect.

Old men sat in the shade of trees and plotted the course of the sun, dogs expectantly patrolled the streets with their tails aloft, small boys played cricket along the riverbank, hawkers silently carried their wares to the entrance of the soccer field. The Constable drove slowly around town in his Land Rover, and the nurses in Casualty checked their instruments.

At sunset the doors opened. People sedately filed into the streets and started walking towards the soccer field. Their voices were subdued at first, until the braying of a donkey disturbed the calm. More people came out onto the streets. Their laughter was carried by the evening breeze to the officials at the Beerfest, who braced themselves for the crowds.

The sound increased in inverse proportion to the receding light. When the Mayor formally opened the festivity, his voice was drowned out by loud singing, laughter and exuberant conversation.

Everyone from the town, the district, and beyond was there: the cattlemen who carried their beer in coarse canvas bags, the touts from the mall, the marijuana-smoking Rastafarians, the shebeen queens, the scruffy, unshaven horsemen who walked with unsteady gaits, the scantily clad prostitutes who congregated at the truck stops, the truck drivers, the bearded maize farmers, the clean shaven government officials, the cleaners from the hospital, musicians and aspirant musicians, respectable and not so respectable businessmen, eager young soldiers, shy and not-so-shy young girls, their worried mothers, and their irresponsible fathers.

Morgan made a brief appearance, drank a beer with Mr. B, and then drove off into the bush. Thomson, the Kenyan and the bespectacled Matron turned a blind eye when they saw some of their patients, still in their blue hospital garb.

Rachel spoke briefly to the Mayor whose wife didn't attend. She looked for Morgan but couldn't find him. She asked Father Michael and Dorcas who sat in a tent counting the growing pile of money, but neither of them had seen Morgan. Rachel shrugged her pretty shoulders and poured each of them a beer, which they drank slowly and appreciatively. Through the opening of the tent, Father Michael recognized most of the members of his parish and wondered who was going to attend his morning sermon.

Mr. B had incorporated the cost of the condoms into the price of the beer. He laughed when he saw the contractors filling a condom with beer to see how much it could take; mothers anxiously looked around for their daughters to warn them about these wild men, and found them in the company of worldly soldiers who could charm the pants off anyone. They joined the company to protect the honor of their daughters and found themselves on the receiving end of the soldiers' charm.

The Constable and his colleagues helped to settle disputes about the ownership of unattended mugs of beer and unattended women, and drank only the occasional beer.

People danced wildly to the music of the official band as well as the music of an impromptu band. An old man in a dog-collared jacket walked around with a trumpet in his hand, keeping time, and now and again cutting the music to shreds with blasts from his horn. The tune sounded familiar to Thomson but he couldn't name it due to the fact that he had tried to measure his drinking capacity against that of Mr. B and the Kenyan.

There was the occasional fight, but it was all in good spirits, and the Casualty nurses listened to the noise and wished they could be at the party.

Nobody noticed the church bell when it rang at midnight and nobody heard the roosters when they started calling just before daybreak. Only when the beer finally ran out just after six, did people think about going home and suddenly, at seven o'clock on Sunday morning, a post-battle silence descended over the town and there were no people on the streets.

In the squatter camp the dogs curled up under the trees, at peace with the world.

A truck stood with one of its front wheels in a ditch, next to a telephone pole bent like an elbow.

The Constable found an unconscious man in another ditch and called the ambulance. The man was only drunk and cursed the Constable for interrupting his sleep.

Patients sneaked back into the ward and slept off their hangovers.

A man was admitted with a broken arm. He vaguely remembered a fight but couldn't remember who had hit him.

The madman disappeared. On Monday morning he reappeared, carrying a portable radio. He had a black eye, which he couldn't explain.

On Tuesday morning his bed was empty. Violet opened his locker. A strange, sweet smell hung around it. 'I am sure he is smoking pot,' she said to Morgan when he came to do his ward round.

'Good for him,' said Morgan. 'A man must have at least one vice.'

'He has many vices,' she said.

'He is a versatile man,' answered Morgan.

The telephone in the nurses' office rang and Violet called him. 'It's for you,' she said and passed the receiver to him. 'Mr. B,' she whispered.

Morgan listened to the effusive greeting with the phone held well away from his ear.

'You will never guess how much money we made,' Mr. B said, and mentioned the amount.

Morgan was astonished and felt his anger stirring. It would have been more than enough for Rastodika.

'The question is,' said Mr. B, 'what do we do with all this money?'

Morgan could think of a lot of things. 'I think,' he said, 'we must discuss this with Father Michael, and maybe a few other people.'

'You must know a lot of people who need help,' said Mr. B.

Morgan looked through the glass partition into the ward and saw Johnson and his friends standing in front of the window. He didn't answer at first and Mr. B said, 'Are you there?'

Morgan said: 'I am thinking.' He kept quiet for a little longer. Why not? he thought, looking at a man staring at the roof. 'Maybe we could buy antiretroviral drugs,' he said. 'But I don't think I should make a decision like that on my own.'

Mr. B reflected for a moment and said, 'I will speak to Father Michael and let you know.'

Morgan met the Kenyan in the passage. The Kenyan was morose, still nursing his headache, and didn't smile. 'That man,' he said, meaning Holmes. 'How can we work for such a man?' he said with the clarity a hangover brings.

'Well,' said Morgan, 'you don't have to.'

'I have a wife and three children,' said the Kenyan. 'I can't just go.'

'I don't have those restraints,' said Morgan, 'and I also can't work for such a man. In my case, he also doesn't want me to work for him.'

They walked through Female Ward and stepped outside onto the veranda where Mary used to sit. Morgan remembered her telling him that she did not fear death. 'Tell me,' he said to the Kenyan. 'If you suddenly found yourself with a sum of money that you could use to help people, who would you help?'

'It depends on the size of the sum,' the Kenyan sat himself down on a dilapidated chair.

Morgan leaned against the railing. 'A large sum,' he said. The Kenyan looked out across the lawn and pointed out the skeletons in blue, as he called them. 'I would help those people,' he said, 'even if I couldn't help all of them.'

'You don't think it would be immoral to help only some of them?'

'It is immoral to help none of them,' the Kenyan replied.

IN THE EVENING, Morgan parked his truck near the water's edge and strolled along the river. He walked past shacks made of corrugated iron, plastic, hardboard, expropriated bricks, planks and bodies of cars.

Loud music came from battery-operated radios, somewhere someone played a guitar, and excited voices of children floated up from the river where they played in the shallows. Men were shouting across the river, a dugout boat was launched, and its occupants paddled furiously to overcome the swift current.

He walked past a shack. Through the open door he saw a double bed illuminated by a kerosene lamp. He continued walking, passed the squatters' camp and sat down on the bank. Lights from the opposite side reflected on the river and he saw the dugout reach the shore. Nearby he heard the frogs, tentatively at first and then louder as it got darker. In Africa, he thought, even in the poorest village, the people always laugh and sing.

In the distance he saw two figures approaching; they were coming straight towards him. He watched as they came nearer, and recognized them.

'There he is,' he heard Mr. B's voice.

'We saw your truck,' Father Michael said.

The lights from the opposite bank reflected on Father Michael's glasses. 'Sit down,' he invited them.

'So?' he asked. 'To what do I owe the honor?'

'We have to talk,' said Mr. B, and sat down next to Morgan.

A donkey brayed and dogs barked excitedly. Morgan smiled. 'Does this place ever come to rest?' he asked.

'So,' Mr. B said. 'The problem now is how to use the money.' He did not mention Rastodika.

Morgan looked out over the water and in the reflected light he saw the ripples of the current. 'There are many worthy causes,' he said. 'Father Michael told you about the orphanage?'

Mr. B nodded. 'We have a lot of money,' he said.

'You told me about a little girl and her mother,' Father Michael's voice came from behind the huge figure of Mr. B.

'We must do something special,' Morgan said. 'We were going to blow almost all of it on Rastodika alone, so maybe we should be extravagant.'

In the dark, he could see Mr. B smile. 'What's on your mind, Morgan?' he asked.

'Why don't we buy antiretroviral drugs?' Morgan said. 'We could help a few people.'

'How many could we help?' Father Michael asked.

Morgan calculated the cost per month. 'Six people,' he said, 'for two years. Then there will still be money left for something else, like the orphanage, for instance, and,' he added, 'in two years' time, we will have to have another Beerfest.'

Mr. B was astonished. 'Six? Only six? Morgan, did I hear you right?

'These drugs are expensive,' said Morgan, 'but we must start somewhere.'

'I can't believe it,' said Mr. B. 'I could buy a big house for that much money, or stock a farm with cattle.'

'Life has a price nowadays,' said Morgan.

Mr. B shifted his weight. 'And how are you going to decide which six?' he asked.

Father Michael laughed, got up, and stood in front of Morgan. 'We'll have a lottery,' he suggested.

'You, of all people,' said Morgan. 'Do you mean a draw?'

'We live in difficult times,' Father Michael echoed Dorcas' words from long ago.

'You're serious, Father?' Light reflected again on Father Michael's glasses so that Morgan couldn't see his eyes.

'Absolutely,' said Father Michael.

Mr. B said again, 'With all that money we can only help six people? I can't believe it. You don't think we should use it for something else?'

Morgan got up, picked up a stone and threw it into the water. 'It's up to you,' he said. 'You hold the purse strings. Why don't you come to the hospital tomorrow, and let me show you what I mean.'

They walked back, weaved their way through a party in full swing, and found themselves surrounded by dancing people who greeted them exuberantly.

MORGAN HAD FINISHED packing his books into crates. He walked outside and stood on the veranda, felt restless, got into his truck, drove out of town and headed south. The road was flooded in places and the water came up to the axles. The grass on the side was as high as the truck and it felt like driving in a tunnel.

Nightjars sat invisibly on the road and flew up as he was about to drive over them. A duiker froze in the headlamps, then ran ahead of him jumping from side to side until it found a gap in the grass and disappeared.

On the straight gravel road, in the middle of nowhere, he stopped at the German's mud-walled pub. The German was glad to see him. 'I thought you had left town already,' he said.

'No, I was just busy.'

'Let's sit outside,' said the German, taking Morgan by the arm. 'It is such a beautiful evening.'

There was not a cloud in the sky and a half moon hung over the plain. They sat down on chairs on the patio that was right next to the road. Far away, across the plain, the lights of the town twinkled.

A huge Bouvier terrier came to greet Morgan. 'This is the chap that always tries to catch Sultan,' Morgan smiled, and rubbed the dog's ears. The dog responded by licking his face.

'Ach, he will never catch him,' said the German. 'Sultan is much too fast.'

'Luckily, Sultan is not afraid of dogs, otherwise I would have bitten the dust a couple of times.' The dog lay down at his feet and Morgan stroked his coat. It was still damp from the rain.

'Sultan is a magnificent horse,' said the German. Morgan wondered whether he should tell the German he was going to give him away. 'An exciting ride,' he said.

'Ach, but he is beautiful,' said the German. 'What can I get you to drink?'

'I will have a beer, thanks.'

A truck came rattling along the road. One of its headlamps was dead. Morgan counted seven people on the back. It came to a halt in front of the pub. A man climbed off and bought a bottle of whiskey from the German. The driver kept the engine running. The man again found his seat on the back and the truck pulled away.

'I'm sure that whiskey is not going to last long,' said Morgan.

'Maybe they come back for more,' said the German, sipping his lemonade.

They sat in silence for a while. The sound of the engine grew softer and then there was complete silence.

There was a ring around the moon. Far to the east, the trees on the edge of the plain stood out against the night sky. 'You are very quiet,' said the German.

'I am always quiet.'

'Not the last time I saw you,' the German laughed. 'Something bothering you?'

'Give me another beer,' said Morgan.

He shifted his chair slightly to have a better view over the plain. 'This is a wonderful place,' he said when the German came back with the beer, wondering why he didn't visit it more often.

'I make a living,' said the German. 'I want nothing more.' A Barn Owl swooped down and picked up something from the road. The German laughed. 'One mouse less,' he said.

The German's wife served them snacks from the bar and they sat talking until late.

'Auf Wiedersehen,' said the German when he left. 'Don't stay away long!'

Morgan stopped in the middle of the plain, got out of his

truck and listened to the jackals. He stood there for a long while and watched wispy clouds gathering around the moon. Then he drove home trying to think about nothing.

43

A stroll through the wards

JUST WAIT A moment,' Morgan said. He called the Kenyan and Thomson, then came back to where Mr. B and Father Michael were standing on the veranda.

'Now,' said Morgan. 'Father Michael already knows what is going on here.' He made it sound like a clandestine operation. 'We will just walk through the wards and I want you to look and remember what you see.'

They started at Male Ward, and Morgan paused long enough for Mr. B and Father Michael to greet the wasted occupants. Johnson was sitting sideways on his bed and Morgan noticed how thin he was.

In Children's Ward, mothers were sitting next to the cots. Yvonne was sitting upright and unsmiling as usual. They looked into each side room and walked on to Female Ward, which had a fresh crop of scarecrows.

'So,' said Morgan when they reached the other side. 'All I can be sure of is that most of these people will be dead in six months' time. Probably less.'

'But there are antiretroviral drugs available?' Mr. B asked. 'Surely, the government can pay?'

'The cost,' said Morgan, 'would bankrupt any government. Even if the drugs were affordable, the bureaucracy would probably screw it up.'

'And we can help only six of these people,' Mr. B said. He turned towards the Kenyan. 'What do you think?' he said.

The Kenyan shrugged. 'Better something than nothing,'

he replied.

'And how are we going to choose them; are we going to play God?'

'Like Father Michael said,' Morgan told him. 'We have a lottery or a draw.'

'What about the other patients?' Father Michael asked the question Morgan dreaded. 'Surely we would be inundated if it became known?'

They were standing on the veranda and watched the men come out of Male Ward and wait patiently under the trees for the ward round to start.

'We put up a smokescreen,' said Thomson. 'We say as little as possible, and just give them the drugs. Anyway, we can discharge some of them and see them as out-patients. That way it will stay a secret for longer. But news will leak out in the end.'

Mr. B laughed. 'I will speak to the other businessmen and tell them I have adopted a patient. They could even make donations. Nobody is going to demand more from an individual; they will be only too thankful.'

Morgan became impatient. 'Let's just do it,' he said. 'That's how much money there is and that's that. Like Thomson said, when they get better they won't be in hospital anymore. Then it should be easier to keep quiet about it.'

The Kenyan reminded Mr. B about the monitoring. 'We can't just dish out the drugs. We must take blood specimens every so often to make sure the drugs are working. And that also costs money.'

'Remind me,' said Mr. B, 'never to become a pauper. It's a costly business to stay alive.'

'We can divide them between two doctors,' said Morgan, ignoring Mr. B's comment. 'That won't be too much extra work.'

He looked at the men sitting under the trees and wondered which were going to be the lucky ones.

Mr. B still couldn't get over the price of the drugs. 'I cannot believe what I am hearing,' he said. 'I thought we were going to help a whole lot of people.' He sat in thought for a moment. 'And after two years?' he asked.

Morgan said: 'Hopefully in that time the drug prices will drop. The government might even pay, who knows. If not, we have another Beerfest.'

'But you are going away,' said Mr. B.

'You will still be here,' said Morgan.

The Kenyan smiled. 'We will drag him back here, some way or another.'

Morgan looked again at the scarecrows sitting under the trees. 'We shouldn't wait too long,' he said. 'These people don't have much time.'

Father Michael and Mr. B looked at each other. 'So we have a lottery then,' said Father Michael.

After Mr. B and Father Michael had gone, Morgan said, 'Now I will do my ward round wondering who will be the lucky ones.'

The Kenyan lingered in the nurses' tearoom. His brief sense of wellbeing had left him, replaced by a heaviness in his chest. He poured himself a cup of coffee and stood with his back against the table in the middle of the room. On the wall opposite, Thomson had put up shelves for the old man's journals.

The Kenyan stepped across the room with the cup still in his hand. He balanced it precariously on the shelf and selected a journal at random. On the cover were comments written in Jenkins' tidy handwriting.

Instantly the Kenyan recalled the journal meetings and the old man's teaching rounds, as well as his attention to detail, picking up signs and symptoms that everyone else had missed, piecing together a difficult case just like Sherlock Holmes. The Kenyan smiled at the coincidence. Definitely not the current Holmes, he thought.

'Old man,' he sighed aloud. 'If you could only see what's happening here now.'

The following day Rebecca confronted Morgan in her office. 'And what is this I hear about a lucky draw?'

She scrutinized his face with her owl's eyes and detected the carefully composed innocence. 'Come,' she said. 'I know you better than that; you can't lie to me.'

'Do you mind if I say as little as possible?' he taunted her. He didn't enquire where she had heard about it. Rebecca knew about everything, even before it happened. Sometimes, he had the feeling she could read his mind.

'Imagine,' she said. 'First, a Beerfest and now, a lottery. You are corrupting the town, Morgan.'

A patient poked his nose through the door. Rebecca fixed him with a stare that almost evaporated him. The man returned to his chair and she resumed her interrogation. 'Are you sure it's fair to do this, Morgan?'

He turned his gaze away from her and looked through the window. Amongst the waiting patients, even from a distance, he could pick out the ones with angel eyes and wasted temples. 'Life is unfair,' he told her.

'You are not answering my question properly, Morgan,' she reprimanded him.

'I don't think there is a decent answer for your question.'

Rebecca reflected for a moment. 'You are playing God, that's what I am saying. How can you decide who lives and who dies?'

Morgan shrugged. 'I'm doing it all the time,' he said, 'depending on whether people have money or not.'

As Rebecca rearranged the files on her desk, a thought occurred to her. 'If only some may have the drugs, then no one should receive them. Why should there be a difference?' she asked.

'That question,' Morgan said, 'you must address to my noble profession.'

Johnson's innocent face haunted him. If I had a say in the matter, he thought, Johnson would be one of the lucky ones, but that will be decided by providence.

Rebecca then changed her line of questioning, 'Why didn't you strangle Holmes good and properly?' she asked, and laughed, 'It would have been a big improvement.'

'The Kenyan stopped me.'

'I wouldn't have stopped you,' said Rebecca. 'I would have encouraged you.'

44

The lucky few

THE DRAW WAS held at Dorcas' shebeen.

The shebeen was closed for business. Around the table in the kitchen sat a panel selected by Dorcas: Mr. B, Father Michael, the Kenyan, Dorcas herself, Morgan, and Rachel.

Father Michael's face was impassive. He gave no indication that he knew anything about the origin of the Beerfest at all. Rachel was her usual beautiful self; Mr. B was still impressed with the success of his venture.

Morgan and the Kenyan wrote the names of all the eligible patients in the wards on square pieces of cardboard. They had recalculated the figures and could possibly afford eight patients, after Father Michael said he would need less for the orphanage. That still left money for unexpected complications such as drug resistance and more expensive medications.

'Let's keep it at six people,' Morgan said. 'That gives us some leeway.'

Dorcas put all the names in a clay pot and gave it to Mr. B to shuffle, which he did with his huge hand that nearly got stuck in the neck of the pot. Mr. B and Morgan's eyes were level with the bottom end of the lampshade that hung over the table. 'So, Morgan,' he said. 'Let's play God.'

'Father Michael can start,' said Morgan.

Mr. B solemnly passed the clay pot to Father Michael, who drew the first name and put it aside: a man from Male Ward. No one spoke. Father Michael slid the clay pot back to Mr. B, who drew the name of a woman who had recently been admitted.

The draw continued. Dorcas drew her card and passed the clay pot to Rachel. She drew a card, turned it up, and read 'Yvonne'.

'I owe you,' Morgan smiled and broke the silence. 'I was keeping my fingers crossed.'

Rachel returned his smile and gave him a wink. Morgan and the Kenyan drew last and Morgan couldn't hide his disappointment. Johnson's name hadn't come up.

'That's life,' said the Kenyan.

'So it's seven,' said Morgan. Yvonne was the only child and they would have to treat her mother.

Morgan wrote down the seven names on a list and then it was over. Dorcas served them beer, which they drank sitting around the table.

'I think we must have another Beerfest,' Mr. B said to Father Michael.

'You will have to wait a bit,' said Dorcas. 'People have spent all their money.'

THE KENYAN AND Morgan wasted no time: they took blood for CD4 counts and viral loads, and immediately put all the patients except Yvonne's mother on treatment.

'Let's wait for her CD4 count first,' Morgan said. 'The others are all sick, so we know they need treatment.'

They didn't make a fuss, just went ahead and did it. Violet was let into the secret, and she kept her mouth shut. 'They are finding private donors,' she told the nurses. 'More people will get drugs that way.'

Morgan felt guilty every time he looked into Johnson's face. 'I can't say I feel too happy about all this,' he confessed to Oumar and the Kenyan.

'It's all we can do,' the Kenyan said.

Oumar was facing them with his arms folded in front of his chest. 'Did you guys think about side effects?' he asked.

'When they go home,' Morgan explained, 'they will be told what to look out for; in the meantime, we just watch them ourselves.'

'It is actually ridiculous,' Oumar turned his head and gazed over the lawn, 'to have to treat only a few people as an undercover operation.'

'That's all we have for now,' said the Kenyan. 'The situation can only change when the government starts to pay.'

Morgan laughed. 'Can you imagine what a stuff-up that would be? Patients flocking in from everywhere. They can't even cope as it is.'

'Maybe,' Oumar reminded Morgan, 'they will be forced to use their imaginations.'

'That,' Morgan replied, 'will be like asking an ostrich to fly.'

HOLMES HAD REGAINED his confidence, and silently congratulated himself. With help from above, he had managed to gag the Health Inspector. True, he was somewhat disturbed that the inspector had issued a report in spite of his efforts to prevent him from carrying out his inspection.

The report was not flattering. The Health Inspector had threatened to shut down the kitchen. Holmes had graciously accepted the report, then invited the Health Inspector to sit down. Had Oumar received a report? He inserted the question into an amiable conversation in which he expressed his regret about the state of the kitchen. No, the Health Inspector told him, Oumar had not received a report.

A day later the Health Inspector received a call from the Regional Superintendent's office, telling him to lay off; Holmes himself was investigating the matter. Holmes destroyed the report and waited. Nothing happened. Morgan's pending departure pleased him even more.

He had given the Regional Superintendent a one-sided, tightly edited version of what happened to Rastodika, concentrating on Morgan's violent outburst. Morgan, he whispered into the Superintendent's sympathetic ear, is an unpredictable man, a loose cannon, not really suitable for the job.

One doesn't want to talk about one's colleagues, he said in an almost apologetic tone, but it is sometimes necessary to make changes. Was it not an opportune time, now that his contract had come up for renewal? They were in complete agreement; the Regional Superintendent himself had been exposed to Morgan's temper during the days when he was in charge of the referral hospital.

Holmes had composed the letter to Morgan with a sense of intense satisfaction. Holmes entered the doctors' meeting with renewed vigor. Opposite him sat Oumar with a disinterested look on his face. Thomson's black eyes were unreadable as always. He followed the Kenyan's gaze and saw Jenkins' portrait on the wall. Holmes suppressed a feeling of irritation.

'Tell me,' said Oumar, after waiting for Holmes to sit down. 'What happened about the Health Inspector's report?' His tone was mild, almost pleasant.

'The matter is being looked into,' Holmes said as nonchalantly as possible, trying not to cause a ripple on a seemingly smooth pond.

Next to Oumar was a sheaf of papers. He took a copy of the Health Inspector's report and passed it to Holmes. 'In case you haven't received one,' he said amiably.

Holmes looked into Oumar's eyes and squirmed like an eel. Calmly, Oumar took a pile of laboratory reports with positive salmonella cultures and showed it to Holmes. 'So what are we going to do about this?' he asked.

All the eyes in the room were fixed on Holmes.

'You realize,' Oumar's voice broke the silence, 'that we can file a complaint of negligence against you. You're lucky Morgan didn't do it in the first place.'

Looking at the faces around the table, Holmes couldn't find a trace of sympathy. Oumar held the papers in his hand, weighing them.

'We are not going to tolerate this and your other nonsense,' Oumar said. 'We are giving you a choice. Either you do things right from now on, or I will personally raise so much hell you'll wish you had never met me.'

'COME IN!' SHOUTED Morgan and was surprised to see Violet enter his office. He was clearing his desk. Violet stood in the middle of the room and observed the overflowing dustbin. 'Why are you throwing everything away?' she asked.

'Papers,' said Morgan. 'I have no use for them anymore. They're mostly junk anyway; I should have done it a long time ago.'

'You need a secretary,' she said and laughed. 'I can imagine what your house looks like.'

'So?' asked Morgan. 'What can I do for you?'

For once she seemed tongue-tied and unable to decide what to do with her hands. At last she folded them in front of her chest. She seemed strangely vulnerable without the duty-book clasped in front of her.

Suddenly Morgan felt embarrassed. 'So?' he said again.

'I am asking you to reconsider.'

'Reconsider what?' asked Morgan.

'Reconsider your leaving us.'

Morgan raised his eyebrows and smiled a sardonic smile. 'I'm afraid I don't have much say in the matter,' he said. Dark eyes, the same color as the deep water in Rastodika's river, Morgan thought, and wondered why he had never noticed it before.

'You could at least put up a fight,' she said. 'The whole town would support you.'

Morgan shrugged. 'I'm not solving anything by staying,' he said. 'I'm tired of fighting futile battles.'

'But it's not futile, you know,' she said with some urgency. 'The patients love you.'

'Fat lot of good I do them,' Morgan said. 'Nursing them to their untimely deaths.'

She took a step closer to him and said, 'But they know you care for them and you know it too.'

Morgan looked into her familiar face with her calm, regular features. For a moment neither of them spoke. 'Sometimes, I think it would be easier if I didn't give a damn.'

'I know you better than that,' she said. 'You really do care.'

'Perhaps that's why I should leave.'

She suddenly reached forward, stood on her toes and kissed him on his cheek. 'Stay, please, Morgan,' she said, and her eyes were unusually bright. 'The place won't be the same without you.'

Morgan was caught by surprise and instinctively rubbed his cheek.

She laughed. 'Don't go away for too long,' she said.

Morgan stood motionless. 'I will give you a rain-check,' he said, and his voice sounded unconvincing, even to himself.

'I want you to know I care a lot about you, Morgan.' She suddenly averted her face, turned around and opened the door. For a moment Morgan caught a glimpse of her perfect figure against the light from the window opposite his office. Then she softly closed the door behind her.

By noon he had restored a semblance of order in the

room. He lingered and stared out of the window. The usual scrawny figures were sitting under the trees; young men in old bodies; wasted, leaning forward and resting their arms on crossed legs.

Morgan recognized a few of the lucky ones. Six months from now, they would wonder why all their mates were dead and they were still alive and on the mend. A controlled trial, he thought. A controlled, macabre, biased trial. Maybe, he thought, I must find something else to believe in. Medicine has gone all the way to hell.

45

Sponsoring a scarecrow

MORGAN RODE SULTAN one more time, then gave him to the wife of a contractor who adored him and wasn't intimidated by his power.

'You want her to break her neck?' asked the contractor.

'Cheaper than a divorce,' Morgan reassured him.

Jake was glad that Sultan was staying, but sad that Morgan was leaving. 'Not the same,' he said. 'Sultan is horse for a man.'

Morgan found an owner for Oscar, sold most of his furniture and lived in an almost empty house.

The leopard was killed. Mr. B phoned Morgan at home, late at night, and asked him to help Elijah, the tracker. Morgan found him in Casualty, sitting in a chair, covered in blood. His shirt and trousers had been ripped to shreds. Deep lacerations caused by the leopard's claws ran across his chest. In his lap, he cradled his grotesquely swollen right hand.

Elijah winced with pain when Morgan touched the hand, but he stoically accepted the discomfort of the examination. Mr. B related the story. Elijah and another man, armed only with wooden clubs, had been tracking the leopard with dogs. It backtracked, sidestepped the dogs, and went straight for Elijah. He managed to shove his right hand down its throat and held it long enough for his friend to club it to death.

The hand was a mess. Two of the metacarpal bones were crushed. Morgan listened with half an ear as Mr. B described the melee: yelping dogs, swirling dust, screaming men, the vicious, snarling leopard and the life-saving wooden club.

'We should have got him on that day you went with me,' Mr. B said as Elijah was wheeled to theater. If I hadn't gone with you that day, thought Morgan, Rastodika might still be alive. Ever since that weekend, he had been blaming himself. He again remembered his reluctance to go out to Mr. B's farm to look for the leopard. I shouldn't have listened to either of you, he thought, looking at Mr. B.

He remembered their encouraging voices. I should have followed my own instincts, he told himself. But maybe it was destined to happen that way. Who can tell?

'All I can do for now, is to clean those wounds as well as possible,' he told Mr. B. 'They are bound to become infected.'

JOHNSON'S WEIGHT GRAPH was showing a subtle but steady decline. His face looked haggard. His beard seemed to be suspended from his prominent cheekbones. His tongue was white from thrush. His eyes had receded into their sockets. The smile on his face seemed forced. Deep lines were visible around his mouth under the scruffy beard.

Another inevitable death, Morgan thought. How long before Johnson joined the long list of lost warriors? Not long, he decided, a few weeks at the most. Against the wall was the tattered fertilizer bag containing a few pieces of clothing and the spirit level.

The end of the spirit level rested against the wall. The bubble in the yellow fluid looked like the slit pupil of a big cat, but slightly off-center.

Morgan felt an uncomfortable stirring of his conscience. Johnson didn't even know about his unsuccessful participation in a lucky draw. Neither, for that matter, did any of the lucky winners. That's the problem with playing God, he thought, you have to stick to your decisions. Some live and some die.

A week from now, I'm out of here, he thought, looking into Johnson's innocent face. I will say goodbye to him and that will be that. Destiny will take care of the rest.

He could almost hear Tesfai's soft voice: 'Some things are beyond our control, my friend.'

Damn, he thought, not if I can help it. Sometimes, only sometimes, you can cheat destiny. Just for the hell of it. When he took blood for a CD4 count, Violet's eyes widened in surprise but she said nothing.

Johnson wanted to know why he was taking blood.

'I want to see what makes you so thin,' Morgan replied.

TWO DAYS BEFORE he left, Morgan drove to Mr. B's office. He found the wealthy landowner standing next to an open window overlooking a courtyard. Just outside the window, men were loading farm implements, bags of maize, fertilizer and drums of fuel onto a truck.

'So, Morgan!' Mr. B greeted him effusively. 'What can I do for you?'

Out of a plastic bag Morgan took a thick wad of banknotes. 'I want you to add a name to the list,' he said. 'Consider it my contribution to the Beerfest.'

'Morgan, you are mad,' Mr. B told him flatly. 'You can't pay all this money!'

They faced each other across the table. Morgan placed the money in the middle. Mr. B sat back in his chair and pensively stared at the money. He lifted his head and scrutinized Morgan's face.

From outside came the sound of something heavy being lifted onto the truck. Men were shouting words of encouragement. Finally, a dull thud, and the creaking of shock absorbers. Mr. B briefly glanced out of the window, then pushed himself forward with his elbows. He took the money, counted it with an almost absent-minded air, and handed half of it back across the table.

'I'll pay the other half,' he said, 'since you are so obviously concerned about this man. We will make this our own, private investment.'

Morgan was embarrassed and shrugged his shoulders. 'If you insist,' he said. 'You don't have to.'

Mr. B's face regained its usual exuberance. 'So we are playing fairy godmother again,' he said, and laughed at his own joke.

'By the way,' he asked. 'How is Elijah?'

'He will be off work for quite some time,' said Morgan.

'Damned leopard,' said Mr. B.

Morgan wrote Johnson's full name on a piece of paper and left it on the table. He started saying something, but their conversation was interrupted by the sound of a tailgate shutting and the noise of an engine starting up. Black smoke and diesel fumes drifted through the window.

Mr. B got up and shouted last-minute instructions to the driver. The noise receded as the truck drove out of the gate. Mr. B turned away from the window and faced Morgan. 'What makes this man so special?' he wanted to know.

I could answer this question in so many ways, Morgan thought. What made me choose this man and not someone else? There was a dream in every one of them. Was one person's dream more important than those of all the others?

'He keeps a spirit level in a bag next to his bed,' he told Mr. B.

'A spirit level?' Mr. B asked incredulously. His massive chest shook with laughter. 'Morgan, you really are mad!'

'It is as good a reason as any other,' said Morgan, 'since I can only afford to help one man.'

A sudden thought occurred to him. 'The drug prices may drop,' he told Mr. B. 'Then maybe you could put more people on the list.'

'And government?' asked Mr. B. 'Surely they must pay sometime?'

Sometime is the appropriate word, Morgan thought. The machinery of government grinds slowly. With blinkered creeps like Holmes and his mates in charge, it grinds even slower. 'Eventually they will,' he told Mr. B. 'A lot of people all over the world are raising hell. Even the politicians might wake up sooner or later.'

But it is not only a question of drugs, he thought as he spoke. How the hell is such a decrepit health system going to cope? Who was going to supervise it properly? It might be another window dressing exercise. We have the drugs; we have a program. It is all on paper. Devil may care about the poor sods in the bush who still have no food in their bellies, or no jobs, or no roofs over their heads, or still no drugs for that matter.

Mr. B's voice was strangely quiet: 'And what about all the people who are dying now?' His big eyes were again scrutinizing Morgan's face. There was no trace of his usual smile.

'There are ample excuses to hide behind,' said Morgan. He thought about his conversation with Oumar. 'These poor bastards are simply not important enough. Nobody cares a stuff about them anyway,' he added.

Mr. B was rocking on his chair, holding onto the tabletop in case he fell. 'But you do,' he said softly.

'Not that it makes a difference.' Morgan was suddenly angry.

Mr. B changed the topic. 'Why do you have to leave us?' he asked. He knew about Morgan's altercation with Holmes. The whole town knew about it. 'I have influential friends,' said Mr. B. 'I could get your job back.'

'No, thank you,' said Morgan. 'It would mean I still have to listen to that fool.'

'Think about it, Morgan,' Mr. B said as he left. 'We like you; you belong here.'

IT WAS TIME for doing last things. A last game of chess with Father Michael, a last stroll around the mall, a last walk next to the river, a last jog along the bush road, a last chat with Jake, and a final pat on Sultan's rump, a last couple of beers with Oumar, Thomson and the Kenyan.

A last night in an almost empty house, with a few suitcases and other gear stacked in the middle of the living room. For a while he lingered on the veranda, smoked a cigarette and listened to the night sounds. A peal of laughter, a whistled tune, uneven footsteps in the road, a car grinding its way up the hill, the braying of a donkey, a brief, decisive dogfight and the tentative call of an Eagle Owl.

He flung the cigarette butt into the garden and surveyed the living room with the paler squares of paint where the bookcases had been, the dull patch on the floor that marked the size of the carpet, the faint mark on the wall left by the headrest of the couch, and the four pale squares made by the feet of the table.

There were only a few things left to pack. Next to a sports bag lay a map, a passport, a notebook, a camera, a few rolls of film, and his sketchbook. He packed the camera with care, wrapping it in a small piece of cloth. He put the passport in his shirt pocket, then picked up the sketchbook and paged through it.

The last sketch was a pastel drawing of Mary, which he had completed after her death, based on a photograph from the funeral program. Absentmindedly he ran his fingers over the face, then packed the sketchbook away.

'AND WHERE TO from here?' asked Oumar. They were standing next to the veranda of Male Ward.

'I don't know,' said Morgan. 'I'll see where the wind takes me. Probably go and travel for a bit.'

'Then what?' asked the Kenyan.

'Who knows?' Morgan shrugged his shoulders. 'I'll probably end up somewhere in the sticks again. I don't think I could bear private practice.'

'Somehow I couldn't imagine you wearing a tie,' Thomson said.

The Kenyan laughed. 'Can you imagine him with decent bedside manners, saying morning madam; how are you madam? What can I do for you madam?'

Morgan shuddered at the thought of so-called civilization. 'I know my limitations,' he told the Kenyan.

He had already said goodbye to the staff and all the patients. Johnson had asked him about the strange new tablets the Kenyan was giving him. Was the Kenyan sure of what he was doing? Johnson wanted to know.

Morgan assured him that the Kenyan was doing exactly the right thing.

'Is it for my weight?' Johnson asked.

Morgan was non-committal. 'It might help for that too.' Suddenly he was in a hurry to get away. 'Cheers,' he said. 'I don't believe in long goodbyes.' He took Oumar's hand and shook it.

Oumar smiled his usual enigmatic smile. 'Let us know if you find a nice place,' he said. 'I might be next on the list.'

'Take care,' said Morgan. 'I will let you know anyway.'

'Enjoy whatever you do,' said Thomson. 'I envy you, you bastard.'

Morgan's eyes rested for a moment on Rastodika's favorite tree, then he looked across the grounds. Holmes and Thunderbird were inspecting the renovations on the office building.

The Kenyan saw the flinty look in his eyes and followed his gaze. 'Now don't get any ideas,' he laughed, and shook Morgan's hand.

46

A sunny day

THE JACARANDA TREES had long lost their bloom. Kikuyu grass grew right up to the red earth of the footpath. Birds flew into the bright sunlight and disappeared again amongst the leaves. Up on the hillside, cattle grazed.

Morgan walked up to Mary's grave. On it and around it stood several vases filled with wilted and dead flowers. For a moment he stood next to the graveside, then sat down on a stone. A funeral was in progress and he could hear the voice of the preacher. From where he sat he could see the solemn faces of the mourners.

The preacher stopped talking and the monotony of his voice was replaced by singing that overwhelmed the birdsong. It was a hauntingly beautiful song. Morgan sat and listened, and nobody paid any attention to him.

With him he had a water bottle and ten red roses. He took the dead flowers out of a vase, filled it with water from the water bottle, put the roses into it and carefully placed it at the head of the grave.

The singing carried on. 'So,' Morgan said. 'I have come to pay my respects. I must also inform you that I find you difficult to forget.' The singing stopped and he heard the preacher's voice again. He looked at all the fresh graves. A new block was being opened and he saw five open, freshly dug graves. Africa is dying, he thought, and only the preachers, undertakers, nurses and doctors seem to know about it.

The preacher was stressing a point but Morgan couldn't